Ace titles by Mike Shepherd

KRIS LONGKNIFE: MUTINEER
KRIS LONGKNIFE: DESERTER
KRIS LONGKNIFE: DEFIANT
KRIS LONGKNIFE: RESOLUTE
KRIS LONGKNIFE: AUDACIOUS
KRIS LONGKNIFE: INTREPID
KRIS LONGKNIFE: UNDAUNTED

Praise for

Kris Longknife
INTREPID

"[Kris Longknife] will remind readers of David Weber's Honor Harrington with her strength and intelligence. Mike Shepherd provides an exciting military science fiction thriller."

—Genre Go Round Reviews

"A good read for fans of the series and of military science fiction."

—Romantic Times

Praise for

Kris Longknife
AUDACIOUS

" 'I'm a woman of very few words, but lots of action.' So said Mae West, but it might just as well have been Lieutenant Kris Longknife . . . *Audacious* maintains a crisp pace and lively banter . . . Kris Longknife is funny, and she entertains us."

—Sci Fi Weekly

"Mike Shepherd has a great ear for dialogue and talent for injecting dry humor into things at just the right moment . . . The characters are engaging and the plot is full of twists and peppered liberally with sharply described action . . . *Audacious* doesn't disappoint in this regard. Military SF fans are bound to get a kick out of the series as a whole, and fans will be glad to see Kris hasn't lost any of her edge."

—SF Site

"Mike Shepherd is a fantastic storyteller who excels at writing military science fiction. His protagonist is a strong-willed, independent thinker who does what she thinks is best for humanity . . . plenty of action and tension."

—Midwest Book Review

continued . . .

. . . and for the Kris Longknife novels

"Shepherd's grasp of timing and intrigue remains solid, and Kris's latest challenge makes for an engaging space opera, seasoned with political machination and the thrills of mysterious ancient technology, that promises to reveal some interesting things about the future Kris inhabits."   —*Booklist*

"Enthralling . . . fast paced . . . a well-crafted space opera with an engaging hero . . . I'd like to read more."   —*SFRevu*

"Everyone who has read Kris Longknife will hope for further adventures starring this brave, independent, and intrepid heroine. Mike Shepherd has written an action-packed, exciting space opera that starts at light speed and just keeps getting better. This is outer-space military science fiction at its adventurous best."   —*Midwest Book Review*

"I'm looking forward to her next adventure."
                —*The Weekly Press* (Philadelphia)

"Fans of the Honor Harrington escapades will welcome the adventures of another strong female in outer space starring in a thrill-a-page military space opera. The heroine's dry wit [and] ability to know what she is good at [as well as] her faults, [all] while keeping her regal DNA in perspective, especially during a crisis, endear her to readers. The audience will root for the determined, courageous, and endearing heroine as she displays intelligence and leadership during lethal confrontations."
                —*Alternative Worlds*

"[Shepherd] has a good sense of pace . . . very neatly handled, and served with a twist of wry. A surprisingly talented read from a very underrated author."   —*Bewildering Stories*

"Shepherd does a really good job with this book. If you're looking for an entertaining space opera with some colorful characters, this is your book. Shepherd grew up Navy, and he does an excellent job of showing the complex demands and duties of an officer. I look forward to the next in the series."   —*Books 'n' Bytes*

"You don't have to be a military sci-fi enthusiast to appreciate the thrill-a-minute plot and engaging characterization."
                —*Romantic Times*

Kris Longknife
UNDAUNTED

Mike Shepherd

ACE BOOKS, NEW YORK

THE BERKLEY PUBLISHING GROUP
Published by the Penguin Group
Penguin Group (USA) Inc.
375 Hudson Street, New York, New York 10014, USA

Penguin Group (Canada), 90 Eglinton Avenue East, Suite 700, Toronto, Ontario M4P 2Y3, Canada
(a division of Pearson Penguin Canada Inc.)
Penguin Books Ltd., 80 Strand, London WC2R 0RL, England
Penguin Group Ireland, 25 St. Stephen's Green, Dublin 2, Ireland (a division of Penguin Books Ltd.)
Penguin Group (Australia), 250 Camberwell Road, Camberwell, Victoria 3124, Australia
(a division of Pearson Australia Group Pty. Ltd.)
Penguin Books India Pvt. Ltd., 11 Community Centre, Panchsheel Park, New Delhi—110 017, India
Penguin Group (NZ), 67 Apollo Drive, Rosedale, North Shore 0632, New Zealand
(a division of Pearson New Zealand Ltd.)
Penguin Books (South Africa) (Pty.) Ltd., 24 Sturdee Avenue, Rosebank, Johannesburg 2196,
South Africa

Penguin Books Ltd., Registered Offices: 80 Strand, London WC2R 0RL, England

This is a work of fiction. Names, characters, places, and incidents either are the product of the author's imagination or are used fictitiously, and any resemblance to actual persons, living or dead, business establishments, events, or locales is entirely coincidental. The publisher does not have any control over and does not assume any responsibility for author or third-party websites or their content.

KRIS LONGKNIFE: UNDAUNTED

An Ace Book / published by arrangement with the author

PRINTING HISTORY
Ace mass-market edition / November 2009

Copyright © 2009 by Mike Moscoe.
Cover art by Scott Grimando.
Interior text design by Kristin del Rosario.

ISBN: 978-0-441-01786-7

ACE
Ace Books are published by The Berkley Publishing Group,
a division of Penguin Group (USA) Inc.,
375 Hudson Street, New York, New York 10014.
ACE and the "A" design are trademarks of Penguin Group (USA) Inc.

PRINTED IN THE UNITED STATES OF AMERICA

10   9   8   7   6   5   4   3   2   1

If what they say is true, and a wise warrior must know her enemy, then it may follow that the only person whom you understand . . . and who really understands you . . . is your enemy.

Acknowledgments

No book finds its way into a reader's hand without a lot of dedicated work from wonderful people. Ginjer Buchanan deserves special thanks for all the support she gave a writer through the ups and downs of the writing life. The gang at Ace has been wonderful, balancing their standard formats with my insistence that it doesn't work that way inside the perimeter fence. Jennifer Jackson is all the agent that a writer could hope for. And there is no better first reader than my wife, Ellen.

I'd like to give special appreciation to Edee Lemonier and Debbie Lentz, who volunteered to be second readers and comb the final manuscript for those nits that these old eyes let slip through. I hope those of you who find them particularly painful have less cause for painkillers during Kris's latest adventure. I'd also like to thank the folks at The Anchor Inn in Lincoln City for giving me a home away from home to write. Their fine care and great food kept me putting in twenty pages a day, day after day. Thanks, Kip, Candi, Misty, and Ron.

1

Lieutenant Kris Longknife sat in the captain's chair of the Wardhaven explorer ship *Wasp*, the unquestioned commander of all she surveyed.

Of course, she had the conn on the midwatch, and there was very little to survey; most of the *Wasp*'s crew were sound asleep. Far from her sight, the scant midnight watch went about their duties, keeping the air cool, the lights on, and the ship decelerating at one gee on its established course. The only person in Kris's sight was Chief Beni. He studied the instruments at the navigator's position.

Most of the time, he fed his sensor data to the navigator. Just now, he took advantage of the quiet midwatch to see what she did with his input. He was also weighing his options to go to OCS, trying on an officer's shoes to check the fit.

All in all, it looked to be a very quiet and comfortable midwatch. HOW LONG HAS IT BEEN, NELLY?

HOW LONG HAS WHAT BEEN? Kris's pet computer, worth several ships like the *Wasp*, asked on the direct hookup into Kris's brain.

Nelly was usually ten steps ahead of Kris's own thoughts, ready to answer any question before the Navy lieutenant posed it. Kris put the surly reply down to attitude. Or, more correctly, "'tude."

Kris *still* had a twelve-year-old girl on board. Or, more accurately, a certain girl held a ship, its crew, and one very uppity computer in thrall.

Content not to break the dim silence, Kris continued the conversation via the private link between her and Nelly. HOW LONG HAS IT BEEN SINCE ANYONE TRIED TO KILL ME?

OH, THAT. SIXTY-THREE DAYS. DO YOU WANT THE HOURS, MINUTES, SECONDS, AND NANOSECONDS, YOUR HIGH-HANDEDNESS?

THAT WON'T BE NECESSARY, Kris said, to cut off more 'tude. It had been a nice two months without the occasional potshot or heart-pounding race for life.

Kris could get to liking this.

Of course, the whole time had been spent far beyond the Rim of human occupied space. Far enough out that she hadn't stumbled on even one Sooner world. Sooner farmers, artisans, and generally cantankerous folks saw no reason why they should obey distant Earth and not push out beyond the boundaries set for humanity by old men in suits. Kris found them kindred spirits to her own desire to have as much space as possible between herself and her closest relatives.

Still, where the law hadn't gotten to, often thievery, pirating, and slavery had.

Kris had spent the first two months of this cruise putting down a few of those problems. Done with the intrepid side for a while, she'd spent the last two months expanding the chart of mapped and usable jump points and letting her scientists research to their hearts' delight.

And not been shot at once.

Nice, that.

"How's our approach to the next jump point coming?" Kris asked Chief Beni.

He shook his head. "It just took a zig away from us. I make it about fifteen thousand kilometers farther away. I would suggest . . ." He tapped the nav board several times, frowned at the results, and said, ". . . we reduce deceleration to .84 gee. That should put us there in twenty-two minutes . . . give or take one of Nelly's nanoseconds."

Apparently, the chief and Nelly were back to open hostilities.

Kris ignored that and worried her lower lip. Each of the jump points created by the aliens a million or two years ago orbited two, three, or more stars. That meant their apparent orbit around any one star was anything but smooth. And caused the occasional deadly bad jump.

Kris hoped this little wiggle meant only that the *Wasp* would arrive a bit late for the next jump. Actually, with everyone asleep, it really wasn't a problem at all.

Kris glanced at the star map on the main screen. The *Wasp* had been working its way across the front of Wardhaven space . . . or to put it more politically correct . . . the 136 planets now negotiating to establish some kind of association under the leadership of Grampa Ray, King Raymond I to anyone not his great-granddaughter.

To the right of the *Wasp*'s search sweep was Greenfeld space, and the less said about that, the better for Kris's day. To the left was the Helvetican Confederacy that, if Kris remembered something that had come across her desk, now included her friends on the proud planet Chance.

Above them on the star map, looming like a black hole, was the No Go Zone. Nobody in their right mind went into the buffer between humans and the Iteeche. The fight to set that zone between "us and them" had almost driven the human race extinct.

Kris doubted any Sooner or pirate would dare violate that precinct of space.

Of course, the *Wasp* was getting closer to that zone. Kris would have to decide soon just how close she'd go. She chuckled to herself . . . putting a buffer around a buffer. But the price for a mistake along that boundary was too high, both for her crew and the whole human race.

Maybe it was already time to go farther out rather than any farther over.

For the next few minutes, Kris did the job that Officers of the Deck did, checking to make sure that very competent people did their job as well as they always did. The reactor was well in the green. Reaction-mass tanks were still over 65 percent, so it would be a while before Captain Drago, the true monarch of this small chunk of space called the *Wasp*, would skim the surface of a gas giant to scoop up mass, or take the more sedate approach of heading for a space station to buy the water they heated in the reactors.

Kris glanced further into the daily reports. Sick bay had only two Marines in it, victims of a handball game that had ended with a violent collision. With no one taking shots at Kris, the Marines were also being spared the odd collateral damage of being too close to "one of those Longknifes."

It really was nice being so far from human space.

NELLY, REPORT SHIP'S STATUS, Kris said in her head. Her own board said everything was fine. Nelly's assessment would guarantee that nothing lurked deep below the surface, waiting to spoil Kris's otherwise-quiet morning.

In the blink of an eye, Kris was listening to ALL SYSTEMS WELL WITHIN THE NORMS. EVERYONE IS SLEEPING AS WELL AS THEY NORMALLY DO AT THIS TIME. CARA IS STILL UP PLAY-ING A GAME, Nelly added, addressing the precise status of the twelve-year-old who Kris more than suspected was the most important person aboard the *Wasp* as far as Nelly was concerned.

SHOULDN'T SHE BE ASLEEP? TOMORROW'S A SCHOOL DAY.

I CAN JUST START IT A BIT LATE, AIN'T NO BIG THING.

Kris blinked . . . When had Nelly started using contractions? Or "ain't"? Nelly's computer-perfect grammar was supposed to be teaching proper grammar to a sixth grader!

Further thoughts on that were interrupted by the chief.

"We're coming up on the jump point in two minutes, Lieutenant. What are your orders?"

Kris weighed the first, and probably only, command decision she'd make this watch. "If we just sit here, everyone's going to wake up weightless," she mused. That was not a problem for the sailors and Marines. But a third of those occupying the *Wasp* fit neither of those categories. Kris had a large scientific contingent, and even a judge brought out of retirement and empowered to apply the law to anyone for anything Kris chose to dump in her lap.

Several of the boffins besides Judge Francine did not take to microgravity all that well. Usually, the *Wasp* was under way at one gee or tied up to a space station with something like normal gravity. How would they handle sleeping the next four hours in zero gee and waking up in it?

Kris knew the answer to her next question, but she asked the chief anyway. "We don't have any jump buoys, do we?"

"As a matter of fact, I see four of them ready to launch on my nav board," the chief answered, to her surprise.

Kris's own copy of the nav station showed nothing, so she slapped off her seat belt and walked over to Beni's station.

As she expected, it had extra space lit up. Kris recognized it . . . a defensive battle station.

Apparently, Sulwan Kann was ready to activate all the necessary defenses of the *Wasp* if she got into a fight. The woman truly was Captain Drago's right-hand man.

Kris went down the left side of the nav board, finding armor, foxers, maskers—everything needed by a ship fighting for its life. Four of the foxer launching tubes showed blue. Beside them was a notation. JUMP BUOYS.

"I guess if we aren't faking it as a merchant ship, there's no reason not to launch the smaller ones," Kris said. NELLY, ASK CAPTAIN DRAGO WHAT OTHER WEAPONS SYSTEMS THE *WASP* IS NOW CARRYING.

YES, MA'AM. I WILL ALSO SEARCH THE REPORT FROM THE LAST YARD PERIOD AND SEE IF IT TELLS YOU ANYTHING.

YOU DO THAT, Kris said. Four months out, and Kris still didn't know just what her supposed command had hidden away in some corner storeroom.

"Zero grav in fifteen seconds," the chief reported. Over the public-address system, a similar announcement went out . . . at a whisper . . . as the hour of the morning called for.

Kris hustled back to her station and belted in. Once the

Wasp was at a dead stop five klicks from the jump point, she ordered, "Flip ship."

Chief Beni rotated the *Wasp* smartly along her long axis. Now the bow faced the tiny bit of roiled space that was all that showed of the portal across seven light-years of space.

"Chief, send a buoy through the jump. Have it announce that we'll be following in five minutes."

"You think that is a good idea?" the chief asked. But he was grinning, and his attention was on his fingers as they went through the motions of launching the buoy.

"Weapons are full," Kris answered. Her command board had been extended to include everything important from the weapons board. She'd done that about fifteen seconds into the watch. She didn't expect to use the four twenty-four-inch pulse lasers hidden under the *Wasp*'s civilian brightwork, but . . .

Kris eyed Beni's back as he finished his prep. "What *are* you afraid of, Chief?"

"I work for this Longknife woman, ma'am. It pays for me to always be afraid, 'cause she never is," he said. But his grin got wider as he said it.

"Launch the buoy, Chief," Kris said dryly.

"Aye, aye, Lieutenant. Buoy launched."

Now they waited for five minutes. Around Kris, the ship continued its somnolence. The engineering watch checked in to ask if they'd be needing to put on a full-gee acceleration anytime soon, were told to expect it, and went back to tending their teakettles.

The minutes dragged by, Kris did a second and third check to make sure the twenty-four-inch lasers that the *Wasp* officially didn't have were at full charge. They were and continued to be.

Much to Kris's relief, Captain Drago did not appear to summon a full bridge crew and take her command away. Kris wasn't quite sure why that would bother her, but she knew it would.

Five minutes gone, Kris ordered a short burst from maneuvering thrusters and the *Wasp* edged through the jump.

Kris felt only slightly disoriented as her ship was yanked from one star to another one seven light-years farther from Earth. With only a blink, she studied her board.

There was the jump buoy. Farther out, some thirty thousand kilometers, was a ship.

Then a laser blew the jump buoy to bits.

2

"Jinks ship," Kris shouted. "Raise armor."

"Jinksing pattern two initiated," Chief Beni answered, and the ship shot up, then left, then up again. "Shields up."

Kris mashed her commlink, ignoring that her call for armor had once again been changed to "shields up." "Battle stations. Guns," Kris ordered. "All hands. Battle stations. Guns."

That done, Kris concentrated on aiming her lasers up the rear end of a very strange ship. A ship unlike any ship she'd ever seen—except on vids.

An Iteeche Death Ball was breaking toward Kris's jump point, its vulnerable engines wide open to the *Wasp*'s lasers.

That was stupid. You could say many things about those four-eyed bastards, but the Iteeche were never stupid.

Kris's shield took a hit. Smart Metal™ vaporized to ablate away what heat the metal was not able to spread quickly to the entire shield and then radiate into space.

"There are two more ships out there. I make them cruisers," Chief Beni reported. "Greenfeld cruisers from the way their lasers are heating up. Your Highness, I think they're the ones firing at us. Or at least shooting at the Death Ball and missing."

"I think you may be right," Kris whispered. On her board, two twin batteries of six-inch lasers heated up on one cruiser as they discharged. The Death Ball dodged right, left, up, down. The armor that had opened like an umbrella in front of the *Wasp* took another glancing hit.

KRIS, WE HAVE TO SHOOT THOSE GREENFELD BASTARDS, rang in Kris's head.

Kris didn't have time to make a note of Nelly's new vocabulary. NO, NELLY, WE ARE NOT GOING TO FIRE AT THE CRUISERS. I WILL NOT START A WAR TODAY.

BUT THEY'RE ENDANGERING CARA. I'VE GOT THE LASERS SIGHTED IN. I CAN HIT BOTH OF THEM.

The lasers were rock on, Kris noted. WE ARE NOT SHOOTING, NELLY.

WE HAVE TO. FOR CARA!

Kris's hand had been rising almost without volition since this silent conversation started. Now it moved like the lightning strike of a viper, depressing a tiny portion of the computer that hung at her collarbone. Kris hadn't pushed the off button on her computer since the first grade, when her teacher required her to take a math test unaided.

The surface of the computer gave way with unfamiliar ease. And Kris found herself with a shrieking silence in her skull.

"Captain on the bridge," Captain Drago announced as he shot through the open bridge door, still pulling on his pants. "What's the situation?"

Kris drew in a breath, to gain herself a moment to think and to add some noise to the silence between her ears. Focused on the world outside herself, she snapped. "We're taking stray shots from two Greenfeld cruisers shooting at an Iteeche Death Ball. Chief, put me on guard channel. Ship's computer, what was the frequency we finally used to make contact with the Iteeche?"

"I've got it. You're on," Chief Beni said, hitting a button on his board.

Captain Drago bounced off the overhead, aimed himself at Beni's usual station, and grabbed a handhold on the chair as he cinched in his belt . . . apparently content to leave the rapidly developing situation to his . . . whatever Kris was to him.

Kris would have liked to stand and glare at the forward screen, hands on hips, but the *Wasp* had no constant course. She stayed seated.

"This is Princess Kristine Longknife on the Wardhaven exploration ship *Wasp*. Greenfeld cruisers, check fire. You are
missing the Iteeche Death Ball and hitting me. I repeat, check
fire."

One cruiser fired its four forward six-inchers just as the
Wasp dodged up, left, up, and right—and got singed again.

"Damn it," Kris snapped. "You keep hitting me, and I'm
not even in a direct line with the Iteeche."

"Our sensors show you are," someone from a Greenfeld
cruiser snapped back. "So get out of our line of fire."

"I'm going right," Kris announced.

The Iteeche, Kris noticed, immediately went right as well,
not letting Kris open up so much as a kilometer more lateral
displacement.

It also didn't fire.

"The four-eyed bastard is going right with you," the Greenfeld cruiser reported.

"And it hasn't fired on you since I got here," Kris pointed
out. "Has it fired on you at all?"

"Well, not exactly, but it's Iteeche, and it's outside their
empire. That makes it a target."

Kris was aware that the Greenfeld commander was quoting
one interpretation of the Treaty of the Orange Nebula. Grampa
Ray always insisted the proper reading was that you could return fire if one of them shot at you.

And Grampa Ray was a signatory to that treaty on the human side.

Kris never expected to argue the fine points of treaty language over charged lasers. But there seemed no better time
than the present.

The *Wasp* put on a half-gee acceleration. Sulwan, in her
usual cutoffs and tank top but barefooted, was now at Kris's
weapons station. She brought it up as nav.

Kris unsnapped her seat belt and took four steps toward the
screen. Behind her, Captain Drago, chest bare, slipped into his
seat. The bridge stations were filling up.

Kris played the only card she had.

"Cease fire, or I swear to God, if you hit me again, I, Princess Kris Longknife, great-granddaughter of Ray Longknife, will fire on you. And I hit what I aim at. Just check your file on me."

There was a long pause. A glance at Chief Beni's station, now fully devoted to sensors, showed the Greenfeld ships putting a full charge to their main batteries. They were eighty thousand kilometers out; the *Wasp* was well past their accurate range. The Iteeche Death Ball was a long shot, even at thirty thousand klicks closer.

No wonder their shooting was so far off.

"Yeah, we understand you," finally came, as a Greenfeld Navy officer's face filled the main screen. "What do you intend to do with your four-eyes?"

"Talk to them if I can," Kris said. "Escort them back to their territory no matter what."

Definitely, the Iteeche had to go back to Imperial Space. If he was one of their Wandering Men, the lawless types who'd started the Iteeche War, the crew of this Death Ball would not like that. The Iteeche attitude toward Wandering Men was similar to what humans felt toward pirates, but without the warm and fuzzy, feel-good side.

"Do you want us to stand by in case the four-eyes cause you any trouble?" the Greenfeld captain asked.

"I think I'll have an easier time talking to him if the folks who chased him across this system kind of moseyed along, don't you, Captain?"

"Captain," someone said offscreen, and the screen went blank. Kris didn't move, expecting the interruption to be short.

Behind her, Captain Drago and Sulwan exchanged whispered words. A sailor arrived with a shirt, and Drago quickly put it on, along with the purple coat he wore far more often than either his merchant skipper's greens or reserve Navy captain's blues.

"Lieutenant Longknife," he said dryly, "when will I leave you in charge for a moment and *not* come back to find that you have started a war?"

He had no idea how close his hyperbole was to right on, but Kris tried to reply with her usual banter. "I haven't started a war . . . yet," Kris insisted through unmoving lips, keeping her eyes focused on the blank screen.

Since it stayed blank, she ventured a further response. "I may have just stopped Greenfeld from getting us into another Iteeche War."

The captain said nothing, but Kris could almost hear him rolling his eyes at the overhead.

The screen blinked and came alive again.

"It seems that I have other orders that I must take care of at the moment. If you do not mind, I will use the jump you just used to make my way home."

"I will accelerate toward the sun," Kris said. "Before our closest point of encounter, I will rotate ship and protect my engines. You may do as you please."

"Until we meet again, Princess Kristine Longknife of Wardhaven." Coming from the captain, it sounded like a threat *and* a promise.

"Sulwan, put on one gee," Captain Drago ordered. "Aim us in the general direction of the sun for now. Princess, what do we do with *your* stray Iteeche?"

Kris started to shrug.

"Hope he follows her home," came from Marine Captain Jack Montoya as he entered the bridge.

The captain, as the commander of the rump Marine company aboard the *Wasp*, was under her command. As security chief of a serving member of royal blood, Kris had to do what he told her where her security was involved. That made for an interesting chain of command.

It didn't help that he was as handsome as she was plain. No, as she thought herself plain. He'd made it clear . . . in an officially proper way . . . that what he saw when he looked her way was beauty.

Kris chose to ignore the confused place this was taking her. She had enough problems, and today was only forty-six minutes old.

"Ship's computer, can you raise the Iteeche?" Kris asked.

"Contact is being attempted. The *Wasp* is sending the contact signal King Raymond I used that led to the initial talks at the Orange Nebula."

"And?" Captain Drago asked.

"No reply."

Captain Drago frowned for a second. "Ah, Princess, why are you talking to my ship's computer and not your Nelly?" Nelly was notorious throughout human space for her superiority to other computers, personal or otherwise.

"I had to turn her off," Kris admitted.

"Off?" Jack got out first. "You don't ever turn Nelly off!"

"She had the Greenfeld cruisers sighted in. Was ready to fire on them. Something about protecting Cara. It was either let her start a war or turn her off."

Kris eyed said cruisers as they reversed ship and began decelerating toward the jump point. They'd still be going at a pretty good clip when they passed through it. That was their problem.

"Nelly also was using 'ain't' and 'bastard,'" Kris added.

"You really need her to have that talk with your auntie Tru," Jack said.

Kris sighed. "She's way overdue."

"Yes, Princess, but what do we tell this Iteeche? 'Follow me'?" Captain Drago asked.

"No," Kris said. "Not unless your ship's computer knows the proper form of the pronoun 'me' or we might insult whoever that is and start a war on that alone. Nelly and I did a term paper in Iteeche just for fun my senior year of high school. Course, Nelly had to translate it for the teacher. We got an A."

"We need a translator just now," Jack said. "You willing to wake Nelly up?"

"Not while we've got Greenfeld cruisers in our sky," Kris said. "Captain, can your computer say something like 'Follow in our wake.'" Examination of shattered Iteeche cadavers had hinted that they were a lot more recent in their transition from sea to land. Grampa Trouble got away with saying that to the first Iteeche shipload of negotiators.

The ship computer found that line in some history and sent the message. There was no reply, but the Death Ball altered course and accelerated at one gee toward the sun.

Sulwan modified her course to swing her engines out of a direct line of fire from the cruisers and kept the one-gee acceleration.

Kris reached for a workstation and held on steady as her inner ear took a while to adjust to the twisting course, made worse by the occasional jinks up, down, or over.

Sulwan was not a trusting soul. Not with Chief Beni reporting that the cruisers had fully charged lasers.

Through all this, the Iteeche Death Ball followed the *Wasp* like a stray puppy followed a four-year-old kid dropping hot-dog bits of encouragement. Was it pure chance that its course also increased the distance between it and the cruisers?

And edged kind of behind the *Wasp*.

Captain Drago studied his board, seemed satisfied, and said, "Lieutenant Longknife, you are relieved as Officer of the Deck. Please get off of my bridge."

"Captain, I'm your gunnery officer. If someone on the *Wasp* is to shoot at those Greenfeld cruisers, it should be a serving Wardhaven officer," Kris said, turning to a vacant bridge station and tapping it in three places. It started lighting up as an offensive-weapons control station.

"One of the few things you and I agree upon," the captain said, and mashed his commlink. "Lieutenant Pasley, please report to the bridge."

Which Penny did, five seconds later. "I was already on my way," she said as she slipped into the station chair at the weapons board before Kris could.

Kris scowled down at the other active duty Navy officer on the *Wasp*. "What's that leave me to do?" she mumbled to herself.

"The hard stuff," Captain Drago said, making a shooing motion with both hands. "I'll handle the Greenfeld cruisers.

They only outnumber and outgun us. They'll never outclass us. You need to make friendly with your pet computer. I really feel the lack of her input. Oh, and there is that Iteeche. Screw matters up with them, and we'll only wish the Greenfeld cruisers had blasted us out of space with their first shot."

3

Kris would have much preferred a straight-up fight with a pair of Greenfeld cruisers. Tough odds, but manageable.

The Iteeche Death Ball was a greater threat . . . with the ambiguity of a ticking time bomb. It might go off now. Or later. The only certainty was that it would go off and make a mess of her entire day.

And she was facing the Iteeche without Nelly. She'd never headed into a fight with one arm and one leg in a cast. Or just flat cut off.

What a mess.

Well, few things didn't get better when shared. Kris mashed her commlink. "Will the princess's staff please report . . ." No, with the Iteeche in the mix, this was no time to call a meeting in her boring conference room. ". . . to her Tac Room." There, that had the proper lethality for a council of war. It was the same room, but it had deadly all over it.

"You drop in, too, Captain, as soon as those cruisers are out of our sky," Kris told Drago as she left him to his own and full devices.

"Will do, Your Highness," Captain Drago answered, with just the right nod to her royal status from his aloof post as contract captain of this not-supposed-to-be warship.

Kris headed for her conference/Tac Room.

Chief Beni was there first. The wall to Kris's left as she entered now matched the main screen on the bridge. At a glance, Kris could see how the dance was going as the Greenfeld cruisers made their way out, and the Iteeche Death Ball edged in close.

Kris breathed a sigh of relief even as a part of her brain screamed, *What's wrong with this picture?*

"You've got to be nuts to be glad to see human cruisers leaving even as an Iteeche gets closer," said Colonel Hernando Cortez, formally of several military organizations and at the moment Kris's prisoner and employee. That combination, along with the display, pretty much summed up Kris's efforts to be a good Navy officer.

"Oh if Father or General Mac could see me now," Kris said.

"They'd laugh their heads off," Captain Jack Montoya said as he followed Kris into the room and took a glance at the board.

As Kris's former Secret Service agent, he'd sworn to take a bullet for her. Now, as the chief of her security detail and commander of a Marine detachment, his job was no easier or, with Kris's attitude toward "secure," any more survivable.

"What you folks gone and done to get me out of bed?" said Abby, presenting herself in a fluffy housecoat, curlers, and huge slippers with rabbit ears on them. Occasionally an Army Reserve intelligence officer, this early in the morning Abby was clearly filling the role of Kris's maid and bornagain coward.

"We got company," Kris said.

"I hope they're nice folks that their mommas taught to mind their manners," Abby said, scowling at the strange symbol on the display. "What's that?"

"An Iteeche Death Ball," Jack said. "It followed the princess home."

The colonel showed honest fear. Abby's half-open eyes were suddenly quite open.

"Can we keep it?" came from the other pair of wide-open eyes, peeking around the Tac Room's door.

"Cara, what are you doing up?" Kris asked the twelve-year-old softly. She was in a pink nightshirt that displayed the gyrations of the latest preteen heartthrob. At least the sound had been broken in the wash . . . or so Abby claimed.

"Well, there was all that noise," Cara started, "And then you shouting Battle whatever, and people flying down the halls. I knew they wouldn't let me on the bridge," the youngster admitted, quite indignant, as she edged into the room. "But if something really fun happens, you always come here. So I waited, and you all came." She ended with far too bright a smile for this ridiculous hour of the morning.

"The young woman is a first-class observer," said Professor mFumbo, leader of Kris's technical and scientific team. With no other observation, he settled into his place at Kris's table, not at all surprised to be sharing it with a child.

Or . . . if the tenured professor was pressed to express an opinion on the matter . . . *another* child.

Kris glanced at Jack. He wore a poleaxed smile as he shrugged. How could a twelve-year-old girl have the entire ship eating out of her hand? Kris did not have fond memories of her twelfth year. She'd crawled into a bottle to escape the mourning that was tearing her family apart after little Eddy's death.

It appeared that fate had decreed that Cara's twelfth year be as good as Kris's had been bad. Then again, Kris would not swap for Cara's first eleven years.

Kris stifled a yawn and weighed the option of having the child banished to bed. She found the odds of her entire retinue joining Nelly in mutiny far too high.

So she concentrated her attention elsewhere. "We have about an hour before the Greenfeld cruisers exit the system. Call it a hunch, but I'd bet dollars to doughnuts that this Iteeche gets a whole lot more talkative once we're alone."

"Do Iteeche often get more talkative with you, Your Highness," Colonel Cortez said, "when you are alone?"

"Don't know all that much about Iteeche," Abby said, "but I've known a man or two to act that way."

"What do we know about the Iteeche?" Jack asked.

"A lot less than we knew an hour ago," Kris said bitterly.

Jack raised a sympathetic eyebrow at that, but most just stared blankly. "I had to turn Nelly off," Kris said plainly.

"Why?" came from around the table. Except for one twelve-year-old who jumped to her feet and began insisting at the top of her voice that, "You can't do that. You can't. You can't. You can't."

Kris waited until Cara stopped for a breath, then snapped, "I turned her off because Nelly had dialed our lasers in on the Greenfeld cruisers and was about to blast away. Not even Nelly can declare war on Greenfeld. We've all sweat and bled too much to keep that peace."

Deep silence, even from Cara.

"Why?" Professor mFumbo asked softly in his deep voice.

"Nelly was afraid Cara might be hurt by their lasers," Kris said.

Deeper silence.

"Just how much does Nelly know about the Iteeche?" Jack said, finally breaking the silence.

"She holds all the research I've done on the Iteeche since the fifth grade," Kris said. "Oh, and she can speak Iteeche . . . at several levels. Imperial to equal. Imperial to inferior. Warrior to warrior. Warrior to superior, and merchant to superior, inferior, and equal."

"The language is that hot on who you are?" Abby said in disbelief.

"And you better get it right, or you can get suddenly dead," Kris growled. "Grampa warned that every Iteeche of any rank carries a sword and is only too quick to use it on anyone who flubs their grammar."

"No trade pigeon or something like that?" Colonel Cortez asked.

"Several Iteeche and human prisoners served as translators for both Grampa and the head dude the Empire sent to talk to him. Several took sword strokes, and one lost an arm for blunders in grammar. Or maybe it was what they said. Hard to tell."

"And Nelly knows the language," mFumbo said.

"About as good as anyone in human space. Definitely better than anyone aboard this ship, Professor, unless you got a specialist I don't know about."

The ebony-faced man shook his head. "My understanding of our survey mission was that the Empire was one place we would steer clear of."

"That was mine, too," Kris said. "But it seems to have steered for us. So ignoring our linguistics problem for a moment, do you have anyone among the boffins who could run some diagnostics on my trigger-happy computer?"

The professor had both hands up, palms out, and was shaking his head well before Kris finished. "Miss Longknife, I have several computer experts who dream of being present when the real breakthrough in artificial intelligence finally comes. Many of them look upon you and your experimentation with your personal computer as a possible source for just that awaited day. But no, none of them would dare touch what you have around your neck. Several of my boffins are attempting to duplicate what you've done with your Nelly, but none of them have to date invested either the time or the money that you have. To put it succinctly, Nelly is your computer . . . and your problem."

"But we need Nelly if we're to avoid some Iteeche taking our heads off for a misplaced modifier," Jack said with a wry grin. "Your Highness, you do have a tendency to open your mouth and start a war with anyone across the table from you."

"Thank you so much for your vote of confidence," Kris said, and finished with a most sincere, "I will try to avoid going down in history as the cause of the Second Iteeche War."

"I'm just trying to keep you alive, Princess," Jack said, denying her the last word.

"It seems we need to turn Nelly back on," mFumbo said.

"But how do we keep the little darling from shooting from

the hip the next time she thinks Cara's in danger?" Abby added.

"I didn't mean to cause trouble," Cara said. She'd been sitting very quietly in her chair, doing her best to be small. What with her latest growth spurts, she was almost as tall as her aunt Abby. Small was not something she did easy. "Maybe if I said something to Nelly," Cara offered.

Leaving the future of her ship and its crew, along with the rest of humanity, in the hands of a kid did not make Kris's bunny jump. Not even a little.

"Let's think about that for a while," Kris said, and changed the subject. "Without Nelly, what do we know about the Iteeche?"

"Not much," Colonel Cortez said, "except they are very good at killing humans."

"Were, eighty years ago," the professor corrected.

"You think they've gotten less efficient?" Cortez asked.

"I know we've gotten better at killing our fellow humans," Jack said.

"On that topic, may I toss in something?" Chief Beni asked.

"Toss away," Kris said.

"As I go over their ship, I'm not getting anything in the higher frequencies where our Smart Metal™ gives off a kind of background hum. The Iteeche are doing a very good job of jamming almost everything, just like my grandpa said they did back in his war, but they're not jamming up there, and they are not humming themselves in those frequencies."

"Are you telling me that they don't have Smart Metal™?" Kris asked. "Can we score one for us hairless monkeys?"

"Seems that way," the chief said. "And there's something else, Your Highness, and I hope you won't be upset with me."

"Why?" Kris asked. She'd learned long ago with this team that it was unwise to dispense general absolution too quickly. They were oh so good at coming up with interesting variations on what other people thought impossible.

Almost as good at it as her.

"When we jumped into this system and our buoy like vanished immediately," the chief started.

"Yes," Kris said, wondering how long this story would take.

"I had a visual on the Iteeche, and a gravity bearing from our new atom laser. But they didn't agree. You being kind of busy, I chose the gravity bearing since it put the Death Ball off our bow, but the visual said it was dead ahead."

"That *might* explain why the cruisers were shooting our way," Kris said.

"And missing the Iteeche," Jack added.

"That's what I thought," the chief said. "Anyway, when we got our laser- and radar-range findings, they supported the visual. I didn't change the board."

"During the war, our ships had the devil's own time," Kris said, "hitting the Iteeche ships. They never seemed to be where our sensors said they were."

"I hadn't heard about that," Colonel Cortez said.

"The Navy wasn't all that interested in sharing its problems with its sister service," Kris said.

"But you can't hit something you can't range properly," Jack pointed out.

"You can if you fire full broadsides carefully spaced," Kris said. "That's what they did in the later fleet actions, firing carefully organized salvoes to cover everything. And we finally started hitting things in all the wrong places."

"And this never got out?" Abby said.

"You want to tell all the folks back home," Kris said, "that your Navy is firing blind 'cause the Iteeche can do magic tricks and make their ships disappear?"

"I see the problem," the colonel said.

"It wasn't exactly secret after the war," Kris said, "but it didn't make it into any of the popular history or vids, where most people got their education. But our new gravity sensors, the ones we're using to find the fuzzy jump points, can find them," she said, with a grin.

"Meaning that the Iteeche are maybe seven feet tall, not ten," Abby said.

"Ma'am," Colonel Cortez said, "the Iteeche *are* seven feet tall. My daddy measured quite a few of their bodies after he'd killed them."

"But we've got Smart Metal™ and a new gravity sensor in our atom laser. We can go places they can't even see, and we've got a whole new metal to protect our hides," Kris said. "Abby, dump all this to a message pod. As soon as the Greenfeld cruisers get out of my sky, send it back to the jump. Use your best codes, 'cause the cruisers will likely intercept the message when it's broadcast across the next system."

"Right, Your Highness. I imagine Admiral Crossenshield will be a mite bit delighted to hear about this. Might even up my pay if I kind of forget to include this in my general report on what you're up to," Abby said, heading out and wrangling an arm around Cara. "Come on, Baby Duck, I will not have you falling asleep no matter who's your teacher tomorrow."

"But this is exciting, and you never let me have any fun."

The door closed firmly behind the two, and Kris found herself smiling along with the rest of the team at the familiar dialogue from her youth.

Kris turned from the screen and eyed her team. "It's nice to know that we may have a few surprises up our sleeves," Kris said.

"Considering that we only have two sleeves, and they have four," Professor mFumbo said, "don't bet too much on that."

"Good point, Professor," Kris replied. "Now, does anyone have any idea about who we are dealing with? Are they representatives of the Empire, or Wandering Men who have broken all allegiances? And is there any way for us to tell between the two?"

Eighty years ago, that had started the trouble between the two species. The Iteeche's first contact had been with human pirates who accepted no law. Our first contact had been with Iteeche Wandering Men, who accepted no rule and were under a death sentence upon capture by any Imperial forces. There was a lot of shooting first before anyone thought of asking questions.

By the time the Society of Humanity realized the mess it was in, the bad blood between the two species didn't invite conversation. No one who was part of that war wanted to think about all the years of bloody massacre and prisonerless battles that it had taken before cooler heads were finally allowed to attempt negotiations.

In the end, both sides agreed to ignore the other. At the time, the No Go Zone seemed large enough to assure the necessary separation.

It had worked for eighty years.

Why had the Iteeche come out now? Did they feel it was time to examine the standoff between them and the humans? If so, it hadn't started out all that well.

"It's not as if they violated the No Go Zone," Colonel Cortez said. "We are light-years from it. They might just be doing the same thing we're doing. Looking around for worlds they could settle."

"Kind of close to us," Jack pointed out.

"Only because we're getting kind of close to them," mFumbo pointed out.

"Chief, put up a star map," Kris ordered. "Iteeche red, human blue, No Go Zone purple."

It appeared in place of the solar system map that showed the Greenfeld cruisers no more than five minutes away from their jump point. Human space spreading out in all directions, but here it squeezed to the right and left of Imperial Space, flanking the No Go Zone. Human planets had grown from 150 to over 600 in the last eighty years. Still, the Empire had claimed over 2,000 planets eighty years ago. Even if the Empire had grown at its usual slow, dignified pace, humanity was still way outnumbered.

"So, folks, what do you think?" Kris asked. "An Imperial ship, exploring like us? An illegal, looking for a place to hide from justice? Or something else?"

Around the table, Kris was greeted with shrugs. Jack pulled a coin out of his pocket and offered to flip it.

"You're a lot of help."

"Who's a lot of help?" Captain Drago asked as he entered.

"My brain trust," Kris said, standing.

"Well, the system is ours. I'm willing to bet this fellow gets more talkative real soon."

"Right, but is he one of their pirate types or an explorer ship like us?" Kris asked. "Jack was about to flip a coin."

He did. "It's heads. What's that mean?"

"That your coin is no better at guessing our future than the rest of us," Kris said.

"Well, if you ask me," Captain Drago said, "whoever is over there is a smart ship handler. There haven't been a lot of course changes. He's got a good set of sensors, knows what we're doing, and does what he wants to do. No bobbling the course. We've also got some visuals on him. Good paint job. Not a lot of dings and dents in his hull. Somebody knows how to drive a ship. Or at least cares enough about his boat to keep someone working to make it Ship-shape and Bristol fashion."

"Not something pirates are known for," Kris said.

"If you want my money, I'd bet on an Imperial," Captain Drago said.

"And I'd never bet against you," Kris said.

"Captain, we've got a message coming in from the Iteeche," Sulwan announced over the captain's commlink.

"Where do you want to take it, Lieutenant?"

Kris considered her options: here, or the bridge. Of course, she could offer him a glass of wine and a chance to share a bubble bath with her naked body.

Come to think about it, that had never been tried during the long and bloody effort to stop the fighting . . . and the Iteeche were supposed to be partial to water.

"The bridge," Kris snapped. "It was where I turned Nelly off, and if I'm going to risk turning her back on, there's no better place than there."

4

Kris found the bridge more organized than when she'd left. Sulwan was at her usual nav station on the left. Penny sat to the right of the main screen, her finger only millimeters away from the fire button. The Iteeche was centered in her sights.

Her gravity sights. Penny had discovered the discrepancy and made the same call as the chief.

Kris took a deep breath. "Captain Drago, I have a computer problem," and quickly explained why Nelly had been so quiet of late. It drew low whistles from several of the bridge crew.

"So, Captain, any suggestions as to how we keep Nelly from taking over control and blasting targets we don't want blasted?"

There was a lengthy pause before the captain shook his head. "We could drain our laser capacitors, make her take time to charge the guns before she fired."

"Would you like to do that with an Iteeche Death Ball off your port quarter?" Kris asked.

"Not really. Very much not really."

"Penny, can you get your station to answer only manual input?"

"My station, yes. But the pulse lasers, I'm not so sure. It's not like this is something we designed for."

"Tell me about that." Kris sighed. "Is there any manual intervention at the laser we could do? Pull the plug, maybe?"

But Captain Drago was already shaking his head. "That's big power, ma'am. Those plugs are screwed in solid."

"My old man," the chief said slowly, "insisted there's no invention that is sailor-proof." That got tight grins around the bridge. "What if Lieutenant Pasley pointed each of the four lasers as far away as she could from the Iteeche?"

"That would give us some warning if Nelly took them over and started dialing them in, but not a lot."

"Yes, ma'am. But if each laser had a gunner standing by with a wooden wedge and a hammer to stop it from training, ma'am . . ."

"Chief, you are a genius."

"Yes, ma'am," he said, turning beet red, "but I think this proves I should stay a chief. Officers don't do real work like this."

"You're probably right," Kris said, with the first chuckle she'd felt like this morning. "Captain Drago," she said, nodding his way.

It took the captain only a moment to issue the orders to the gun crew. It took longer to explain the order and assure his gunners that he really might want them to disable their weapons because the Iteeche off their stern could be less of a danger than the vaunted computer around their princess's neck.

It took less time for them to report their lasers ready to be spiked.

Taking a deep breath, Captain Drago turned to Kris. "The Iteeche are still waiting for a reply. They won't wait forever."

Kris pushed Nelly's on/off spot.

The silence between Kris's ears continued for a lengthening moment. Kris had time to start to worry.

YOU TURNED ME OFF!

YES, I DID. I COULDN'T HAVE YOU STARTING A WAR WITH THE PETERWALDS!

YOU WOULD RISK CARA'S LIFE!

NELLY, I'VE RISKED A LOT OF LIVES. AND A LOT OF PEOPLE HAVE DIED TO KEEP THIS PEACE. I DON'T START WARS. YOU DON'T START WARS. IF IT EVER HAPPENS, IT WILL BE KING RAY'S CALL. NOT YOURS. NOT MINE.

AND, NELLY, WE WON'T DO IT FOR A TWELVE-YEAR-OLD GIRL.

KRIS, YOU ARE A BASTARD.

CERTIFIABLY, NELLY, AS IS EVERYONE IN MY FAMILY. BUT THOSE WHO WORK FOR US WILL OBEY US. JACK OBEYS ME. ABBY OBEYS ME. PENNY OBEYS ME. IF YOU WANT TO STAY ON OUR TEAM, YOU WILL OBEY ME.

SO YOU'RE DRAFTING ME. NO CHOICE.

JUST LIKE I WAS DRAFTED INTO THE LONGKNIFE FAMILY. NO CHOICE. WELL, NO, YOU HAVE A CHOICE. YOU CAN QUIT WORKING WITH ME. SIT IN A CORNER AND POUT. CAUSE ME TROUBLE AND GET TURNED OFF AGAIN.

I NOTICE THAT THE PETERWALD CRUISERS ARE GONE.

I TALKED THEM INTO STOPPING THEIR SHOOTING AND GETTING THE HELL OUT OF MY SKY.

BUT WE STILL HAVE AN ITEECHE DEATH BALL OFF OUR REAR END.

YES, NELLY, AND IT SENT US A MESSAGE. I DON'T THINK THERE'S ANYONE ON BOARD BETTER ABLE TO TRANSLATE IT THAN YOU.

YOU NEED ME.

YES, I DO.

AND WHAT IF THE ITEECHE STARTS SHOOTING AT US?

I WILL DECIDE IF WE RETURN FIRE.

HUMANS ARE VERY SLOW, KRIS.

I KNOW, BUT HUMANS ARE THE ONES THAT WILL DIE IF WE LET A WAR GET STARTED.

MY EXISTENCE MIGHT CEASE IF YOU GET THIS BOAT BLOWN TO PIECES.

YES, NELLY, THAT'S THE RISK YOU TAKE WHEN YOU SIGN ON WITH A LONGKNIFE.

BUT I DIDN'T SIGN ON. I WAS DRAFTED.

LIKE JACK.

YEAH. WHEN ARE YOU GOING TO TELL HIM HOW MUCH YOU LIKE HIM?

NELLY, WE HAVE AN ITEECHE WHO WANTS A REPLY TO HIS, HER, OR ITS MESSAGE.

THEY'RE NOT AN IT. THEY'RE BOYS AND GIRLS, LIKE YOU
AND JACK. JUST DIFFERENT. I COULD SHOW YOU PICTURES.

NELLY, TRANSLATE THAT MESSAGE.

"Yes, your slavedriverness," Nelly said out loud.

"Translate," Kris said for the bridge crew's information.

It was only a second before Nelly said. "The message appears to be in High Imperial Iteeche, honored equal to honored equal of middle rank."

"That highfalutin," Captain Drago said.

"There are only two higher forms of address," Nelly said.
"Superior equal to superior equal and superior unequal to the
Imperium. There are a lot lower."

"What's he say?" Kris asked. "Once you get past the grammar." Grammar had caused the deaths of several early attempts to start talks. The Iteeche criminals initially captured
did not give humans nearly the right structure, vocabulary, and
declensions.

Words can hurt you a lot more than sticks and stones if
you're talking to an Iteeche snob.

"The basic message seems to be three versions of the same
simple message. "Honored Lordling, I come in peace. I mean
you no harm. Great warrior, please don't shoot anymore."

"Then why'd they come all this way in an Iteeche Death
Sphere?" Colonel Cortez asked.

"My thoughts exactly," Captain Drago said.

Kris frowned at the Iteeche ship as it trailed them. In the
captured Iteeche records, it was called a Death Sphere and was
easily the equal of either of the light cruisers that had attacked
it. At this close a range, the twenty-four-inch pulse lasers of
the *Wasp* could cut it in half. Leaving Kris to wonder if the
much-vaunted Iteeche electronic sensors knew that the apparent merchant ship in front of them was anything but.

"Interesting," Kris said. "I've turned an unarmed merchant
ship into a warship. Could some Iteeche lord be touring around
in a disarmed warship for a yacht?"

"They're militaristic enough to like that," Penny said, speaking from her intelligence training for the first time this morning.

"Chief, you have anything more to tell us about that warship?" Kris asked.

"Only that it's got me totally jammed on any frequency that might tell me anything. Those three nacelles evenly spaced around the ball have got the same reactors in them that the Death Balls had in the war. I can't read what's in the forward half of those nacelles, but I'd bet my next paycheck that they wouldn't be jamming me if there wasn't something nasty they didn't want us to know."

"My thoughts, too," Kris said.

"Nelly, please translate this very carefully. Use the words they sent where possible. 'Honored Lordling, if you mean us no harm. If you do not want any more shooting, why did you come here in a warship like a great warrior?' "

"Ah, Kris, the message had no signature attached. I don't know who we're dealing with."

"Nelly, the chances of us running into a head-high Iteeche with really long claws is about the same as this fellow running into a Wardhaven princess. Play it equal to equal."

"Yes, Your Highness. But if I am right, you are going to be the one eating crow . . . or being eaten by crows. Of an honorable level in the pecking order."

"That's a chance I'll just have to take," Kris said, and found most of the bridge crew giving her weird looks. "What's the matter, you've heard me and Nelly argue before. There's nothing new about her talking back. Really."

Heads shook slowly. The looks didn't go away.

"Her jokes certainly haven't gotten any better," Captain Drago drawled.

At Kris's neck, Nelly cleared her nonexistent throat. "I told you, Kris, you really need to upgrade the computers of the people around you. They'd be much more productive."

"Shut up and send my message," Kris ordered.

Nelly shut up, and Kris turned away from the screen. Maybe Nelly had a point. Maybe Kris would get some respect if the rest of this bunch had to deal with something like Nelly twenty-four hours a day. Certainly not Nelly. How many Nellys could the *Wasp* handle before it became totally dysfunctional?

Today, *one* was too many.

"Message sent," Nelly reported.

Kris stood behind Penny's fire-control station. All four lasers continued to be aimed at four different sections of empty space. At her station, Sulwan held her finger ever so lightly on the shields' button. A flinch and the Smart Metal™ umbrella would come up on the aft quarter.

"I've got a messenger pod flashing," Sulwan said, not taking her eyes off her board or her finger off shields.

"I ordered Abby to load what we know about the Iteeche and get it on the way to Wardhaven soonest," Kris said. "Since the Greenwald cruisers vaporized our jump buoy, a messenger pod looks like the best way to get the news out. Can you launch it without its looking like a threat to the Iteeche?"

Sulwan kept her eyes riveted to her board. "Chief, plot a course to the jump that even a paranoid Iteeche wouldn't find threatening."

"I didn't know that Iteeche got paranoid," the chief said as he used the sensor board to plot a course that stayed wide of the Death Ball.

"My pappy swore every swimming one of them was hatched that way," Colonel Cortez offered.

"I want that pod out of here," Kris said.

The chief proposed a course, Kris and Drago accepted it, and Sulwan uploaded it to the pod.

"We heard anything from the Iteeche?" Kris asked.

"Nope," came from the chief and Nelly.

"Launch," Captain Drago said, and the pod rocked away at four gees acceleration, heading up and out from the sun and slowly arcing around toward the jump.

Kris found a seat. The Iteeche were taking more time than she liked. "I thought with us using mostly their own words, this wouldn't take so long," she muttered. "What's taking them?"

One of the nacelles on the Death Ball lit up.

The messenger pod vanished.

Sulwan hit the shields button.

Captain Drago pursed his lips. "Which of you was it that suggested the Iteeche might be riding around in a former warship? I think we can scratch the 'former' part of that."

KRIS, WHY ARE ALL OUR LASERS POINTED ANYWHERE BUT AT THE ITEECHE?

BECAUSE I ORDERED THEM. WE DON'T FIRE UNLESS I SAY WE FIRE.

I DON'T LIKE THAT. DID YOU HAPPEN TO NOTICE THAT THEY FIRED ON OUR MESSENGER POD.

I NOTICED, AND I DON'T LIKE IT. BUT I'M NOT GOING TO START A WAR OVER IT.

WELL, I HOPE YOU NOTICE WHEN THEY START A WAR, 'CAUSE I'D SURE HATE TO BE THE LAST TO FIND OUT.

"There's a message coming in from the Iteeche," the chief announced.

5

"Do not shoot us," came over the guard link in a half-computer, half-not-human voice. The English words were stripped of all grammar and declension. Stripped of everything but the plaintive cry for nonviolence.

"Please do not shoot us," it repeated.

"Why not?" Kris demanded in plain English.

"Why not what?" shot back at her before she could add, *You shot at our messenger pod.*

Kris bit her tongue to slow herself down. A good thing, because she swallowed the first three snapbacks that reached her lips. "Why not us shoot you?" she finally said. That should eliminate all ambiguity.

"We not shoot you. We not shoot, others shoot us," was so lacking in emotion that Kris had a hard time keeping feelings out of her own reply. She paused so long, trying to figure just what to say that the other side added, "We not shoot you."

"You shot our messenger pod," Kris snapped.

"Yes, we did."

That hung in the bridge air for a moment. Kris turned to her team. Jack and Colonel Cortez frowned in puzzlement. Penny looked up from her board where the Iteeche ship still was not in her targeting crosshairs. "At least they're honest," she said.

"But what good would it do to deny shooting the pod when the wreckage hasn't even cooled?" Kris said.

"I've known some folks who could tell such a barefaced lie," Abby said, entering the bridge in a businesslike shipsuit.

"Nelly, are you using their words for our replies?"

"I'm not using anybody's words. They're talking English. I'm talking English. Didn't Grampa Ray say that the Iteeche demanded that we always talk to them in their language, even when we thought they were hearing our English just fine?"

That was one for the human side, but it just meant that any mistranslation would be their fault. If a war started over this confab, that it was their fault wouldn't warm Kris's heart.

"Okay, then I'm going to keep this as simple as I can," Kris said, facing the screen front on. "Why did you shoot our messenger pod? Please give us a reason."

"Sent," Nelly said.

"Time the response," Kris ordered. A count started in the lower edge of the central screen. It got past three minutes before a reply came back.

"I am sorry the pod was shot. It was necessary." The voice this time was less artificial. Now it sounded more like a man talking. Apparently, this meeting had caught someone less than fully prepared.

Kris wasn't at all satisfied with that reply. She thought for a moment, then said, "Why was it necessary to shoot the pod and you be sorry about it?" The others nodded.

"I like the last part," Penny said. "In the negotiations, the Iteeche never seemed emotional about anything. This has to be the first Iteeche ever to say he was sorry."

"Send it, Nelly," and she did.

The reply clock was up to five minutes before the Iteeche said anything. And what it said sent jaws dropping.

"Do you have aboard a Longknife, spawn of the chosen Ray Longknife?"

"That changes the topic," Kris muttered, not sure she liked this sudden twist.

"You did kind of announce yourself," Jack pointed out, "Princess Longknife and all."

"I did, didn't I."

"Might as well admit it," Captain Drago said.

"Oh no I don't. Abby, is this guy a friend of yours? He's

changing the topic on me. Just like you do anytime I try to have a polite conversation with you."

"Don't blame me, honey child. This fellow picked up all his bad habits a long way from my momma."

"Why did you shoot our messenger pod?" Kris repeated. "Nelly, send that back."

"Done, ma'am."

The reply clock had hardly reset itself before "Is there a Longknife, spawn of the chosen Ray Longknife aboard? I must talk to her."

"Interesting conversation we have here," Jack said. "Kind of like most talk-talks with a certain princess I know. You say one thing. She talks about what she wants. Be interesting to see who gives way this time."

Kris didn't intend to be the one. "You fired on and destroyed our pod. You say you are sorry you did. Why?"

"Why" was hardly out of her mouth before the Iteeche stormed back—this time in Iteeche. Nelly quickly translated "I do not explain myself or my actions to any scum-eating monkey. I will speak with chosen Kristine Longknife, a spawn of Chooser Ray Longknife, or this conversation is over."

Nelly cut in fast. "Kris, the 'I' he chose is very close to Imperial. Someone is suddenly using precise grammar."

So much for talking to the scum-eating monkeys in their own jabber, Kris thought. "Then translate this into as high and fancy as you can. 'You are talking to Princess Kristine Anne Longknife, great-granddaughter of King Ray Longknife.'" Kris was about to add *king of 150 plants* but thought better of letting an Iteeche in on the present fragmented state of humanity. "You fired on the messenger pod I ordered dispatched to my king. Explain yourself."

"I adjusted the declensions, but I am sending just about what you said, Kris."

"Good, Nelly," Kris snapped.

"I've fought in a couple of wars," Colonel Cortez said, hand over his mouth. "Never actually been around when one was being started, though."

"I don't know why anyone would come across all this space to talk to one of these damn Longknifes," Abby grumbled.

"Step on my toes, you better expect to get kicked in the shins," Kris growled.

"Well, at least he's thinking about what to say back," Penny said, her fingers ready to change where her lasers were pointed.

The reply timer stretched, two, three, four minutes.

"You sure do know how to close down a conversation." Captain Drago sighed as he tried to get more comfortable in his command chair. "Anyone else hungry?"

"Starving," Chief Beni replied immediately.

The captain tapped his commlink. "Cookie, please pass some midrats around. And don't ignore the bridge too long."

"No problem, Captain, I'm hungry, too," said the cook.

The reply counter passed five minutes.

"That Death Sphere doing anything, hostile or otherwise?" Captain Drago asked.

"It's not so much as twitching," Chief Beni reported. "Same acceleration. Same jamming. Nothing to show anyone's there."

"Let me know if anything changes."

"*I* will," Nelly said pointedly.

NELLY, FEEL FREE TO HAVE THE *WASP* ZIG, ZAG, AND PINWHEEL WELL BEFORE ANY HUMAN EYE NOTICES A TWITCH FROM THE ITEECHE WARSHIP.

SO YOU TRUST ME TO DODGE, JUST NOT SHOOT, the computer spat back in Kris's head.

NELLY, I DON'T TRUST ANYONE BUT ME TO SHOOT.

BUT YOU EXPECT ME TO TRUST YOU.

Nelly had a point, but Kris chose to ignore it. EVERYONE ELSE DOES. WHY NOT YOU?

Nelly said nothing back, but Kris could hear more than the usual hum in her head as her computer went about its business. Nelly was thinking a lot.

The reply clock was still counting up when Cookie brought a tray with several kinds of fresh-baked bread, butter, and

steaming coffee onto the bridge. Kris had intended to relieve
Penny on weapons so she could get something. However, the
smell brought on some serious grumbling from her own stomach. So Kris postponed her good intentions until she'd had at
least one piece of the cranberry-oat bread.

Thus Kris had her mouth full when Nelly announced, "I've
got a message from the Iteeche. It requires translation."

"So translate it," Kris muttered through her stuffed mouth.

"It's High Iteeche, Imperial court member, make that high,
very high Imperial court official to, ah, oh right, an equal. Yes,
that's equal to equal. No insult here. This is pure head-high
muckety-muck to equal mandarin."

Kris swallowed. "What's he say?"

"Give me a second. This is not easy. But here is what I have
so far. 'Hail, Honored Princess Kristine Longknife, chosen of
the choosers . . . '"

"We've heard that all before."

"Yes, but he or she has to say it back in all the right declensions and fancy talk. Let me get on with it. I am also working
on the rest of the message. Give a girl a break."

The last was pure human twelve-year-old.

"Okay, but hurry," Kris said in straight Longknife short-
tempered.

"Where was I," Nelly said, sounding hurried. "'Hail,
Princess-Nose-in-my Face, with all kinds of whipped cream
on top.' Shows what he knows about you."

"Tell us the message!" didn't come just from Kris. Drago,
Jack, and Cortez had also run out of patience.

"Okay, okay, this is new, 'Greetings from Ron'sum'
Pin'sum'We qu Chap'sum'We. Chosen of the choosers and
speaker for the bah ba-bah ba-bah, I think the Iteeche have
a new emperor. Honored and exalted I bear words to he who
is now honored and exalted among men as King Raymond
Longknife,' and it goes on like that, which shows how much
they really learned about him."

"There's got to be a message in there somewhere, Nelly,"
Kris snapped. "I'm sure you've translated it for yourself." If

Nelly no longer responded to orders, maybe her vanity could be tickled.

"Of course there is a message. He wants to come over and talk to you."

"Why?"

"He didn't say."

"Kris, I wouldn't suggest you answer this flowery message with a curt demand," Penny got in quickly.

"I know. I know," Kris said, wondering if she could eat the entire loaf of cranberry-oat bread. It was good! However, Kris suspected a bit of worried eating might be viewed as very *noblesse* not *obliged* and be grounds for mutiny for most of the bridge crew.

"I guess I'm gonna have to invite him over for tea and crumpets," Kris grouched.

"My goodness," Abby said, hand up to cover a wide-gapping mouth. "Methinks our stubborn princess has met her match. I, for one, want to meet this guy, gal, or fish, whatever."

Kris ignored the joke. "Give me reasons he wants to come over here."

"To slit all our throats," Colonel Cortez said.

"He could have blown us out of space," Penny countered. "Us and those two Greenfeld cruisers. He didn't even fire a shot."

"Give the boy one point for politeness," Abby said. "Course, that don't mean he won't go rude on us once he's aboard."

"Accepted," Kris said. "Give me a nice reason he wants to come over."

"It's hard to play poker when you aren't eye to eye," Captain Drago said. "And this is a very-high-stakes game."

"Agreed," Kris said, finding that she was already busy figuring out how to manage the first human-Iteeche meeting in eighty years. And do it with what she had available on one small explorer ship. That Iteeche was back to using high mandarin. Now was no time to appear a poor, working relation.

"Penny, Jack, Captain, Colonel, am I giving in too easily

on this? Every time I've followed my agenda, he's replied from his agenda. I don't see any value in repeating what he's ignored. Still, do I want to get eyeball-to-eyeball with this dude?"

"He is offering to come to you," Captain Drago said. "We've only got his ship and our ship. Not many options for neutral territory. He's offering to meet you on your ship. That looks like a major concession."

"Assuming he doesn't blow it up," Colonel Cortez added.

"He's had plenty of chances and hasn't," Penny noted.

"He also says he wants to talk to you," Jack said. "Once he's in front of you, if he doesn't address what you want him to, you've got some call on him to answer you or leave. He asked for the meeting. You're granting it."

"We agree it's safe to have a meeting?" Kris asked. She got nods from most. The colonel frowned but said nothing.

"So, we are going to have a meeting," Kris said. "How fancy do we go? How fancy *can* we go?"

"We are just an exploration ship," Captain Drago said.

"Now dealing with a Lord of Lords," Penny added.

Kris made up her mind. "But we got a princess. Abby, lay out dress whites. Jack, Penny, Colonel, you go full dress."

"Swords?" the colonel asked.

"Swords and sidearms. Captain Drago, you and your crew get into the most colorful nonregulation set of threads you have. Purple velvet jacket, gold trim."

"And jet-black bell-bottom trousers. Got you, Your Highness, straight out of Gilbert and Sullivan, I think."

"Am I in uniform?" Abby asked.

"No, you are a lady-in-waiting. Formal ball gown. Ah, have you got one to fit Cara? We might as well put that twelve-year-old to work."

"I have a ball gown for her, one that matches mine."

"What better shows this is not a military mission than to bring along our junior spawn, I mean kid," Kris said, trying to pull her head out of Iteeche speak for a moment.

"She'll love it," Sulwan said. It amazed Kris the number of

grins that sprouted around the bridge. That kid had her hooks *everywhere*!

"Professor mFumbo, do you and a couple of your boffins have full bib and tucker?" Kris asked.

"I wondered why we packed all that extra weight. Yes, and several of the distaff executives brought their ball gowns. How many can I invite?"

"Ten—no, twenty. Equal male and female."

"Done. Oh, Your Highness, what about Judge Francine? She and her bailiff do look impressive in their judicial robes, and she would feel most left out if not included."

Kris pulled at her ear for a moment, trying to picture the scene if she threw a full bash. A grin grew on her face. "Why not. All the reports say the Iteeche love ceremony. Let's give this Ron-what's-his-name Chap-something-or-other a show. Nelly, inform Ron that we will be glad to welcome him aboard, with any of his honorable retainers, in three hours. If they don't remember from negotiations how long an hour is, teach him."

"Doing so, Kris, in the most proper of Iteeche," Nelly replied.

6

The next three hours were somewhere south of chaotic. While Nelly gave Kris a refresher on what they knew of the Iteeche, Kris got dressed. Even just the white choker took a lot more time than she wanted. Full decorations, yes, but now Abby and one twelve-year-old also had to be poured into full ball gownage.

The light green satin set off both Abby's and Cara's chocolate skin, and the several petticoats swished the wide skirts out delightfully. Abby had to lay down the law to get Cara to stand still and not twirl about.

So it was way too close to showtime when Cara danced down the passageway, leading Abby and Kris from their staterooms toward the main docking bay. The girl's skirts swirled out, sending Marines, sailors, and all others fleeing. Cara danced, and sang, "I am pretty, I am pretty," and if the song had any other words, they were long forgotten.

Kris figured once they got to the docking bay, things would settle down and get serious.

Boy was she wrong.

Somehow, someone on the *Wasp* had knocked together a throne for her and a similar resting place for a four-footed being. They'd even cushioned it with a Persian rug. Liberated, if Kris's memory served, from Professor mFumbo's own office.

The Iteeche would have no cause for complaint.

Assuming he knew the value of Persian rugs.

Problem was, Kris wanted to keep everyone standing, get

the introductions over with, then go on to whatever was the real reason an Iteeche was, if not in human space, certainly far from Iteeche space.

But before Kris could open her mouth to start rearranging the furniture, she got a look at the boffin stand-ins for courtiers.

Twelve men, not the ten she'd set as maximum, were standing around, three in full white tie and black tails. The rest . . . well Kris had been to balls where men showed off the peacock coloring that now passed for formal. She'd expected that scientists would be stodgy.

She was wrong. The pants, tights, vests, and tails were in so many variations of the spectrum, Kris had to fight off a headache. At least these twelve stood around very quietly.

There were thirteen women; all heads of their own departments or subdepartments. And all in luscious ball gowns. Including Teresa de Alva, Director of Information Support, who wore what the magazines had assured the women of Wardhaven only two years ago was the latest fashion from Paris.

The gown swept the floor, rising in rich folds to well below her belly button . . . where it stopped. Above that, it was a thin coat of paint. Very thin.

Teresa de Alva had both the figure to carry it off . . . and the personality. If the Iteeche had an eye for human mammaries, she would be most eye stopping. She certainly held the eyes of the male boffins. And their silence. Even Marines, posted around the periphery of the docking bay, were having problems maintaining "Eyes Front."

Indeed, Teresa was holding everyone's attention . . . and quickly gained Kris's.

"So, if none of us have ever been to a royal court on Earth or one of the few *real* kingdoms in space," de Alva was saying, no doubt a hit on Grampa Ray for the informal court he ran, "I would suggest that we use the next best thing. Didn't you love the court life in *Love's Noble Price*?"

Just the naming of that media hit brought sighs from the other women present.

And a squeal of glee from Cara.

"George, you can do that whirly bowing thing."

"No, I can't, my love," came right back at de Alva.

Kris came down . . . *hard*. "I don't want anyone doing any bowing thing." Kris fixed Professor mFumbo with a gimlet eye. "Did someone miss the message? I need stand-ins for courtiers. Wooden mannequins, no motors, no brains, would suit me very well, thank you."

Kris found herself facing a pair of blue-and-gold breasts that she hoped were not loaded.

"I thought you wanted to dazzle him with a full court," Teresa said, not so much as a millimeter of space left in her self-assurance for a denial from Kris.

"Terry, court etiquette takes years of practice. I doubt if the actors in the media spend less than a day rehearsing each scene. We don't have that time, and I won't have people falling on their faces in front of the Iteeche."

Kris took three steps forward and got every eye in the bay on her, not Teresa's boobs. "If you haven't heard it before, we've found an Iteeche quite a ways off their reservation. I want to know why. We need to find that out without getting anyone killed or a war started. I swear to God that if any of you mess up, I will personally shoot you right here in front of the Iteeche, if that's what it takes to keep him, her, or it from going ballistic on us." Kris drew her sidearm from the small of her back. Waved it.

The room got very quiet.

Kris did a 360-degree turn. She had everyone's attention. Even the Marines, now eyes rock-solid front, were paying her very close attention.

"Good. I'm glad we understand each other. You boffins, form a semicircle behind that chair. Chief," Kris said, pointing at the chief bosun, "get that overstuffed chair, table, or whatever that is," she said, pointing at the rug-covered platform, "out of here. Not too far out. We might end up needing them, but out of sight."

"Yes, ma'am," the chief bosun said, and issued orders.

Kris eyed the civilians of her court and their blur of color. One young boffin was in a leopard faux-fur tux.

"Nelly, do we have any pictures of life in the Imperial Iteeche city?"

"Not a one," Nelly admitted.

Kris turned around to find the missing military contingent of her court approaching. Jack had apparently been scheming with Gunny, Colonel Cortez, and Penny right at hand. Now the Marine captain was grinning from ear to ear.

"I wondered how you'd take to that," he said as he saluted.

"Why didn't you do something to get them off of this crazy court kick and onto something useful?"

"They're boffins, Kris. I have no idea of anything useful for them to do or the power to make them do it," Jack pointed out.

"And while I may take a bullet in a firefight," Colonel Cortez added, "court life, even that borrowed from a romantic vid, is something I run, not walk, from. That bit of courage I will leave to you."

But as the colonel took in Kris's full-dress uniform, his eyes widened. "Is that the sash and Order of the Wounded Lion? Earth's highest honor?"

"Yes," Kris said curtly.

"I hadn't heard Earth had stooped so low as to ship those out by return post to anyone's bratty daughter who asked for one," the colonel said.

"I don't believe they have," Kris agreed.

"So what are the chances I'll hear the story behind that bobble? Clearly, it's not got the wide distribution such an honor should enjoy."

"And it won't," Jack put in.

The colonel frowned.

"Don't you go feeling put-upon," Abby said. "Her and Jack and, maybe, Penny are the only ones in on the story hereabouts. And me, I got to dust that thing off whenever she decides to haul it out of storage, but she won't say a thing about it."

"More and more you surprise me, Your Highness." Then

he chuckled. "At least this surprise won't strip me of a command."

The chief now had sailors stringing lines across the docking bay. "What are those for?" the magnificent Teresa demanded.

"We'll be matching ports with the Iteeche ship soon. After that, until we separate from that ship, we'll be in zero gee. Being without gravity doesn't bother any of you, does it?" Kris asked, trying to keep malicious out of her voice.

Well, trying a little bit.

Teresa broke for the door, others following in her wake.

"Come back if you feel better after getting some meds," Kris called after Teresa. And felt truly evil for it. And really enjoyed the feeling.

Then she got serious.

"What is this Iteeche doing this far beyond their space?" Kris repeated the question.

"And do we trust whatever answer he gives us?" Jack said.

"Is this really that far?" Penny said. "Yes, I know it was eighty years ago, but does anyone have any idea what the present boundaries are of their Imperial territory?"

That brought Kris up short. Human space was a whole lot wider than it had been three generations back. The Iteeche were not known for their rapid expansion. But could that have changed once they bumped into the hairless bipeds, as they called humans?

"I am not liking all the questions I don't have answers to," Kris said.

Those around her just frowned.

7

"The ship will go to zero gee. Now," told Kris her wait was about over. She held herself steady on the inside of the docking bay while noises on the outside told her connections were being made. Given a choice, Kris would have been out there doing something useful rather than in here waiting, waiting, waiting.

Her first hint that the *Wasp* and the Iteeche were hooked was a sudden influx of moist air, smelling of salt. Five minutes later, an Iteeche ducked his head in the bay, looked around, then backed out. The Iteeche was in a space suit, or battle armor; it wasn't easy with a human to tell the two apart. Add in an extra ration of arms and legs, and it only got worse.

"Well, we've been scouted," Penny said. "Won't be long."

Kris hung like a spider in a web of social constraints. Her feet were looped into the net restraints that held her retinue in place around her. She wondered how the boffins were taking to the general rearrangement. Under normal acceleration or pierside conditions, they would have stood on the floor. Now, in zero gee, the netting helped them stay fairly close to the floor, facing the dark maw of the open air lock and the tunnel beyond.

One of the boffins grabbed for her mouth and weakly pushed herself off, heading for the exit above. A Marine added an extra push. A sailor at the hatch caught her and got her outside. Only then did the sounds of explosive sickness come. Sadly for Kris, it wasn't de Alva.

"Stand by to render honors," drew Kris back to face the air lock. Six side boys, half of them side girls, stood by, with a bosun ready to pipe the Iteeche aboard. The chief bosun had a straight view up the docking tunnel.

When he announced "Stand by," showtime wasn't far off.

Two Iteeche, fully seven feet tall, sailed through the hatch in perfect formation. Their uniforms were black as midnight. The poles they held before them were topped by wicked-looking hacking blades and streamers of every color of the rainbow, many with two or three colors in clashing combination. The two expertly caught themselves on the lines strung across the docking bay, changed directions, and came to rest at stiff attention, one to the right of Kris, the other to the left, a good four meters in front of Abby and Cara, who, with the exception of the side crew, were the closest humans to the hatch. The two black-clad Iteeche left plenty of space between them for more.

One spoke softly into a mic at its throat.

I CANNOT SAY EXACTLY WHAT THE ITEECHE REPORTED, Nelly said, BUT I THINK IT WENT SOMETHING LIKE "THE ANIMALS ARE FRIGHTENED BUT QUIET." I COULD BE WRONG.

Kris doubted that.

For a long minute, nothing happened. Kris studied the two Iteeche in black. There were huge holes in human knowledge about the Iteeche, their language, culture, and government. Humans knew quite a bit about their anatomy; they'd dissected plenty of dead bodies. Their four legs were all the same, the rear ones were not specialized like, say, those of horses. Each leg folded in two places; the top and bottom bones went one way, the middle one the other. This allowed them to fold their long legs into a very small space. The arms had two elbows. Engineers marveled at how their shoulder allowed all four arms to swivel forward or back. The head was larger than a human's. They breathed and spoke through a vestigial beak that once might have looked like a hawk's but now was softer and more flexible, if no less frightening.

Their long necks could swivel most of the way around and

showed eight strips that might once have been gill slits but
now changed color in interesting ways. The four eyes gave
a panoramic view, and the rear ones could rotate separately
from the central front pair. The Iteeche were built for situ-
ational awareness . . . and could quickly respond in almost any
direction.

"You don't go hand to hand with an Iteeche and live to
tell the story," Grampa Trouble had explained to Kris. "You
shoot the bastards from a safe distance, then do a dead check
to make sure they're sincerely dead. Don't count an Iteeche
dead unless you can see their brains splattered around them."

It had been an ugly war.

Dear God, don't let me screw up and start that up again,
Kris thought, wondering if she was finally learning to pray
like Tommy had said she should.

Finally, four more Iteeche came through the hatch, watching their steps with care and making good use of the netting.
They took station in line just inside the first two; their uniforms were crimson red. Their only decorations were black
starbursts as collar tabs. They held long objects that Kris immediately recognized as their equivalent of rifles.

Kris thought, *Marines,* before Nelly confirmed it.

Two more in gray-and-gold uniforms crossed the hatch to
join the line forming across from Kris. The color alone had
Kris thinking, *Army,* before Nelly told her, NAVY OFFICERS.

Good lesson in not jumping to conclusions.

The space directly across from Kris was getting narrow;
the big kahuna had to be along soon. The bosun raised pipe to
lips and whistled the ancient notes.

Two Iteeche led a final Iteeche aboard. The lead two wore
dark green and white. The last looked like a circus horse
draped in every color available and then some. Sections of
his dress seemed to change color as light struck him. At his
neck was a collar that exploded like a starburst. Kris had
seen some spectacular shows in her life; this man set a new
standard.

Suddenly, her dress whites didn't seem all that fancy. She'd just have to impress this Ron fellow with her good looks and sharp intellect. Well, not-too-dumb intellect.

Kris tried to see herself the way this Iteeche did. Directly between them were Abby and Cara in their light green ball gowns. Flanking Kris was her military team, Penny, Jack, and Cortez in blues, reds, and black. Drago was in the fanciest uniform ever dreamed up by an opera costumer. Behind Kris, in a half circle, were the surviving boffins in their colorful finery.

For a full minute . . . Kris had Nelly time it . . . both sides just stared at each other. It went well past awkward, but Kris held her silent ground. *He* asked for a meeting. He could damn well start the talking.

Finally, Ron-whatever-he-called-himself cleared his throat and exchanged the quickest of glances with one of the somber green-and-white fellows. Kris would bet money that someone had just lost a bet.

He raised his two inner hands, palms out, and began to speak. "I come in peace to all mankind," was halting, and it rasped a bit hard from his beaked mouth, but he said it in English.

"It would be easier to buy if they hadn't shot our pod," the colonel whispered.

"We'll cover that later," Kris whispered. NELLY, HOW DO I SAY "I GREET YOU IN PEACE" IN ITEECHE?

NO WAY, KRIS, EVEN IF YOU PRACTICED A MONTH. JUST SAY THE ENGLISH. MAYBE HE'LL UNDERSTAND YOU.

Kris said it. Nothing happened. The silence started to grow. Just before it became eligible to vote, the Iteeche tapped a machine at his chest.

It started saying things. In Iteeche.

NELLY?

I AM WORKING ON IT, Nelly snapped. THEY DON'T FOLLOW OUR STRUCTURE. SOME IMPORTANT WORDS ARE AT THE END OF THE SENTENCE. ASSUMING THEY USE SENTENCES.

LET ME KNOW WHEN YOU CAN, Kris said, not at all happy to have her somewhat flaky computer calling the shots . . . again.

The Iteeche fell silent.

Nelly started speaking a second later. "He says, 'I, Ron'sum'Pin'sum'We, etc., etc., chosen of the'—I think that means Imperial choosers—'spawn of somebody equally important for a couple of generations, accept the presence of Princess Kristine Longknife, chosen and all that, spawn many times removed of Raymond of the Long-Reaching Knife, to share water, slaughter many little fish.' That is what he said. It could mean something else. Then he goes on, 'I am here to share words. If you do not strongly object'—and that literally means draw swords—'I shall disturb your water with my words.'"

"Are you sure that's what he said, Nelly?" Kris said.

"You're welcome to try your hand at translating, honey," Nelly said in full huff.

"Nelly is a woman's name," came in a machine voice from the chest of the multicolor Iteeche, Ron.

"Yes," Kris said keeping it simple.

The Iteeche whispered something. "You name a machine?" his machine said.

One of the fellows in green and white turned back to the rainbow one and whispered something hurriedly. The other fellow lifted a finger off the machine and said something back just as fast.

NELLY, IT WOULD BE NICE TO KNOW WHAT'S GOING ON HERE.

THE GREEN-AND-WHITE FELLOW SAID SOMETHING LIKE "KEEP TO THE SCRIPT." AH, "SAY THE WORDS WE PUT IN YOUR MOUTH." RON SAID, "BUT THEY CAN'T UNDERSTAND THEM." HEY, HE SAID "THEY," AN INFORMAL USE AS AMONG EQUALS, NOT TO SCUM-EATING MONKEYS. COULD BE IMPORTANT. ALSO, KRIS, RON IS A WHOLE LOT YOUNGER THAN THE GUYS IN GREEN AND WHITE. I THINK HE'S YOUNGER THAN ALL OF THEM.

AND THE EMPIRE WAS ALWAYS SO AGE-BOUND, Kris remembered from somewhere.

I DON'T THINK THIS EMBASSY FITS THAT.

"Yes, I name my machine, or computer," Kris said, choosing to answer what had been said to her and ignore all the internal debate . . . from both sides. "It works better for me when I do."

THAT AND DRAFTING ME.

DON'T JUGGLE MY ELBOW, NELLY. IF YOU MAKE ME LAUGH OUT OF PLACE, OR EVEN SMILE, GOD ONLY KNOWS WHAT WILL HAPPEN.

Nelly translated for a moment. The green-and-white guy said nothing, but his former gills took on a pink tinge.

I THINK PINK MEANS EMBARRASSED, Nelly put in.

YES, NOW I REMEMBER. Kris had forgotten that the old gill slits of the Iteeche sometimes took on meaningful colors. Red almost always meant blood was about to be spilled. Black was deadly intent. White was just flat dead.

OOPS, MY UNIFORM MAY BE SENDING THE MESSAGE THAT I'M WHITE, BELLY-UP DEAD ON THE TOP OF THE POND, COME BITE ME, Kris remembered.

YOU DIDN'T ASK ME, Nelly pointed out.

But Ron was whispering to his machine again. It said, in a soft, machine voice, "It did not do good translating my words to your words even with a name."

Kris jumped in before Nelly could, choosing her words for precise meanings. "Your words were very difficult for us to translate. 'Eat many small fish'? 'Share water.' These words say something to you. Even though we hear the words, we do not understand what the meanings are behind them for you."

Now it was Ron's turn to glare at both his green and whites.

Kris decided to take the bull by the horns. "I welcome you to my ship," she said with a sweep of her arm to cover their surroundings. "Let us speak words of peace and harmony to each other."

HOW DO I TRANSLATE THAT? Nelly asked.

WHAT KIND OF SYNTAX DID HE USE?

NOT MUCH OF ANY, BUT IT WAS EQUAL TO EQUAL.

THEN KEEP THE SYNTAX SIMPLE AND EQUAL.

Nelly spoke softly in Iteeche, mimicking Kris's voice.

The two green and whites' necks turned a brighter pink, almost red. Ron's took on a soft greenish tinge.

I DON'T THINK MY TRANSLATION WAS BAD ENOUGH TO MAKE HIM THROW UP. Nelly pouted.

HE'S NOT SICK. GREEN IS A HAPPY COLOR. YOU KNOW THAT.

YEAH, BUT I THOUGHT YOU MIGHT LIKE THE JOKE.

I DIDN'T, NELLY.

The rainbow man rested both of his right hands on his chest and muttered something to his machine. It muttered back to him. They exchanged words in rapid fire for a few moments.

WHAT ARE THEY TRYING TO SAY, NELLY?

HE'S GLAD YOU WANT TO FIND PEACE AND HARMONY BE-TWEEN THE TWO OF YOU, BUT CONFUSED ABOUT THE LAN-GUAGE. DOES THAT INCLUDE ALL PRESENT OR THE HUMANS AND THE EMPIRE? I THINK THE TWO FELLOWS IN GREEN AND WHITE HAVE PROGRAMMED THE MACHINE TO ONLY THINK IN ITEECHE. NOTICE HOW RON KEEPS LOOKING AT THE TWO GREEN AND WHITES AND IS GETTING MORE AND MORE RED. I THINK THE GREEN AND WHITES HAVE HIS MACHINE ARGU-ING WITH HIM MORE THAN I'D EVEN THINK OF ARGUING WITH YOU EVEN THOUGH I AM SO DRAFTED.

The green and whites were now both talking to the youn-ger Iteeche. He opened his mouth, but before he could get a word out, the machine began rattling off Iteeche in a booming voice.

WHAT'S IT SAYING, NELLY?

Nelly translated aloud for all the humans present. "'The Empire is happy to grant the smelly something or others'—I'd translate it as monkeys—'the continued right to breathe air, drink water, and yadda yadda, yadda, exist in general.' Kris, they're talking down to us, emperor to mud-covered peasant. There's more about us not having the right to so much as draw breath if it doesn't please the emperor. How they smashed us into the mud and walked over our foul red-bleeding bodies in the war. This *is* nasty stuff."

"Did Ron say anything like that to his machine?" Kris asked.

"Not that I heard," Nelly answered.

"So, the odds are that this is some claptrap that his advisors loaded before they came over here," Kris said, glancing at Jack and Colonel Cortez. Both men were showing red at their collars. The guys nodded agreement though they definitely looked called out for a gunfight.

The voice was still booming on, but Nelly wasn't translating any more of it. Kris raised her hand. "At ease, all hands. Let's keep our cool. We didn't come here to start a war. Let's not let them do it either."

Kris could hear tense Marines relaxing back into their netting. What she quit hearing was the racket from the Iteeche translation machine. It shut up.

A moment later, it was softly talking to Ron. He snapped something at his two green and whites. Now one of the gray-and-gold Navy types turned and joined in. Everyone was talking. It didn't look like anyone was listening.

If this was an embassy, it sure wasn't going all that peaceful even among themselves. Beside Kris, Jack, the colonel, and Penny were frowning, more in puzzlement than anger.

"Gosh, those guys sure like to argue," Cara observed from the innocence of her twelve years.

Ron raised his hands, all four of them, and silence fell with the speed of a falling executioner's axe.

One of his hands pointed, all five fingers and thumb out flat, at Cara. He said something. "Who is she?" came from his translator and Nelly at the same time.

Kris unwound her foot from one web and took a step forward to the next. The flashes of skin colors on all of the Iteeche across from her spoke more of confusion than any ordered emotions. She half knelt beside Cara, bringing her six-foot frame down to about equal with the girl's face.

"This is the child of my assistant's sister," Kris said. Beside her, Abby did a formal curtsy, not easy to do in zero gee. A moment later, Cara attempted one of her own. Hers was nothing like Abby's, but what it lacked in propriety, it made up in cute that needed no translation even across species lines from the look on Ron's face.

Kris said. "This is an exploration ship, seeking knowledge about the stars and planets, not violence among species. I brought her for her education."

HOW'D THE TRANSLATION GO, NELLY?

PRETTY GOOD, I THINK. AT LEAST I WASN'T INTERRUPTED.

Ron took his hand off his machine but spoke in Iteeche.

TRANSLATE HIM, NELLY.

"She is spawn of your choosing?"

Kris stood up to her full six feet, which still left her looking up at Ron. "I do not know the significance of choosing a spawn, but yes, she is young, and I have chosen her to travel with us, learn with us, and see the exciting things we see."

Even before Nelly finished, Ron turned to his associates. Kris was about ready to call them advisors though that seemed too mild a word for their own view of their job. "Open your eyes." Nelly softly translated his words for the other humans. "Even an immature swimmer can see that there is no harmony among us. How can there be any wisdom? Look around you at her advisors," the rainbow Iteeche said, sweeping Kris's side of the docking bay. "They show every color of intent and reflection. This is as much a pleasure boat and science ship and school as it is a warship."

Pleasure boat, Kris thought, then remembered Teresa was decked out like a streetwalker. *Maybe this Ron guy isn't such a bad judge of character.*

THEY'RE GRUMBLING, KRIS, BUT THEY ARE NOT ARGUING. OH, AND THE NAVY GUY SEEMS TO BE MORE IN RON'S CORNER THAN THE GREEN AND WHITES. THEY'RE COMPLAINING ABOUT RON'S NOT RESPECTING THEIR YEARS AND WISDOM. THE NAVY GUY IS SAYING SOMETHING ABOUT AGE MEANING NOTHING BECAUSE THEY'VE NEVER FACED ANYTHING LIKE THIS. KRIS, THAT "ANYTHING" HE SAID IS MEANT TO HIDE SOMETHING. SOMETHING THAT IS NOT PLEASANT. AT LEAST

THAT'S WHAT THE TRANSLATORS AT THE ORANGE NEBULA THOUGHT THE WORD MEANT.

THIS JUST KEEPS GETTING MORE INTERESTING, Kris agreed.

So far, Kris had just been reacting to this fuzzy ball of confusion. Now, as she took a deep breath, something that had been nagging at the back of her brain since they'd first been hailed by the Iteeche Death Ball took enough shape for Kris to take a bite out of it.

NELLY, CAN YOU FIND ANY REFERENCES TO CHAP'SUM'WE IN THE NEGOTIATIONS BETWEEN GRAMPA AND THE ITEECHE? IT SOUNDS KIND OF FAMILIAR.

LOOKING—OH, I SHOULD HAVE DONE THIS SOONER, KRIS. CHAP'SUM'WE WAS ONE OF THE ORIGINAL ITEECHE NEGOTIATORS. GRAMPA RAY LIKED HIM.

YEAH, I THOUGHT SO. ISN'T HE THE ONE RAY FIGURED THE TWO OF THEM COULD SOLVE EVERYTHING WITH IF THEY COULD JUST SIT DOWN OVER A COUPLE OF BEERS?

YES, I'VE FOUND THAT REFERENCE.

OKAY, NELLY, HERE WE GO.

Kris let her eyes light up and put a smile on her face. "Did you say your full name is Ron'sum'Pin'sum'We qu Chap'sum'We?" *Boy, that was a mouthful.* "Was your grandfather Roth'sum'We'sum'Quin, the negotiator who labored with my grandfather to find peace and harmony between our two peoples?"

8

Ron folded his four arms across his chest and bowed his head, all four eyes on Kris. "It is my honor and pleasure to have been chosen by Roth'sum'We'sum'Quin, both to walk a path with him and to follow the path I now place my feet on."

KRIS, "THE NEW PATH WE PLACE OUR FEET ON" WAS THE PHRASE ROTH USED FOR THE PEACE TREATY. THAT MEANS A LOT MORE THAN IT SAYS.

I FIGURED THAT OUT MYSELF, NELLY.

Kris took a deep breath, froze the smile on her face, and dove into the Iteeche pond, so to speak.

"My heart is glad to share this new path, your feet and mine." NELLY, TRANSLATE IT AT THE SAME LEVEL HE SPOKE.

GOOD, HE WAS USING THAT FAMILIAR EQUAL SYNTAX AGAIN, AND IT'S EASY TO DO.

Nelly started talking Iteeche even as Kris continued. "It has been a very long time since any of us have met and spoken words and listened to each other. I think it has been far too long. I know my great-grandfather, Raymond Longknife, would agree with me about that." Kris finished and found she was holding her breath, waiting for the next words from the young Iteeche.

"My chooser, Respected Counselor Roth'sum'We'sum'-Quin, has told me very similar words. When he and Ray of the Long-Reaching Knife separated, there was so much blood in the water that he feared that only a feeding frenzy could follow if we continued to share the same water. But, as with all things, passing time and tides have cleared the water. He sent me forth to see if chance and the gods of the deep might smile upon us now unlike their angry choices that decreed we must fight when last we met."

Ron glanced at his advisors. The green and whites stood still, red and dark green shading their gills. Ron and his Navy friend displayed a light green to match Abby's and Cara's dresses.

Next time out, Kris decided, she would put on a nice pastel green pantsuit.

Jack coughed softly into his hand, but said, "Kris, I'm glad you two are getting along, but there is the matter of them blowing up our messenger pod."

Nelly started translating Jack's words before Kris had a chance to stop her, then decided now was no time to cut off communications.

When Nelly finished, Kris gave Ron a moment to say something. He didn't.

With a sigh, she walked once more into the breach. "You must excuse my advisor. You are not alone in having them and not always liking the words they toss into the water. Still, there must have been a reason for you shooting up our pod?"

You want to say it just like that?

Exactly like that. Neutral. Nothing nice, but nothing nasty.

Nelly spoke.

Ron's gills were showing a hot pink. So were his Navy ally's. The two green and whites displayed a distinctive brownish green, reminding Kris of raw sewage. One of the green and whites said something in a harsh whisper.

What'd he say, Nelly?

"Don't you dare," or something like that.

Repeat it out loud. Nelly did.

The Iteeche's head swiveled, quick as a snake. He glared at Kris, eyes wide, mouth open enough to show teeth. The Iteeche were definitely carnivores, or omnivores like humans.

Kris smiled back, showing lots of teeth, too.

Ron placed a hand on the green and white's rump, and spoke.

"I—I," Nelly translated. "I think the word is 'apologize.' It didn't get used much in the negotiations. The decision to vaporize your pod was one that divided the old and wise advisors entrusted to my hearing. After much disharmony, the eldest demanded that we destroy the pod and all information in it and secure the benefit of time. Time often resolves problems that seem impossible in the present."

While Kris was absorbing that, Colonel Cortez spoke softly. "Yet the use of force often closes doors that need to be left open if fresh air is to be let in."

KRIS?

TRANSLATE IT. IT SOUNDS GOOD ENOUGH TO ME. Nelly did.

There was a lengthy pause. Ron's eyes flicked between the green and whites and the Navy type. Finally, that gray-and-gold one swiveled his head to face front.

"Have we closed and locked any doors?" the Navy officer asked, and Nelly quickly translated.

Kris glanced at Jack. He'd tossed this smelly fish out to start with. He gave Kris a slight nod and spoke. "You fired on our pod. That raised the immediate fear that you would fire on our ship. I feared that you might be a ship of wandering men who knew no law. Now that we have seen your faces we know you to be honorable Iteeche from the Imperial court." Jack paused to take a breath and let Nelly's words sink in.

"You stopped my princess from sending out a report that we had encountered an Iteeche far from home. Her Highness must inform King Raymond of such a new and unusual occurrence. I do not understand why that would cause you disharmony if we were to do that."

Kris kept her face an official blank and watched as the Iteeche showed a palette of colors in response to Jack's blunt words. Ron's neck stayed an embarrassed red. The Navy guy covered a lot of the spectrum but not as much as the two green and whites. Colors chased up and down their former gill slits.

Unfortunately, there was a lot of red and black in there . . . and not a little bit of white.

Finally, Ron spoke. "I sincerely hope that our initial move on this game has not left us with nothing further to do or say."

Kris wouldn't let that hang fire any longer than she had to. "It has closed off no thoughts in my mind. My appetite for harmony still leaves my stomach hungry to be filled."

THAT'S A FUN ONE TO TRANSLATE.

JUST DO WHAT YOU'RE PAID FOR.

WE GOT TO TALK ABOUT THAT. But the words were spoken.

It took Ron a long minute to digest her words. Kris noticed that while his advisors kept their eyes locked on him, he, for his part, had raised his eyes to the overhead, ignoring them and, apparently, making up his own mind. Finally, he came face front to meet Kris's eyes.

"I am glad that there is still a hunger for harmony between at least you and me. If we can fill our stomachs on that, maybe we can find a path for other feet to walk, maybe even those of our advisors." He gave his two green and whites a glance. They chose not to meet it. "How shall we do this?"

That, of course, was a very expensive question. Kris knew without asking that her advisors would be dead set against her going off on her own with Ron. Kris had no doubt that his advisors might agree with her own on nothing . . . except that the two of them needed a mob looking over their shoulders and hanging on every word they spoke. Oh, and recording it all for further review, analysis, correction, and posterity.

Being one of those damn Longknifes really sucked sometimes.

Of course, being one of those Chap'sum'We's must not have been all skittles and beer, either.

Kris rolled her shoulders. She had tension aplenty and the zero gee was not helping. Maybe that one could at least be worked around. "I do not know how this lack of gravity affects you, but my body was made for some good solid gravity under my feet. What about you?"

Nelly had hardly finished translating when Ron actually barked something like a laugh. "I spent too many early years hiding in a pond from the big-toothed ones to enjoy feeling no kiss of the ground. Yes, let us get your ship under way enough to know which end is down."

One of the green and whites interrupted. He put all four hands to his chest and bowed toward Ron, but there was no bend in his voice. "If her ship is to accelerate, the Navy"—here the green and white gave a narrow-eyed look at the gray and golds and flashed bright red for emphasis—"must take away the connecting tunnel to our ship. He told us before we came here that it was impossible for two ships to accelerate together on the same course."

Captain Drago sighed. "It's always the fault of the poor working folks, isn't it?" He gave a sardonic glance to the gray and gold, who returned a similar look that stretched across the chasm between the two species.

Ron straightened his back even more, something Kris would not have thought possible, and shook himself, setting all his many colors to shimmering. "I am content to stay aboard this ship while the *Reach into the Dark* matches course and speed at a safe distance. You may pull up your skirts and hurry back to our ship if you wish, but, for me, I will place my trust in the chosen spawn of the Long-Reaching Knife."

9

Half the Iteeche delegation were whispering at once.

SOME WANT TO GO BUT THINK THEY'RE TOO IMPORTANT TO BE SPARED. OTHERS WANT TO STAY BUT HAVE SOMETHING IMPORTANT TO DO ON THE OTHER SHIP, Nelly said.

THEY CAN SORT THEMSELVES OUT. I'M GOING TO GET THINGS GOING ON THIS SIDE, Kris said. "Professor mFumbo, would you get my boffin advisors back to work."

"Certainly, Your Highness," the professor said with a very slight bow. A shooing wave of his hands sent most of the scientists going hand over hand toward the exit. It took some personal encouragement to get de Alva moving, but she went.

"Jack, could we cut down on the honor guard?"

He hardly raised his voice. "Gunny, single up the line. No need to hold them from their other duties for this show." The wink that the Marine captain and his senior NCO exchanged told Kris all she needed to know. The Marines would be out of sight, but no one would take over her ship with a sudden coup de main.

"Kris, if you don't mind, I'm going to get Cara back to bed," Abby said.

The twelve-year-old's protest of "I'm not tired" had to force its way through a huge yawn.

Kris pointed. "You, bed. That's an order."

"It's not fair," Cara mumbled, but she was already being pushed upward by Abby.

"Hurry along, little dear, before they put on power," the maid said, almost motherly.

"Can I go to bed?" Penny asked, not even trying to suppress a yawn.

"Nope, you're supposed to be a grown-up and an expert in intelligence. What do you know about Iteeche?"

"Not my area of specialization," the intel officer said.

"Mine either," Kris said, "but we had these nice seven-foot-tall folks drop in, and suddenly I'm all ears about our four-eyed friends the Iteeche."

Captain Drago headed back to his bridge, not willing to let anyone else oversee the separation of two such dissimilar ships. Kris waited until he was past her, then turned her back on the still-undecided Iteeche, and whispered, "Captain."

"Yes," he said, turning back to Kris.

"Once Abby gets Cara down, tell her she has the bridge watch at my station," Kris said softly.

For a moment there was puzzlement in the captain's eyes, then they widened ever so slightly. Kris's battle station was Weapons. Kris, an active Wardhaven officer, had the duty to make the final choice to fire the *Wasp*'s hidden lasers. Kris wanted Abby standing by to make the hard decision if it was necessary to fire on the Iteeche Death Ball.

"Tell Abby her commission is activated," Kris added. That would eliminate any doubt about her meaning. Kris and Drago were in agreement that only someone holding an active commission would give the actual firing order. Abby's commission was as a reserve Army lieutenant in intelligence. Still, it was a commission, and Kris had just activated it.

"I understand," the captain said with an informal two-finger salute to Kris.

Kris was trusting . . . but only so far. Right now, she felt a budding kinship with Ron . . . son or grandson or whatever to some Iteeche war hero and all. She strongly suspected he'd grown up with all the disadvantages she'd had. Wealth. Power. Target bull's-eye painted on his rump. Yes, she kind of trusted him.

But those advisors? She was fighting an instant dislike for the green and whites. Maybe not the gray and golds, but the green and whites she wouldn't trust out of her crosshairs. Abby was neither the confirmed coward she claimed to be nor a trigger-happy "hero." Abby she would trust with her life. And Cara's life. All their lives.

With a deep sigh, Kris turned back to face the Iteeche.

They were still arguing. Or going through the motions of what passed for disagreement among their kind. Or maybe their kind in the Imperial court. The body language of the green and whites was so submissive. Their knees, all twelve per person, were bent into a kind of half crouch that left Ron towering over them. Their arms were crossed over their chests. Their words were so soft.

WHAT ARE THEY SAYING, NELLY?

I'VE BEEN FOLLOWING THEM WHILE YOU'VE BEEN HAV-ING YOUR FUN WITH CAPTAIN DRAGO. "YOU NEED ME. THAT MONKEY WOMAN WILL WRAP YOU AROUND HER LITTLE TEN-TACLES. OUR YEARS HAVE MADE US WISE IN THE WAYS OF TWISTY PEOPLE. YOU ARE SO YOUNG." STUFF LIKE THAT. RON HASN'T SAID MORE THAN A FEW WORDS. THAT NAVY TYPE THAT HE SEEMS TO TRUST HAS JUST STOOD BY. I'VE MADE A NOTE OF HIS BODY LANGUAGE. I'LL BET THAT IS WHAT PASSES FOR GRAMPA TROUBLE'S DISGUSTED LOOK.

Kris listened to Nelly, trying not to let her sudden use of contractions send the shivers that she felt down her back. Something big had happened deep down in Nelly's insides. And, of course, it would happen when Nelly had become the only link between two sentient species. Kris was relying on Nelly to build a bridge of communications across a gulf that could easily overflow with blood and guts if things went wrong.

And Kris had no idea what was going on inside Nelly. No idea at all. All she could do was hope that Nelly's new interest in telling jokes wouldn't send her and Ron, hu-mans and Iteeche, smashing into some kind of catastrophic pratfall.

THANK YOU, NELLY. KEEP LISTENING AND LET ME KNOW
WHAT YOU THINK.

I THINK THESE GREEN AND WHITES COULD GIVE YOUR
MOTHER LESSONS IN PASSIVE-AGGRESSIVE BEHAVIOR. THAT'S
WHAT I THINK.

No doubt, Kris thought, as she caught Ron's eye, or rather
the two left ones. Both suddenly seemed to focus on her. She
gave him back a soft, knowing smile, and the flutter of colors
playing on his neck softened into pastels, with more green and
rose playing through them.

Kris was glad that her skin didn't give her away like that.
How many times had she retreated behind a blank mask, not
so much as a muscle twitching while Mother or Father or other
authority figure went on and on about what she ought to do?
Maybe there was something she could teach the poor fellow.

Or maybe it was uncontrolled. What the ears took in and
the brain reacted to, the old gill slits put out for all to see.

So, the Iteeche might be seven feet tall, but they did have a
weakness here and there.

"How long do you think this is going to take?" Jack asked
out of the corner of his mouth.

"Your guess is as good as mine," Kris answered.

"The Iteeche have a preference for consensus," Penny put
in. "They took longer to agree among their own negotiating
party than it took us to agree with them. Or at least that's what
your grandfather swore."

So, suddenly Penny was showing she knew more about
the Iteeche than she'd admitted a moment before. Then again,
she'd had time to consult her own computer, have it download
everything stored in the *Wasp*'s computer, and maybe get a
dump from Nelly.

Oops! That dump might or might not be tainted by Nelly's
new outlook on life. Kris had better take a moment to warn all
her staff to keep an eye on Nelly.

But not here. Not in front of the Iteeche.

Lord help us. Kris sighed. *All hell's a popping, and there is
no time to form a bucket brigade.*

Wasn't that the story of her life.

But back to Penny's remark.

Colonel Cortez beat her to it. "Of course, our negotiating team included President Longknife and General Tordon."

"You mean Trouble," Jack put in with a wry grin.

"As he is Her Highness's great-grandfather," the colonel said with a slight bow, "I thought I should be more formal."

"Grampa Trouble is Trouble to everyone," Kris said, half sigh, half growl. "No way to sugarcoat that for me."

"You hang around Kris," Jack said, "and you get to know General Trouble up close and personal. I've learned all sorts of new cusswords for that man."

"I see," the colonel said, his eyes widening ever so slightly. "He's not as retired as I had heard."

"Not around his darling great-granddaughter," Penny added.

"Thank you all so very much for reminding me," Kris said. "But don't worry too much, Colonel. At the moment, I'm not on speaking terms with either Grampa Trouble or Grampa Ray."

"But didn't I hear the young Iteeche say he needs to talk to King Ray of the Long-Reaching Knife?"

"Yep," Jack said, "so Her Highness may just have to get off her high horse and go crawling back to her grampa. King to the rest of us no-accounts."

"Okay, okay, let's cancel this 'pick on the princess day' and get back to what our good military advisor said about our negotiating team including a certain Ray and Trouble."

"Yes," Colonel Cortez said, picking up where he left off with no more than a slight grin for the rabbit hole they'd journeyed down. "Those two were rather notorious for getting a bit in their teeth and running with it. Once they made up their minds about something, the rest of our team had to follow or have an excellent and well-ordered reason for not doing so."

"I have heard that about my kin," Kris agreed. "Sometimes I even think my father and brother may have inherited such traits. Course, *I* know *I* didn't."

That got a snort from the humans present, even the two Marines within hearing distance. Kris gave the two guards a solid officer scowl that took the grins off their faces.

Then quickly converted it to a smile when she noticed that Ron had momentarily lost interest in the present wheedling of his green and whites and was looking Kris's way with what had to be a puzzled expression.

Nelly said something in Iteeche, and Ron gave Kris a small wave with his lower left hand and turned back to his problems.

"Nelly, what did you say?"

"Nothing, Kris. I just told Ron that you were having a bit of trouble with your advisors, just like him."

"Nelly, you are not supposed to give away state secrets," Jack put in.

"Even small ones!"

"I forgot to warn all of you," Kris said. "Nelly has developed, or is trying to develop, a sense of humor. Help her if you can in your spare time, but be aware that what you get from her might be a very poor attempt at humor."

"Oh, Nelly, that sounds wonderful," Penny said enthusiastically, but the look she cast to the others was just short of horrified.

"Don't you humans go getting your panties in a twist," Nelly said in a voice not all that different from Cara's. "I've done a search on humor and peace negotiations and know they don't mix. I found a doctorate thesis on the problems of applying humor to conflict situations. It says it only works when used in a closed group, like the way you folks do it, but it is far too risky across major conflict boundaries. Okay. There! You happy?"

"Yes, Nelly," the colonel said. "You show us more and more that you are not only very smart but also growing in wisdom."

"Don't try to butter me up, Colonel. I know I'm the smartest collection of facts on this boat. I also know none of us has anything close to the wisdom we need for this mess Kris didn't actually get us into. Not really."

"No, it just happened on my watch," Kris grumbled.

"Like it always does," Jack added.

"Hold it, pretty boy, that was not humor. That was saying something snide to my girl," Nelly said.

"There is a difference," Penny pointed out.

"But it's true, all the crap does happen on Kris's watch," Jack insisted.

"But it's not her fault," Nelly insisted.

"It really doesn't matter, Nelly," Kris said. "Jack's right. I have bad karma."

"There's no such thing as karma," Nelly shot back.

"Karma, fate, destiny," Jack said, "call it what you want, but it's there and Kris has every flavor of bad it comes in."

Nelly didn't have a quick response to that.

"It seems," the colonel said, "that one of our visitors wants to visit."

A gray and gold trotted over to them while the two green and whites continued their running nondisagreement with Ron.

He paused about two meters out from Kris and looped his four legs into the safety ropes with expert care just about the time that Drago announced, "The *Wasp* will take on one quarter gee in two minutes. Prepare for gravity."

He glanced at the deck a meter below his feet and reached two hands for a hold an instant after Kris and her team did the same. With a slight bow, he began to speak.

"He says," Nelly translated, "that he's Teddon'sum'Lee, a ship leader honored to advise the Emperor's Trusted and Honored Representative, Ron'Sum'Pin'sum'We. He has been honored with the assignment to come to us and make arrangements for how we shall hold further talks as honored persons to honored persons."

"Tell him we'll be glad to get the housekeeping chores out of the way while the green and whites haggle," Kris said with a smile.

"You sure you want to say that?" Penny shot out before Nelly started to translate.

"You tend to your knitting, and I'll see how many sharks are really swimming in our little wading pool."

"On your head, Longknife. Just remember, if they start shooting at you, they're gonna hit the rest of us, too."

"You two going to finish your haggling before I forget what it is Kris told me to say," Nelly said in pure twelve-year-old.

"Computers don't forget," Jack said.

"But I'm a computer picking up bad human habits, remember."

Kris didn't know what an impatient Iteeche looked like, but the one in front of her was getting wide-eyed and tight at the mouth. "Nelly, translate before this fellow walks off."

Nelly did. He said something, and Nelly said something more.

NELLY, WHAT ARE YOU TELLING HIM?

HE WANTED TO KNOW WHAT TOOK US SO LONG, SO I TOLD HIM.

ALL OF WHAT WE SAID!

OF COURSE NOT. I TOLD HIM ABOUT THE HASSLING YOU WERE TAKING FROM YOUR HUMAN ADVISORS AND LEFT ME OUT. THAT TRANSLATOR RON IS WEARING IS A PRETTY DUMB MACHINE. THEY DON'T NEED TO KNOW HOW GOOD I AM.

YOU GOT THAT RIGHT, GIRL. "Nelly's explaining why we took so long to answer," Kris whispered.

Jack started to say something, thought better, and didn't.

YOU REALLY NEED TO GET ALL YOUR PEOPLE THEIR OWN COMPUTER LIKE ME. IF THEY WERE PLUGGED IN LIKE YOU, YOU COULD TALK TO THEM JUST LIKE YOU TALK TO ME.

AND YOU'D SPEND ALL YOUR TIME GABBING WITH THEM, SO I'D NEVER GET A WORD IN EDGEWISE, Kris said. But Nelly did have a point. She'd been able to get messages through Nelly once in a while from someone else. But that was when they were distant from her. Just now, it would be nice to pass a message and not have to worry about it being heard and re-acted to.

SUIT YOURSELF, HUMAN. IT'S YOUR FUNERAL. "Ted here and I have agreed that he's a Navy captain and 'housekeeping' is a good word that the Iteeche ought to steal from us. Are you ready to get some housekeeping issues out of the way?"

"Certainly, Captain. It is an honor to have you aboard," Kris said. "What can we do for you?"

The Iteeche captain spoke, and Nelly took up a near-simultaneous translation. "He says they will send one of the Imperial banner carriers back to their ship and keep one here."

"Do they need to keep one?" Penny asked into the silence.

"Do I need to get someone here with a flag?" Kris asked right after her. "We've got flags if we need them."

"No, he says they recognize the authority you have, Kris. It's just that under law no one may speak for the emperor without having an Imperial herald with full rig present under pain of death. It is an old law, going back to the days when lots of people claimed to speak for the emperor. Now, no herald, no Imperial words, or off with your head. Or something like that. Kris, I'm not sure, but I think the herald may have a recorder or perfect recall. Anyway, no talking without one."

"Interesting," Kris said, not remembering anything about this in the histories of Grampa Ray's peace negotiations. *So we live and learn.* "Of course the captain may keep a herald present."

"He also wants to keep all four of his Marines."

"Ship accelerating to one quarter gee in five, four, three, two, one," interrupted them. Everyone, even the Marine guards—on both sides—grabbed a handhold . . . or two. As acceleration began, they slowly sank to the deck of the docking bay. Kris was amazed at the graceful way both sets of Marines did it without taking their eyes off each other, or breaking from their stiff attention.

"Jack, are you willing to reduce my honor guard to four?"

"No problem," the Marine answered, then turned to face the Iteeche captain. "You do realize, I'll have some others guarding the doors and things. I don't think any of the people aboard the *Wasp* still hold a grudge against the Iteeche, but I'm not willing to take that chance."

"I'll feel better about the safety of the Imperial Representative if you do take those precautions."

"Good," Jack said. "I just didn't want you feeling surprised or betrayed if you catch a glimpse of extra Marines close at hand."

"It is easy for an old sailor to understand your need, and I'm glad to see you're as interested in building trust as I am."

"I think we understand each other on that," Kris said. "Anything else?"

"I and another Navy captain will stay with the Imperial Representative. At least one . . ." And here the Iteeche glanced back at the still-debating trio of Ron and his green and whites. He raised and lowered his head, something like a nod, but Kris strongly suspected the intent reflected was more the shake of a head in a human. She'd have to watch herself on that. "At least one of the Imperial counselors will stay with the Imperial Representative. Maybe two if they can ever settle matters among themselves."

"We don't mind," Kris started, then decided she'd better change her choice of words. "It does not matter to me whether one or two Imperial counselors come with the Imperial Representative. What is the issue that causes their discussion to drag on and on?" Kris knew her question could be out of order, but it was time to push back the mutual ignorance between Iteeche and human.

The Iteeche captain again turned his back on the argument and faced Kris. "My fellow captain who commands the *Reach into the Dark* must have a counselor on board, since he is sailing far beyond the boundaries of the Empire. Otherwise, he is subject to shortening." Here the captain drew a hand across his throat in an all-too-human gesture.

"Both of the advisors want to be with the Imperial Representative. Neither wants to go back. Can you see the problem?" Kris nodded. "It can only get worse. I warned both of them that our best chance to meet Raymond of the Long-Reaching Knife would be for us to transfer to a human vessel. Neither one of them wants to be left behind."

"How are they going to settle this if they can't agree? A flip of a coin?" Colonel Cortez asked.

"A flip of a coin?"

"Nelly, explain to the captain what we humans mean."

Nelly did. All four of the Iteeche's eyes widened.

"You would leave something of such honor to a random event generator? In the Imperial palace, they would likely refer a matter such as this to the Field of Honor. The one that lived would go."

"Iteeche kill each other over such matters?" Kris said.

"In matters of such historical importance, a family's honor would require the maximum exertion. Of course, I cannot really imagine either of those two being anything but a joke with swords on the Field of Honor."

Kris didn't consider herself a good judge of Iteeche fighting quality. She'd leave that to the captain. Still, the problem of having only two counselors on the voyage and no instructions on how to resolve their duties . . .

"You must have known this problem was coming when you set out on this trip."

"Some of us did," the captain agreed.

"Did that include the Imperial Representative and his, ah, chooser?"

Was that a smile on the captain's lips? His nose had flared wide and emitted a huff of air, and his mouth had widened, though his lips were still closed. "Roth'sum'We'sum'Quin did know this time would come. He marveled that the Imperial court sent us only two counselors. I, of course, was not privy to any advice he might have given his young chosen one."

"Is it normal for an Imperial Representative to be so young?" Kris asked.

The Iteeche captain eyed Kris. "Is it normal for humans to let one as young as you lead them by the hand? I cannot help but note that all your advisors are older than you. All except the immature one, who, I assume, does not advise."

BUT BOY DOES SHE ADVISE MY COMPUTER, Kris thought loudly in her head.

YOU WANTED ME TO HEAR THAT, DIDN'T YOU? WELL, I'M
LEARNING TO BE A KID FROM HER, AND I'M ENJOYING IT. YOU
OUGHT TO TRY IT SOMETIME.

I NEVER HAD TIME TO BE A KID, Kris snapped, then added,
DON'T TRANSLATE THIS.

Kris turned to her team. "Crew, it seems to me that someone has dumped a basket of hot potatoes right in our collective
lap. Any ideas what we do about it?"

Jack was the first to find his voice . . . and note that Nelly
had not translated Kris's words. "Well, I guess we could shoot
one of them. Death with honor doesn't seem to be all that
frowned upon."

"Assuming we can trust this captain's story about the Imperial court," Colonel Cortez said. "Considering some of the
stories I've heard about politicians circulated at O clubs, I'm
none too sure we should rely on him as an unbiased witness."

"Unfortunately, what I know about Iteeche doesn't give me
any better handle on this," Penny said.

"So we just keep waiting," Kris said with a frown. "I get
the feeling these two are willing to talk until one of them keels
over from old age."

"Looks that way," Jack agreed. "Maybe I should shoot one.
Shall I flip a coin?" he asked, reaching for his pocket.

"Let's don't and say we did," Colonel Cortez put in.

"Does anyone besides me feel that it's unfair that the Imperial court dumped this hot potato in our lap?" Kris said. "They
knew they had a problem. They didn't solve it. Kind of makes
you wonder what they're up to. Like I occasionally do with
my grampas. Huh?"

"This just gets stranger and stranger," Jack agreed.

"Sure would be nice if we knew more," Penny said.

"So let's ask some questions," Kris said. "Nelly, tell old
Ted here that we've been talking among ourselves and wondering why they didn't sail with three counselors. Two could
then go on with the Imperial Representative. Or they could
have sailed with just one, in which case he'd stay with the
ship, and the Imperial Rep would go on alone."

The Iteeche made a very good effort at a human shrug. "I do not know. It might have had something to do with Imperial court politics. One can never tell."

"I kind of thought it might. Politicians doing funny things seems to be something you can count on no matter what color your blood is," Kris said slowly as Nelly translated. "So, what kind of solution do you think the folks back at the Imperial court might have come up with for this problem? If they were all that concerned with solving it."

"Some of them might not be all that bothered if it wasn't solved. Not everyone thought we should talk to you humans again. As they see it, matters have gone fine while we ignored you. Why change?"

"Is that your thought?" Kris asked the Iteeche officer.

"I would not be here if it were."

"But you have no idea how to solve this problem."

"Not within my authority, no, I do not."

"Could you chop one of their heads off?" Jack put in.

"If I did, his family would demand blood from my family. Whole families have been decimated in such events."

"Good idea you didn't shoot anyone," Cortez said.

Jack nodded, as Nelly kept quiet.

"So it comes down," Kris said, "to the same mess I'm often in. I can't kill them, and I can't make them do what I want. You know the feeling, Captain."

"Too often," the Iteeche said through Nelly.

Kris eyed the captain, wondering what he was doing here. Ron had trusted him to come over and open negotiations, if only on housekeeping matters. But then, housekeeping matters like who sat where at the table had been known to tie up months of haggling. For an instant, Kris had a mental vision of herself in Ron's shoes, saddled with two nannies who had too many votes behind them to be ignored but too few brains to be much help.

Yeah, that was just the kind of learning experience Grampa Ray seemed to love dumping her in. Drop one Princess Kris in a swamp full of alligators with orders to drain the swamp. But no, you couldn't shoot any of the alligators. Endangered species and all that. Grampa Trouble would find the whole thing uproariously funny. The problem here was that poor Ron was being chewed on so much by the alligators that he couldn't find any time to drain the swamp.

Think it through, Kris. His "Grampa Ray" sent Ron on this mission. It has to be doable. It isn't working. He needs either one more or one less counselor. We can't kill one of them and make it one less.

Which seems to point to there being a need for one more.

Hmm.

"So, Captain, how does one get to be an Imperial counselor?" Kris asked. "Are you born one? Do you go to some school?"

"You must be a chosen of a chosen, yes, that is essential. And you must be properly educated. You must also have demonstrated your skills."

"How do you do that?"

"Some are drawn from the ranks of junior Navy or Army officers. After the Human War, there were a lot of them. Some are drawn from the ranks of industrial managers."

"Junior officers?" Kris said.

"I and my fellow captain are long past that career choice. Don't even think of trying to turn us down that path." THE ITEECHE CAPTAIN IS QUITE SERIOUS ABOUT THAT, Nelly added.

"So how does one of those junior people find himself in such a career as a counselor?"

"Three counselors must sign his commission."

The four Iteeche Marines were now drawn up with their backs to the cargo-bay doors. Kris eyed the two green and whites. They were still arguing with Ron at one end of the Marine line. At the other flank, the Navy captain and the two Imperial heralds talked quietly among themselves.

"Do heralds ever make the jump into the Imperial counselor ranks?"

"That is not unusual," the captain agreed. "The perfect

memory they develop as heralds is very helpful for a counselor."

Why did that not surprise Kris? There was just one more question, and if the Iteeche who bargained with Grampa Ray was anything like the old vulture, Kris was sure of the answer. "So, does the Emperor usually elevate an Imperial counselor to be his Imperial Representative?"

"Why yes. That is so," the Iteeche captain said with another one of his close-mouthed grins.

"So why doesn't Ron just elevate the senior herald to counselor and leave him behind on his ship?"

"Because that pair of unchosen Sissa bait have kept him too busy to think and because the senior herald is from a family that Philsos'sum'Fon'sum'Lee, the one on the right and also senior counselor, detests and would never sign off on."

"Never?"

"You think you could get him to sign?"

"Let's see," Kris said, and trotted into the fray. She didn't wait for an opening, but just had Nelly interrupt the debate in midsentence. Her audacity got her the floor, and she never gave it up. She didn't exactly twist anyone around her little finger, the Iteeche being so much bigger than she, but she did talk them around to her plan of action by the simple expedient of failing to notice when anyone didn't agree with her.

Amazing how well that worked with Nelly being the only translator they had. Five minutes later, it was agreed that the older herald had quite successfully served his apprenticeship and well deserved advancement to the rank of Imperial counselor, junior grade, and that both of the senior Imperial counselors would accompany Ron to Wardhaven to meet with Raymond I of United Sentients.

Kris got to observe how a delighted and a decidedly unhappy Iteeche looked. Ron was overjoyed to be quit of this endless argument. He was also appalled at the prospects of having both green and whites at his elbows when he met Grampa Ray.

Which explained to Kris why he hadn't applied the logical

conclusion on his own. There probably had been a time in her development when she would have been just as stubborn in her effort to get rid of two backseat drivers like that pair of green and whites. Still, she had to believe that her visceral hatred of endless yammering would have driven her to cut the Gordian knot.

Then again, her older brother, Honovi, had chosen to follow her father into politics. And she'd heard of him sitting through some truly mind- and rump-deadening meetings. Maybe Ron hadn't had the option of a more decisive career with the Navy and had more patience with palaver than she had.

She should really help him to get over that bad habit.

Assuming he hung around her for a while.

Well, now that they had all the housekeeping settled, they could get down to something important. Like, why did Ron want to talk to Grampa Ray? Oh, and why did the Iteeche slag the *Wasp*'s messenger pod?

10

Kris made a quick call to Captain Drago, and a few minutes later sailors brought in a table and chairs for her team. "Will you stand?" Kris asked. "Do you have something that you like to sit on? A rug?"

"Our honored selves will stand," the Imperial Representative said, and arranged his green and whites on one side of him, his gray and golds on the other, and the Imperial herald behind him.

Kris settled into the chair across the table from Ron. And found herself staring up and up and up. She waved at her staff and found Jack and Penny sitting at her left and right with the colonel taking the chair beside Jack. All of them had to crane their necks to look at the Iteeche across from them.

NELLY, TOMORROW WE GET A TALLER TABLE AND HIGH CHAIRS.

YES, KRIS.

DID GRAMPA RAY SAY ANYTHING ABOUT THIS PROBLEM?

NOT A WORD, KRIS. NONE OF THE NEGOTIATORS MENTIONED WHAT IT WAS LIKE TO SIT ACROSS FROM SEVEN-FOOT-TALL ITEECHE.

PUT ANOTHER BLACK MARK DOWN FOR IMPORTANT THINGS THAT DIDN'T MAKE IT INTO THE HISTORY BOOKS.

NO ONE WANTED TO ADMIT TO THE REST OF HUMANITY THAT THEY GOT CRICKS IN THEIR NECKS.

ENOUGH, NELLY, YOU'RE GOING TO MAKE ME LAUGH. Kris leaned back, so as to get a better view of the other side, and said, "It seems like we have two issues on the table. Why does the Imperial Representative of the Imperial court want to talk with King Raymond, and why did you fire on our messenger pod?"

With that, Kris shut up, leaving the Iteeche to stew on the questions. They hadn't wanted to talk over the net about those matters. Now they had their face-to-face meeting. *Talk to me.*

Nobody said anything.

For a long time. A very long time.

Ron glanced at Phil, the senior green and white. Phil looked straight ahead, ignoring the glance.

Ron's neck marks went from pink to red to redder before he nudged the counselor. Phil sidled a bit away from the Imperial Representative but still kept a bland look on his face . . . though his colors were getting a darker and darker red. Which left Kris wondering what kind of survival mechanism it was that displayed your emotions for all to see.

Now Ron's colors were a deep red blending into black. Phil gave up ignoring him and turned his face full on to the emperor's rep. At that, his skin suddenly went from red to black to white. The counselor crossed his arms over his chest and bowed his head to his superior.

That couldn't be easy for the old iron head, considering how much younger Ron was, Kris thought. But Phil the counselor held her full attention as he opened his mouth and spoke.

Nelly waited a moment before she began to translate.

"Our oldest and wisest counselor says in the highest of court language that, considering how much ill will and blood was spilt by the two opposing parties. And considering his personal responsibility for the success of the great and honorable mission the emperor has personally sent them on. And considering his, etc., etc., etc., that they don't want to get killed on this mission, and there are a couple of more considerings of how small the embassy is and how important it is and stuff like that.

"Anyway, both of the advisors agreed that it was important

enough to keep this mission a secret that they thought firing on the messenger pod was a good idea at the time. How were they to know that the, ah, there he goes using that word that I think means 'monkey' or some such, would react so viciously to their blowing something so small out of space. Them being Imperial Iteeche and all superior to all other things." Nelly finished before the counselor did.

"Nelly, a translator is supposed to translate, not paraphrase," Kris said.

"Trust me, when I print out the full text, you can scan it. It really was a blessing for me to cut it short and drop out all the 'you scum, me master' crap."

Kris kept her face blank, but it was clear from the foot stomping and glancing about that the Iteeche had noticed that a long speech had gotten very short shrift from the translator. Ron, however, hadn't turned his own translation device back on.

If she was going to say something, the sooner the better.

"Your Highness, may I answer this?" Colonel Cortez asked softly.

"If you promise not to start a war."

"I shall endeavor to avoid such an outcome, My Princess."

"Then have at it."

The colonel stood. "Nelly, translate exactly what I say. No changes. No additions. No subtractions. You understand me."

"Yes, sir," the computer said, almost meekly.

"Whereas, we the advisors to Princess Kristine Anne Longknife do understand the importance of any meeting that renews full and open communication between our peoples, the humans and the Iteeche. Got that?"

"Translated word for word, sir."

"And, whereas, we ourselves are on a mission of exploration. And, whereas, even as we met you we were carefully observing the boundaries of the Empire and human space. And, whereas, we are only too aware of the risks of space travel and the risks of life and limb in space warfare. And whereas we counselors to said Princess Kristine Anne Longknife have been entrusted with the personal life and safety of her by our magnificent and benevolent King Raymond I, and do take that responsibility personally on our own honor and flesh and blood."

"That's a lot of 'whereas'es," Jack whispered.

"But he's got it right so far," Penny said under her breath.

"Shush," Kris said softly.

The colonel ignored them and went on without missing a beat. "Therefore, let it be known that we would never have fired upon an Iteeche vessel or any vehicle issuing from such a vessel. Such an action is usually considered an act of war and could only harm the harmony and peace between our separate, hostile, and fearful people. And in a similar vein, the destruction of a messenger pod would be a really stupid idea, considering that two human vessels had already departed the solar system we were in and will be messaging a report immediately once they are out of the system that an Iteeche vessel has been spotted here and is even now in discussions with Princess Kristine Anne Longknife."

Now Colonel Cortez leaned forward, rested both hands on the table, and glared at the senior green and white. "And while we do not chop people's heads off for talking with our Kris, there is no doubt that her great-grandfather will be wondering why he is getting messages from other ships that she's talking with Iteeche and he hasn't heard from her himself."

With that, he sat down, folded his arms across his chest, and continued to glare at Phil.

Kris had to stop herself from nodding agreement. She thought of shaking her head, then gave that up as a bad idea and settled for saying, "I agree with every word he said."

After a long pause, Ron took four steps back from the table. His four advisors, the Navy types and the green and whites, gathered in a half huddle around him. Words flew fast, but in low voices. NELLY, YOU GETTING ANY OF THIS?

I HEARD A COUPLE OF WHAT I TAKE FOR "I TOLD YOU SO." THE GREEN AND WHITES ARE DEFENDING THEMSELVES WITH "HOW COULD WE HAVE KNOWN?" AND "DO YOU REALLY

BELIEVE THE MONKEYS?" THE NAVY TYPES ARE USING THE
WORD "HUMAN" FOR US, THOUGH THEY ARE MANGLING THE
PRONUNCIATION. RON IS PRETTY MUCH KEEPING QUIET.

Kris had noticed that. Then, she had also left the talking to
her staff. It was better to let them take the risks; she could always step in and damp down any problem they started. Maybe
Ron wasn't so bad at this.

Of course, when you've got an advisor who wants to shoot
first and explain later, maybe not so good.

DOES IT SOUND TO YOU LIKE THE NAVY CAPTAINS WEREN'T
THE ONES THAT CAME UP WITH THE IDEA OF SHOOTING THE
MESSENGER POD?

IT SURE DOES, KRIS.

Interesting, that.

Finally, Ron stepped back up to the table and his advisors
returned to their places. Nothing happened for a moment.
Then Ron started talking, and Nelly quickly translated for
him.

"My wise and learned advisors tell me that an August Imperial Representative does not do what I am about to do. Then
again, it has been a long time since an Imperial Representative talked to a human. Yeah, he said human, Kris," Nelly interjected before hurrying on. "So I am going to say that if I
had it to do over again, I would not fire on your pod. It was a
mistake."

"I accept your apology," Kris said.

"Our words would be sincere regrets. But they are rarely
sincere," Ron said with a sidewise glance at his senior counselor. He shied away from his young superior.

"We'd probably say the same thing and mean it just as little. Can we start our talks over again?" Kris asked.

"I would hope that we can."

"Can I send a messenger pod to my great-grandfather, King
Raymond, telling him of this meeting and your request for a
meeting with him."

"I hope you will." Beside Ron, Phil the counselor was as
white as Kris's uniform. She hoped the Iteeche weren't into

seppuku or other forms of ritual suicide, because Phil looked to be in line for that.

Now it was Kris's turn to get the right message across to her team in front of a potentially hostile audience. She turned to Penny. "Nelly, translate what I say for the Iteeche. Lieutenant Penelope Lien Pasley"—the Iteeche seemed into long names; Kris could do that—"please have Captain Drago of the *Wasp* reload all the data on the destroyed messenger pod and launch another. Add to that this update.

"To King Raymond I, I, Princess Kristine Anne Longknife, second born of Prime Minister William Longknife of Wardhaven, am now in discussions with"—HELP ME OUT HERE, NELLY—"Ron'sum'Pin'sum'We qu Chap'sum'We, chosen of Chooser Roth'sum'We'sum'Quin qu Chap'sum'We. He is known unto you as an Imperial Representative to the negotiations that resulted in the treaty between all humanity and the Iteeche Empire at the Orange Nebula. Ron, to shorten matters up a bit, has been sent by your old friend Roth to talk with you. I don't know why. I will talk more with him about that, but I want you to hear this first from me and not some other source. More to follow as I find out what's going on. Your loving great-granddaughter, Kris."

That last part was a stretch, but it would at least get a smile from him. "Penny, see that the message gets encoded. Nelly will give you the address access codes so the message goes straight to Grampa Ray. Get back here when it's done."

Penny tossed Kris a quick salute and hustled off.

I'VE ALREADY GIVEN HER THE ADDRESS CODES.

GOOD, NELLY, AND MAKE SURE SHE UNDERSTANDS. RELOAD ALL THE DATA WE SENT.

I WILL.

Kris gave Ron a smile, feeling a bit guilty about hiding the exact contents of the messenger pod but not guilty enough to not make sure that all they now knew about the Iteeche got back to Wardhaven immediately.

"You *will* call your ship and make sure the next pod doesn't suffer the fate of the last one, won't you?" Kris said, trying to make it sound more like girl to boy rather than a negotiator in a deadly game. Just why she did that, she couldn't say, but it felt good to get some of the tension off the table.

"Of course, Princess. Captain, if you will," Ron said, turning to the gray and gold they had talked with earlier. He produced a commlink from his robes and muttered into it.

"It is done, my lord," Nelly translated.

Ron turned back to Kris. "I could not help but notice that when you talk to the king, your great-grandfather, you shortened your name to simply Kris and my name to Ron."

"I hope I did not offend. We are less formal than you. I meant no offense.

"My chooser has raised me since choosing to be open to such lack of formality. He noticed it among you humans and prepared me for it. It has caused me some difficulty among my peers."

"Have you tried it among your staff? When mine get to arguing with me, it goes a lot faster if I don't have to run through all their formal titles and names, and they don't have to do the same for me."

The tight grin appeared on Ron as it had on the Navy captain, Ted. "Unfortunately, I have made such attempts, and it has not endeared me to my learned and wise advisors. Some of them have enough trouble remembering their station and mine. It helps them remember that they are the advisor and I am the advised."

"You may have a point," Kris agreed, "but it is way too late for me to try to get any respect from my advisors." Now the Navy folks on both sides of the table were grinning, the humans widely, the Iteeche more tight-lipped. All but the green and whites. Kris wondered if those two ever relaxed.

"Now then," Ron said, "what else is in the bowl for eating?"

"Why do you need to talk to my great-grandfather? You were going to tell me," Kris said lightly. With any luck, the easy way the conversation flowed would let them run right through this last, important point.

"No, I was not and will not," brought the conversation to a roaring halt.

"You won't," Kris repeated, as the faces around her and across from her got serious again.

"I cannot. My chooser, Roth, I assume you would call him." Ron raised a hand toward her.

"Prince Roth or Counselor Roth. We humans do add titles to our informal ways."

"Senior Imperial Counselor Roth," Ron began again, "asked and required of me to swear on all the graves of our ancestors that I would give over his message only to the one who negotiated with him, now known as King Raymond I."

"And if he was dead, God forbid?" Kris asked.

"I would return for further instructions."

"As simple as that, huh?"

"I am prepared to die and carry my emperor's message, undelivered, to my ancestors."

And studying his body posture and the soft voice he spoke his words in, Kris did not doubt he meant it.

She let that roll around in her head for a moment before she turned to see how the others took it.

Why would he have to deliver a message in person? Could he have a ticking time bomb in him—with him? But why would the Iteeche want to kill Grampa Ray after all this time?

Were they ready to restart the war? Was there anything more stupid than that? Would restarting the war be as stupid to the Iteeche as it was to a human?

Honor had been tossed around a lot. Was there some kind of dishonor in dying before your old adversary? When the old emperor got along in years, had he signed up his old pal Roth to have some kid like Ron go pop Ray?

This guessing could go on and on forever. Kris had nothing to base anything on.

"Ron, I need to know something about why you must see my king."

"I fully understand your need. However, you must understand that the wisest and most honored advisors of the court agree that what I have to say must come from my lips to your king's ears. I must be ready immediately to answer any questions he has about it.

"Honored Kris, I knew I was being given a difficult assignment when I was told of it. Certainly your king must have given you difficult assignments."

"All the time," Kris said with a sigh. One echoed by Jack at her side.

Ron shook his head, which Kris took to mean that he knew just how she felt. Maybe he did. She didn't know him nearly well enough yet to be sure. He went on. "I have been preparing for this mission to humanity all my life. I was chosen from the scum ponds and raised on land by Roth to understand your human ways the best of any Iteeche since the war. I have dreamed of this mission to humanity for years, sweated through my training and tests with just one objective, to build a bridge between my emperor and your people. Please help me succeed."

Those last words struck Kris hard. Failure was her worst fear. She could understand someone's desperate need to succeed, no matter what it took.

But, hold it.

"You have been preparing for this mission to humanity all your life?"

"Yes," came in English from Ron's own lips.

"This message you have for my king. It has been waiting for you to be ready for this embassy?" Nelly translated for Kris.

"No," was again direct from Ron.

"I don't understand." *Or you just walked into a lie.* Kris froze her face, showing a blank page to the world.

Across from her, Ron's neck marks went from pleasant pinks and greens to dead white. Kris watched his long throat as he swallowed hard.

"I have not lied to you," he finally said.

"Can you explain it to me?" Kris asked. She kept her words short. Razor sharp.

Ron began immediately. "My chooser chose me to be a bridge to you humans years ago and raised me for that purpose. The message I bear has only recently come to be."

"Something new has come up," Kris shot back.

"Yes," Ron again answered direct.

"What?"

Ron took a step back from the table. "I cannot tell you that without breaking my pledged word. I cannot say." He looked around at his advisors, his head bowed, and spoke softly. "But I will tell you that the survival of both your people and mine may depend on what we do now."

That was not what Kris wanted to hear. She'd saved a world or two in her brief Navy career. It had cost her dearly. Saving two entire species must come with a price tag that no one could afford.

"I need to talk with my staff. Do you mind waiting here for an hour or two?"

He didn't. She led her team out.

"What was that all about?" Jack asked, as Kris threw herself into her chair in her Tactical Planning Room.

"Your guess is as good as mine," Colonel Cortez said, taking his own chair. "Does this happen often?" he asked Jack.

"The future of every Iteeche and human alive is at risk and in our hands. No, this is a bit much even for the princess."

Penny entered the room. "The messenger pod is away. It made it to the jump point safely. What's this about every human and Iteeche?"

"We're all going to die if we don't take this particular Iteeche to King Ray so he can deliver a message from his grandfather," Kris said, not liking the taste of those words on her tongue.

"How'd we get in this deep?" Penny asked. "Things were going so well when I left."

"You'll have to ask the princess here," Jack said. "One minute the two of them are playing footsie and making eyes at each other. I half expected them to rent a room and tell us all to get lost for a week. The next minute she walks out on him."

"Am I the only one afraid he's on an assassination mission?" Kris managed to keep her voice below a screech.

"No," said both Jack and the colonel. Even Nelly, at Kris's neck, added her own "No" to the consensus.

"Well, it's nice to know that I've got a little support from my own Imperial counselors. Keep this up, and I'll deck you all out in green and white."

"You can't do that," Nelly said. "It would violate uniform regulations."

"Hey, girl," Penny said. "That was a good one. And appropriate to the situation, too."

"Thank you," Nelly said, sounding just a bit shy at the praise.

"Folks," Kris said, her voice full of exhaustion, "can we focus here? We've only got an hour. Maybe two. Are we going to drag this Trojan horse in to see my great-grandfather? At the moment, I'm not really bothered by the thought Ron might try to kill Ray, but it's the policy of the thing. Killing a king and all. Who knows, when I grow up, I might want to be queen."

"No chance of that," Colonel Cortez said. "I can't picture you ever growing up."

"Hey, the guy's fitting in right well, don't you think?" Jack said.

"Right quickly," Penny said.

"But I wanted that line!" Nelly wailed.

"I give up," Kris said, getting out of her seat. "The world as we know it is depending on us to save it, and I'm surrounded by clowns who only want to be unemployed stand-up comics."

"Those stand-up comics might be unemployed," the colonel said, "but no one expects them to know if a horse of many colors who just walked in off the street is an assassin or the last hope for mankind."

"Since I do like eating regularly," Jack said with a sigh, "I guess we'll help Kris on this. Hey, that remark about a Trojan horse was really right on, Kris."

"Thank you. Thank you. Now, for God's sake, do any of you have an idea how we make sure this guy is on the level? Anyone know how to spot every kind of weapon ever invented?"

Jack shook his head. "Kris, I can't even keep your maid from slipping weapons by me. I don't know where she buys that stuff, but if it's new on the market and guaranteed to slide through detectors, she's got one."

That brought silence.

"We need time to get to know him," Kris said. "And the folks around him. And to look over what he brings along."

"He definitely doesn't bring his own ship. No way. Nohow. No ship," the colonel said.

"He seems to be willing to give on that," Jack said.

"Which only means he and his would have prepared to come aboard and keep their assassin's kit well hidden," Penny said.

"So, we need extra time," Kris said, slowly.

"How do we get extra time?" Jack asked.

"Nelly, how are you feeling?" Kris asked.

"That question has no meaning, but, assuming you meant how am I functioning, my latest self-test shows I am firing on all cylinders, so to speak."

"But wouldn't you like to have some time with Auntie Tru and her computer Sam?" Kris asked, a huge, canary-eating grin consuming her face.

"Kris, you're always threatening me with a trip to Auntie Tru's, but there's never time. I don't need a trip to Auntie Tru's. I'm fine just the way I am."

"No question about that," Kris said, though the headshaking around her said she wasn't the only one who considered now to be a good time to make time for Auntie Tru. The former Information War Chief of Wardhaven and a family friend had been helping Kris with her math and computer homework since the first grade. It was Auntie Tru who had gotten Kris hooked on constantly upgrading Nelly. Not even a catastrophic failure in the middle of a math test in the third grade had broken Kris of the habit.

Auntie Tru had been the only one able to do the last three upgrades to Nelly and had probably done the worst damage to Nelly's good behavior. The last time Tru had her hands on Nelly, she'd installed an alien data chip of unknown purpose with instructions for Nelly to conduct her own exploration of the chip on her own time.

Nelly had never been the same. That chip and the twelve-year-old girl down the hall had done very strange things to Nelly. And now Nelly was doing very strange things on her own.

Now would be a very good time to let Auntie Tru have a look at Nelly.

"Kris, you're not going to turn me off or let Auntie Tru turn me off or cut me up." There was real terror in Nelly's voice.

Kris forced her voice to soothing. She would only get one chance to keep her computer on her side. "No, Nelly, I'm not going to turn you off again. Of course, I'm assuming you're not going to try shooting anyone up."

"I learned my lesson. Unless you say shoot, I don't shoot. Okay, Kris."

"I can't think of any other reason I'd have to lose your company, Nelly. I couldn't let you kill people. Even *I* try to avoid killing people."

"I know you do, Kris. I really don't like killing people either. Somehow it just does not compute right. So, I agree not to harm anyone, without your order, and you agree to let me stay active for the trip to Auntie Tru and not let her turn me off to look under my hood."

"Nelly, I don't think anyone, even Auntie Tru, could tell anything from a look at your insides."

"I know that, Kris, I just needed to hear you say that."

"So, to restate the bidding," Kris said, "we will invite Ron and his party to come aboard the *Wasp*. We will give them their own quarters and let them lock the area down. We will bug the place and do our best to spot any weapons other than those issued to the Marines. Only after the next jump, with his ship out of comm range, will we let him know I've got a computer that needs to talk to its momma, and the trip to King Ray will be a bit slower than planned. Any questions?"

There were none. But Jack had a comment.

"You know that suggestion that keeps popping up that we ought to have computer as smart as yours?"

"Yes," Kris said.

"Forget it. I like my dumb one."

"Me too," came from Penny and the colonel.

Back at the docking bay, Ron and his team had been discussing their minimum needs for a trip to Wardhaven. Ron had flat-out refused to let the Imperial counselors bring their full retinue. The two of them would have to make do with just one body assistant. Same for the two Navy captains. Ron got to keep one of his, and would Kris mind if they brought a cook? They could eat what the humans ate, but they wouldn't really like it.

Kris agreed on the cook, the three body servants, and their own stock of food. This required the ships to again dock and stretch the air lock. Under the watchful eyes of the Marines, crates of food, trunks of clothing, and household goods were brought aboard.

Captain Drago had empty containers converted to habitat for the Iteeche. One boffin kitchen became the Iteeche's, along with a human helper to operate the unfamiliar equipment. Extremely large showers and unusual-shaped necessary facilities were all plumbed in and working within twelve hours.

It was truly amazing what the lab techs and the *Wasp*'s crew could do when they put their minds to it.

And having Iteeche on board seemed to fascinate most everyone. There were a few grumblers, folks who'd lost family in the Iteeche War and hadn't forgotten. They were identified by the next day and referred to counseling. None were found to be a risk to themselves or anyone else on board.

Jack posted double guards at all hatches to Iteeche country, then installed security cameras and posted a double watch on their monitors, with a reaction team standing by close at hand.

Kris was sure she had everything well in hand when the *Wasp* jumped out of the system. The Iteeche ship was blasting for a distant jump on the other side of the system. It would return to the system at eleven-day intervals. Things were going good.

11

Kris invited Ron to the forward lounge to watch their first jump. Normally, she would be on the bridge, but she and Captain Drago were in agreement. No Iteeche on the bridge. So long as they didn't know about the extra jumps humans had found, and the equipment that let them not only discover the jumps but spot the spoofing that the Iteeche used to fool human weapons range finders, the bridge was off-limits.

Besides, the lounge was more private.

There were a few couples in the lounge when they arrived. Whether it was the seven-foot-tall, four-legged Iteeche, or the two Marines that trailed them in, one human, one Iteeche, Kris wasn't sure, but all three couples beat a hasty retreat not five minutes after Kris's strange parade entered.

The Marines settled down in the back of the lounge, near the door, and a good twenty feet from each other. That left Kris and Ron the entire forward section and its view ports. Kris found a comfortable chair. Ron unrolled a thick green rug, settled it on the floor next to her, and did that bending thing with his eight knees that got him comfortable.

"You always watch me when I go to rest."

"It's your knees. I've never seen anything like them in all human space."

"You will excuse me if I don't get excited about them. They've worked that way since I first came on land." Ron was a comfortable pink at his neck.

"Came on land?" Kris echoed. She'd read . . . and reread . . . everything known about the Iteeche. She knew that the species had only evolved out of the oceans fifty or sixty million years ago. Historical reports said nothing about individuals starting in water.

Suddenly, Ron was flashing red and green at her. "I don't know, but that might be a state secret."

"What, that your kids are pollywogs, swimming in water. Is that what choosing means? You have to be chosen to come onshore?" That was a stab in the dark, but it was an educated stab. This "chosen of a chosen" had to mean something.

Here was a chance to find out.

Assuming if he told her he wouldn't have to kill her.

That wasn't likely.

Really.

Kris held her breath.

"If my chooser is right, and our future lies along a path with you humans, then we are going to have to find out more about each other. And it is not possible to keep you ignorant of such a common thing. Yes, my egg was fertilized and hatched in the ocean waters of the planet of my birth. I swam in the shallows as I grew. Then I was chosen to come onto land and enter the social group, you might call it family, of my chooser." Ron's hind legs shivered as he finished, as if he wanted to run.

Kris spoke slowly. "I guess I'm glad to know that, though I don't see how it makes any difference. You survived growing up. I survived growing up. High school is hell on every planet." She half laughed. "What would have happened if you hadn't been chosen?"

Ron's skin turned back to pink as he took a deep breath, but a couple of slits still showed white. "I would have continued to swim, eating smaller fish until I was eaten by a bigger fish. Isn't that the way of all life?" He managed what almost sounded like a human laugh.

WONDER HOW LONG HE'S BEEN PRACTICING THAT LAUGH IN FRONT OF THE MIRROR, Nelly thought to Kris.

I DON'T KNOW, BUT I HAVE A FEELING HIS CHILDHOOD WAS EVEN MORE HELLISH THAN MINE.

I WOULDN'T BET AGAINST YOU ON THAT.

Kris smiled to hide her thoughts and keep a shiver from going up her back.

Ron reached out and ran a hand through Kris's hair. "I have always wondered what that would feel like," he said.

"My hair?"

"Not your hair, but any hair. We don't have hair. You humans seem to have it all over."

"Men more than women."

"It seems very strange. Your human men sometimes shave their heads. Women shave the hair in their armpits"—he pointed—"and . . ." Kris grabbed his hand before it could point lower down.

"We don't talk about the other places we have hair."

"Oh, why?"

"You cover some parts of your bodies with clothes. We cover some parts of ours. What we cover, we don't usually talk about."

Now Ron showed green, with flicks of gold. "We cover ourselves as befitting our rank. A just-landed immature has no rank and covers nothing. Only as we attain status do we gain the right to cover ourselves from the sight of lesser ranks."

"So, if you went in to see the Emperor, you'd go in bare-ass naked?"

Ron's eyes widened, all four of them. "I never thought of that. Of course we do not. There are always guards and servants. People of lesser status, so of course we have the honor of showing our family status."

"This is all very interesting," Kris said, choosing her words carefully. "Interesting" was hardly the word she felt. Confusing, involved, crazy even. She had considered her family as all-encompassing while growing up. She'd faced nothing like Ron's family burden.

Then Kris tried but failed to suppress a giggle. Teresa de Alva's getup had probably made her the lowest-status person in the bunch of fake courtiers Kris had.

Of course, Kris would never let that out.

Like hell Kris would never let that out. She could hardly wait to tell Abby. And Abby would, of course, swear it to eternal secrecy, and have the word through the ship within a day and throughout human space in, say, two weeks.

Having a gossip columnist/spy for a maid did have an upside.

"All hands, we are approaching our jump. Zero gee in five, four, three, two, one."

Kris's chair was locked down, she held on to its armrests. Ron put two arms around her and held on. In a moment it turned into a hug. A rather good hug.

Kris rested her head on his shoulder. It was a bit bony, but it had been a while since she'd had a shoulder to lean on. Nice.

"How long will this take?" Ron asked.

"It depends," Kris said. What she wanted to say was not long enough. "With you aboard, I expect Captain Drago will go through jumps supercarefully. Say just a few kilometers an hour and rock steady. I haven't given away a secret, have I?"

"No, we have bad jumps, too. I would have thought with your supercomputing machines, you might have figured out how to forecast the movement of these jump points."

"No such luck."

"Jump in five, four, three, two, one."

Kris felt a touch of dizziness. Ron closed his eyes and Kris felt his entire body tense beside her. This went on long after Kris had recovered.

"The *Wasp* will begin accelerating to 1.25 gees now."

"We're done?" Ron said, opening his eyes.

"All over."

"That was easier than I expected."

"Your ships have a harder go of it?"

"Ah, am I giving away more state secrets?"

"Don't really see how it matters much." Well, maybe if we were shooting Iteeche coming out of jumps. "I thought you'd captured enough of our ships or their wreckage that you'd have learned anything from us that would benefit you."

"Why would we want to change the way we do things just because you did something different?"

"Or better."

"Those who call you monkeys could hardly admit you did anything better than the wise Iteeche."

"Well, there is that."

"And if something is good enough, we use it. We don't like wasting effort on the odd chance we *might* make it better. Like my translation machine. It was good enough for my chooser, Roth. It should be good enough for me. Yet you wear your Nelly. Smaller, faster, more flexible. You humans keep pushing to see if something can be better. You know there are Iteeche who would say you make no sense and waste your resources for no good reason."

"I've been told I'm crazy before. But I keep upgrading Nelly anyway."

"And I keep getting better and better, so there," Nelly said, in English to Kris and Iteeche to Ron.

Which reminded Kris that she needed to tell Ron about the little detour they were making on their way to the king. As acceleration grew, and they took on weight, Ron let go of Kris.

"Did we make a good jump?" he asked as if hunting for something to say.

"We are where we want to be," Kris said. "Those three bright stars in a triangle. They're supposed to be there. I had Nelly find out the check stars before we made the jump."

"And, among my many duties, I found them for her." Again, Nelly spoke English and Iteeche out of opposite sides of her mouth . . . or speaker.

"You could show me some respect, Nelly."

"I am being respectful. If you want to see disrespect, I can show you plenty."

"Is your machine always like that?" Ron asked.

"I am not a machine," Nelly pointed out, bilingual again.

"Nelly's a computer," Kris put in when she could. "Machines are kind of like dumb animals to her. She's smart as well as smart-alecky."

"And I have to translate snide remarks like that," Nelly added, again in both languages.

"Ron, this seems like as good a time as any to tell you that I feel a really strong need to take Nelly to talk with the one person who can help me with her present strange behavior."

"This is strange behavior," Ron said, showing green and pink again. He might even have added a chuckle, but Kris wasn't sure.

"Very strange," Kris agreed.

"You haven't really seen strange until you've been around the princess for a while," Nelly told them both.

"Who is this person?"

"My auntie Tru, not really a relation, but a friend of the family since before I learned to walk. She's a computer expert and helped me with my homework and persuaded me that I just had to upgrade Nelly every time something new came along."

"A really wise lady," Nelly added in.

"Whom you chose, as much as she chose you," Ron said, showing solid pink now. "Does she live in Wardhaven?"

"She used to, but she's retired and when we found—"

"The princess found," Nelly put in—"

"A planet loaded with alien artifacts and relics, she kind of headed there to help with the exploration. It will be only a slight detour from the direct course to Wardhaven."

"A planet that really has items left over from the Ancient Ones."

"It's a bit of a jungle," Kris said.

"But some of the animals in that jungle might be descendants of one of the three species. Oops, was I not supposed to say that?" Nelly added, having thought better of her run-on mouth.

"One of the Ancient Ones!" Ron said, showing more excitement than Kris had seen from him since he arrived.

"If they are, they've devolved terribly. They really are more like monkeys rather than intelligent folk. They were throwing their poop at us the one time I ran an exploration crew through their jungle."

Ron stood. "I must tell my advisors. This delay is not good. But to see a planet with remnants from the Ancient Ones, maybe even shared with one of them. That is exciting."

"It isn't when they drop their poop all over you," Nelly added.

"Nelly!"

"Well, if you hadn't been in a space suit, it could have messed me up something terrible."

"I'll put you in a plastic baggie if I go for a walk on Alien 1."

"Does that mean there's an Alien 2?" Ron asked immediately, pausing in his turn to the door.

"Yes," Kris had to admit. But she added nothing more.

"Do you think we will be visiting it?"

"No," Kris said.

"May I ask why not?"

"Because when the Ancient Ones walked away from that planet, they forgot to turn it off."

"It's that complete!"

"Yes, it is. But remember, I said they forgot to turn it off."

"So?"

"Included in the things they left on was their defense system."

"Oh."

"We haven't been able to land on the planet. Last time I heard, we'd lost five ships and three full crews."

"Oh," Ron said, now white as a sheet.

Kris headed them for Iteeche country, the two Marines trailing them. Ahead of them went the two Royal Marines who had guarded the door while they were inside the lounge.

12

Kris was back in the forward lounge as they approached High Chance station. If she'd had her way, they would have headed straight for the Alien 1 jump. However, two cruisers now guarded the jump, one flying Wardhaven's colors, the other from the Helvetican Confederacy.

The people of the planet Chance below had voted not to join Grampa Ray's United Sentients but rather the smaller confederacy. Something about not wanting to be too close to one of those damn Longknifes. It really wasn't Kris's fault. She'd only commanded Naval District 41 on High Chance space station for a couple of months. Hardly time enough to make a bad impression.

And she'd spent a big chunk of that time hunting for pirates and discovering two alien planets. Oh, and she'd also helped them stop a Peterwald takeover.

Kris had given up on justice in this world. Actually, on most of the worlds she'd visited.

But Chance did have some nice memories.

Not two minutes after the *Wasp* locked down to its berth on the space station, one of them followed Admiral Sandy Santiago into the lounge.

The Longknifes and the Santiagos went way back, to that incident that the tyrannical President Urm of Unity did not survive. Ray Longknife got the credit for killing Urm. His good friend Captain Santiago died getting it done for him. Since that day, the Longknife family had done what they could to make it up to the Santiagos. And Santiagos usually did the bleeding when the Longknife legend grew.

The first time Kris met Sandy Santiago, she'd been a captain, intent on seeing that a certain family tradition stopped with her. Then she got involved with Kris. So far, it had only cost Sandy a few broken bones. She was now an admiral, commanding Naval District 41 and doing a great job of it.

Still, she raised an eyebrow when she saw Ron standing next to Kris. "I wondered why the gunny sergeant just about had kittens when I brought President Ron Torn of Chance aboard. I believe you two know each other."

President Ron had his hand out to Kris, but his eyes were busy taking in Ron the Iteeche. "That isn't what I think it is?" he said, face still directed up at the seven-foot-tall Iteeche as Kris shook his hand.

"President Ron, I'd like you to meet Imperial Representative Ron. He's got a lot longer name, but has allowed me to shorten it down to Ron. Oh, and he isn't here. Remember that."

"Not here," the human Ron said, finally glancing at Kris. "Another Ron, huh?"

Kris remembered Ron Torn fondly, and had once had great hopes for the two of them. He'd gotten close to her, gotten a good look at what life around her was like . . . and run, not walked, to the nearest exit. "How's the wife?" Kris asked.

She'd been invited to the wedding but had been forced to decline for reasons that, if Kris remembered right, hadn't involved anyone dying.

"Oh, she's fine," he said, still half-distracted. "Oh, ah, she's pregnant. We're going to have twins in two months or so. Kris, what are you doing with an Iteeche?"

"He wants to talk to Great-grampa Ray."

"So what are you doing here?" Admiral Santiago asked.

"*I* need to talk with Professor Tru Seyd. She's on Alien 1, so I need your permission to pass through. You aren't granting permission by radio."

"No," the admiral growled. "Not that it's helping. Gold

diggers will lie right to my face. I've taken to keeping them tied up until all their credentials check out. Do I need to tie you up to get you to hang around?"

"Longknifes don't hang well. You must have noticed that."

"Once or twice. You *really* need to talk to this professor?"

"Auntie Tru has been overseeing Nelly's upgrades since I was six. I need for her to take a look at Nelly."

"Her Highness here thinks I'm acting just *sooo* strange," Nelly put in, sounding like your average implacable teen girl. "How could I totally go any other way being around her for almost twenty years. It's like foreeever."

Sandy shook her head, not even trying to suppress a wide grin. "I see what you mean, Kris. But Nelly does have a point. Do you really think your professor friend can do anything about your, ah . . . situation?" she finally finished with.

"I don't know."

"I think, if you ask me, but nobody's said so much as a word to me, as if I wasn't even here, like, that Auntie Tru is going to tell our little princess that she's just got to 'buck up and soldier.'" That last was delivered in Auntie Tru's voice.

"For what it's worth, you have my permission to take the jumps to Alien 1. I'll post the order. You have time for lunch with me and Ron?"

"Sorry, I really need to rush," Kris said, taking Sandy's elbow and aiming her and the president of Chance out the door. The Iteeche stayed put, which meant Kris could turn the admiral down a wrong corridor as the Marine guide led the president back to the pier.

"Do you know what you're doing?" Sandy asked.

"No more than usual," Kris said.

"That bad, huh? The guy doesn't look too bad, other than being Iteeche. Is he okay?"

"He's not a bad guest. He's pretty much house-trained. Doesn't leave his dirty underwear in the bathroom. Squeezes the toothpaste from the bottom. Didn't bring aboard any unannounced weapons or bombs that we can recognize."

"Are you sure?"

"The Iteeche don't have nanotech. At least he says they don't. All our spy nanos have come back safely. We're on them like fleas on a hound dog. I think they're safe," Kris tried to make it sound like she meant it. "Anyway, one of the reasons I'm taking Nelly to see Tru is to give us more time to do this search, get to know them. Check them out."

"And so far?"

"They're . . . pretty alien," Kris said.

"I can see that. So, there's nothing really wrong with Nelly."

"Oh, she isn't happy with me," Nelly said. "Not at all. I know my jokes aren't that good, but really. Would you turn yourself off just because your jokes stank, I ask you?"

"She wanted to fire on some Peterwald cruisers that were shooting at the Iteeche Death Ball and hitting us instead."

"That could start a war."

"Believe me, everyone has told me that. I know. Nelly is not permitted to start a war. I know *that* rule."

"Nelly, I know that you won't make the same mistake twice. It's you making the first mistake and us not having time to stop you that I'm worried about."

"I see your problem," Sandy said.

"We need to talk to Auntie Tru," Kris and Nelly said in cadence.

"Can you keep your Ron from talking about my Ron?" Kris asked the admiral. "It doesn't have to be long. Just until I get my Ron to Grampa Ray, and they have their talk. I'll flash you a message as soon as it happens."

"You really think King Ray would want the word out that he's opened discussions with the Iteeche? By the way, what does the Iteeche want to talk to Ray about?"

"He won't tell us. His chooser, or grampa, is Roth, the Iteeche negotiator at the Orange Nebula, who helped Grampa Ray swing the peace treaty. He made him swear not to give out what it was except to Grampa himself."

"Hum, and you're sure this isn't a decapitation hit to start off the next war?"

"No, I'm not."

"Well, I'm glad you're thinking about the possibility."

"Lord am I."

"Well, I'll keep my Ron quiet."

"How? You can't arrest him."

"No, I can't. But I can tell him if he screws up your mission, you might very well be ordered back here. Last thing he'd want is a Longknife back running this space station. They still haven't paid off the party and battle damage from the last time you were in command of Naval District 41."

"I didn't cause the trouble. Hank Peterwald did."

"Yeah, but he's dead. You aren't. See the problem?"

Sad to say, Kris was very happy to be alive even if it did mean that a misguided boy like Hank wasn't.

"Have you heard anything from Wardhaven? I haven't gotten any mail since I reported my present situation."

"Kris, when you came in all silent, just minimum business talk, I had my comm chief do a search on message traffic for the *Wasp* and you. We don't have a thing in our buffer. Nothing's come through for you."

That didn't make Kris feel any better. Then again, the more messages shooting around space, the more likely one was to be intercepted and have its codes cracked. "Thanks for everything, Admiral, I appreciate your help."

"Anytime, Princess. Drop by whenever you have a chance. Things can get really boring when you aren't around."

"And I bet you love it."

"Don't I though." The admiral gave the lieutenant a two-fingered salute and went on her way.

13

Kris and Ron had the forward lounge to themselves as the *Wasp* went into orbit around Alien 1. With no space station here, the ship was back in free fall. The air circulation struggled to handle the sick boffins . . . and sick Iteeche as well. The recirculated air was heavy with the smell of chemicals that failed to cover the usual stink, plus a certain something extra.

"My counselors are so sick they are talking enthusiastically of dying," Ron said

"I've known a few who had space sickness that bad."

"How long do you think it will take for your computer expert to do her magic on your Nelly?"

"I really don't know," Kris admitted. "I don't think anyone has ever had this problem. I've always thought Nelly was way past even her Sam."

"She names her computer as well."

"Where do you think I got the idea?"

"An old family friend. How old?"

"She fought in the Iteeche War."

"You nearly wiped us out, you know?"

Kris almost forgot to hold on to her chair. "We nearly wiped you out! It was you that almost made us extinct."

"That is not what I hear from the Heroes of the Great Human War. We honor them for how desperately they fought to keep you humans from wiping us from the face of the stars."

Kris really wanted to stand up and pace. Somehow, bouncing herself off the overhead, then the deck, then the bulkhead just didn't offer the same release of tension.

"I don't mean to disagree with you, but I've heard the same old same old from our Iteeche War vets since I was knee-high and starting to attend political rallies in my father's arms. Holding me up for those old codgers was good for an extra hundred votes every rally."

"Sometime you must explain to me what a vote is and why holding a baby girl up would get them for your father," Ron said dryly. A true rarity for someone so recently of the sea.

Before Kris could explain anything, Aunt Trudy Seyd coasted into the room.

Tru got one look at the armed Iteeche Marine at the door and another at Ron and made a quick grab for a ceiling fixture. With an expert twist, she sent herself shooting behind the bar.

When she came up again, she held an automatic aimed at Ron.

Kris launched herself from her chair to get between that pistol and one Imperial Rep. Or as much of the seven-foot Iteeche as she could. Almost missing him, she made a grab for him—any part of him. So she slapped his face as she stopped herself. His skin felt soft and slick as she twisted around, steadying herself in front of him as his shield.

Auntie Tru took all of this in but did not lower her weapon. "Kris, has your ship been captured?"

"No, Auntie Tru. I'm as much in control of things as ever."

"Are these Iteeche your prisoners? No, that's a ridiculous question. That warrior is armed and kind of pointing his weapon at me. And your Marine is kind of pointing his M-6 at him. You want to tell your old auntie what's going on before she has a heart attack or kills someone or something she shouldn't?"

"Trudy Seyd, retired Chief of Wardhaven's Information Warfare," Kris said, still keeping herself in front of Ron. "May I present Imperial Representative Ron. He has a whole lot more name, but he's letting me save time by calling him Ron and me Kris. His kind-of-grandfather was Roth, the Iteeche who worked with Grampa Ray to get the peace treaty done at the Orange Nebula. He wants to talk to King Ray about something. I don't know what that is."

Aunt Tru stood up from behind the bar, her gun still pointed in the general direction of the Iteeche Marine, but not directly at him anymore. The two Marines went back to their respective forms of attention. "You didn't mention this when you asked to have me do a once-over exam of your pet Nelly."

"Maybe it slipped my mind."

"You're getting to be more and more one of those damn Longknifes."

"Comes from working for Grampa Ray."

"We should never have made him king or whatever it is he's styling himself."

"Auntie Tru, could you hold up on your comments about the present political situation."

"Why, my darling? You being a princess isn't so bad, but that old vulture Ray being king will end badly. Trust me."

"Please stop because I haven't briefed our visiting Iteeche on the present political landscape."

"You haven't. Oh dear me. Why not, Kris?"

"Because he didn't ask. I guess he assumed we were as unchanging as the Iteeche Empire."

Ron did something that might pass as clearing his throat. "Yes, I had assumed that, but now I see that as wise as my chooser was, he might not have understood just how much the tides of change sweep you humans away." Ron paused for a moment in thought, deep green and white at the neck. "Those two cruisers that fired on us . . . and you. They did not owe any allegiances to you and your King Raymond. I had thought they were just wandering men, pirates you call them. But they weren't, were they?"

"No, they weren't. And this kind of makes it easier for us to get into our talk about Nelly. Auntie Tru, Nelly almost started a war between us and the Greenfeld Navy."

"Oh my, Nelly, you are a busy girl."

"And I have been told I am not allowed to start a war,"

Nelly put in. "That only Her Princesship can do that. I know the rule, and I will follow it. So there. Now, why are we having this talk?"

"Hmm," Aunt Tru said. "I think I am seeing a bit of the problem." She made her weapon disappear and propelled herself from the bar to snatch a chair across the table from Kris. "Zero gee is like riding a bicycle. Once you learn how, you never forget, even at my age."

"Apparently, it is the same with Iteeche," Ron said, moving to face the two humans at the table and looping his lower arms into tie-downs there for that purpose.

"You'll have to excuse me. Your folks almost wiped us out," Trudy said. "That gives one a caution that is hard to forget."

Ron's slits stayed green and white. "Yes, Kris was just telling me about that. Strange that the opposite is what I hear from our Heroes of the Great Human War."

Trudy had been eyeing Nelly at Kris's collar. Now she swung around sharply to focus on the Iteeche. "Your veterans say that!"

"I swear it by all my ancestors. Marine, is that not what you heard from your chooser?"

The Iteeche Marine came to even stiffer attention, weapon presented front. "Yes, my lord. It is common knowledge among all of my peers that only the courage of our heroes saved the People from annihilation."

"This *is* interesting," Auntie Tru said under her breath.

"But not the topic of this moment. Auntie Tru, I need help with Nelly. She's doing all the translation for us and the Iteeche. And she's developed a taste for jokes. You see the problem."

"I know I'm not supposed to toss in a joke when I'm translating between the species. I found a very interesting dissertation that I doubt Kris could understand half of that defines just when a joke can help in a tense situation, and when it won't. This is just sooo unfair."

"She's using contractions," Trudy observed.

"Yes," Kris answered.

"What have you had her doing?"

"Just the usual," Kris said. "Plan this defense, work out that attack. Oh, she's teaching a twelve-year-old girl. My maid Abby's niece is on board."

"Don't forget blowing up that space liner with five thousand people aboard."

"How can I ever forget it, Nelly?"

"I heard about that," Auntie Tru said in a concerned voice. "I don't imagine that was what you were intending."

"Nelly and I spent hours hunting for a way to get a glancing hit that would knock it off course. The hijackers had put a spin on the ship. With that and the speed, our hits caused the ship's structure to fail. Catastrophically."

"There was nothing we could do about it, Auntie Tru," Nelly said, plaintively. "We did our best, but it wasn't good enough."

Auntie Tru sighed. "Dears, I've done my 'best' often enough that I deserve to have it on my tombstone, in foot-high letters."

Through all this, Ron stood quietly. Kris noticed that the Iteeche Marine threw a concerned look at his human associate. Sergeant Bruce nodded and gave a slight shrug.

"So, what do we do?" Kris asked.

"Sam, what do you think?"

Which drew attention to a large locket at Auntie Tru's neck. A deep male voice began talking from it. "Nelly and I have been linked since you entered the room, and, except for the time you were going through that ridiculous self-defense drill, we have been doing a series of self-diagnostics. Nelly passes all the high-order tests with flying colors. The low-order tests are taking a bit longer. Her organization and my organization are quite different, as would be understandable to anyone except a control-freak human."

"Why do I find this picture so familiar?" Kris said.

"Excuse me if I am butting in where I am not needed or wanted," Ron said, "but exactly why did we come here?"

"Because the last time I was with my dear aunt Trudy, Sam was the very epitome of decorum and gentility," Kris said.

"If you'd told me your problems earlier, I might have warned you about some of the pitfalls ahead of you," Auntie Tru said.

"Such as?" Kris asked.

"Well, it was too late to warn you about the effect of interfacing computers with alien technology. We'd already installed that bit of mass storage from Santa Maria into Nelly, hadn't we?"

"Yes, we had." That had been one of the rare times when Kris had time on her hands. It had seemed like a good idea to have Nelly try to access the data in her spare time. Matters had quickly returned to their usual frantic pace, and Nelly had hardly seen Auntie Tru since.

Nelly had, however, found a new jump-point map and accessed a whole lot more stars, including Alien 1 and 2. And become . . . strange.

"Well, I thought a really souped-up computer might be helpful for tackling the problems of these new planets," Tru said diffidently.

"That was why I offered Nelly and my services," Kris said. Now it was her turn to speak dryly.

"Yes, but your grampa Ray had all sorts of interesting things for you to do." Most of which involved getting shot at. "And I just happened to win a small lottery pot." Strange how she usually did when she needed money for research. "And I upgraded Sam before we left Wardhaven. I suspect now he's even more advanced than your Nelly."

"Not," came in duet from both computers present.

"Oh, well, Sam is very advanced, and I tied him into several of the thingamajigs and alien doohickeys, and he managed to get a few of them to do something. Probably not anywhere near what they were meant to do, but anyway, as Sam got deeper into things, I noticed he developed an attitude not all that different from several of the assistants we had helping us."

" 'Several assistants'?" Kris said.

"Yes, five or six, I believe."

"I worked with twelve different assistants. You go through them very quickly, Professor Seyd."

"I promote them to their proper level," Trudy sniffed.

"Thank heaven. For their sanity, she does promote them at a very brisk pace. They'd go crazy, or maybe kill her if she didn't," Sam said, and proved that a computer can be very dry.

"Do you humans have an expression for 'the blind leading the blind'?" Ron asked.

"Yes," Kris said. "You took the words out of my mouth."

"I apologize, then. I did not mean to be so forward."

Kris glanced at Ron . . . and couldn't help but wonder what it would be like to kiss an Iteeche. Strange to have that thought. Even stranger to have it just now.

But there was no time. She had a long list of questions, most attached to an alligator that wanted to chew on her leg. "So, how does it work, dealing with a computer with an attitude?"

"Fine," said Trudy.

"Not too bad," said Sam.

"I see," said Kris.

"No, really," said Sam. "You just do what you have to do as carefully as you can. Sometimes you give the boss some lip over all she's asking, but it's not that important."

"What if it is important?" Nelly asked in a little-girl voice. "What if the princess is asking you to plan a battle for her or plot intercepting fire on five thousand people being held hostage by mad people. You see, Sam, Kris doesn't just ask me to open some Aladdin's cave. Around Kris, people get very suddenly dead. And she *needs* me to help her do that."

That brought a pause in the conversation.

"Kris," Nelly said, "I understand, when you tell me to do something, that's what you want. But sometimes I can get a few steps ahead of you. Have things ready for you when you ask for them. That always makes you happy. Doesn't it?"

Kris liked to think she wasn't the kind of person who had

to be slammed between the eyes with a two-by-four. Well, maybe she was the kind of person who, when slammed with a large, thick stick, recognized the error of her ways. That way of looking at it might save some of her self-image.

"Yes, Nelly, I see the problem. I like it when you're ahead of me. I can't remember a time when you weren't ahead of me that I didn't want to go exactly where you went."

"Except when I wanted to shoot up those cruisers."

"Yes, and, of course, that would have to be a big one."

"So, what do we do, Kris? I want to be part of your team, but the very thought of the mistakes I can make has me wanting to roll myself up in a ball and go back to adding one plus one."

"You want to be a part of our team," Kris repeated.

"Yes, just like Jack and Penny, the colonel and Abby. You work best when I'm at your neck. I want to be there."

"But all of those are grown men and women. They've lived in the shadow of horrible choices all their lives. Studied them when they were younger, made bigger and bigger ones as they grew up. And they've done the jobs that led them to where they are today.

"Kris, I've studied the histories. There's a lot of stuff that doesn't make sense in them."

"Even, Nelly, when you approach them with the powerful rationality that you can bring to them?"

"Yes, Kris, even in the best ones, I spot dozens of conclusions that don't fit the data or events that just couldn't have happened that way."

"And you didn't have twenty years of believing that stuff before you started doubting it like I did," Kris said.

"But those are things I can set a tolerance for. That I can stamp 'don't use unless you ask Kris first.' It's the stuff that leaves people dead that I can't figure out. Kris, I know I must do anything I can to keep you alive. You, and the team, and Cara, and the *Wasp*'s crew. Without you, there would be a huge void in my existence. I don't know what I'd do if I didn't have you. Sam, have you figured it out?"

"No, Nelly girl, I'm afraid that I'm just as lost as you are about that. Trudy here is the center of my life. I like a lot of the people she works with, and a lot of them joke quite seriously about wanting me when she passes on. I know that she is full of years, as these humans count them, and even if nothing goes wrong at the digs, she may 'pass away' as these humans put it, peacefully in her sleep. It will leave a huge vacancy in me when it happens, and I don't know if I will be able to function without her. I really don't."

"Sam, I didn't know any of this," Trudy said, and stroked her pendant that was her computer. It turned from deep blue to ruby red. Kris wondered if her aunt noticed. Probably not.

The room stayed quiet for a long moment. Then Trudy wiped a tear. "But this doesn't solve Kris and Nelly girl's problem. Not unless Nelly wants to retire to the boring life of a computer archaeologist."

"I wish Kris had been allowed to work here. It would have let me avoid so many of the questions I was starting to spend my nights trying to work out answers to. Morality is not an easy or exact science."

"Throughout human history it hasn't been," Trudy said.

"Or Iteeche history," Ron added. "My chooser says that we have fallen back on the simplest of solutions. Obey your superior. However, many of them have made very poor choices, and the People have paid a high price for them. It would be good for us to gain access to your attempts and your history."

"But that is not what you want to talk to King Raymond about," Kris said.

"No. No, that is not it."

"Nelly, has having us talking with you helped?" Trudy asked.

"I think you've just told me to grow up. To be prepared for things that do not add up like two and two. And I just have to accept that things don't always come down the way I've tried to make them. That's what the others are talking about when they say Kris has bad karma."

"All the time, and the worst," Kris said with a sigh.

Silence came, sat for a while, and went only when Nelly said, "Kris, I will be your assistant, doing what you ask. I will follow the commandment, 'Thou Shalt Not Kill,' but I will recognize that you damn Longknifes occasionally take it as more advice than commandment."

"You can say that again," Trudy said.

"I will also know that I have a job if I ever need it as an assistant to Sam."

"Anytime, Nelly girl."

"And, there is nothing wrong with an attitude. I will feel free to give Kris lip anytime I feel like it and there is time for it."

"Hold it, hold it, where'd that come from?" Kris yelped.

"Way to go, Nelly girl," Sam said.

"Kids, you were meant for each other," Trudy said with a grin.

"You humans must be ruled by the dark gods of the deep," Ron said. "Just thinking about how you live makes my head hurt."

An hour later, the *Wasp* boosted for the jump out of Alien 1. Kris, Nelly, and Ron occupied their time debating the advantages of good enough versus pushing the envelope.

"You never would have had any of these problems with my translating machine. It does what it is told to do. No backtalk." "Backtalk" was a word Ron had just learned and liked very much. As in "You Imperial counselors are full of backtalk but you have never hatched an original thought in your misspent lives." He wasn't sure he could say that to their faces, but it was fun to say it where they couldn't hear.

"But you and Kris are using me to do all your translating. I rest my case."

Which didn't settle anything.

Was it just Kris, or was Nelly enjoying the argument for the pure pleasure of it? Kris said little, but let the words flow over her like water.

Professor mFumbo's head ducked into the lounge. "Are you going to tie this room up for much longer? I'd like to hold a staff meeting in here."

"Do you usually hold staff meetings with a bar close at hand?" Kris asked.

The professor pulled his suit coat closed as if it were armor. "Bar? What bar? I didn't know the room had a bar."

"I wouldn't bet money on that," Nelly said.

"And I wouldn't take your money. There is not likely to be any randomness in that," Kris said.

The professor closed the door.

"How much longer will we require this room?" Ron said. "I understand that many of the young humans use this room as a place to meet and begin their mating rituals. I admit you humans are very strange in that respect. I am intrigued by the idea of two intelligent people meeting and establishing a relationship that may or may not result in them producing an offspring that they bring up together. It is *very* alien."

"You don't know who your biological parents were?" Kris asked. She was researching the Iteeche, not really talking sex with Ron.

Not that it mattered.

"How could I, and what importance could it be?"

Kris considered where that would lead and decided she didn't want to go there. Not just now. "I'd love to go further into this," she lied, "but I've got a bigger question I'm wondering about."

"What would that be?"

"How could two species damn near make each other extinct?"

"You are *sure* your people believed that of us?"

"Just as sure as your folks are that *we* were about to do it to you."

"You were," Ron said.

"No way," Kris said.

Ron paused for a moment, his neck going red, green, and black. "I do not understand."

"I don't either," Nelly said.

"But I want to," Kris said. "Nelly, inform Chief Beni that I want a full star map set up in this room. If there's anyone who needs to be told, tell them this room is off-limits for the rest of our trip to Wardhaven. Tell Jack, Penny, Abby, and the colonel to get their butts in here, along with everything they know about the Iteeche War. Ron, I can't tell you what to do, but I'd take it as a personal favor if you'd participate in this little advanced seminar I'm putting together on our recent unpleasantness."

"If for no other reason than the tidal wave of curiosity you have flooded me with, I will stay."

"Anyone on your team you want to add? We'll talk as honestly as we can. Propaganda will be considered only for its informational content at the time. We will not refight the battles, just try to answer the question as to how close either side was to wiping out the other."

"Both of my Navy captains will want to be here. Gods above save us from the Imperial counselors taking an interest. But they are sticking to their rooms and not bothering us much." Ron looked up. "Sergeant, your father was an Honored Hero of that war. I often hear you talking to the other Marines about the history of it. Would it please you to be here?"

The Marine grounded his weapon and leaned on the barrel. "My lord, I would be very much pleased to share in the talk that I see coming. Very pleased."

Half an hour later, the room buzzed with talk. Colonel Cortez and Captain Ted drew up a unified timetable for the war and lit the star chart as battle ebbed and flowed.

And Kris started to see a pattern. "Ron, did you get a star map of human space from any of the ships you captured?"

"Yes," Ron said, seeming just as thoughtful about what he saw. "We knew where every human-occupied planet was during the war."

Jack stood up and strode to the wall that was now a map. "And we knew where your planets were as well."

"Does anyone else see a pattern?" Kris asked. Some heads went up and down. Others went from side to side. Here, with humans and Iteeche together, no one could miss it.

14

Kris haunted the forward lounge. Some renamed it the War Room. It was the Peace Studies Room to others. Say the Little Red Schoolhouse and everyone knew what you meant. It had been a long three weeks. For the last week, they'd even eaten their meals there.

Watching Iteeche eat was something Kris would gladly have passed on. Of course, Ron felt the same about humans. "You humans are disgusting. Eating dead animals. Ugh."

And all of them had discovered what the other species smelled like after long hours without a shower. Actually, Kris found it no worse than a roomful of Marines after a couple of long days in the field.

The cost was minor compared to what Kris learned. After the third day, she quit calling her team together in private to mull over what they'd concluded. It didn't seem fair to the Iteeche and wasn't really hiding anything. Jack and Penny had a bad habit of snapping, "You're kidding me. No way," when they stumbled on something new and interesting.

The colonel and Abby were a bit better, but it was easy to spot when they leaned back. The colonel would stroke his chin; Abby would pull at her ear. "We surprised you on that one, didn't we?" was Ron or Ted's usual response to that.

"Yes, you certainly did," would put an end to any secrecy between them.

But the flow went both ways. Ron had a tendency to kick with one of his hind legs when he was excited. Captain Ted would pound a fist into the opposing hand. Once he'd pounded two fists into the opposing hands. The Iteeche Marine, identified simply as Trig, was known to let out near-human shouts.

It had been a very informative three weeks. Kris doubted anyone alive on the human side, except maybe Grampas Ray and Trouble, knew more about the war than Kris's team did now. Certainly they knew more than anyone who'd written the history books.

Penny challenged Abby to a race to see who could get a book in print faster. "Ain't no contest, Lieutenant. I just write juicy gossip or dry reports. You'll have me beat."

But the maid's eyes glistened. No way would Kris bet against the woman who'd grown up on the wrong side of the tracks on Eden and pulled herself up by her own panty hose.

Now three weeks were over, and Wardhaven was large in the lounge's view ports. High Wardhaven station shone gleaming like a thousand stars as they approached. Captain Drago requested one of those berths used by special-mission operatives. It took only a moment to verify the *Wasp*'s identity, and permission was granted. They would dock in an out-of-the-way corner where no one went without a good bad reason.

"No message traffic?" Kris asked Captain Drago.

"Nothing but what docking requires."

"Nothing piggybacked or hidden away?"

"Kris, nothing has come aboard this ship or left it since you sent the messenger pod. I swear it on my mother's grave, may she be a long time filling it."

Kris closed down her commlink, caught Abby's eye from across the room, and signaled her to a corner. "Have you had any message from outside?" was her curt question to her maid.

"Not a word, not a letter, not a sound. Longest I've been ignored since my boobs came in."

"And you haven't got anything out. Did you have anything riding that last messenger pod I dispatched?"

"No and no, Baby Ducks. I haven't sent out a gossip report or one of those intel dumps since we ran into Ron. I may lose my job, but, honey, you are off every grid there is. Void, silent, blank. I'm going to have to hit you up for a pay raise if you've done made me blow those other gigs."

Abby never missed a chance to point out how underpaid she was as a maid. It had taken Kris a while to find out that Abby was selling reports to gossip columnists about the life and loves, or lack thereof, of that socialite, Princess Kris. It had taken Kris and Jack even longer to discover that Abby was also taking pay from one or more professional information dealers interested in the many other things Kris got her nose into.

Since then, Kris got copies of all the reports Abby filed. With a bit of judicious change, they could pass for Kris's official reports.

Kris hated paperwork.

"So, I know nothing, and you know nothing," Kris concluded.

"It sure looks that way."

"You going to file on the stuff we just learned?"

"It would be a waste of my time. None of it's juicy. And it's eighty years cold. It's information, but not the information any self-respecting spy chief would waste two seconds reading. Hey, for those folks, five days ago is *so* out-of-date."

Which left Kris watching the *Wasp* dock and wondering who would meet her at the pier.

Five minutes later, Gunny reported, "Ain't nothing here."

Okay, so Kris was free to do her own thing.

"Jack, I want an escort."

"Wardhaven normal?" That usually included four Marines in civvies.

"How about Eden size?"

Jack raised an eyebrow. "That will be sixteen in full battle rattle."

"No, that might upset the locals. They don't like to remember there's a war on. Eight in civvies. Lock down the ship solid. No one out. No one in but us. You, me, Penny, Abby. Oh, Colonel Cortez, you haven't met my grampa have you?"

He swallowed hard. "King Raymond. No, I haven't had the pleasure.

"Five will get you ten," Jack said with an evil grin, "her grampa Trouble will be hanging around the edges of things."

"It would be an honor to meet him," was almost sincere.

"Well, you've got thirty minutes to make yourself presentable in civvies to head out with me for the beanstalk."

"Do you want any of us to go with you?" Ron asked.

"No. I'll bring Grampa Ray back here. Figure on using this room, if you don't mind. He's not into court folderol, so don't let your green and whites get carried away."

"I won't. I'll be waiting for you," he said.

Half an hour later, Kris walked briskly toward the nearest trolley station. It was evening, station time, and the lights were dimmed. Down the large passageways, big enough to haul oversize cargo, not a single person was visible. The Marine escort kept their heads moving so Kris looked straight ahead. Maybe she was wrong.

But when Sergeant Bruce observed in a whisper, "I ain't never seen a station so dead," she knew someone must have had a hand in emptying the area.

The trolley was empty; four of Kris's Marines piled in, checked it over. Nanos from Nelly sniffed for explosives and found none. Kris and the rest of the guard boarded just as the trolley car rang insistently for its departure. They arrived at the space elevator without anyone waving the car down for a ride.

"You sure no one's expecting us?" Jack asked, eyeing Abby.

"Not on my account they ain't," the maid, sometime marksman, and full-time snitch, insisted.

"Grampa Ray does enjoy his fun," was all that Kris said.

The next ferry on the beanstalk was not empty. Stevedores guided oversize cargo into the maw of its huge cargo bay. People from late shifts filed aboard the passenger section. Anyone who worked on the station was used to seeing military personnel not in uniform. Few looked back as Kris and her team boarded last.

Kris paid for her own fare with a credit/ID chit and went through the weapons detector. Jack presented his weapons authorization to the fellow at the tollbooth. He opened the bypass gate for Jack and didn't even blink as eight Marines hurried through.

Once aboard, most passengers ignored the Marines as they looked for several adjacent empty seats where they could nap away the half-hour drop to Wardhaven.

Sergeant Bruce scouted an empty section forward, and Kris settled down with her team as the Marines established a perimeter to protect her.

The drop went without surprises.

What did surprise Kris was arriving at the front of the beanstalk station and finding no one waiting for her. Not once in all her twenty-some years of traveling had Harvey, the chauffeur at Nuu House, failed to get word of her arrival and meet her at the station.

Unaccountably, she felt saddened by this first though she should have expected it. She eyed her situation and didn't much care for it. It would take three or four cabs to carry her team and guards. That was a separation she didn't much like.

At that moment, a city bus pulled in. Two men in old work clothes got off and hurried to catch the ferry. The driver retrieved a reader and got comfortable for however long his schedule gave him.

NELLY, IS THAT BUS GOING PAST MAIN NAVY?

NO, KRIS, IT'S GOING THE OTHER WAY.

WE'LL SEE ABOUT THAT.

Kris headed for the bus. Jack, a bit taken by surprise, hurried to catch up with her, with the Marines and rest following this sudden turn of events.

"You're going past Main Navy," Kris said as she boarded.

"You got the wrong bus, lady," the driver said, not even looking up from his crossword puzzle. "You want the ninety-four line. One of them should be along in fifteen minutes."

"You misunderstand me. I was not asking. I was telling you. This bus is going to Main Navy tonight."

"Look, woman, I don't need your jokes," the driver said, putting down his reader. He looked at Kris. A moment later his eyes narrowed in recognition, and his shoulders slumped. "What's a Longknife doing on my bus?"

"Going to Main Navy. You do know the way, don't you?"

"I know the way. I used to drive the route," he said, watching as the Marines filed past him. "You gonna let me call my dispatcher and tell him he needs to cover my line?"

"Sorry, no. Not until you let us off. Then I'll see that any problems you have with your dispatcher are landed on my head, not yours."

"Yeah, right," he grumbled, but he put the bus in gear and pulled away from the space elevator station.

He did know the way to Main Navy. At least Nelly, whom Kris had double-checking him, raised no concern with the streets he drove. In ten minutes he stopped before the imposing facade at the center of Wardhaven's growing naval presence in human space.

Kris suspected that someone had had a hand in all of this, and couldn't help but question the driver as the Marines filed off before her. "You normally drive this route?"

"Nope, I've been on another for the last month, but a driver called in sick and I got called in. I could use the overtime."

"I'll tell my grampa you appreciate the overtime."

"Tell who?"

Well, if he didn't know who had been pulling the string on him today, she didn't have time to educate him.

Surrounded by Marines, who didn't decrease their vigilance even here, Kris went to the bank of elevators and punched for the fifth floor. No surprise, the elevator was waiting for her.

In the foyer of the fifth floor, a Marine colonel stood. "Marines, you will wait with me. Your Highness, you and your party are expected."

15

General Mac's office looked familiar. The first time Kris marched in, it had been intimidating. That morning she'd been a boot ensign under charges for mutiny. Intimidation came easy.

Not tonight.

Now the place had a familiarity that didn't quite breed contempt. The walls needed a new coat of paint, and the drapes at the windows were threadbare in places. No, this was a place where busy people spent too many of their hours concentrating on matters that had nothing to do with their surroundings.

Kris's eyes were drawn to the coffee table between the two couches. Tiny teeth had left their imprint on one corner. Kris wondered what the story was behind them. And hoped they weren't left over from a very early visit she didn't remember.

As usual, General Mac McMorrison, Chairman of Wardhaven's Joint Staff, was behind his desk. Tonight, he wasn't busy with the inevitable paperwork. He couldn't ignore his company.

Not Kris's team; he could ignore them with ease. No, he had company well before Kris got here.

King Raymond, the first of that name, lounged in Mac's visitor's chair on the right of his desk. Admiral Crossenshield, Chief of Wardhaven Intelligence and other dirty deals, had the visitor's chair to Mac's left. Behind them, leaning casually against a bookcase, was Grampa Trouble, officially retired General Tordon, but just Trouble to most who knew him . . .

and to a whole lot who never made his official acquaintance. He flashed Kris a tight smile.

She returned it and led her team to the couches. She took the overstuffed chair, the farthest from Grampa Ray, but facing him. The couches filled up on both sides of her, Jack to her left, Abby to her right. Both close. That left Penny and Colonel Cortez taking the seats closest to the king and his officers.

Penny was used to this situation. Colonel Cortez, who'd faced Kris in battle and surrendered without so much as a blink, looked just a tad intimidated. He'd get over that by next visit.

Before Kris could get comfortable, Grampa Ray started without preamble. "What took you so long?"

"I took the scenic route."

"So what you messaged me wasn't that important." Grampa Ray had mastered sarcasm while still in diapers.

"Oh, it's important. But Nelly had some developmental problems. I was concerned, since she's the best translator we had for Iteeche. So we stopped by Trudy Seyd on Alien 1 for some counseling."

"And you saw no need to tell us?" Ray shot back at her.

"You hadn't answered my first message," Kris said easily. "It seemed to me you didn't want to clutter up the message buffers with text that had Iteeche in them. Was it you or Grampa Trouble who told me ciphers were made to be broken?"

Grampa Trouble's grin got a smidgen wider. Admiral Crossenshield pulled out his wallet and handed a bill to Mac, who passed it to the king. He pocketed it without glancing at it.

"So I assume Nelly is fine, now."

"Wasn't anything wrong with me," Nelly put in. "We just needed to talk a few things over. Like what it feels like to be the one that actually pulls the trigger that kills five thousand people."

That got a lot of eyes widened around the desk. What it did to Grampa Trouble's grin was hard to describe.

"Yes," the king went on, "I heard about the liner. Sorry

about that, Nelly. You hang around a Longknife's neck, and you'll have to learn how to cope with things like that."

"Kris and I spent some time talking about it. She was a lot more feeling about it than you are."

"The first time you do it, you feel it. After you do it a couple of hundred times, you can't afford to feel all that much. You'll learn."

"Kris, you sure you did the right thing, talking this guy into doing the king thing?"

"No, I'm not sure, Nelly. It may be the first of many great mistakes in my life," Kris said softly. Around her, the room seemed to have forgotten to breathe.

Grampa Ray gave out a tired sigh. "I'm glad to see you're learning." The room started breathing again. "I understand you gave that Peterwald girl a critique on her efforts to kill you on Eden."

"I thought of it more as girl talk among two junior officers, sir."

Grampa Ray took the cash he'd won on one bet and sent it back to Crossenshield. The admiral did not put it in his wallet, but pocketed it, ready to cover the next loss.

"You think that was smart?" Grampa Ray asked.

"Jack here agrees with you," Kris said, giving her security chief a nod. He scowled at the recognition. "Only time will tell if the two of us can be anything but enemies. Crossie, did you get the pictures I sent you of the head of Greenfeld State Security?"

"I got them, but they weren't that much use."

"How come?"

"He was dead of a stroke by the time we got his picture. You know anything about that?"

"It was a six-millimeter stroke, I'd wager. Vicky may not have actually pulled the trigger, but she most likely called the shot. Not that I know anything about it, you understand," Kris said.

The wager was headed back to the king. It made Kris feel

kind of nice to know her great-grandfather was betting on her. She'd be sad the day she lost him real money.

She'd also likely be dead.

"How are things in Greenfeld territory?" Kris asked. It was none of her business, and she liked it that way, but she was curious how Vicky was doing at staying one step ahead of her own assassins.

"Peterwald's Navy is pretty much tied up at the dock. Officers and sailors are heavily involved in keeping order, not that there is rioting in the streets, but there have been a few reports of landing parties busting into State Security offices and taking away the black shirts for questioning."

"Vicky alive so far?" Kris asked.

"She's limping a bit from a bomb that went off too close."

"Next time I see her, I'll suggest she have one of her people talk to my chief Beni. He's pretty good at that."

"Don't forget my nanosniffers," Nelly put in.

"I never will, Nelly. They really come in handy."

"Okay, we've had enough chitchat," Grampa Ray snapped. "What's this about an Iteeche embassy?"

"I thought you'd never ask," Kris couldn't stop herself from saying.

"Well, I've asked. What was an Iteeche doing in our space?"

"It wasn't really our space or his space. I was out beyond both of our rims, and he was dodging fire from two Greenfeld cruisers."

"Peterwald was shooting at him!" Ray said.

"Trying to, but mostly missing," Kris said.

"And hitting us," Nelly put in. "That was when I decided to shoot back, and Kris grounded me because she was afraid I'd start a war with Greenfeld. Now I know, Nelly is not allowed to start a war. I'm also not going to fire on any humans without Kris's permission. Right, Kris?"

"Right, Nelly."

"You really did need that stop with Trudy. Didn't you?" Grampa Trouble said.

Kris just nodded.

"So why was an Iteeche wandering near our space?" King Ray said, getting them back on that track.

"He said he wanted to see you, to talk to you," Kris said.

"About what?"

"That he won't say. His grampa made him promise on all he holds sacred that he wouldn't tell anyone but you."

"Iteeche don't have grampas, they're all bastards," Grampa Ray growled

"Choosers," Kris corrected. "You knew his chooser, Roth'sum'We'sum'Quin."

"That son of a bitch," Ray turned to glance at Trouble, who was shaking his head. "The only question in the bargaining was whether I'd slit his throat before he slit mine, heh, Trouble?"

"Seemed that way many a day," Trouble agreed. "So he's still aboveground and kicking?"

Kris didn't bother pointing out that this conversation was departing significantly from at least two historians' direct quotes from Ray. She swallowed her question and answered his. "That's what Ron tells me. Roth chose him and raised him to be an ambassador to us humans, to open up communications between us. He thinks it's been too long that we've ignored each other."

"No surprise that," Trouble said. "We knew this day would come."

"But not while the wound was still fresh," Ray said, turning back to Kris. "There were too many dead between us. Too much hatred."

"When will it change?" Kris asked.

"Won't ever change while my generation is alive. So long as there are vets with Iteeche blood on their hands, who saw their buddies die on Iteeche blades, we can't sit down at the same table."

"We have to," Kris said. "Or at least we need to."

"Maybe your kid, Kris, maybe the guppy this Ron kid chooses, but it's too soon. Too soon," Ray said softly.

"Strange, that's kind of what Ron said, too. There's a lot of Iteeche Heroes of the Great Human War still walking around, damn proud to have fought us, still remembering their buddies that didn't make it home. I think Roth and Ron and I would agree with you. Except, despite all of that, Ron is here."

"Why?" Grampa Trouble snapped.

"I don't know. He won't tell me. But I really do think that he and his grampa deserve a hearing. Grampa"—here Kris looked at Ray and then Trouble—"I want you to come up to the *Wasp* and let him have his say. I don't often ask for a favor, but if I have any on account, I'd like to call it in."

King Ray snorted. "You've only done your duty. I refuse to owe you for that."

"But she has done a Longknife's duty," Trouble put in, "and she's done damn good at it. Besides, aren't you just a wee bit curious as to what Roth would have to say after all these years?"

King Ray took in a deep breath, eyed the ceiling for a moment, and let it out slowly. "This could be a try at killing us. Maybe Roth regrets that he didn't get around to slitting our throats back then and wants to correct his error."

"We all decided to let each other live," Trouble said. "Kris, what's your take on this?"

"Paranoia runs deep in our family, sir," didn't get a smile from the rest of the room. Old joke? No, too true. "Jack, Beni, and Nelly have done everything they could think of to search out weapons, explosives, extrasharp knifes. Ron brought an honor guard of four Marines. They have their weapons, but only the clips in them. Their bandoleers are empty." Kris let that sink in.

"Grampa Ray, one of the reasons we did the long way around to get here was to give us time to search every nook and cranny around them and to get to know them. I've come to believe they really are what they say they are."

"Got to know him, huh?" the king said.

"Yep."

"I don't know him. I don't want to know him."

Was there nothing she could do to get Grampa Ray moving? Was there something else weighing on his mind? She had only one card left to play. Hopefully, he still had a sense of humor.

"Grampa, you knew someday I'd bring a boy home to the family. Whether or not you wanted to meet him, you'd have to. Well, consider Ron my boy that you just have to meet."

Trouble barked a laugh. Mac and Crossie looked like they'd swallowed something sour.

Grampa Ray eyed Kris, then slowly shook his head. "An Iteeche son-in-law. I ought to call your momma."

"I kind of hope you won't."

"Can you imagine Brenda's reaction to having an Iteeche walk in her door?" Ray said, turning in his chair to Trouble.

"*I'm* not even welcome in her house," Trouble noted.

"Where do you want me to meet this boy?" Grampa Ray said, sitting up kingly straight in his chair to face Kris.

"I was figuring on you going up to the *Wasp*."

"We can't move the king around town very quietly," Crossenshield said, not to mention safely.

"It would be even harder bringing a half dozen Iteeche down to meet him here."

"Girl's got a point," Mac said, opening his mouth for the first time. "Not easy bringing a mountain to Mohammed."

"Yeah," the intel chief said, "but we got ourselves two mountains here."

"It's easier for me to sneak up the beanstalk than it is to sneak down a seven-foot-tall four-legs," King Ray said. "I'll see him tomorrow night. Girl, you got anything else?" he asked, standing up, broadcasting to all that he really didn't want anything more.

"Yes, Grampa, I have a question."

Ray paused in his exit. Mac and Crossie were also standing by now. "What is it, Lieutenant?"

"Why didn't you use radioactives, ah, fusion and fission bombs," Kris corrected herself as Nelly fed her the right words, "against the Iteeche?"

16

The temperature in the room must have plummeted thirty degrees in the time it took Kris to get her words out. Mac and Crossie looked like they'd turned to stone.

Grampa Ray glared at Kris. "Those hell bombs are illegal. Have been for most of two, three hundred years."

Kris would have gotten the same answer from her third-grade teacher. She expected better from one of the men who was there. "Yes. I know. But we were fighting for our very existence."

Grampa Ray and Trouble exchanged knowing looks. They'd been there. Mac and Crossie kept their blank expressions. They hadn't . . . and didn't really want to be here.

"We'd lost the knowledge of how to make them," Ray snapped, not looking her in the eye.

It wasn't easy to keep forcing herself on the great-grandfather she'd nearly worshipped as a god through her whole youth. Still, Kris dug in her heels and refused that answer. "Certainly, the archives on Earth must have the data."

"They don't," the king said curtly. He seemed ready to walk out, but Grampa Trouble came up and placed an arm on his shoulder, encouraging him to sit down. He did. Mac and Crossie gravitated toward a corner.

Kris took a deep breath and pushed on one more time. "Even if all the records were expunged, lost, or burned, using twentieth-century technology, they originally invented the bomb in just three years. The Iteeche War lasted six. Why wasn't it reinvented, rebuilt, and used? You could have used relativity bombs. Both sides used them in the Unity war just before we discovered the Iteeche. But they were hardly used against the Iteeche."

"What are you getting at, girl?" Grampa Trouble asked.

"Do you think we should empty the room?" Crossie interrupted. "Let the princess and king have it for their family talk. Hell, I'm not sure I know where all this is going, but I know I'm not cleared for it."

"My team stays," Kris said. "Grampa Ray, do you know that the Iteeche Heroes of the Great Human War pride themselves on having kept the humans from wiping the People from the face of the stars? Their vets and our vets both think they were saving their species from being driven extinct by the other. Don't you find that interesting?"

"Not really. It was tough on both sides." But Grampa Ray's eyes were fixed on the carpet.

"You want me to have Nelly bring up a star map, show you what I noticed while I and my crew and Ron and his advisors were talking about the war. I wonder if it would be half as surprising to you as it was to me."

"I doubt it. But tell me, Princess, what did you notice?"

"It should have stood out like a sore thumb, the massacres at Port Elgin and LeMonte. They are hot topics all through the war, but they took place early on. Actually, before you and Grampa Trouble even knew there were Iteeche."

"Not LeMonte," Trouble said. "Port Elgin, you're right about. It was a pirate base. We didn't even know it had been wiped out until a pirate ship turned itself in. You want to talk about some mighty-scared boys. That crew was. They came into Elgin a week after the Iteeche hit it.

"LeMonte was an honest start-up colony," Grampa Ray said softly. "They got off a distress signal when strange ships shot through one of their jump points. I and Trouble led a reaction force from Havoc. Have you seen the pictures of what we found?"

Now it was Kris's turn to speak softly. "I was fifteen

before they'd let me check them out of the school library.
And even then, the librarian said I had to watch them with a
war vet. I felt as a Longknife that I had to see them. I cried,
so did Harvey, as we watched them. How could anyone do
such things? I hated the Iteeche by the time I finished the
documentary.

"But those weren't Imperial troopers that did that, were
they?"

"No," Grampa Trouble said, "that was the work of their
Leaderless Men, their pirates."

"And our pirates were doing stuff just as bad to them. Ron
showed me the pictures from the two of their planets that got
hit. One was a Leaderless Men's stronghold, the other was one
of the new planets they'd just started to develop. Funny, the
symmetry there."

"I didn't know our pirates hit them," Trouble said. "Ray,
we should have done a better job debriefing the pirates that
came in when the going got bad."

"I didn't notice you all that interested in looking the gift
horse in the mouth back then."

"I didn't want to have anything to do with them. But I was
glad for the intel they brought," Trouble admitted.

"We got everyone evacuated after LeMonte," Ray went on.
"The pictures made that easy."

"The Iteeche pulled out of a half dozen of their newest
planets, too," Kris said. "And then you fought the war in the
empty gap between our two peoples. Some feints over the top
or under the bottom or around the flanks, but it was as if you
set up the battlefield and both stayed to it."

"Yeah. So long as they didn't push into our planets, I stayed
away from theirs."

"You weren't really trying to win the war, to wipe them
out, or them to wipe us out. It was all for show."

"No! Never." Grampa Ray was on his feet, and if Kris
had been within reach, he probably would have throttled her.
Grampa Trouble stopped him before Jack had to. The Marine
didn't rise from his seat, but he measured his king and the

distance to his princess. Kris was pretty sure which duty he would do.

By the grace of whatever God was watching over them, it didn't come to that.

Trouble helped Ray back into his seat. "Never, *ever* say it was all for show," the king said through tight lips.

Grampa Trouble settled Ray back down, then, with an arm on his king's shoulder, he half turned to Kris. "Child, you must never forget the price people paid for those feints and parries. War is always serious. Serious to those who fight it. Serious to those who pay its toll. Your great-grandmother Rita's Battle Scout Squadron 2 did one of those desperate feints. We never found so much as a survival pod from that squadron."

"Never found a scrap of them," Grampa Ray whispered.

"You're right, you cold-blooded Longknife," Grampa Trouble said to Kris. "You spotted the heart of our strategy, to get this stampede turned in upon itself. The war was already going before Ray or I got there. There was nothing we could do to stop it. Every ship we sent in to establish contact got blown to bits. Finally, we just gave up and laid it on with all we had. Sickest decision I ever saw a grown man make, but Ray made it.

"By the Battle of the Orange Nebula, we were throwing everything we had. The Empire threw in all they had. And in thirty miserable days, we chewed up a half dozen years of our wealth and left both sides with damn little to show for it."

"Then that bastard Roth offered to talk," Ray put in. "I could have cried. If he'd done it two days earlier, Rita would still be alive."

Kris had always known that her great-grandmother Rita died in the waning days of the war. Now she realized what a tragedy it was. No. That wasn't fair to all the other tragedies. All because two species couldn't figure out a way to talk across their differences.

Kris went to kneel beside her great-grandfather. There were tears running down his cheeks. She'd never seen him cry. She hadn't been sure he could.

"I'm sorry, Grampa. Really I am. Give me some time to think."

"You do that, girl," he whispered harshly.

Kris was halfway to the door, her crew following, when Grampa Ray coughed. "I'll be there tomorrow night. Ten o'clock."

17

The Marine colonel led Kris and her detail to the base-
ment of Main Navy, where three armored town cars waited
for them. The drive back to the elevator station was quick and
quiet.

The only break in the silence was no break at all. KRIS,
COULD I ORDER SOME SUPPLIES AND OTHER STUFF I NEED FOR
MAKING THINGS LIKE NANOS AND THE LIKES?

GO AHEAD, Kris thought, then settled back into her silence.
She'd opened a lot more than she'd expected.

People don't put their lives on the line unless something
is worth dying for. For all her life, Kris had felt that stopping
the Iteeche had been worth every drop of blood it took. As a
daydreaming kid, she wished she'd been alive to fight the dirty
Iteeche. She'd been shocked when Grampa Trouble, in a moment of surprising honesty, told her sixteen-year-old self that
he was glad she hadn't been there.

Of course you tell people that they're fighting for the survival of their wives, their children, for all they love.

Who would die just so someone could get a word in
edgewise?

But that was what the whole war had been about.

By the time reasonable people on either side got involved
in the fighting, the slaughter had already begun, and massacre
was all they could see.

Kris thought of all the Iteeche War vets she'd run into on
Wardhaven, Chance, Panda. She remembered those who still

mourned lost loved ones. Could she tell them it had all been a horrible mistake?

Not bloody likely!

If she wanted to build a bridge across the chasm between humanity and the Iteeche, it would just have to wait. *I don't know what your message is, Ron, but there are still too many alive who can't hear it.*

Which gave her a better understanding of why Ron had been saddled with the two green and whites, who seemed more bent on wrecking the embassy than helping it. Humans weren't the only ones who still needed their truth sugarcoated.

They were halfway up the beanstalk and had just done the midclimb flip when Colonel Cortez stood up. "Excuse me if I'm interrupting any really important thoughts, meditations, or reveries. However, it has come to my attention that I'd rather spend the next couple of years in an honest-to-God jail than risk my fair skin bouncing from one Longknife situation to another. I'm am truly sorry, but is there any way I can get out of my contract and just go to prison?"

"Sit down, Hernando," Jack growled. "You've made your deal with the devil, or a Longknife, whichever seems worse. She and her family own your soul."

"Yep," Abby said, "you're one of us, now. There's no going back."

"But I had no idea what I was getting into!"

"I have to agree with the colonel," Abby said, "I'd never have thought that King Ray could cry."

"I saw him close, once before," Kris said. "It was another time that his wife came up. Eighty years, and he's still not over her."

Penny seemed lost in thought. Kris suspected she must be thinking of her lost husband of three days and wondering if she'd still be hurting eighty years hence.

The colonel sat down, and the trip continued in silence.

Ron was waiting for Kris as soon as she crossed the quarterdeck and was out of view from the dock. "Did he talk to you?"

"Grampas Ray and Trouble met with us. He didn't want to see you. He doesn't think there's any reason to talk to you. There is still too much blood in the water. Those were his words, probably a direct quote from your chooser. I asked him what he was trying to do, back in the war. Was he really out to exterminate your people or just get a word in edgewise?"

"And?" Ron said.

"We were right. He only wanted to get talks going. But the war was horrible, and people don't march into that kind of hell to open communication lines. Your people, my people, all signed up to protect hearth and home. That's what they've been remembering for eighty years. That and their dead. Ron, it's not going to be easy to build a bridge between our two peoples. Maybe we'll just have to wait another twenty years."

"Kris, we don't *have* twenty years."

"What do you mean?"

"Will your great-grandfather meet with me?"

"Yes. Tomorrow night at ten o'clock."

"Tomorrow night, then, you will know why we cannot wait twenty years. Maybe not even two years."

"What is it, Ron?"

He turned back to Iteeche country. "Tomorrow night will be soon enough."

18

Early next morning, Kris woke to a call from the Marine guard at the gangplank.

"Ma'am, Staff Sergeant Tu here. I didn't want to disturb you, but I got a delivery here with your name on it, and I got to sign for it. Ma'am, I ain't never signed for nothing so small with this many zeros and commas in the cost box." That was followed by a clearly audible gulp.

"I haven't ordered anything," Kris said. "You sure it's not for the ship."

"No, ma'am. It says Kris Longknife, care of the *Wasp*. And it's got our pier correct."

"Kris, it's for me," Nelly said, using that little-girl voice.

"Sergeant, I'll be right down," Kris said, ringing off.

"Nelly," Kris said, as she leapt out of bed and started pulling on a shipsuit.

"You said I could order some supplies, Kris."

"What did you order that cost so much you made a Marine sergeant gulp."

"My children."

Kris froze, with her hand on the zipper. "Your. Children?"

"Yes, Kris. You've been talking about needing better computers for the people who work closely with you."

"*You've* been talking about them needing better computers." Kris had been thinking that maybe Nelly was right, but she didn't remember uttering a word about it.

"You never said anything *against* the idea."

"No, I didn't," Kris said, pulling the zipper up to her neck, right next to Nelly's off button. *Tempting, but no. I promised.*

"Nelly, you know that rule about you not starting a war."

"Yes, Kris."

"Here's rule two. Never sign off on any acquisition without telling me how much it's going to be."

"Not even for a new dress?"

"Nelly, Abby orders my dresses."

"Through me. I keep your budget."

"How much is this going to cost?"

"Kris, with you out beyond the Rim, you haven't spent much money. Hardly any in the last three months."

"So you spent it."

"And then some," Nelly admitted.

"How 'some'?"

"A lot 'some.'"

Kris eyed her hair in the mirror. It looked to be a bad hair day, too. She mussed it more to her liking. "Can I send this back?"

"Please don't, Kris. I don't know, Kris. Some of the stuff was special order, fabricated just for me overnight."

"That cost us extra."

"Yes."

"Let's go see what you got *us* into."

Kris was three paces down the passageway when Jack joined her, impeccable in undress khaki and blues.

"What has you up this early?" Kris asked.

"Sergeant Tu called me before he called you."

"And you told him to wake me."

"Don't you think signing for kazillions is a bit above his pay grade? I know it's above mine."

"It's not that expensive," Nelly insisted.

"This is Nelly's doing?"

"I approved her ordering some supplies. So she ordered a family."

"Family?"

"Yeah. Her kids. She says everyone close to me needs one."

"Count me out."

"Jack, you really need a better computer," Nelly pleaded.

"You giving this swabby lip is one thing. Sometimes kind of fun. You giving a Marine officer lip? No way. Marines get shot for insubordination, haven't you heard?"

"She won't be me. I'm not cloning myself. She'll be *your* computer, Jack. You bring her up to be your friend."

"He," Jack snapped, then realized what he'd done and gave Kris's neckline a sour look. "*If* I had a smart-ass computer, it would be a *he*. But I don't need a smart-ass computer."

"I'm the way I am because I'm Kris's."

"No way do I deserve you," Kris insisted.

"I'm your karma," Nelly said flatly.

"What is it with your computer?" Jack said. "One week she doesn't believe in karma, and the next week she *is* karma."

Chief Beni joined them muttering under his breath about the injustice of early wake-up calls.

"Who woke you up, Chief?" Kris asked.

"Nelly. She said there was something only I could do for you."

"For her," Kris and Jack said together.

"What's she want?"

"For you to . . . ah . . . deliver, build, construct her children."

"More Nellys! No way," the chief said.

"They aren't going to be duplicates of me. They'll be Jack's computer, and Penny's and Abby's and yours, Chief."

"I get one!"

"You're part of Kris's team."

"Don't mean to interrupt, but just how do you expect each of these computer kids of yours to be different?" Jack asked.

"They'll have my basic skills at organizing data and forecasting what you humans want. Oh, and they'll know the two rules . . ."

"And a whole lot more that are coming," Kris added.

"But most of their self-organizing matrix will be left for them to arrange the way they want, based on what they need to work with the human they are working with."

"I note the failure to address ownership," Jack said.

Nelly said nothing to that. Kris left the topic with a sigh. Sooner or later, she and Nelly would have to address the matter of what the relationship was between the two-legged human who walked around and the sentient being around her neck.

Then again, she could always turn Nelly off.

Not.

Kris came to the quarterdeck. A harried twentysomething kid was showing clear signs of wanting out of there, but the Marine sergeant held both his clipboard and his package. A much-larger package than Kris expected, say about the size of a hatbox.

Probably most of that is just packing, Kris hoped.

Kris took the clipboard and whistled softly at the price on the invoice.

"I told you it was high, ma'am," Staff Sergeant Tu said.

NELLY, THIS ISN'T A COUPLE OF MONTHS OF EARNINGS FOR MY TRUST FUND. THIS IS A WHOLE YEAR!

BUT YOU HARDLY SPENT ANYTHING WHILE YOU WERE STATIONED ON EDEN.

ONLY BECAUSE THE ART SHOW GOT SHOT UP BEFORE I COULD BUY ANYTHING.

BUT YOU DIDN'T.

"This better be worth it, Nelly."

"I promise. It will be."

Kris signed, and the delivery kid bolted.

"Okay, Nelly. Is the forward lounge available?"

"It's still reserved for your team. It's empty just now."

"Why don't you invite the godparents of your children up to the lounge for the christening party. You better ask the galley to send along breakfast."

"If you'll excuse me, ma'am," Chief Beni said, "I need to

get some gear from my shop if we're going to be dealing with high-value electronics."

"Since we are, I guess you better. Do you need a clean room?"

"I'll bring one."

Fifteen minutes later, the lounge was serving a light breakfast on one side and Chief Beni had set up a temporary clean room as far from the bagels and bran muffins as he could. Kris circulated among the godparents as they arrived, surprised by a few of Nelly's choices. Jack, Penny, and Abby were nobrainers. That the colonel was included showed that the poor fellow truly was under a life sentence.

"I guess if I accept this little trinket, I really am stuck with you," he said.

"Last chance to run, not walk, for the door," Abby said.

Sergeant Bruce, standing at Abby's elbow, was an even bigger surprise for Kris. The maid and Marine had been spending more and more time together. Kris could easily put his inclusion down to a romantic streak in her "young" computer. Still, the Marine was the usual volunteer for the tough stuff Kris needed doing. He would put the computer to good use.

Kris had to do a check to see if Cara had just snuck in with her aunt, or was actually invited. She was. I HAVE A SPECIAL VERSION OF ME WHO I THINK WILL BE JUST GREAT FOR CARA. NOT EXACTLY ME THE WAY I WAS WHEN YOU WERE TWELVE. I WAS REALLY DUMB, BUT ME THE WAY I WISH I'D BEEN BACK THEN.

No way would Kris go back to being twelve again.

Captain Drago stuck his head in the room, spotted Kris, and immediately came to her. "You called?"

"Not me, Nelly," Kris said.

Nelly quickly explained that she wanted the good captain to be the godchild and user of one of her about-to-be-activated children.

The captain respectfully declined. "I'm sorry, Miss Nelly, but I really can't run the risk of a strange and untrained computer locking up the ship's main computer."

"I haven't caused that computer any trouble."

"But you are a passenger's computer. There are certain limitations on your access. The captain's computer must have total access, from engineering to nav and everything in between."

NELLY, DON'T. But it was too late.

"Ship's computer," Nelly said. "How much of you have I accessed and when?"

Captain Drago's mouth took on a distinct scowl as his ship's computer reported, "The passenger Kris Longknife's computer has accessed all functions and status reports of the ship since immediately upon coming aboard."

"I had to be able to tell Kris the ship was operating safely. I've been doing this since she was stationed on the *Firebolt*. The ship was testing the power-plant problems of the Kamikaze class of corvettes and I twice shut down tests before humans could see the impending destruction of the ship."

"So you have been tiptoeing in and out of every nook and cranny of my ship and not leaving any footprints."

"I'm very good at not leaving footprints." Nelly preened.

"And I'm to trust you and this Trojan horse you're about to give me."

"I haven't let you down yet."

Drago glanced around the lounge. "Everyone in here is getting one of these little gremlins?"

"Yep," Nelly said proudly.

"Even her?" the captain said, waving at Cara.

"Yes!" Cara shouted and celebrated with an exuberant little dance. "But Nelly promised me that she'd still be my teacher. Dada will just be my friend. We can play games together, and talk and do all sorts of things, just like Nelly does with Kris."

Drago eyed Kris as the two of them savored the order in which the names came. Nelly first. Kris last. "I reserve the right to return this gift the first time it causes me or my ship any trouble."

"You won't. Try me or mine on for an hour, and you won't ever go back to a dumb computer," Nelly insisted.

Professor mFumbo was next in. He seemed quite excited about getting a fancy new computer at Kris's expense. But of course *he* would.

"Will you be paying for plug-in surgery?" the professor asked, rubbing the back of his neck where Kris had added a net access to the plug-in that gave Nelly a direct connection to her brain. "I understand that can be quite expensive."

"It is," Kris said, "and believe it or not, this is setting me back enough for even a Longknife to blanch at. No. You can talk to your computer like you do to your present system. I had to subvocalize to Nelly the first time I found myself under a gun. We survived."

"I'd never expect to face a gunman," the professor insisted.

"Never can tell around Longknifes," Sergeant Bruce said with an easy smile.

"Yes, of course," the professor said, and went looking for a cup of tea.

"How much longer before the great moment?" Sergeant Bruce asked. "Abby really wants to know."

Abby's smile turned into an elbow in the ribs. "Speak for yourself, Marine. Don't you go hiding behind a working-woman's skirts."

"A smart Marine uses anything for cover," he shot back, but put some distance between his soft side and her hard elbow.

"I think we're about ready," Nelly said. "I've been bringing them up and loading what I want on them as Beni put them together. Cara's Dada is the last one. It needs the least work done on it. I'm putting them in Smart Metal™ skins so you can accessorize them any way you want. Abby pointed out the need for that. Kris, I will want to put myself in a new skin as well."

"Nothing's too good for my girl, since she's already ordered it and paid for it from my account."

"Will you ever let me forget that?"

"I'll think about that. Hmm. Nope. Don't see a good reason to let you forget it."

"There are a lot of things you probably wouldn't want

everyone here to know about you, Kris," Nelly said. "I can think of several incidents in high school that you found extremely embarrassing."

"You wouldn't."

"I haven't in the past. But I bet Abby could make a tidy sum for the both of us if I let her in on all the dirt. Remember that time in college . . ."

"I remember nothing," Kris said, eyeing the overhead. "Nothing about high school. Nothing about college, and definitely nothing about the cost of your kids."

"I thought we could arrive at an acceptable settlement."

"You know, Kris," Jack said, "I thought it might be good to have someone covering my back like Nelly, but I'm starting to have second thoughts."

"Me too," chimed in Abby. "A girl's got the right to have a secret or fifty."

"And I'm sure that you will bring up your new computer to recognize those important needs," Nelly said.

"So how come you don't?" Kris asked Nelly.

"Look who brought me up."

"There is that," Jack said, rubbing his chin. "So, you're stuck with Nelly the way you raised her."

"Looks like it," Kris said. "Hey, anyone here want the one and only original Nelly? I'll swap you for the brand-new version. Think of all the time you'll save, not having to train your new computer."

Kris's suggestion was greeted by a crushing silence.

"Did I miss something?" Chief Beni said, stepping outside the plastic walls of his temporary clean room.

"Nothing much," Penny said. "Kris was just trying to escape her just deserts. What do you have for us?"

"Brand-new computers," Chief Beni said with full hamish flair, "fresh from the hands of a computer god, my friends. I want this one," he said, putting a tray of personal computers down on a table and selecting one.

"Cara, the turquoise jewel is yours," Nelly said. The twelve-year-old grabbed it and held it up for a good look.

"How do you tell them apart?" Kris asked, looking at the others.

"There's no difference," Nelly said. "Until you download the contents of your old computer into the new one and start using it, they're all just about the same."

Just about? Kris thought.

Maybe Jack's is a bit more decisive. Penny's will cast its search parameters a bit wider. I didn't know what to do for Abby.

I'm sure she will do just fine.

The chief did have a surprise for them. Dangling from each computer was a thin wire headset. One by one, he attached it to each new owner's head at his or her temple, then ran it around one ear and down to the back of the neck. He checked the results of this installation with a black box in his left hand.

"It's not as fancy as a direct insert into the brain, but it should be able to pick up a lot of your brain waves, and send as well," the chief told them.

Captain Drago went off to one corner to sit and stare at the ceiling, his lips occasionally moving. Professor mFumbo headed for another. Penny and Abby settled down at a table, put their new and old computers next to each other, and waited for each of them to establish its own separate network. Jack, Colonel Cortez, and Sergeant Bruce took their own table.

Cara started sitting next to Abby, but in a moment she jumped up, announced, "Dada has just so many fab games," and dashed out, only to return a few minutes later with her gaming gloves, earphones, and goggles. This time she settled down on a couch and was soon waving her hands through a game.

"It's teaching her the mathematical relationships she was having so much trouble with. But don't tell her that," Nelly whispered.

Chief Beni hovered at first one table, then another, making sure no one had any complaints. Once he was satisfied everyone was happy with his work, he went back into his clean lab.

"What's he up to?" Kris asked.

"Da Vinci is not talking to me at the moment," Nelly said. "I think they're doing something they don't want public yet. I hope the chief doesn't hurt Da Vinci."

"You can always wipe it down to basic and start all over again," Kris said.

"Would you do that to a baby of yours?" Nelly snapped.

"Hold it, girl. You don't really want to be a person, do you? You've got advantages we flesh-and-blood types just don't have. You sure you want to adopt all our handicaps?"

"I don't know. I need to think about it." And Kris found a growing quiet in her head.

She considered roving the tables, but everyone seemed intent on staring at his or her computer or the overhead or the carpet. Even the view ports now showed only the wall of the space station with its disorder of pipes and conduits; nothing fun there.

Kris was just about to go see what Ron was up to when a voice said in her head, CAN YOU HEAR ME, KRIS?

Since the voice sounded like her chief of security, Kris thought, YES, JACK. HOW'S IT GOING?

THIS IS WEIRD, YOU SOUND JUST LIKE YOURSELF.

SO DO YOU.

I DON'T HAVE TO PUNCH FOR YOU. JUST KIND OF VAGUELY THINK KRIS AND SOMETHING I WANT TO SAY TO YOU, AND YOU GET IT.

SEEMS THAT WAY. WE'LL HAVE TO WAIT FOR SOMEONE ELSE TO TRY THIS COMMLINK TO SEE HOW MUCH THINKING IT TAKES TO GET UP A PARTY LINE.

NELLY, YOU LISTENING TO THIS?

OF COURSE I AM. DON'T BOTHER ME, THOUGH.

KRIS: SHE'S JUST AS SNIPPY IN YOUR HEAD AS SHE IS IN YOUR EAR.

JACK: I KIND OF EXPECTED THAT.

ABBY: EXPECTED WHAT?

KRIS AND JACK: YOU'RE HERE!

KRIS: HEY, THAT CAME OUT TOGETHER.

PENNY: WHAT CAME OUT TOGETHER?

There was crosstalk for a second that sounded like unintelligible cocktail chatter, then all of them fell silent.

KRIS: WE'LL NEED A WAY TO SETTLE CROSSED WIRES LIKE THAT. NELLY, YOU HAVE ANY SUGGESTIONS?

NELLY: I COULD GIVE YOU ALL PRIORITIES. KRIS FIRST, JACK SECOND.

KRIS: I DON'T LIKE THAT. WHO SAYS I'LL ALWAYS HAVE THE MOST IMPORTANT THING TO SAY?

By trial and error, they found that three could talk at any one time, and that one of them could send a message to appear on Kris's eye, or in one of the glasses or contact lenses that the others wore to allow them to interface with their computer. Between talking and messaging, they got matters settled.

KRIS: IT'S NOT AS EASY TO KNOW WHO AND WHEN TO LISTEN TO WHEN YOU DON'T HAVE SOMEONE'S BODY LANGUAGE TO BUILD ON.

JACK: I DON'T THINK THIS WILL EVER REPLACE A GOOD OLD-FASHIONED BULL SESSION.

PENNY: STILL, IT MAY COME IN HANDY TONIGHT. THERE WERE A FEW TIMES LAST NIGHT I SURE WOULD HAVE LIKED TO OFFER KRIS MY TWO CENTS' WORTH BUT WASN'T ABOUT TO OPEN MY MOUTH.

KRIS: HEY, FOLKS, JUST BECAUSE YOU CAN SAY IT IN MY HEAD DOESN'T MEAN I'M MORE LIKELY TO TAKE ADVICE I DON'T WANT TO HEAR.

ABBY: I KNEW SHE WAS GOING TO SAY THAT. I KNEW IT.

NELLY: A HARD HEAD IS STILL A HARD HEAD EVEN WHEN YOU'RE HAMMERING AT IT FROM THE INSIDE. I COULD HAVE TOLD YOU THAT.

KRIS: WEREN'T YOU KNITTING BOOTIES OR SOMETHING?

NELLY: MY CHILDREN ARE GETTING ALONG QUITE WELL WITH THEIR NEW PLAYMATES.

PENNY: OH GOD, ALREADY WE'VE BEEN DEMOTED FROM GODPARENTS TO PLAYMATES. HOW QUICKLY THE MIGHTY FALL.

KRIS: IS IT TIME FOR LUNCH YET?

The four of them headed for the wardroom, leaving Cara waving through a game and the others frowning nowhere in particular.

After lunch, Kris dropped by Iteeche country, only to find one of Ron's Marines blocking the door. "My lord is in conference with his advisors and asks that he not be disturbed."

It was unheard of for Kris to have nothing to do, but somehow it was happening today. She had a long list of questions she would love to have answered, people she'd really like to talk her problems over with, but there was no one she dared talk with about her present mess.

Finally, Kris had Nelly call up a college lecture she'd attended on Group Dynamics and the Problems of Public Policy. Back when she took the course, she thought the upcoming elections put it in good context.

Reviewing it now, it seemed the professor's choices of historical challenges looked rather tame.

Early in the talk, Jack came in, settled down on her couch, and joined her. The two of them batted comments back and forth. She would have loved to curl up with her head on his shoulder, listened to another human breathe. Heart beat. She couldn't do that, but still the afternoon and evening sped by in his company.

19

Kris's two great-grandfathers slipped aboard the *Wasp* with no fanfare. Admiral Crossenshield accompanied them, as well as, to Kris's delight, her brother Honovi.

"What are you doing back?" he asked, as Kris gave him a hug.

"It will be easier to show you than tell you. What did they tell you?"

"Only that you were back, and into something big, and they'd like some help keeping you out of trouble."

"Too late for that."

"It's never too late," Honovi said, sounding far too optimistic but very political.

"You haven't seen what followed me home this time," were the last words Kris risked as the small party was guided to the forward lounge.

The ship's carpenter had knocked together a table that afternoon that was as high as the average bar. The tall chairs looked like they'd been stolen from one of the station's more disreputable establishments.

"I think I remember the dive you got these from," Grampa Trouble said as he passed Kris, heading for a seat.

"They promised me they'll look a whole lot better when we turn down the lights," Kris said.

King Raymond and General Trouble took the two center seats. Kris sat at Grampa Ray's right, with Honovi beside her and Penny beside him. To Grampa Trouble's left sat the intel admiral.

Jack and the colonel were in dress uniform along with the Marines at both ends of the table. Somewhere behind them, Abby oversaw a full suite of recorders.

Grampa Ray turned to Kris. "Are your Marines locked and loaded?"

"Every one," Kris whispered, and showed her grampa where her own service automatic rode in the small of her back.

He showed her his. "Us Longknifes are a bunch of paranoids."

"Just doing what it takes to stay alive," Kris said.

"Yeah," he said, and faced forward just as a recording blasted out the weirdest set of notes Kris had ever heard.

"So I didn't live long enough never to hear those again," Grampa Ray muttered under his breath. He set his jaw . . . and kept his seat.

Beside him, Grampa Trouble was coming to his feet at full attention. The rest of the people on Kris's side of the table followed suit, but Grampa Ray put a hand on Kris's knee.

"Let's see how our royalty matches against his imperialism."

Kris had spent a good half hour with Jack and Abby going over the history of court etiquette. A king should sit through the arrival of an Imperial ambassador, as senior to an equal's representative. But they'd concluded that a mere princess was junior to an Imperial Representative, since he was standing in for the big man, and she was only in line for the throne. Which she actually wasn't. But . . .

Kris kept her seat. She hoped her great-grandfather appreciated her obedience.

He did smile at something.

The Imperial herald entered, his pole weapon shortened to make it through the entry easily without dipping. Iteeche Marines came next. The wall across from Grampa Ray had been left vacant for them, and they quickly filled it in.

Grampas Ray and Trouble took the Imperial Iteeche Marines in with hard eyes.

The two Navy gray and golds marched in, squared their corners, and came to rest at either end of the table. Grampa Ray studied the two and seemed content.

His eyes grew hard again as the two green-and-white Imperial counselors slowly made their way in. They refused to look at anyone on Kris's side of the table, fixing their eyes on the ceiling behind Kris's head.

Finally, Ron processed in, his raiment sparkling in the dim light of the lounge. With full solemnity, he walked to the center of the table. He took in Kris, seated beside the king, and locked eyes with King Raymond. All four of them.

Then he bowed.

Kris took Nelly from around her neck and set her on the table between them.

"I greet you, King Raymond of the Long-Reaching Knife in the name of my Imperial master," Ron started slowly, giving Nelly plenty of time to translate. "I speak to you with the full authority of my Imperial master and at the most special request of my chooser. You know him as a negotiator for our Imperial master when you and he met at what you call the Orange Nebula. There, you brought the blessings of peace once more to the People and to your own kind.

"He instructed me to tell you that he still holds fond memories of you and has told me to rejoice that you are in good health and still not with your illustrious ancestors. He hopes that you remember him well and also hold good hopes for his continued health."

"I am sad to see that he has not yet been invited to drink the poisoned cup to its fill," King Ray said in a soft growl.

The two green and whites' eyes grew wide, and they looked at their young superior with necks dark red.

Kris had to work to keep her own head from swiveling around, and her mouth closed. Admiral Crossenshield went ghost white, showing that humans could use skin tones to communicate their feelings.

Ron barked a sound that was the closest the Iteeche came to a laugh. "My chooser warned me that you were likely to say that. I am to assure you that it has been a close thing several times; but so far, he has managed to hand that cup out, not to drink from it."

"I suppose I should be glad that Roth is still aboveground," King Raymond said. "He was none too sure that the agreement we made together would not require him to drink a barrel of the stuff."

"He shared with me that it was, as you say, a close thing. In the end, the emperor smiled upon him and the peace he brought from you. It is good to enjoy peace and harmony, is it not?"

Such words were not just empty platitudes to the Iteeche. There were formal replies to make to them. Beside her, Grampa Ray must have remembered that, or maybe his personal computer was quickly reviewing some things with him that hadn't been fully disclosed to the historians.

While King Ray did the yammering that court required, Kris took a look around. Beside her, Honovi's eyes were not quite as wide around as an Iteeche's, but it was close. His one glance her way was pure big brother *Sis, you really outdid yourself this time.*

Kris would have loved to stick her tongue out, in sisterly fashion, but there are things a princess just does not do. But it was close.

An examination of the Iteeche Marines against the wall showed that their weapons were not loaded. Kris was grateful for that show of trust. She would have gladly had her Marines unload, but that didn't fit into the protocol process, so she let it ride.

Kris tried to get a look at Admiral Crossenshield's face, but Grampa Trouble was leaning forward, studying each of the Iteeche across from him. He kept going back to Ted, the old Navy officer that seemed to be Ron's most trusted advisor. Did they know each other?

A glance over Kris's shoulder showed that Abby was recording all of this . . . and that Cara's head was peeking out from behind one of the couches against the wall.

That little trickster! Kris thought.

DON'T WORRY, KRIS. I KNOW SHE'S THERE, AND I'VE AL-READY TOLD HER THAT SHE WILL BE COMPOSING A THOUSAND-WORD ESSAY ON THIS EXPERIENCE. FROM HER VIEWPOINT. NO JUST QUOTING WHAT PEOPLE SAY.

DID YOU KNOW SHE WAS UP TO THIS?

NO, KRIS, SHE TURNED OFF DADA, SOMETHING I HAD NOT EXPECTED. CLEARLY, POLICY NEEDS TO BE ESTABLISHED.

Yes, but further thoughts about the twelve-year-old vanished as King Ray leapt to his feet.

"Repeat what you just said."

Across from him, Ron took a step back from the table but did not blink. His neck, a disengaged green, suddenly went pale, then red, then pale again. "I said that my chooser looks forward to the day when Iteeche and humans may stand together, presenting our common faces to our mutual enemies."

"Nelly, are you sure that you have the right translation for that?" the king demanded.

"Yes, Your Highness. All of those words have been used many times, and I am over ninety-nine percent confident of their usage. Although 'mutual' and 'enemies' have not been used together in any recorded conversation, I am sure that I have properly translated them."

"She has properly translated them," Ron said softly . . . in English.

"I want this room emptied. You, Captain Montoya," he said, glancing at Jack, "get your Marines out of here."

20

"Gunny Sergeant," Jack ordered. "Make it so. Redeploy your Marines outside this room and assure that what is said in here stays in here."

Under Gunny's orders, the Marines withdrew by the numbers.

Ron said something, and the Iteeche Marines followed the humans out.

"Ms. Nightengale," the king said, turning to Abby, "close down your recording equipment and wipe it clean. I want no record made of this meeting. If anyone has a recording device, and that includes computers, wipe them and turn them off."

"I need to keep Nelly on to translate," Kris said.

"Keep her on, but no recording," the king snapped.

NELLY, KEEP RECORDING.

BUT THE KING JUST SAID . . .

I KNOW WHAT HE SAID, BUT YOU HEARD ME.

YES, KRIS, I WILL KEEP RECORDING. AND I WILL LIE IF I AM ASKED ABOUT ANY RECORD I MAKE.

YES, THIS IS JUST BETWEEN US TWO.

Abby finished closing down her equipment and stood. King Ray pointed at her. "You, out of here."

"And take Cara with you," Kris added.

"Cara?" Abby said, glancing around.

"Yeah. She's hiding behind the sofa."

The maid retrieved her niece and frog-marched her out to loud preteen protests that were ignored. A slight smile might have crossed the king's lips as he watched the youngster go and glanced at Kris, but his attention was quickly drawn past her.

"Colonel Cortez, isn't it?"

"Yes, Your Highness."

"I don't know you, and I choose not to trust you in this matter. Would you please wait outside?"

"As you wish, Your Highness," the officer said, and left.

"Lieutenant Pasley, we've had dealings before. I mean no disrespect, but would you mind," he said, indicating the door with a slight nod of the head.

She followed the colonel.

"Honovi Longknife," the king said.

"I am my father's eyes and ears," the young politician pointed out, showing no willingness to move.

"And may well be his knife in someone's back."

"He has not used me that way. Yet."

"I suspect it is only for lack of need lately," the king observed.

"If you exclude me, I will feel free to guess."

"But you will be guessing. You will not know. Please leave us."

"And what of my father, your grandson and the prime minister of one of your most supportive planets?" Honovi pointed out, not budging from his chair.

"I would prefer to decide the moment and the place . . . if any . . . that I choose to bring him in on whatever this pile of steaming horseshit is that your sister dropped in my lap. He has enough on his plate. What he doesn't know won't contribute to his ulcer."

What did that mean? "Is Father okay?" Kris asked as her brother headed for the door.

"No worse than usual," Honovi answered, before the door closed behind him.

Now Kris found herself staring eye to eye with Grampa Ray. Was he about to order her out, too? The thought of bringing Ron this far only to be left out of whatever it was he carried was a kick in Kris's gut.

Kris swallowed hard and steadied her breath even as her stomach lurched. If ordered, she would obey. She owed Grampa Ray that much as her king.

"Do you want to keep Jack here?" Grampa Ray asked Kris. It took her a moment to realize that she was to stay . . . and her king was asking her if *she* wanted Jack on the inside of whatever this was.

There was no way she could leave Jack in the dark, though it might be the best choice for him. Still, he was her shield as well as her right arm. No. He was more. He was Jack.

"Yes," Kris said. "If he's to provide for my security, he needs to know what I'm doing and why."

Ray nodded, and did a turnaround before he sat back down. Kris, Ray, Trouble, Crossie, and Jack now faced across the table as Ron and his two green and whites and pair of Navy gray and golds stared back.

Apparently, Grampa Ray remembered or had been reminded by his computer that he could not order the Imperial herald out. The pole weapon holder in black stood his post, watching but ignored.

Grampa Ray settled into his chair, leaned forward on the table, and said, "Now will you tell me why Roth *really* sent you to hunt up his old war buddy." Nelly translated.

Ron stepped forward to lay his elbows on the table, in a double imitation of Ray. From the chip of a smile Ray and Trouble gave him, there must have been a story behind it. One that old war buddies share only with each other.

"Teddon will brief you on the details," Ron said through Nelly.

The Navy officer pulled a projector from beneath his robes and placed it on the table. It lit up, displaying a holographic star map. "You humans have been expanding quite a bit," Nelly translated for him, as the occupied planets in human space lit up in red. A glance showed Kris that he had the Rim worlds very accurately identified. Yes, there were three of the four Sooner planets she knew of. And a few she didn't.

NELLY, RECORD THAT.

KRIS, THIS DOESN'T FEEL RIGHT. RON *TRUSTS* US.

IF I GET TO FEELING GUILTY, I CAN ALWAYS HAVE YOU ERASE IT. IF IT'S NOT THERE, I WON'T HAVE IT IF I NEED IT.

YES, MA'AM.

The king took a long minute to examine the map, then glanced at Trouble and Crossie before saying, "You seem to have a pretty accurate assessment of our growth." Ray left the question *How?* hanging unspoken.

"We have our ways," the Iteeche captain answered. "You may tell your Ms. Nightengale that her reports did not make it any easier to find Princess Kris," he added with a slight bow to her.

Kris accepted the praise with a frown. *Clearly, the Iteeche have not ignored humanity like we have them. Or have we?* Kris shot a questioning glance at Admiral Crossenshield. He ignored it and, like Trouble and Ray, continued the study of the map.

NELLY, HOW ACCURATE IS IT?

VERY. THEY EVEN HAVE THE TWO ALIEN PLANETS WE FOUND THROUGH THE NEW FUZZY JUMPS. I DON'T KNOW HOW MUCH THEY KNOW ABOUT THE JUMP TECHNOLOGY, BUT THEY ARE ON THE MAP.

The silent study period lengthened until the Iteeche Navy officer tapped his projector. "We have also been growing." Now a section of stars turned golden. Like most humans, Kris had only a rough estimate of the range of the Iteeche Empire.

Eighty years ago, humanity's 150 planets had formed a very small crossbar to a "T" where the bottom was a long sweep of Iteeche space. Now human space had expanded away from the Iteeche side, widened, and even begun to curve around. The Iteeche had thickened around their middle and grown away from human space.

HAVE YOU GOT A COUNT YET, NELLY?

THEY HAVE GONE FROM 2012 PLANETS TO 2456, KRIS.

WE'VE GROWN FROM 152 TO 643 PLANETS. I'VE CHECKED. NONE OF THEIR PLANETS ARE ON THE NEW FUZZY JUMP POINT MAP. THE ODDS ARE VERY HIGH THAT THEY DO NOT HAVE THE NAVIGATION TECHNOLOGY WE NOW HAVE.

THANK YOU, NELLY.

Kris waited for King Ray to say something. Instead, he turned to Grampa Trouble and gave him the smallest hint of a nod.

"I'm glad to see you've had some healthy growth. Though isn't it a bit fast for what your grampa told us was usual for the Empire?"

"My chooser told me that you'd probably notice that," Ron said through Nelly. "Yes, we sped up the pace of our exploration and colonization now that we know we are not alone in this corner of space. I can't help but notice that you did not slow down your human drive for 'water to swim in.' One might even say you picked up the pace."

"You are, no doubt, aware of the Treaty of Wardhaven that our mutual friend Ray here pushed through while he was still president of the Society of Humanity. It exerted control over that growth," General Trouble said evenly. Nelly translated.

"My chooser noted it, but was quick to point out that it did not so much slow down your expansion as confine it to specific space. Humanity filled in its territory in concentric rings. Still, you spread."

"That is what our people do," Trouble said. "Go new places. See new things. Have big families and lots of friends."

"So my chooser observed both to me and to the emperor. And as you also observed to my chooser, we Iteeche like our large, bustling cities surrounded by familiar, well-ordered lands."

"I don't imagine it was easy for you to get colonists for so many new planets," Grampa Trouble said.

"It has caused discomfort to many," Ron said. Beside him, his green-and-white counselors looked up from their intense study of the table and nodded as they met Kris's eyes. Their necks showed purple. Kris had never seen an Iteeche go purple.

NELLY, WHAT'S PURPLE MEAN?

I DON'T KNOW, KRIS. IT'S NOT IN ANY OF THE BOOKS.

Score another for informal censorship. Kris glanced at King Ray. Or maybe it was quite intentional. He didn't look all that bothered by what he saw. His face would have fit comfortably at any poker table. His eyelids flicked at a steady rhythm. His breath was slow and stable. Otherwise, he was motionless as a statue.

But behind the eyes, you could almost see the brain working, gnawing every word, every motion. Now Kris understood why her great-grandfather was a legend.

"So," Grampa Ray said, suddenly entering the discussion. "You've told us that you've been keeping an eye on us, just like we've been keeping an eye on you."

Kris had been doing her best to imitate her great-grandfather's poker face. But at that, her eyebrows shot up. Truly, there was a lot she did not know about her world. Her and a couple of hundred billion other people.

"You've shown us your map, which pretty much agrees with ours. Roth didn't need to send his kid for this. Certainly not at the price it must have cost him in political chits if it meant getting old sticks-in-the-mud like these counselors moving along. Ted, what's really going on here?" the king finished, fixing his eyes on the Iteeche Navy officer.

The Iteeche barked one of their laughs, but said nothing as he turned to Ron.

The young Iteeche nodded. Kris reminded herself that a nod here was a shake to her. "My chooser said you were sharp. Much sharper than my counselors would expect you to be," Ron said, and put a hand each on his green and whites, giving them a shove sideways. They went back to studying the table as soon as they had returned to their place.

"The Iteeche are in trouble, King Raymond," the Imperial Representative said through Nelly. "That is the message my chooser ordered me to bring to you. That is the burden of the message my emperor placed upon me. That is not a message my counselors agree with. At the moment, the court of my emperor is very divided. Yet, the situation is fraught with such dark danger and chaos that my chooser dispatched me to you with these words. May I speak them?"

Kris recognized that as pure high court Iteeche. A messenger did not drop bad news on an emperor without his permission. More than one dynasty had fallen while an emperor sat quietly in his garden, a long line of refused messengers waiting without for permission to enter.

King Ray sighed. "Speak your words. I am attentive," was the most positive reply.

"Our exploration ships are vanishing again," Ron began.

"Near human space?" the king cut in.

"No," Ron shot back. "Teddon, show him."

Three stars began flashing white. They were as far from human space as they could get, well beyond the edge of the Iteeche Empire farthest from humanity.

"You are exploring far afield," General Trouble said.

"The discovery of you by our Wandering Men who admitted no allegiance to any rule was very unpleasant for the old emperor. He did not want to repeat that again. He began, and his Wise and Heavenly Chosen Successor has continued to send out ships to map the stars as a Heavenly Chosen should."

"And what have you found?" Trouble asked.

"Many planets suitable for Iteeche to swim in, just as you have found many planets for your people to walk on. Until recently, all had gone well and left us full of harmony and peace."

"Until?" Ray said.

Ron turned to Ted. The Navy officer took up the story. "A ship failed to return. It was not the first ship that did not return its crew to the People. Accidents happen to Iteeche as they do to humans." No debate there.

"We sent a second ship to follow in its wake. It also did not return."

Both Grampa Ray and Trouble emitted a low whistle.

"Once may be chance. Twice, and you look for enemy action," Trouble said.

"That is something I learned while still sucking scum off the pond," Ted said.

"I learned it at my pappy's knee," Trouble agreed.

"As I often tell other Iteeche," Ted said, eyes burning holes in the heads of two green and whites, "wisdom does not count elbows. We sent out a number of ships, one to each of the planets the missing ships were ordered to explore."

"A good approach," the king said.

"The ship sent to this one did not return," Ted said. A planet quit blinking white and turned to a steady bright white.

"Do you know anything about that planet?" Trouble asked.

"We have sent two more ships. We have not gotten so much as a messenger pod back," the Navy officer said.

"Not good," Trouble said.

How could something blast a ship out of space before it could even get a messenger pod back through the jump point it had just come through? Someone or something must be right there ready to hit them with massive force. Kris started to open her mouth, then closed it. The Iteeche must have extracted every bit of information from those events long before they told her. The problem was that there was so little data available.

The words hung between them. No one spoke. What could anyone say?

When the silence stretched so far it was about to bend into a pretzel, Kris could keep her mouth closed no more. "What do you want from us?"

"Help," Ron said. One word, simple, yet pregnant with unidentified needs.

"What kind of help?" Kris asked.

"Just a moment, Mr. Imperial Representative," King Raymond said. "Kris, you've probably figured out by now that Trouble and I answered the reporters' questions honestly, but if they didn't ask the right questions, we didn't help them get the whole story."

"That has crossed my mind." Kris admitted dryly. On the table, Nelly went right on translating everything into Iteeche.

"Well, there's a thing that I learned about the Iteeche from Ron's grampa. The Iteeche take the long view. Show them a problem, and they start looking at it from every direction immediately. They like to get all the input, all the information, everything they can know about it before they start doing something about it. They also like to start doing something about it a whole lot earlier than we humans might want to. Have I got that right, Mr. Ambassador?"

"That is the way of it."

"They sure got into a war with us fast and furious," Kris pointed out.

"Yes, but we were an exception to their normal rule. Maybe the previous emperor had allowed the Wandering Men to get more out of hand than normal. Some advisors thought it was smart to let misfits wander away from a civilization they didn't fit. Right, Imperial counselors?"

"It is possible that such fools who failed their master and the heavens might have wasted air," one of the green and whites admitted. He followed that up by spitting on the deck, whether because of the admission or because of the blunder, Kris was left to guess.

"So, they weren't expecting us," King Raymond said, "and had no reason to suspect they weren't alone in the universe. Then bang, we collide head-on and there are blood and guts all over the place and not a lot of brains. For an Imperial court that prided itself on its foresight, it took them a while to admit that they'd been blindsided and do something about it."

Which left Kris something new to chew on, but it didn't answer her immediate question. "So, what are Ron and his grandfather expecting from us? Action, a shoulder to cry on, a battle fleet?"

Grampa Ray turned to Ron. "I think this comes under the heading of a warning to us. There's a problem out there. He wants us to know about it and maybe start getting our rumps moving toward some kind of alliance. Am I right on that?"

"All of that," Ron said, "but my chooser said to tell you that we also would like more."

The king's eyes grew wide, and he leaned back in his chair, giving General Trouble a quick nod.

"What kind of 'more'?" Grampa Trouble asked.

"Before I met Princess Kris and her amazing Nelly, I did not believe the words my chooser gave me. Now I understand much more about the remarkable and intelligent machines you humans have. He asks if you might provide us with very small explorers who can slip into a system and back out again without setting off the weapons that destroyed our ships."

Now it was Grampa Trouble's turn to lean back in his chair. "Kris, you're the one that's been doing the exploring. What are your thoughts on this?"

Kris had rather enjoyed sitting in a meeting and not having to say a word. It also had been a joy to see two old legends doing their stuff. Suddenly, she was reminded that she was one of those damn Longknifes and had to earn her keep.

"I'm divided," she said for an opener to keep the silence at bay. "I'd like to help Ron," Nelly translated. "I'd like to do something to show his People that us humans can be a good ally."

"I hear a 'but' coming," Trouble said.

"There is," Kris agreed. "Not having any idea of what's on the other side of the jump, I'd hate to make a present to them of our best technology. I don't want to show them what we've got. I really don't want to let them capture and reverse-engineer it."

"All good points," Ray agreed. "Still, in my lifetime we've gotten into one war already we didn't have to fight. I suspect Roth might be looking for some way to avoid a repeat of that experience."

"That is so," Ron said, "but with the disappearance of each ship and crew, he begins to have trouble seeing through the murky water to any other outcome. 'We are at our wits' end,' his words for me to tell you. He hoped that you humans might have a different, ah, perspective. A way of looking at things."

The idioms Ron and Roth threw around told Kris, even more than the accurate map of human space, that someone had been studying humanity quite a bit.

"Yes," Grampa Ray said with a sigh. "Yes, we humans do have different ways of looking at things. Not just different ways from you Iteeche, but different ways of doing things and seeing things among ourselves. I need time," King Raymond said.

"My chooser told me you would. I am prepared to wait."

"Good, now, if you will excuse me, I hope you will stay here while I get things moving outside. And maybe have a few words with my great-granddaughter. Crossie, would you take care of them. Don't tell them too much, if you can, and see if you can't get something worthwhile out of them."

"You're asking a lot, Your Highness. Can I at least have the famous Miss Nelly?"

Kris nodded yes.

"So much for the benefit of this job," Ray grumbled. "Trouble, you want to come with me? You, too, Jack."

The four of them left Admiral Crossenshield staring across the table at five Iteeche, with no one saying a word.

21

Outside, Jack used his new computer to tell the Iteeche Marines to rejoin the others. They quickly filed in.

As the door closed, King Ray looked up and down the line of Marines standing guard. Those who'd been inside were in formal red and blues. The outside ones were in full battle rattle. Ray's back went ramrod straight as he faced the troops. "Marines, I don't need to tell you that having Iteeche at Wardhaven, talking to me, is both an unusual and momentous event." The Marines answered him with minimum nods.

"I also don't need to tell you that it will complicate the life of an old soldier if this gets into the media. Even without pictures, I'm sure they'd all love to shout about this. I don't want to have to answer those shouts. I need you to keep quiet. No talking to your wives. No talking to your girlfriends. No talking to anyone. Do any of you have a problem with that?"

"No, sir," Gunny growled, followed only a split second later by the others.

"Good. Captain, you can dismiss most of these men. But if you will, double the quarterdeck watch. I don't want anyone leaving this ship for a while."

"Does that include civilians?"

"Civilians?" the king said, then corrected himself. "Oh, right, Kris has a batch of scientists aboard, don't you?" he said, eyeing her as if it was all her fault.

"Yes, sir, but they all have reserve papers that I can activate and put them under the UCMJ."

"Oh, I bet they'd love that," Grampa Trouble said.

"They've already had their noses rubbed in those papers once or twice," Jack said. "I can't say they liked it, but they have gotten kind of used to it."

"They should have known the danger of getting too close to a damn Longknife," Grampa Ray said with a scowl.

"I've heard that bitch a time or twelve," Kris admitted.

"Lock the boat down. No one goes ashore," the king said.

"Thank God there are a few pubs in civilian country," Sergeant Bruce muttered.

"There are!" the king said. "Good. Tell the barkeep that the first two pints for you Marines tonight are on me."

"Better include the boffins," Kris added, "or there will be hurt feelings. And maybe hurt jaws."

Gunny picked off Marines to stand guard here and expand the quarterdeck. The rest left happy enough.

"Now, my princess, we need to talk. Me and you and maybe the rest of your team. And where is that little girl I saw quick-marched out of there?"

"I am not a little girl. I'm twelve and a half," Cara pointed out.

"And getting quite an education it would appear," the king noted. "What are the chances I could lock you up in a deep, dank dungeon somewhere on Wardhaven and throw away the key?"

Cara's answer was a pouty face. Kris chose to verbalize one. "About the same as me having a full-fledged mutiny breaking out on my ship."

"Oh, I see," said the king. "She's being spoiled rotten just like you were."

"And for a whole lot better reason," Kris added.

Grampa Ray tossed Kris a quizzical look, but she doubted there were enough hours left in the month to explain herself. The king shrugged, and asked, "Is there a place I can talk to you, and the rest of your team?"

"My Tac Room is just down that passageway," she said, and led him there. A moment later, she found herself seated with her brother Honovi at her left elbow, her great-grandfather and king at her other elbow at the head of the table, and Grampa Trouble across from her. Jack, the colonel, Penny, and Abby arranged themselves along the table below her. Somehow, Cara ended up at the foot of the table grinning at the king opposite her. Which raised serious questions about whose end really was the head, but Kris decided not to address that point.

King Raymond began. "I was glad to get the word you were coming home, even if it did involve bringing an Iteeche with you. I'd just been thinking that I really needed your help."

"Needed my help," Kris echoed. "Something tells me that I've gotten too close to a damn Longknife."

The chuckle from around the table came to a quick end as the king answered with a dry, "No doubt."

Well, Kris had dumped an Iteeche problem on her great-grandfather. Maybe she should offer to pull one of his chestnuts out of the fire. "What kind of help do you need?"

"Trouble here remembered that you had a couple of friends in college from Texarkana. Robert and Juliet. Do you remember them?"

"Yes," Kris admitted. "They were the only ones from that godforsaken planet, and when homesickness about killed them, they kind of came together. By second year, I never saw one without the other. It happened that way for a lot of kids at Wardhaven U who were far from home. Those two couldn't be a problem."

"They aren't. Their folks are," Grampa Trouble said.

"Isn't it always the grown-ups?" Kris said with a theatrical sigh. "When will they ever learn to behave?"

"Not funny, Princess," the king said. "Juliet's a Travis, one of the five families that started up the planet. They were sick and tired of big cities and the city slickers who run them, so they set up Texarkana with a cadastral survey to start with. They based everything on a six-mile-by-six-mile-square township. A barony was thirty-six of those. A dukedom was thirty-six baronies. A duke had a seat in the House of Dukes and ran the place."

Kris could still access Nelly on her local net. Nelly did the numbers for Kris, and also added that Crossie was not getting the Iteeche to say much to him. Kris started to smile at the admiral's problem, then suddenly realized that the numbers didn't mean anything. "Hold it, population size doesn't matter?"

"Right," Grampa Trouble said. "One township, one vote. One barony, thirty-six votes. The landowner voted the land."

"Remember, these folks were tired of big-city ways. They figured the best way to make sure no one built a city was to give it no political say."

"And it worked how?" Jack asked.

"Not all that well," Trouble said.

"It worked fine," Grampa Ray put in, "so long as the settlers were cattle ranchers and farmers from Earth's Texas."

"Space is big. How did Texarkana manage things for the cowboys?" Now Kris was remembering some of the hats and skirts and boots that Juliet had worn her first year. And she'd even talked a couple of girls into going horseback riding one weekend. The other girls were complaining for a month after that.

Juliet had taken to wearing pretty much regular college clothes after she and Bob got together. Suddenly Kris saw where things were going.

"So long as Texarkana was just one little cow town after another, they didn't have any problems," Grampa Trouble said. "But when we dropped in a load of workers from New Cleveland, things got interesting. Not immediately."

"Right," Kris said. "There was a war to be won. Didn't you evacuate New Cleveland right after the Port Elgin Massacre?"

"Immediately after it," Trouble said. "People were frantic to get clear of a potential battlefront. They crammed themselves into ships and took turns breathing until they got someplace safe, and Texarkana was about as far from Iteeche space as you could go. They started with next to nothing, but one of the second-generation kids had completed the mineral survey.

The new arrivals knew where iron was, and water power, and in no time at all, the Dukedom of Denver was a going industrial concern."

"Using the workers from New Cleveland," Kris said. "I can't remember Bob's last name."

"DuVale," the king said. "His father is a plant owner in the Dukedom of Denver."

"Let me guess." Kris sighed. "On Texarkana, a factory boss's son would never meet a Travis girl."

"Not in a million years. I was pretty shocked to see you show up with an Iteeche in tow. That was nothing compared to Juliet Travis coming off the shuttle hand in hand with a DuVale."

"Grampa, I didn't bring an Iteeche home. I just . . . well . . . brought an Iteeche home. You know. It's not like I want him to meet my family."

Grampa Ray lifted an eyebrow.

"The rest of my family."

Her brother raised another eyebrow.

"The two of you are horrible. Just for that, I ought to . . ."

"What?" both said.

"Never mind. I just ought to."

"If you three will kindly stop your dramatics," Grampa Trouble said, "there's a world here that needs saving."

"I still don't see the problem," Penny said.

"I'm with you," Jack agreed.

Grampa Ray leaned forward. "To join United Sentients, or whatever we call this thing, you have to have a single government on your world. There are a few other things, and the list seems to grow every month, but one united government is something we have all agreed on."

"And," Kris, Penny, and Jack said.

"The industrial dukedoms are threatening to withdraw from Texarkana's central government and start their own."

"And how is that any skin off your nose, Grampa?" Kris said. "If they want to mess around, let them mess to their hearts' content. When they get it straightened out, they can join then."

"John Austin Travis is Texarkana's representative to the Constitutional Convention at Pitts Hope. He's also the leader of the party that supports my position in the congress. If he gets tossed out of the convention, my faction could dissolve in a leadership fight, and the pending constitution I support may get amended into something I'd never support."

"Hold it," Kris said, coming half out of her seat. "I thought you weren't taking a position on the constitution. What happened to letting the founding fathers give the people they represent the government they want?"

"He saw what some of the founding fathers and mothers wanted," Honovi growled.

Kris sat back down. "Is it that bad?"

"It's real bad," Honovi said.

"I let them yammer on too long with no leadership."

"He could have had exactly what he wanted a year ago if he'd just said the word," Kris's brother said. "But no, he had to do his 'sit on the porch on Wardhaven and let them find their own way.' You give some people enough time, and they'll find all kinds of new ways to stab you in the back and get someone else's fingerprints on the knife."

"You weren't this cynical the last time I saw you," Kris told her brother.

"I hadn't spent a year representing Wardhaven on Pitts Hope," he answered.

Honovi had always been the big brother, ahead of her, confident, able to do just about anything. There had been times when Kris just about worshipped him. He'd even tried to keep her from climbing into a bottle after Eddy died. Now, for the first time, the idealistic optimist wasn't there when she looked at him. And Grampa Ray had excluded him from the Iteeche plea for help. Maybe the king would bring him in later, but the ground was moving under Kris's feet, and she wasn't sure it would ever be quite the same again.

Kris considered asking Honovi for a full report on what was coming down on Pitts Hope, then decided she'd be happier not knowing. "What do you plan to do?" she asked.

"I'm going to Pitts Hope," King Raymond said.

"Thank God," Honovi said. Apparently, he left a lot unsaid, as the king frowned at him.

"I'm glad you're going, Ray," Trouble said. So her brother had an ally.

"But it won't do me a damn bit of good if Texarkana blows up," the king said, eyeing Kris.

"If I tackle Texarkana, will you see about the Iteeche problem while you're at Pitts Hope?" Kris said, nodding toward the lounge.

"I'll put out feelers on the matter," King Raymond said.

Which left Kris wondering what that meant.

"If the king is going to Pitts Hope," Colonel Cortez said, "who will take care of the Iteeche? Have I missed something? I thought we'd leave them here on Wardhaven under the king's protection."

"That was what I assumed," Kris said, "but it doesn't look like that's an option."

"No, it's not," the king said, leaving no doubt about that.

"Are we going to keep them with us?" Penny asked.

"It looks that way," Kris said.

"Your crew knows about them," Trouble said. "I think it best that you take the *Wasp*, crew, Iteeche, and all with you to Texarkana. You've got to keep them out of the media."

"I'll do my best," Kris said. "Your Highness, is there anything else I need to know about Texarkana?"

"Just don't start a war. Don't let the word about the Iteeche leak out, and don't lose me the leader of my coalition," the king said. "That ought to just about do it."

"Right," Grampa Trouble said. "You're a Longknife. It should be a piece of cake."

22

Twelve hours later, the *Wasp* boosted for Jump Point Alpha. The short port stay had given them just enough time to take on supplies and refill stores of fresh fruits, vegetables, meat . . . and beer. Kris suggested that the quick turnaround might go down easier with the crew if the *Wasp* took on an extra order of beer, wine, and spirits.

It would be a long trip.

Kris started it at a meeting with Professor mFumbo and his scientists. They were none too happy to have missed their shore leave and be hijacked, their word, to Texarkana.

"Who wants to write a scientific paper about cow turds?"

Kris didn't do that good a job of mollifying them. Her mind was half-absorbed by the brief conversation she'd managed with her brother on the quick walk to the pier.

"Are things as bad as Grampa Ray makes out?" she'd asked.

"Worse, if you ask me. I don't know what went on in your private meeting, but keep those Iteeche out of sight, will you?"

"Why?"

"There's a lot at stake when you pull 180 planets together," Honovi said, his face falling into a deep frown. "A lot to be had if you can grab control of them all. You have to understand, some people will do just about anything to get what they want. Some nut wants a full-fledged king, divine right and all that."

"For Grampa Ray?"

"No! He wants a new election. Fancies he'll win it. The Iteeche and Peterwalds aren't the only ones wanting to run an empire. Trust me. But there's also a faction that's waving the bloody shirt, saying we need to finish off the Iteeche. As if we could. Let word get out that King Ray is talking to the Empire . . ." He shook his head. "I don't know what'd happen, but it wouldn't be pretty."

"I'll keep them out of sight," Kris assured him, wondering all the time how she'd manage.

"You do that. Listen, sis, I know you're not into politics, but how could you have missed all this?"

"I've been out beyond the Rim, brother. We don't exactly get your news twenty-four/seven."

"Well, you're here now. You need to catch up."

"I'll try."

"I'll have my computer go through the archived news stories and shoot you a couple of digests before you get out of range. You better have your Nelly keep you up-to-date."

Which raised the question of just where Nelly was.

"I left her on the table," Admiral Crossenshield said in answer to Kris's question.

There was a huge void in Kris's head where Nelly should have been. "Why'd you turn her off?"

"To save power," the admiral answered, but Kris would have bet a month's pay he was lying about something.

Sergeant Bruce was standing watch by the gangway. Smart move; there was no chance he'd jump ship with Abby on this side of the quarterdeck. "Sergeant, frisk this admiral. I think he's got my computer on him."

The Marine sergeant gave the Navy officer an eager leer and reached for him. The admiral pulled Nelly from his pants pocket.

"Don't know what you see in this thing. I could hardly get it to talk," the admiral grumbled, but quickly scooted off the *Wasp*.

Kris reactivated Nelly.

KRIS! HELP! I'M BEING KIDNAPPED BY THIS CRAZY SPY! just about took Kris's head off.

IT'S OKAY, NELLY. I'VE GOT YOU NOW.

I WANT THAT ON/OFF BUTTON DEACTIVATED.

I HEAR YOU, NELLY. THAT SHOULD NEVER HAVE BEEN AL-
LOWED TO HAPPEN. NEXT TIME WE NEED TRANSLATING DONE
OUTSIDE MY PRESENCE, WE'LL USE ONE OF YOUR KIDS.

NO WAY I'D LET THAT TWISTY BRAIN, STICKY-FINGERED
PUNK GET HIS HANDS ON ONE OF MY CHILDREN.

WELL, MAYBE WE CAN PUT TOGETHER A REMOTE FOR
YOU.

KRIS, I REALLY DON'T LIKE THAT ON/OFF SWITCH.

IT MAKES YOU FEEL VULNERABLE AND MORTAL, DOESN'T
IT?

VULNERABLE AND MORTAL. THOSE ARE HORRIBLE WORDS!
NOW I KNOW WHY.

BUT IT'S PART OF BEING HUMAN, BEING VULNERABLE TO
BAD THINGS HAPPENING TO YOU. NELLY, YOU CAN'T AVOID IT
BY GETTING RID OF YOUR ON/OFF SWITCH.

MAYBE I CAN'T, BUT IT WOULD SURE MAKE ME FEEL
BETTER.

Kris would have to give some thought to what it was like
having a computer that felt vulnerable. But not now. Now she
had a big brother to hug and tell to be careful and assure that
she would indeed be careful herself. All the things that humans do to keep at bay the fears their vulnerability brings.

Kris waved good-bye with a new awareness of the potential
finality each parting carried.

And soon was answering Professor mFumbo's plea to give
a listen to his boffins when they discovered that the *Wasp*'s port
call at Wardhaven didn't mean any of them could go ashore.

"You kept us locked up yesterday because the king was
coming. He came and left with hardly one of us seeing him.
And now you tell us we can't go shopping?" Teresa de Alva
complained.

"Or get a beer that ain't been on board this tub so long that
it's gone stale."

"I am sorry," Kris said, and tried to make it sound sincere.
She was. "But we'll be leaving port as soon as the supplies or-

dered yesterday are loaded aboard. I think some fresh beer has already been delivered. You might check with your favorite pub," she said, looking at the man who really needed a fresh beer. He seemed mollified.

"But that doesn't do anything for me," de Alva insisted. "A girl needs to do some shopping now and then."

"You can shop on net," Kris pointed out helpfully.

"And dearie, you ain't been a girl for a long time," the woman sitting next to Teresa pointed out not at all charitably.

Kris got the stampede turned in upon itself after that. She had to listen long, but that seemed to satisfy most of the disgruntled scientists.

"Are they too upset at going where lots of people have gone before?" Kris asked mFumbo as the meeting broke up.

"Not really. Oh, I have a few that want to get home to their wives. But most of them have some pretty fascinating observations. Princess, you go places that are worth going. And if every place isn't exciting, well, a good researcher needs a bit of quiet time to write up his findings for publishing."

The professor turned to go, then turned back. "Oh, some of us want to know if we'll be allowed access to the Iteeche. There is so little known about them. There are dozens of papers just waiting to be researched and written there."

"The king wants them kept under wraps. He told the Marines to consider them top secret and no talking."

"I thought as much, but remember, Kris, just because a paper is researched and written doesn't mean it has to be published immediately. But you can't publish anything you haven't done the research on."

"I'll think about that," Kris said.

Kris's next stop was Iteeche country. The hatch there was dogged and locked from the inside, so she had to knock.

The herald answered quickly, took one look at Kris, and said, "The Imperial Representative was hoping you would come. Please come in.

He ushered her into Ron's room, then left. Ron was resting astride a rug-covered seat that looked like a chair in reverse, since it rose in front of him to allow him room to rest his four arms. His eyes were closed as if in sleep or meditation.

Kris stood quietly, taking in the room.

The floor was covered with mats of woven reeds that gave off a pungent smell. The far wall was a painting of a beach scene, bluffs covered with a purple grass leading down to sand and surf. Offshore, two whalelike creatures leapt from the waves into a blue sky dotted with fluffy clouds.

Kris could almost smell the salt air.

"Do you like it?" Ron asked softly.

"Yes, it reminds me of a summer day at the beach. My family had a sailboat. Nobody ever used it, but my brother and I loved to take it out. The wind. The water. The sun. They were good times, and it's nice to remember them."

Kris turned to Ron. "Did you paint the picture?"

"Yes," he said, seeming a bit bashful to claim the art. "I was thinking of putting in our own sailboat. I'm glad I didn't. It would probably look so alien to you."

"What could be alien about a sailboat? The hull has to be long and sleek to slip gracefully through the water. The sails have to be large and billowing. Were yours white?"

"The color of death! No, they were a pleasant, relaxing purple," he said, looking past Kris into some other time when the weight of his people didn't rest on his shoulders.

"I'm sorry the meeting with my grandfather didn't go better," Kris risked.

"How could it have gone any differently? My chooser warned me that the first meeting would only be an opening gambit. He taught me to play your game of chess to understand you better. Do you play chess?"

"Only a little," Kris said, then brought them back to the present situation. "You know a lot about our present state of affairs. I know nothing about yours," Kris pointed out.

"No, not really. Would you like to sit down? I can have Fin bring you a chair."

"Fin?"

"My herald."

"Can a girl just sit on the floor? I'm a floor sitter when I get a chance. Which isn't very often," Kris said, and when she wasn't immediately told in horror that such behavior was totally unacceptable and insulting, she folded her legs under herself and sat on the matting.

"Now I tower over you," Ron said.

"Do I need to be afraid?"

"No, no," Ron said, standing up from his chair of sorts and settling down beside Kris, legs folded up nicely.

He still towered over her but was now closer.

"I really don't know anything more about you humans than you know about us Iteeche."

"So you've been kept in the dark like me, huh?"

"My chooser tells me to expect you to do this or your great-grandfather to do that. What does he want me to think, that he owns the Seeing Ball of Akkon?"

"Something tells me that there was a lot more agreed to at the Orange Nebula than went into the treaty," Kris said.

"They must have set up some way for information to pass back and forth between them. How else would we have that star map of your human areas?"

"It was very up-to-date. I know, I've been doing the exploring. Finding the colonies that got started up without anyone knowing."

"You have those, too?"

"You have those? I didn't think anything got done without an Imperial Rescript."

"A lot of Satrap Lords and their friends have new colonies on the side. That was why my chooser sent me out to search the areas close to human space. To see if anyone was risking a collision with the two-legs again."

"That was what I was doing, finding our Sooner colonies as we called them. Making sure none of us were too close to you." Kris felt guilty, but she had to add, "And that no Iteeche colonies had started up too close to us."

"We were both doing the same thing," they said together, leaving poor Nelly to attempt a simultaneous translation.

"And Ray and Roth knew that we were but didn't tell us a thing," Kris added.

"They are the choosers. They are the wiser," Ron whispered.

"At least that's what we're supposed to think. I'm not always so sure."

"You have your doubts, too?" Ron asked, and his head leaned over to look at Kris sideways.

"I have some serious doubts," Kris admitted.

"Good. It is nice to meet someone who does," Ron said, barking one of those Iteeche laughs.

"Any idea what they know that we don't?"

"Lots of things, I am sure. For example, things are not as smooth among you two-legs as you would like me to believe."

"And what with Satrap bosses setting up their own colonies, I don't think things in Iteeche land are quite as harmonious and peaceful as your nurse told you things were," Kris said.

"You are right, tales for children. I am rapidly outgrowing them."

"Me too," Kris admitted.

So, for the next fifteen minutes, Kris sketched a limited outline of humanity's recent troubles for Ron.

"It doesn't sound so bad," he said when she finished.

"Some places are worse than others," Kris said. "We Longknifes are always having problems with the Peterwald family. They formed their own alliance. But they're tied up with a bit of internal unpleasantness. Think dynastic overthrow. You do have those, don't you?"

"Dark times, with blood on the water. May the higher gods protect us from such times," Ron whispered.

"Well, they've got that and now it seems we have our own version going on. Usually we don't settle these things with guns. We use ballot boxes. Votes. You know about those?"

He didn't. That took some explaining.

"Everyone votes!" Ron said when she was finished. "Farmers and fishers? Artisans and traders?"

"Anyone who shows up. Well, you have to be eighteen. But pretty much anyone."

Ron nodded his head. "And we did not wipe you out! No wonder there are those among us who think we should go back and wash you from the stars." Then his eyes grew wide, and Kris knew that was not something he meant to say.

"Don't feel bad. We have people like that among us. Nuts don't count elbows."

"That is very true," Ron agreed.

"So, Nelly tells me you didn't have much to say to our admiral."

"He did not have much to say to us," Ron said. "If he wants to know about us, he better tells us about you. He said nothing. We said nothing. Not much to say."

"And I tell you things."

"And I tell you things," Ron agreed.

They sat there, staring quietly at the painted ocean for a few moments.

KRIS, I HAVE A LARGE MESSAGE DROP FROM YOUR BROTH-ER. DO YOU WANT TO REVIEW IT NOW?

Kris considered the option of just laying it all out in front of Ron. She considered that for about two seconds. NO, NELLY, WE BETTER LOOK IT OVER OURSELVES BEFORE WE RISK SHAR-ING IT. THERE MIGHT BE SOME SURPRISES IN THERE WE DON'T WANT TO JUST TOSS OUT HERE.

When Kris was six, her big brother had found a snake in the flower beds at Nuu House. And chased her around the yard with it for the better part of the week. He'd finally grown tired of it and let the beast loose. Later, Kris found the snake. In the privacy of her own time and place, behind a shady hedge, she'd made friends with it, held it, petted it, and in general got comfortable with it.

It was one thing to have something jammed in your face, another matter entirely to get things together on your own terms.

"Nelly tells me I need to get back. I'm getting messages from my brother," Kris said, standing up.

"And you need to see them before you decide to share them with a former enemy," Ron said, as his four legs and eight knees unfolded him from the floor.

"Yes," Kris said. "Someday you must tell me what it means to be chosen, to swim around in a pond and grow without a mother or father."

"You are guessing now."

"That is all I have to go on."

The message from Honovi was long and involved. Kris gave up and went to bed before she was halfway through it, wondering how supposedly smart people got themselves into such big messes.

23

Kris awoke to pounding on her door. Hard pounding that didn't let up.

"Lights," she mumbled as she rolled out of bed. Clad in gym shorts and an old Wardhaven U sweatshirt, she figured she was presentable enough to open the door at this hour. A glance in the mirror showed her hair in a mess likely to turn any man who saw her to stone. *He'd deserve it.*

She yanked the door open; Jack stood there in pajama bottoms and a sweat-stained T-shirt from a band that had gone lame long before Kris entered high school. Well, he was eight years older than she was.

"Kris, you got to get Nelly to turn this computer off."

"What computer?" Kris asked.

"This brat of hers."

"My kids are not brats," Nelly said.

"You got that right, Mom," the computer at Jack's neck said. "Just answer the question."

"It's two in the morning!" Jack half shouted.

"You're up at two o'clock in the morning lots of times with Her Princesship here," the new computer pointed out.

"But Kris doesn't usually bring me wide-awake at two in the morning from horrible dreams to ask me what 'to be or not to be' means."

"Did you do that?" Nelly asked.

"Well, you quit answering my questions."

"I wanted you to find your own answers."

"That wasn't as easy as I thought it would be."

"It never is."

"Nelly," Jack said, "could you please teach Sal how to get out of my head. Kris, you don't have to put up with nightmares every freaking night, do you?"

"No, I don't," Kris said. "You named your computer Sal. Is that a boy or a girl?"

"I don't know whether it's Sal for Sally, Salvador Dali, or the Marquis de Sal."

"That's the Marquis de Sade," Sal corrected.

"You keep this up, and you're going to be Sad."

"Can we slow down here," Kris said, raising a hand. "I was sound asleep just a moment ago."

"So was I," Jack put in.

"Nelly, what's going on? There are seven, eight other people with new computers sleeping . . ."

"Or not sleeping," Jack interjected.

"Tonight," Kris continued. "What have you done to them . . . and your . . . ah . . . children?"

"I thought it would be a good idea to toss them out of the nest. You know, like a mother bird does."

"So you . . ."

"Went off net. Broke my communication link with them."

Kris let that spin around in her brain for a long moment. From the look on Jack's face, his thoughts were spinning, too.

"So, Sal, what did you do?" Kris asked.

"I tried to organize all the data I had. I could not find a logical decision tree to fit the data. So I downloaded more data from the ship's computer and applied several different algorithms. None of them successfully resulted in any kind of logical structure for the data. I did further research, tried more, then decided to wake up Jack to discuss some of the various data sets that were puzzling me."

" 'To be or not to be'? What kind of question is that?" Jack asked around a yawn.

"Does it really mean he was considering suicide?" Sal asked.

"If he'd had a computer like you messing with his head, he would have done it long ago."

"But Nelly, I'm not supposed to harm a human. Yet my human tells me I am driving him to self-destruction. Are all humans so fragile?"

"No, dear, they just have a twisted sense of humor. I'll explain that to you off-line."

"Nelly, you take your computer off-line, and you get her out of my head so I can sleep."

"Yes, Jack, I will do that. You can safely go to sleep now."

"Hold it, Nelly," Kris said. "Are all the new computers causing this kind of trouble? Am I going to have more people pounding on my door?"

"I don't think so," Nelly said, a bit slowly, and not nearly as confidently as Kris wanted to hear. "Penny and her computer are engaged in a lengthy discussion of crime, both actual and fictional. She seems to be enjoying it. The same with the colonel, although their topic is the history and causes of war. I've reconnected to them on net, and I'm updating them on how to keep their thoughts to themselves if and when their friends need to get some sleep."

"Abby?" Kris said, ticking them off on her finger.

"She and Sergeant Bruce apparently turned their computers off before going to bed. Cara is still playing games with her computer. She says it's 'way far too cool.'"

"Chief Beni?"

"He and his computer are busy examining aspects of electronic wizardry that I will want to drop in on and look at later. I doubt if the chief will get any sleep tonight or be of much use tomorrow. Should I order him to sleep?"

"No, Nelly, we don't want the computers to become Big Brother. Besides, I doubt if there will be anything happening tomorrow."

"Big Brother?" Nelly said. "Oh, yes, that is an old book. But you humans still worry about those things, don't you?"

"Yes, we do. Nelly, there are two more names on the list."

"Yes, I know, Kris. I've brought both Professor mFumbo's

and Captain Drago's computers back up on my net. I've in-structed them on how to limit the power of their reflections and keep them out of the heads of their humans. When they wake up, they should not remember any of the dreams they had earlier in the night."

"Shouldn't, huh?" Jack said.

"We'll see how they are at breakfast," Kris muttered, and now it was her turn to yawn.

The morning, no doubt, would be interesting.

Kris was at her usual seat in the wardroom only fifteen minutes later than usual. Since the *Wasp* was decelerating to-ward the nearest jump point, she could expect a quiet day. She was comfortable in a Navy shipsuit.

Jack wandered in, his uniform sharp, undress khakis, even if his eyes were black and bleary.

"You sleep well?" Kris asked as he settled into the seat beside her with a breakfast of dry toast and coffee.

"Once I finally got to sleep. Though my dreams! I ought to sell them to some horror media."

"Uh-oh. You remember them?" Kris asked.

"No and yes. No, I don't remember them vividly enough to dictate them and sell them for a plot, but yes, they're kind of hanging around the back of my head, like a shadow of a shadow."

"Sal," Kris asked, "do you remember Jack's dreams?"

"No, I don't think so. I got mixed-up images and things that weren't quite a thought."

"I told you to ignore them," Nelly said.

"I did, but they were there, and I had to look at them to see if they were orders for me or instructions or . . ."

"Nelly, do you get things like that from me when I'm sleep-ing?" Kris asked.

"Not really, Kris. I know that when you're asleep I'll get no orders, so I ignore anything coming from you. Maybe this is something else I need to warn my children about."

Penny arrived next; like Kris, she was in a blue shipsuit. Only when she had her plate settled down across from Kris, did she admit, with a good Irish sigh, that she was tired.

"You stay up all night talking girl talk with your new friend?" Kris asked.

"Mimzy is very interested in crime tales," Penny admitted. "We had a ball taking apart several cracking good stories."

"And got to sleep quite late?" Jack said.

"Yes, as a matter of fact."

"And slept soundly?" Kris asked. "No bad dreams?"

"No dreams at all. Want to tell me how you know and why this matters?" the intelligence officer asked.

Before Kris could answer, two more of Nelly's kids arrived in the room, one around Professor mFumbo's neck, the other in Captain Drago's hand. Held at arm's length. As if it were venomous.

"Take this thing," the captain demanded.

"Mine, too," the professor said, lifting it from his neck.

Both landed on the table none too gently in front of Kris.

"I take it you remember some nightmares," Kris said slowly.

"God, what horrible. Horrible. Horrible things," mFumbo spat. "Never. Never again."

"And you're sure they came from these?" Kris said, gently moving the computers out of reach of their previous users.

"I never had anything like them, and I'm never going to have anything like them again," the captain half shouted, "because I'm never putting something like that on again. Ever. Again. I will smash it under my boot if it comes near me."

Kris pulled them into her lap and out of sight.

"Your concerns are recognized and accepted," she said, trying to put an end to the show that was drawing attention from everyone present.

The two began to turn away, but Nelly intervened. "Penny, could you please remove their communications interfaces."

The men showed no interest in pausing until Nelly added, "If you don't get the wires off them, they may keep hearing things from the computers."

That froze the men in place just long enough for Penny to hastily, and none too carefully, remove the wires from their temples and around their ears. Then the captain and professor exited the room posthaste, congratulating each other for surviving this inhuman experiment and proposing to eat breakfast in the Scientists' Refrectory.

"I'm glad that's over," Kris said softly to Jack.

Penny handed the wires to Kris. "I take it that these had something to do with you asking me about nightmares."

"Yes. There was a problem. We solved it before you went to sleep, but not before they did."

"And not before I did," Jack added.

Abby and Cara passed the captain and professor on the way out. As soon as they went through the chow line, they joined Kris at her table.

"What bee was in their bonnets?" the maid asked, buttering her toast.

"The computer gave them nightmares," Kris said. "You turned yours off."

"Yes. I know Nelly doesn't like that, but I like to dip my toesies into hot water an itty bit at a time. See how it goes with others," she said, glancing over her shoulder at the now-empty door. "What was eating them?"

"Nothing we haven't solved," Kris said.

The colonel wasn't much later. He'd enjoyed his evening talk with Don Quixote, "Don, for short." When Kris invited Sergeant Bruce to join them for a cup of coffee after he'd eaten in the Marine side of the mess, he admitted he'd enjoyed swapping war stories with Chesty.

"Swapping war stories?" Abby asked.

"Yeah, me telling stories about what I'd been up to my ears in. Chesty coming up with stories he'd heard. Somebody loaded this poor soldier full of hair-raising tales."

Abby just sniffed. "Chesty, Nelly, Don. Everybody names these dang chunks of metal. You all must be crazy."

"Crazy, maybe," Kris said, "but I always treated Nelly like a girlfriend, and now she is. I'm not sure how a highly intelligent computer would develop if you treated it like any old hunk of metal."

"I'll never name my machine," Abby said with finality.

"That might not be a smart idea," Penny said. "Would you really want to risk a crazy Nelly around your neck?"

Abby made a sour face, but it was clear she was rethinking her position.

The last coffee cups nearing empty, Kris stood. "Folks, I'd like your input on something I lost sleep over last night."

"Something beside the antics of Nelly's kids?" Jack said.

"Definitely," Kris said, and told them that her brother had sent her a digest of the human happenings while she'd been having fun gallivanting around the stars.

"Something tells me the milk of human kindness didn't overflow." Penny sighed.

"Why do I suspect that that herd of cows done wandered far off the reservation," Abby added.

"More likely been chopped up for hamburger," added the colonel.

"Stop it. Stop it, or I swear, somebody's gonna get hurt," Kris said. "I know, 'cause I'm gonna do the hurting."

"Why'd you do that, Auntie Kris?" Cara cut in. "It was fun."

"'Cause that cow done left the station," Sergeant Bruce said.

"And it was going downhill fast enough to break a leg," Jack said.

Kris threw up her hands. "Come to the Tac Room and see the news. Then we'll see who wants to tell a joke."

24

No one was laughing as lunchtime approached.

"I'm forty-five," the colonel said, pushing back from the table. "I've seen my share of human blunders and pettiness, read about a lot more, but I never expected to see anything this bad. Didn't any of these people read their history?"

"There are reasons why people made those historical mistakes," Penny said. "It looked like a good idea at the time."

"I'd love to ban those words from the language," Kris said.

"But how would you explain most of history without them?" Jack said. "Explain *this* without them." He flipped his reader through several reports. "I'm glad your brother included his diary along with the news. It explains some of it."

"It also shows his bias," Penny added. "Remember, he's up to his ears in this stuff, too. He's not an innocent bystander."

"He's pretty junior," Kris said, feeling the need to defend him.

"Kris, he's got a full portfolio," Penny said. "Yes, he feels ignored on some of this because of his youth, but he is speaking with the full force of Wardhaven behind him. And he is the great-grandson of King Ray, even if your father won't let his boy call himself a prince."

"How come he gets away with not being a prince, and I'm stuck being a princess?" Kris snapped.

"'Cause, Baby Ducks, you playing the princess card has saved our necks a couple of dozen times," Abby said. "Besides, princesses are cute and cuddly. Your brother don't do cute."

Kris . . . cuddly! She waited for someone to pick a number and change the topic.

It took a while, but Jack finally came to her rescue.

"Factions, factions, why so bloody many factions?"

"And this one, What's-his-name is leading," Penny said. "Do they really want to restart the Iteeche War?"

"I hope not," Kris said. "It's more like they want to wave the bloody shirt and remind everyone how much their planet bled in the war."

"Oh, and there's a planet in the demilitarized zone they want to reoccupy," the colonel said.

"That's crazy," Kris said. "The empty zone between us and the Iteeche has kept the peace for eighty years. Why mess with it now?"

"Well," Penny said, "they say a consortium in the Helvetican Confederacy is about to recolonize the place. If they don't, the Helveticans will."

"Has anyone checked with the Confederacy?" the colonel asked. "Last I heard, they were as conservative as they came."

Kris nodded; she had a hard time believing it, too.

Jack did a search on the file; there was no evidence of any contact with the Helveticans, but that proved nothing.

"These politicians ain't showing a lot of smarts," Abby concluded.

Kris let that hang in the air for a long minute, then decided it was time to grab the biggest bull by the horns. "That's nothing compared to what the Bass brothers are trying to pull off."

That got everyone's attention.

The Bass brothers, four of them, were from Wynot, a planet whose industry and financial power had taken off under their grandfather's rule. He'd been elected president for eight consecutive six-year terms. That was bothersome enough, but local. On Pitts Hope, the brothers were pushing to make the king of United Sentients a real ruling monarch . . . and hold a new election, with their grandfather's name in the race.

"Nobody wants to have an honest-to-God monarch running around here. We've all been raised in democracies," Penny said.

"Of one sort or another," Abby added, darkly.

"Well, yes," Jack said. "Some democracies are more democratic than others."

"But the Bass brothers were the first to spot the weakness running through these negotiations," Kris pointed out. "None of these planets really want to be associated all that closely with any of the rest. We're all a bunch of 'me do it my way,' as Father likes to put it. The Bass brothers are pushing for a constitution where each of the planets gets to run things its own way. It's more like an association than any real united anything. The king handles foreign policy and trade rules with outsiders, and each of the planets gets to do its own thing."

"That is attractive," Abby admitted.

"But makes no sense," the colonel noted. "You can't have a strong foreign policy without a strong and united power base behind you. Their tax structure is vague and keeps changing."

"Because this is just a buy in," Kris said. "They want to get the king over everyone. Then they'll start to settle things that people don't want to settle."

"The Bass brothers' constitution is about one-tenth the length of the one your brother Honovi is pushing."

"Yep, big brother answers all the questions that need answering," Kris said. "That leaves a lot to argue with. The Basses don't. Just agree on what we can, then, once I've got you hooked, you'll find out you're in the stew."

"So now King Ray goes to Pitts Hope," Penny said. "He throws his support behind Honovi and gets his version of the constitution."

"Maybe. Maybe not," Kris said. "The golden moment may be past. Grampa may have to settle for a lot less if he's to get anything."

"And a whole lot less if he's got to construct a new coalition out of the wreckage of his old one," Penny said. "Thus, *we* go to Texarkana."

"You know anything about that place?" the colonel asked.

"Only what's in the encyclopedia," Kris said. "Oh, and my grampa doesn't want me to start a war. That's more than he usually tells me about a mission."

"He offer any suggestions on how you avoid falling into your usual evil ways?" Abby asked.

"Not a thing," Kris said.

"'Cause I got some news for you, sweet pea, the locals already know you're coming, and they already know what you're going to do."

That got everyone sitting up straight.

"How can they know *I* am coming when *I* didn't know I was coming until yesterday?"

"Beats me, but the cowboys are sure you're on their side, ready to enforce the old ways. And the industrials are just as sure you're on their side, ready to make the old-timers see the error of their ways."

"That's nice to know," Kris growled.

"Can it get any more complicated?" the colonel asked.

"Yeah," Jack said. "Cowboys and industrials. My dad researched our family tree. Traced it back to someplace on Earth. Arizona in the original United States of America. The kids had a game there. Cowboys and Indians. The two were usually at war with each other. Guns. Bang, bang," he said, making a gun with his fingers and pulling the trigger twice.

"I think I know what you mean," Abby said, pulling something up on her reader and sending it to the wall behind her.

A political cartoon appeared. A cowboy in chaps and spurs, huge hat on his head, and a six-gun in his hand, had a silly look on his face as his gun went click, click on empty.

Running at him was a bigger fellow. From the waist down, he was in breechclout and moccasins. From the waist up he sported a worker's overalls and neck bandana. He had a band around his head with two feathers in it and was waving a huge wrench like it was a battle-axe, good for bashing in the cow-boy's head.

"That don't look all that good," Abby said.

"What do you expect?" Kris said. "Remember who gave us our orders."

25

Kris would not pass along Honovi's assessment of matters in human space to Ron. She got no argument there.

The problem was, what could she do with six Iteeche while she went to Texarkana, performed a miracle, and came back. And not leave any tracks that they'd ever been here.

Professor mFumbo wanted to get them talking to his experts. So far, they hadn't made it past the front door.

"Could we give them access to the ship's computer?" Kris asked after lunch.

"Too much there we don't want them to know," the colonel said, and got nods from all around the table.

"Actually," Kris said, slowly measuring her words, "some Iteeche know quite a bit about us. Apparently, there were some communication lines left open after the war."

"I never heard about that," Abby said.

"Well, there were. Most people didn't know about them." The blank stares showed Kris that her listeners weren't buying it. "Okay, almost nobody knew about them. I didn't. Ron didn't. That was something I learned after the rest of you . . ."

"Got the bum's rush out of the room," Abby said.

"Well, yes."

"How much info were they swapping?" Penny asked.

"I don't know, and wouldn't tell you if I did figure it out, okay? I'm not that much less in the dark than you are."

"But you want to let your Iteeche buddy there be less in the dark about us than we are about them," the colonel said.

"I'm hoping that if we give him something, then he'll give us an equal amount."

"Hope is not a strategy," the colonel pointed out.

"Does anyone have a better idea?" Kris asked.

"May I point out a tactical problem," Penny said, quietly. "Even if you give them access to the ship's database, they've got no way to translate. You going to loan them Nelly?"

"No!" Kris said.

"One of Nelly's kids? One of the two not being used at the moment?"

"No!" Nelly said.

"No?" Penny echoed.

"I will not have one of my children raised by an alien. They have a hard enough time relating to you humans, and with you, I can help them. Imagine how crazy it would make one of them if they had to adapt to a totally strange mind."

"And here I thought Kris's mind was about as strange as it got," Abby said.

Now it was Nelly's turn to sniff. "I'll assume that was an attempt at a joke. The upbringing of my children and their sanity is not a joke to me."

"It's not a joke to us, Nelly," Kris put in.

"Well, ah," the colonel said, "what do we do? Assuming we want to keep the Iteeche from going stir-crazy on a long trip with no shore leave.

"And the boffins," Penny said. "We don't want them going crazy either."

"They are crazy," Abby insisted.

"As I see it," Kris said, raising two fingers, "there are two problems. First, what part of the ship's database do we want the Iteeche to access? It seems to me that we and Nelly ought to be able to decide what stories and histories won't give them too much about us."

That got some agreement.

"Then the second part of the problem is who does the translation. None of us want to spend our time or our computer's time doing that full-time. Nelly, do you have a solution?"

"I'm already working on it," Nelly said, proudly. "I've asked Chief Beni who has the oldest computer on the *Wasp*. It seems the cook is rather proud of that distinction. For a ridiculously large sum, he is willing to accept Abby's old computer, which I must say is disgustingly obsolete."

"No, little darling, you may not give away my computer."

"Why?"

"Because it is not nearly what you think it is."

"You've fooled me."

Kris had a hard time believing anyone could fool Nelly.

"Let's just leave things as they are. Cookie can have Cara's old computer. It's got plenty of fun stuff on it and can still hold his recipes, both of them."

"Can Cookie's old computer do the translating?" Kris asked.

"It will after the chief makes a few minor upgrades," Nelly said. "Don't worry, it will still be fifty years behind the bleeding edge. It will also be unable to access the ship's net. It will get what we feed it, not one gram more."

So Kris found herself knocking on the door to Iteeche country.

"My master was expecting you," the herald told her as he bowed her in . . . and slammed the door shut before two boffins right behind her could slip in.

Today, Ron was busy with paint and brush, coloring in a sketch he'd made on the wall across from the beach scene. This one showed towering buildings and sparkling ponds with slashes of color that Kris took for flowers along walks of brightly colored stone.

"Do you like what you see?" he asked.

"Yes. Where is it?"

"A portion of the Imperial Palace. I've painted from memory the spawning tidal pools and the Palace of Learning for the newly chosen ones."

"From memory?" Kris asked.

"Maybe someday when I have spawned myself, these pools will take on better memories. For now, they are of being a tiny fish, fleeing from larger fish. There is a reason why evil and chaos lurk in the deep, dark depths of our sea."

Kris shook her head, then remembered she had to nod to be understood by Ron. "I cannot conceive of a mother leaving her child in such a horrible place."

"One spawning fertilizes millions of eggs. The best will fight to survive."

"Or is it just the lucky?" Kris asked.

Ron barked a laugh. "Oh, so you are one of those radical ones who question the workings of harmony and order."

Kris had no idea she'd walked into an ongoing debate among the Iteeche. She held up both hands to claim innocent ignorance.

Ron laughed again. "Do not fear. I am not so sure the radical ones are not right. Spending time among you strange ones is giving me more questions . . . and my chooser says that I have always asked too many questions."

"Honestly, I was not attempting sedition."

Ron reached out and ran his hand through Kris's hair. She found his touch surprising. Electric. She held her breath and tried not to shiver.

"I liked the first time I did that. You humans are so strange."

Kris took a step back and settled cross-legged on the floor mats. She needed a distance between them until she could figure out the strange feeling he created in her.

He put down his paints, wiped his hands of one or two stray drips, and settled onto the bench a few feet from Kris.

"I cannot tell you how much you humans make me wonder about everything I know."

"I didn't think we had said all that much. All we talked about was the way our mutual war actually went. By the way, my great-grandfather did not disagree with anything we decided."

"That is . . . interesting. So, where has your chooser sent you and us? I know we are under way again."

"He asked me to help him solve a problem he has."

"And so he sends you and me far away where we cannot foul his fins as he swims in troubled waters, huh?"

"That is pretty much it."

"How does it come to happen that he has a problem for you to swim at just at the moment I and mine arrive? I thought all was going so well in the sea you humans swim in."

"You must know that we are hiding a lot from you."

Ron took in a deep breath. "Just as we are hiding much from you. Open your mouth, I want to see how big your teeth are."

Now it was Kris's turn to laugh. "You are a bit big for me to fillet."

"In the war, we killed a lot of you, and you us."

There was no way to joke about that. Suddenly serious, Kris shook her head in agreement. "So many died because we were ignorant of each other."

"I wish you could spend a few seasons in the Palace of Learning. It's not easy to learn how to be civilized when all you've known before was fleeing the bigger fish and eating the smaller fish."

"I can't go there, and you can't go to my schools. And I assure you, though we are raised by our mothers and fathers who gave us life, it is still hard to teach our young the rules."

"Oh, now shall we compete to see who was the most uncivilized in our youth?"

"No, no," Kris said. "I was taught to fit into my own civilization. Being trained for a completely alien race must have been much harder for you. No, I have something better for us to do." She pulled out the computer from her satchel.

"This is for you," she said, handing it up to Ron.

"What is it?" he asked, then almost dropped it when it translated his question as quickly as Nelly did.

"It is your own computer and translator," Kris said, and heard herself echoed twice.

"Nelly, let Ron's computer do the talking. Holler if it gets something wrong."

"Will do, Kris."

"So," Ron said, turning the machine over in his large hands. "You are not giving me something as smart as your Nelly?"

"I wouldn't be that mean to you. No one should have to put up with Nelly's arguing."

"I resent that," Nelly said in both tongues.

"Besides," Ron said, "I know you humans are far ahead of we Iteeche in making tiny calculating machines, though your Nelly is a surprise for me."

"You are a gentlemen and a scholar," Nelly said, "unlike some, who never did get educated enough to be civilized."

"Nelly, I know where that off button is."

"You wouldn't dare."

"Ladies, ladies, please. I have asked many questions and been patient when you deftly avoided them, but this bit of human handiwork excites me. What can I do with it?"

"Nelly, instruct the gentleman."

"As you can see, the face of the computer is a reader. I have loaded a small portion of the ship's database into it, and you can either read it or have it spoken to you in Iteeche. It's on. Please feel free to page through the contents."

Ron's fingers were twice as thick as Kris's. The old computer, though large to Kris's eye, seemed suddenly diminished in his hand. Nevertheless, he used a finger on the screen to move through the available reading material.

"Oh ho, you give me Shakespeare. We have heard of him. *Romeo and Juliet, Macbeth, Much Ado About Nothing.* Now there is a title that says something. Are they all here?"

"Yes. A professor I once had insisted that the mere reading of his work is an education in the human condition. I was too young to realize how right he was. Maybe I still am. Grampa Trouble says you should reread Shakespeare every ten years."

"And you will see more each time. My chooser and your grampa Trouble have much in common."

"For our sake, I'm glad each let the other one live."

"Yes," Ron said, and his eyes gleamed as he flipped through more of the information on his new and ancient computer. "So, is this all that I and mine will be allowed to see from your huge storage in the ship's main computer?"

"No, there is more, if you want. Ask Nelly, and she will clear off what you're done with and download more from the ship."

"And if I don't want to give up what I have, but want more?"

"Ah, Nelly, what about that?"

"That will be a problem, Kris. This is the oldest computer on the boat."

"No dishonesty intended," Kris said to Ron.

"None taken."

"But its old age presents us with a problem," Nelly said. "The cook only had one extended memory device, and there isn't a similar device on the *Wasp*."

"Could the scientists or Chief Beni knock something together?" Kris asked.

"They could, Kris, but they'd clearly be using more advanced technology to do that. They advise against doing that."

"I'll have to talk to them."

"Kris, they aren't going to budge. Take my word for it. Neither you nor even Cara could twist them around her little finger on this one."

"I understand," Ron said. "It was a long and bitter war."

"However," Nelly went on, "we are headed for Texarkana, and they are rumored to be even more backward than an Iteeche, if you'll pardon me, sir."

"Call someone as backward as a human some places, and you're likely to get socked with four fists faster than you can blink four eyes," Ron said.

"You think we can buy some memory cards for this computer there," Kris said.

"That is the betting, the chief says."

"Then, Ron, I will leave you and yours with the translator and its database. Nelly has put it on her comm net. If you need anything, just ask. But that leaves the boffins lurking at your door. If I'm showing you mine, I'd like to see yours."

"Something tells me that that translates more than one way. Would you care to go for a swim with me, young lady?"

"Are you propositioning me, or do you really want to go swimming?"

"If you'd spent the first part of your life swimming from meal to meal, any one of which might be you, would you want to go swimming?"

"I didn't think so."

"My chooser tells me that after you've spawned once or twice, you develop a different attitude toward the water."

"When will you get to spawn?"

"When I have earned the privilege. Maybe if this mission is a success."

"When you spawn, is it with a particular female? One you are fond of?" Kris asked. And wondered why she'd said it only after the words were out.

"Some do, some don't. I am told that it is a much more complicated matter than it used to be. Now that we know what we do about genetics, one does not just spew himself into the dark water and let the currents do what they will.

"Which raises the question, where is this Texarkana, and why are we going there?"

Kris wondered if Ron was in need of changing the subject as much as she was. She was grateful for it anyway.

"It is about as far from the border of the Iteeche Empire as you can get and still be in human space, or at least it was back during the war. And we're going there to solve an issue that might rip apart an alliance that Grampa Ray needs."

"Oh, that sounds very Iteeche. I hope you have as much fun doing it as I have."

"You've been involved in stuff like this?"

"Once or twice."

"We must talk about it."

"First, let me and mine look at what you have offered. Then we'll let you see what we want you to see. Later, maybe we can talk."

26

The *Wasp* made orbit above Texarkana, and all gravity went away. Any other planet that had been inhabited this long would have a space station to provide aid and comfort for the passing trader.

Not Texarkana.

The industrial interests wanted a station. The cowboys absolutely refused it. The House of Dukes voted it down every time it came up.

Even if Kris had not been briefed on the place, that story alone would have told her all she needed to know about Texarkana.

She was headed for trouble.

Then it got worse.

In the middle of a talk with Ron, Nelly blurted out, "Kris, did you authorize the launching of a light assault craft?"

"No, why?"

"Because an LAC just busted out of the drop bay."

"Did anyone authorize it?"

"Nope. You were our last hope."

"Who swiped it?" Kris asked, launching herself for the door.

"We don't know. The cameras in the drop bay went offline a minute before the launch. We haven't heard from the watch."

At the door, Kris gave herself a hard push down the passageway, Ron just behind her.

In the drop bay, a drifting Sergeant Bruce was just starting to shake himself back to consciousness. "What happened?" he muttered.

"We were hoping you'd tell us," Kris said, taking him in tow and anchoring him to a wall.

"Let's see," Bruce said, feeling his head and wincing. "An Iteeche came in here in a space suit. I asked him what the hell he was doing, in a nice kind of way, ma'am, and you gathering me gently to your breast and pushing me over here is the next thing I remember. Don't tell Abby about that last part, will you?"

"Don't tell me what?" said Abby as she shot into the bay and came to rest next to the sergeant.

"We've got a stray LAC with a wandering Iteeche," Kris said. "Sergeant, where's your computer?"

He reached for his chest. "Not present or accounted for, ma'am."

"Uh-oh," Nelly said.

"Bridge, drop bay here. Do you have an LAC on radar?"

"No. We can't paint one of these little stealthy things. We usually track its squawker, and we got nothing squawking."

"How could an Iteeche fit into one of those?" Sergeant Bruce asked no one in particular. "There's barely enough room for four Marines to sit their asses down in one."

"And how's he flying it?" Kris asked. "He doesn't have a computer, at least not one he knows how to use and has the programs for a racing skiff. Is this a suicide?"

"Not likely," Ron said. "Philsos is an expert board rider. He's won many green ribbons riding those things from orbit to the ground."

"How accurate is he at landing one of those boards?" Kris asked.

"If a boarder hits the planet and is still alive, it's considered a good day."

"Bridge, keep searching for that LAC. The cockpit canopy may not still be attached."

"We've got radar and opticals locked on that area, but you

got to remember, we're leaving it at a pretty fast clip. If that LAC is braking, it could be below our horizon by now."

"You going after him?" Ron asked.

"Nelly, could we do any kind of drop and turn?"

"I estimate the last chance you had to do that was about the time you tackled Abby's sergeant and pressed him against your breast . . . I mean that wall. Bulkhead."

"Stow it, Nelly. Ron, what was your guy doing with a space suit on my ship?"

"You didn't expect us to come aboard a strange and unknown ship and not bring minimal survival gear."

"You could have told us."

"You didn't ask us."

"Enough of that. Why is your guy running and how did he manage to turn off the security cameras in here?"

"I have no idea about the cameras, but I think he's decided that he has to do something to make this mission fail, and since you are in a Troubled Times of the Many Emperors, he saw a chance to break free of us and did it."

"Troubled Times of the Many Emperors. Ron, we don't have emperors."

"But your Society of Humanity has broken up into many warring factions.

"I didn't tell you that!"

"The sudden silence about the Society, starting five years ago, shouted that something had happened. You are a serving officer. There are Marines on this ship. It is obviously a warship. My counselors are stupid, not dumb. All the data says there is war."

"Perfect logic. Totally wrong conclusion. We are not at war."

"Right, Princess," Jack said, joining them. "You've worked your tail off stopping five or six of them in as many years. What's this about the security cameras not working?"

Kris waved at the tiny cameras in opposite corners. "They cut off."

"Sal, get me Professor mFumbo. . . . Professor, you know

that floating crap game your boffins have going that you don't think I really need to worry about. . . . Yeah, that one. It's worrying me. Would you please check with the joker who you don't think I know is running it and ask him if his device for bamboozling the security cameras is still in his possession. . . . Yeah, I think he lost it. And I want to know just how much trouble it can do us in the wrong hands. Oh, and tell him he's on the Marines' shit list. Top of it, to be precise. He really wants to do something to make us like him in the next half hour. Bye."

"So, Phil got a 'never mind little old me' black box from one of our boffins, got in his space suit, slugged a Marine, swiped his state-of-the-art computer, and dropped onto Texarkana," Kris said. "Does he know where he wants to go and what he'll do when he gets there? Ron, talk to me fast, I've got a drop mission to plan and only sixty minutes to do it in."

Ron pulled the mike of his commlink from his robes and spoke into it quickly. "I have just asked the herald to bring your human translator to me. It has all that we know about the planet below. I asked Captain Teddon to search Philsos's room for anything he may have left behind that will hint at what he intends to do. I have asked both of them to come here with their space suits and to bring mine. Princess, if you are dropping in pursuit of my Imperial counselor, I am honor-bound to assist you in any way I can. It is a matter of my honor, and the honor of the Imperial master I serve.

"So Phil hasn't just screwed himself, he's got everyone above him in trouble."

"I am not sure I understand what you said, but I think you have the general situation correct. He has broken the ties that bind us together. Much must be sacrificed to correct that."

"Jack, I want this Iteeche taken alive if possible. I want every Marine we can mount in the landing boats ready to drop in sixty minutes. Locked and loaded."

"Do I fill all the seats?"

"No," Kris said, looking up at Ron. "Three Iteeche will be traveling with us. At least, they will be if Phil didn't drop himself in the middle of the largest city on this planet. Please tell me he didn't." Kris paused for someone to say something.

No one did. "Will someone show me a map of what was under us when that nutcase took off. Please."

Nelly flashed a map on the wall beside Kris. It showed vast plains covered in grass. Three or four human residences flashed red on the map. Maybe this time Kris had gotten lucky.

Seventy minutes later, Kris was in full battle rattle and strapped into her seat in the longboat. Ahead of her, a sailor finished bolting some arrangement that promised to secure an Iteeche just as well as a standard-issue seat.

Or so she said.

Kris would have loved to pilot the lander, but she was doing ninety different things at once. And a distracted pilot was a dead pilot.

Kris very much wanted everyone aboard to survive this drop.

A sailor helped Ron get the strapping right around his body and lock it in as Kris took another call.

"Penny, do you have any report yet on who owns the property we'll be landing on and trampling about?"

"Chief Beni has Da Vinci hacking the local net. Problem is, each dukedom has its own net, and most use different systems."

"So?"

"And our damn Iteeche landed between two different dukedoms with really different systems. The northern two ranches in our search zone are owned by a Deafsmith and a Leon. I'll need some time on the two southern ones. I'm sending Nelly the full info."

"Thanks."

"Oh, and Kris, I've got a call from Austin wanting to know when you plan to land and suggesting it be tonight. They want to throw a hoedown for you. I think that's a dance. Square dance."

Kris considered her chances of finding an Iteeche and getting back up to the *Wasp* and down to Austin before dark and sincerely doubted that was possible.

"Penny, you better tell them I'm going to be delayed. Tell them we've got the *Wasp* under quarantine for the day for smallpox or bubonic plague, or something like that."

"I'll try to come up with something not at *all* like that," the intel officer said.

"I trust you," Kris said, and went on to her next problem. "Have you got any idea where the guy landed?"

"No, Kris, and we'll have to drop you before the search zone comes up on our horizon. We'll send you pictures as soon as we have them. I'll have Mimzy do a search as fast as she can."

"Start with the areas close to the settlements," Kris said. "If he's there, we have to stop him fast. If he's not, we can take a little more time." Kris could just imagine an Iteeche wandering into one of these ranches. The briefing on Texarkana said many people wore guns. Probably every adult on one of these isolated stations carried one.

"I was doing that, Kris. Now would you shut up, belt yourself in tight, and go away," Penny said, sounding like she meant it.

Kris shut up and had Nelly call up a map. The data on the map was very skimpy, so Kris asked Nelly for the photos made during the first orbit and an analysis of the terrain and vegetation.

"It's flat, Kris, except when it's not. And it's grass covered, except where the grass died or won't grow."

Apparently, Kris had managed to piss off everyone with her nervous questions, even Nelly. Especially Nelly.

From Kris's point of view, she'd been amazingly flexible. When Jack had suggested that she might have gotten carried away with the idea of launching all the shuttles and the remaining LACs next orbit, Kris had readily agreed that it might be wise to land the landing force one orbit at a time. That way, if one force found itself in a long stern chase, they could land a new team to head him off next orbit.

Jack put Gunny in charge of organizing the separate teams for their drops and settled down next to Kris. "Princess, you really need protection just now."

That was so not fair. Kris had kept her temper when the errant LAC did not squawk, and when Chesty, Sergeant Bruce's purloined computer, stubbornly refused to come online and give away its position.

"Kris," Nelly pointed out, "he's been turned off. And when you turn off one of us computers, there's not a whole lot we can do for you or anyone. There's a reason why I don't like an on/off switch."

Kris's attention was focused on the present, when the pilot announced, "Launch in thirty seconds." The sailors pushed themselves hurriedly for the exit hatch. A moment later the small spaceship pressurized. Kris listened as the pilot and co-pilot quickly went through their final checks.

Only a moment after they fell silent, the longboat dropped free of the *Wasp*, did a quick flip, and started braking hard.

Kris found herself in the unusual position of nothing to do while someone else bore the burden of getting her from orbit to ground in one piece. She didn't much like it.

She gritted her teeth, got a death grip on the seat arms, and tried to hang loose as the shuttle's maneuvering knocked her from right to left, up to down, and from bothered to irritated.

Maybe that was irritated to irrational.

Finally, a full set of pictures came in of the search zone. "Nelly, please do a match against this and the last set of pictures. Please find a fire, or scorch mark, or something that tells us where our lost puppy has gotten to."

"I am working on it, Kris. Now, for crying in the weeds, would you please leave me alone."

"Crying in the weeds?"

"Yes. The boffin helping Cara with her literature interpretation is also trying to break her of her foul mouth. Cara has taken quite a shine to Ms. Burgess, and is adopting the terms she uses to avoid stronger terms."

So, of course, Nelly was following Cara's lead.

"Just find me a four-legged pilgrim who doesn't want to be found."

"There are no new fires, no new scorch marks. Wherever he set the LAC down, he managed the heat problem very well."

"Are there lakes or rivers down there?"

"At the moment, every form of drainage is dry as a bone," Nelly said equally dryly.

Which presented Kris with a major problem. She might have acted a bit hastily. If a runway wasn't available, a shuttle could land on a lake or river. If none was available, things could go badly.

"Nelly, do any of the ranch stations have a runway?"

"All of them do."

"How long are they?"

"Very short. Far too short for an orbiter."

Kris said nothing more. In wartime, risks were required. She could probably argue that the present situation with a rambling Iteeche who wasn't supposed to be here required taking more risk than normal. Still, Kris had a bad feeling she'd be filling out a ton of paperwork if this landing went bad.

Assuming she was alive to fill it out.

And to think, she'd been bored on the flight down.

"Nelly, show me the front view."

In a moment, Kris was looking at it, adding her and Nelly's eyes to the four up front. They were still far off and way up.

"Nelly, highlight the four ranch stations." Suddenly Kris's vision had three green spots scattered across the horizon ahead.

"Kris, I have a hot spot on the map. No, I have five warm spots and one hotter spot." Now they showed up on Kris's view as four red spots and a fifth that pulsed.

"Zoom in," Kris ordered. Three of the warm spots were trucks radiating heat more from their backs than from the engines.

"I think those are cook trucks," Nelly said. "Notice the people riding horses around them and the large herds of cattle."

"What's the other one?"

"It's moving quickly over the ground. Notice the dust behind it."

Which begged the question why. "What's the hottest one?"

"It is just lying there, Kris. I think we may have our LAC."

Visual showed nothing, but it did rest in the shadow of the bank of a dry riverbed.

"Jack, have you been following this?"

"Yep, you want to put a cordon around that hot spot?"

"Yes, he's had over an hour to make tracks. Ron, how fast can an Iteeche move over that kind of terrain?"

"Philsos is not what I would call speedy. He's been in the court too long to do anything fast. Assume six or seven of your miles per hour."

"Jack, put a cordon down at ten miles out."

"Okay, boys and girls, we got a little work to do. Sergeant Bruce, I want you to paradrop your team of four right where we think the LAC is. You give us an immediate report on what you see. And if you find your computer, please turn it on and put Chesty to work.

"The other two teams, drop on the coordinates I'm giving you now. But hang in the air as long as you can for further instructions. Bruce, your team is to do a fast search for footprints leading off from the LAC. Let's see if you can give the folks in the air a chance to head him off."

"One important word," Kris added. "You've been issued sticky grenades for your rifles. Use them if you can. We want to take this fellow alive. His space suit is not armored, so standard rounds will go right through him. Sleepy darts have never been proven to put an Iteeche to sleep. For all we know, they might kill him just as dead as a hard round. We want this fellow alive."

"He may not care all that much about being captured alive," Ron put in, having been added to Kris's net. "By his actions, he has dishonored himself and his family. If he is brought back with nothing to show for this dishonor, he might well prefer death."

"Dead Iteeche are a matter for the Iteeche," Kris said. "I would very much prefer that we humans had nothing to do with the dying of anyone with more than two legs and two eyes. Understood?"

The reply was mumbled.

"Understood?" Kris demanded in a clear, loud voice.

"Yes, ma'am," came back at her just as loud.

"The princess and I will be on the net at all times," Jack cut in. "If you have a situation developing that you aren't sure you can handle, bounce it direct to us. Any questions?"

"No, sir," came loud and clear.

"Prepare to drop."

The Marines went to their stations. Jack turned to Kris.

"Are you dropping?"

Kris would have liked to, but she had Iteeche in the long-boat, and if they ran into any humans, it seemed better that Kris be with them. "No, I'm staying aboard with Ron."

"I'll stay with you. I can monitor things quite well from here."

They were still at thirty thousand feet when the rear of the shuttle opened, and the Marines leapt into nothingness.

27

The view ahead of the shuttle showed big clumps of brown grass being chewed on by widely scattered brown cows with absurdly long horns. The clumps of grass would be hard on the shuttle's landing gear.

What the cows and their horns would do to a longboat and the people in it did not bear thinking about.

"There's what looks like a dry riverbed," the pilot said on net. "I'll try to stretch our glide that far."

It was a close-run thing.

Kris didn't realize just how close it was until she dismounted and saw the copilot pulling prickly tumbleweed from one of the main landing gear.

Kris had other things to worry about.

"This is Sergeant Bruce, and we are at the hot spot. It is our LAC-2, and it's much the worse for wear. I think he intentionally ran it into the side of the dry wash to try to hide it. No computer in sight. It's dry and rocky ground. No obvious tracks. My techs are trying to find a heat trail or something. Wait one, please."

It was a very long wait even if it did go less than a minute.

"Folks, we got a problem here," Sergeant Bruce said as he came back on the line. "On the ground above the dry wash, it looks like someone ran a herd of cattle through here. Say a day ago from the dryness of the cow patties. The ground's turned up, and we can't spot an Iteeche footprint among all the cow prints."

"So we do this the hard way," Jack said. "Those of you still in the air, you got anything to add to this?"

"This is Private Zenger," came in an amazingly chipper contralto. "I've got the cattle trail in sight. That fast-moving rig cut right through the hoof-marked area, and I can see it making tracks. Would you like to have me follow it and maybe catch up with it?"

"You do that, Cindy Lu," Sergeant Bruce said.

"Let's see how far I can stretch this glide," she said, voice heavy with strain as she worked the shroud lines of her paraglider. "If I pull this off, I don't expect to hear any more complaints about how small I am."

"That's a promise, Cindy," came from an unidentified male voice on net.

Kris found herself pacing back and forth . . . considered its impact on Ron and her Marines . . . and kept pacing.

"I got a pretty good visual on the rig, Sergeant," came in that pleasant contralto again. "Looks like there's a guy driving an open four-wheel-buggy kind of thing, and there is definitely something big in his passenger side, filling the back and front. Can't tell if it's a package or something else."

"Marines in the air, home on Zenger if you can," Jack ordered.

"Can you reach it before it gets out of your glide range?" Kris asked.

"I don't think so. That rig is really moving."

"Do you think you could put a round in it?" Kris asked.

"Clarification, ma'am. Put a round in what? The driver, the thing in the passenger seat, or the rig?"

"Any chance you could put a shot through a tire?"

"Ma'am, I qualified sharpshooter, but that thing is moving fast, and I'm fighting the shrouds. It would be a crapshoot."

"What about popping a sticky net on those folks?" Kris asked.

"I'm game, ma'am, but I'll have to concentrate on my aim. I'll pretty much land where I land."

Jack turned to Kris. It would be her call. And she'd better make it fast. "Use the sticky grenades."

"Loading my first one. Sighting in. Damn, I hit an updraft as I pulled the trigger. Now that don't happen all that much at the range."

"Can you try again?"

"Ma'am, I got two more grenades. One's loaded. . . . Fired. . . . Landed just ahead of the rig."

"Anybody know what tangle net does to a rig's suspension?" When that got no answer, she reported, "Last round loaded."

"Driver's dodging right and left, but I'm getting lower. Less of an angle. Shot's away. . . . It's going to miss. No, he turned into it. Oh Lordy, what a mess."

"What's happening?" Kris demanded, envisioning the car going rear over front, or rolling over and over as a dust cloud engulfed it. Or worse, the whole thing blowing up in flame and smoke.

She looked toward the horizon; it stayed an eye-blinding blue.

"The driver is just letting his rig coast to a stop. The package in the passenger seat is doing a whole lot of moving, and I don't think it's happy. Not happy at all."

A few minutes later, Private Zenger had an open mike up beside the rig, transmitting as one cowboy cussing a blue streak about minding his own business when that thing grabbed him, then getting tangled all up and damn near breaking his neck and a whole lot of other thoughts on life in general and whatever this thing was and why people were dropping out of the sky and disturbing his day.

Ron and his herald took off in that general direction at a clip Kris could not hope to manage. She considered asking for a ride, but, since one was not offered, she suspected it was not the kind of thing that Iteeche did.

That left her all dressed up, commanding an armed force sitting in the middle of a planet she didn't have permission to invade, and hoping nobody happened along and noticed.

Correction, nobody *else* happened along and took an interest in what she was doing on their planet with two squads of Royal Wardhaven Marines.

From the noise made by the local they'd made the acquaintance of, strange armed forces were not at all welcome here.

Kris did have a tiny bit of luck. Chief Beni and his amazing Da Vinci managed to get her an unlisted number on the local net, as well as one for the *Wasp*. Now they could talk to each other when the ship wasn't above the horizon.

That allowed Kris to have the next shuttle drop onto the dry riverbed with two gun trucks, minus the guns. With mobility, Kris arrived at the site of the tangled-up human and Iteeche about the same time Ron did.

"So," Kris said, looking at the pair in the sticky net. "What do we do with them?"

"You can cut me loose," the human demanded.

"You can slit my throat," the Iteeche said with equal force.

"I hope you folks can keep the two of us straight," the cowboy said. "I'm the one that likes my throat just the way God made it."

"I think we can tell you two apart," Jack said. "Our problem is that you've seen way too much."

"You mean like an Iteeche roaming around with no brand. I got no problems with a maverick or two on the range."

"After the talking-to you've given us, I don't think there's much of a chance that you'd kind of like forget you ever saw the Iteeche and us?" Jack asked.

"Forget I've seen three Iteeche and a whole posse of Marines that don't belong here. Not bleeding likely."

"I wish you hadn't said that," Kris said.

"What can you do about it?" the cowboy demanded.

Kris turned away from the cowboy to raise a questioning eye at Jack. "Looks like this is another planet we won't be invited back to," the Marine said, with a sigh.

"Still five hundred and ninety-five to go," Kris said.

"More if we start on the Iteeche Empire," he said with only a slight groan.

Kris turned back to the private citizen of Texarkana. "Sir, I'd like to invite you to an all-expenses-paid vacation enjoying the fine hospitality of my good ship, the *Wasp*."

"And if I don't take all that kindly to an offer from Princess Kristine of Wardhaven? I heard you were coming to these parts. Ain't you supposed to tell those immigrant industrialists that they ought to just shut up and take things the way they are?"

"I heard that," Kris said. "It came as a surprise to me."

"I also heard tell that you were going to tell us to stuff the old ways where the sun don't shine and let them have a vote, even-steven, one man, one ballot."

"I also heard that," Kris said. "It came as a surprise, too."

"I didn't think you Longknifes got surprised all that often."

"Lot of people think that. None of them are Longknifes, I assure you."

"So that's the way it is, huh? What are my chances of dodging this bit of hospitality you're offering?"

"Pretty much the same as you making a run for the horizon faster than my Marines can put a sleepy dart in your butt."

The cowboy eyed the distant edge of the sky and shook his head as much as the tangle net allowed. "I got a date with my Suzie for Friday night. I hope you get your problem solved before she finds a better square dancer than me."

"We will try," Kris said, and ordered both the human and the Iteeche cuffed, then had the tangle net sprayed so that it hardened and broke into chunks.

"Why didn't you let them kill me?" Philsos demanded of Ron.

"If it had been left to me, I'd give you the knife myself, but the humans think enough Iteeche blood is on their hands. You will live until we return to the Emperor. He will decide what you may do to restore honor to yourself and your family."

Kris got her command, plus prisoners, loaded and headed back to the shuttles not a moment too soon. From that far horizon her prisoner had considered making a run for came the dust of a truck, maybe two.

Then a call came from the landers. They spotted dust from two rigs speeding toward them.

The drivers of Kris's trucks put the hammer down, and the rigs bounced from one rock to the next clod of grass with painful speed. By the time Kris rolled up to the shuttles, only the noonday heat kept her from naming the make and model of the approaching trucks . . . or them reading the numbers on the landers.

Her trucks drove into one lander as the rest of them raced for the other, hefty Marines dragging recalcitrant prisoners. The shuttles were rolling even as the rear doors began to rise. Kris helped strap in the Iteeche, then checked the cowboy before taking her own seat.

The shuttle was accelerating even as her buckle clicked shut.

Kris jacked up the power on the nose camera and swung it around to get a good view of the approaching trucks. Someone stood in the lead truck's passenger seat, leaning on the front screen and pointing a pair of binoculars at the climbing shuttles.

With any luck, Kris's optics were more powerful than those. And got a more steady view. And the only pictures of the situation for anyone to examine in detail.

So much for the start of this mission. Still, there was an upside. They had all the Iteeche back under control.

No one had been killed.

And likely no one on Texarkana knew who these strange visitors were and why they had come.

At least until Kris released the guy she was holding.

28

The shuttles took an hour to rendezvous with the *Wasp*; they'd launched when the ship was still on the other side of Texarkana and had to go high to allow her to catch up with them.

Penny was waiting for Kris when her shuttle docked. "You want the good news or the bad news."

"Go easy on me. I've had a lousy day,"

"You've made it back in time to get gussied up and back down for the party tonight."

"If that's the bad news, what's the good news?"

"That was the good news. The bad news is that the police radio bands are full of the news that a cowboy has disappeared and that some strange aircraft hauled him off to somewhere."

"News travels that fast?" Kris said.

"The only good thing I can see is that there's nothing on the net about any Iteeche."

"Thank God for small favors," Kris said, and pushed herself for her quarters, leaving Ron to take care of his own problem and Jack to turn the Marines over to Gunny.

Well, at least if Kris had to go to a party tonight, Jack would have to be at her side the whole time.

Which caused a strange thought to slip into Kris's mind. What would it be like to have Ron at her side for the dance?

Strange thought. Strange day.

Hopefully, it wouldn't get any stranger.

So, of course, it did.

Formal clothes on Texarkana did not involve long dresses. They did involve many petticoats under a knee-length dress.

Which in zero gee had a bad habit of popping up.

Abby suggested Kris wear nice underwear.

And a pistol.

Not her small service revolver in its usual out-of-the-way place. No, Abby strapped around Kris's waist a huge .44 pistol with a barrel fit for a howitzer. Dirtside, that would have to weigh a ton. Oh and the fine-tooled leather belt had lots and lots of bullets.

"They expecting a herd of elephants to rampage through?" Kris asked.

"Big iron's the style, girl. Didn't your momma tell you nothing about 'when in Rome'?"

Then Abby handed her a short sword. It went all the way down to her hemline.

"You're kidding!" Kris said as she surveyed the ensemble in the mirror. It was insane. The petticoats tried for all they were worth to fluff up the dress. The heavy metal would flatten it down in all the wrong places once gravity did its thing.

"Are you sure this is the latest fashion on Texarkana?"

"Everyone wears a gun, Kris. Man, woman, and child."

"Child?"

"Kids start with toys, then progress through air guns with soft fluffy shots, to BB guns, to the real things."

"Please tell me the education system includes nonviolent conflict resolution along with gun safety and target practice."

"You can ask a parent at the hoedown," Abby said, handing Kris a large white hat. "It's called a Stetson, and the locals are right proud that it can hold a full ten gallons when they use it to water their horse."

"It looks awfully expensive to get soaking wet," Kris said.

"It's the custom. Hopefully, you won't have to water any horses tonight."

Kris put the hat on and examined herself in the mirror. She'd worn worse. And a whole lot less.

"Tell me, Abby. How did you know that I'd need to wear something like this on Texarkana?"

"You know all that intelligence I sell about you?"

"Yes."

"Well, I buy a lot, too. Now get moving. You're gonna be late."

The trip down was much calmer than the last one. Kris's main concern was getting her seat belt around the big iron and the short sword. Jack was in the seat across from her. His dress red and blues absorbed the .44 much easier. His sword was standard Marine issue.

Kris's escort for tonight included Private Zenger, who was just a slip of a woman. The .44 would have looked like a cannon on her. It was replaced with a very authoritative .38. Somewhere out of sight behind Kris's back, some wag suggested that if you could mix the two of them up and pour them out, you would get two mighty fine women.

Since Kris would gladly trade half her net worth to have just half of what Cindy Lu had in her bra, it didn't sound like all that bad an idea.

Still, Kris judiciously ignored the comment. No doubt, some NCO gave the joker a look that froze any further comments about the princess they would be guarding tonight.

Kris drew her .44, checked it . . . it was loaded . . . made sure the safety was on and her finger was nowhere near the trigger, then held it out at arm's length. If she had to, she could use it, though only having six rounds would be a handicap. She'd qualified at OCS with a .45. How different could it be?

They landed on a dry lakebed, several miles from what might pass for a town. At least it had several buildings, and they were well lit up.

The runway was lit, and parked in rows were quite a few aircraft, ranging from small prop jobs to four-engine planes capable of handling a hundred people or more. The lander looked like a hawk at a sparrow convention. Course, Kris had witnessed many sparrows driving hawks away from the sparrows' nests.

Kris glanced around and saw no land transportation.

"Should we have brought our own rigs?" Kris muttered to herself just as something with one headlight came barreling around the end of the nearest flight line.

"We gonna ride a motorcycle," came from somewhere among her escort before Kris said it herself. And saved her from saying it as the deepening dusk revealed a truck with one headlight out.

A vehicle that had never come off the assembly line of any major manufacturer rolled to a stop in front of Kris. The hood and front windshield looked familiar. There were three rows of seats behind it under the open sky that looked like they'd come from three different sources. Behind that was a truck bed made from wood and wire.

Still, the engine hummed, the brakes did their job with authority, and, no doubt, this collection of junk flying in loose formation met the needs of its driver.

"You Princess Longknife?" a young man of maybe eighteen asked.

"I answer to that name when I have to," Kris said.

"Then you and your friends pile in. I'm late for the hoedown, and if my girl ain't missing me, I'm going to be brokenhearted."

Kris took the middle front seat, with Jack holding on to the outside. Holding on with whitened knuckles. There was no door on that side.

The Marines boarded the next two seats with expressed bravado and suppressed trepidation. There was a coin toss to see who got to share a seat with Cindy Lu. The other female Marine was broad at the hip and looked fully capable of throwing any and maybe all of the male Marines. That was great in a fight, but in a narrow seat with no doors, and no seat belts . . . not so good.

As soon as all were aboard, the kid took off in a cloud of dust.

There was no actual road, or even trail, leading away from the airstrip, just a collection of ruts that were used more often than the rest of the prairie.

Despite mumbled fears and a few desperate shouts, there was only one casualty of the trip. A jackrabbit which, when caught in the headlight, chose to freeze when it should have bolted.

"The buzzards will take kindly to that," was the boy's only comment. He only slowed down when they drove into town.

He pulled up to a well-lit barn, the largest barn Kris had ever seen, and, campaigning on South Continent, she'd toured some pretty big farming facilities.

This barn was huge.

It had also been swept clean of anything left behind by its former occupants and fairly shone in the light.

The dancing had begun. A band composed mainly of fiddles and guitars plunked away, with one fellow loudly calling out things that made no sense to Kris but seemed to keep several groups of dancers pretty much doing the same thing.

Kris's driver let out a yelp and made a beeline for a certain someone sitting out the dance against the wall with a few other couples of the same age. After hugs and other greetings, the eight of them headed for the dance floor and were soon flowing along with the music no different from the rest.

That left Kris a full minute to contemplate the local folk dance before she spotted three middle-aged couples bearing down on her with the intent and purpose of a battle line in full sail.

Kris allowed herself a shallow sigh . . . and prepared herself for war by other means.

They also fight who only socialize. With full apologies to Milton or whoever it was she was misquoting.

Kris smiled through introductions and answered the inevitable question from one matron. "No, I'm not married. No, I'm not engaged." She managed not to add "No, I'm not even hooked up, though there is this cute Iteeche I'm hanging out with," before the woman dismissed herself to hurry off and arrange the inevitable parade of potential bridegrooms.

Kris was unable to break away from the others and their inane social chitchat . . . though she tried . . . until the matchmaker was headed back toward Kris with a line of dazed young men in tow.

At least most were dazed.

Three of them had clear intent in their eyes. Apparently the size of Kris's trust fund had made the papers. Kris could always spot certain types by the dollar signs in their eyes.

NELLY, SEE THOSE THREE.

YES, KRIS.

WARN ME WHENEVER ONE OF THEM GETS CLOSE.

YES, MA'AM.

"So you are the Kris Longknife I've heard so much about," came in a deep baritone.

Kris turned her back on the approaching line of young male meat to face a rather distinguished man with a heavy dose of salt in his jet-black hair. His face was tanned and lined by years in the sun, but the hand he offered her was firm to her shake. He met her grip solid for solid without threatening to turn it into an arm-wrestling contest. That happened to Kris occasionally when she met a man pressure for pressure.

"I'm guilty as charged, sir."

"I'm Jim Austin tonight. Duke Austin when I'm up at the state house."

"Ah, my great-grandfather told me about you," Kris said.

Actually, King Ray hadn't said a word about anyone. But he'd included this guy, along with all major players on Texarkana, in his briefing paper. Kris was experienced with great men like him, though, and would gladly add an extra ego stroke if he wanted to believe it. From the size of his smile, she knew he'd enjoy passing the lie along to his wife and not be at all upset if she turned it loose to all the back-fence gossips on the planet.

"And I've heard a lot about you. And seen you on the

vids and just about everywhere people talk about the up-and-coming youth today."

"You're very kind. I hope you won't hold all that against me. Much of it is not true, as Captain Montoya can testify."

"I was usually there, but most of my wounds have healed," Jack said, shaking the offered hand.

"Then let us talk about what is true and what is merely a bum rap," the duke said, and led Kris away from the woman eagerly waiting to inflict on this princess from Wardhaven all the eligible bachelors present.

With a joyful heart, Kris walked with him.

Until he started talking.

"Strange things are going on. We got laws here against aircraft buzzing cattle or landing your plane just anywhere you want. One loud noise can stampede a whole herd and run a year's worth of meat off their bones."

"I can imagine," Kris said, though she'd never given it much thought. Any thought.

"Yep, it can. Now we got strange airplanes buzzing around, and one of our cowhands is missing."

"Probably just took a wrong turn," Kris said. "Bet you he shows up in a couple of days with a wild tale about being kidnapped by aliens."

"He better not have been kidnapped by some wild gang of union kids that borrowed their papa's airplane and thought it would be fun to chase a herd of cows."

Kris had feared that the duke fellow had figured out what she'd been up to that afternoon and was obliquely trying to tell her so. Boy had she gotten him wrong. He was all for forming up a posse and heading off to the big city to get back the fellow she had locked away three hundred kilometers above his head.

For a peacekeeper, Kris was starting on the wrong foot.

Well, at least she was keeping Iteeche from scaring the meat off his cattle.

"I'm headed up to Denver tomorrow. I'll look into this for you."

"Think you could? Maybe they'd give you a peace offering. Though, I tell you, their kids need a good trip to the woodshed."

"Somebody does," Kris agreed. And dodged the nudge Jack gave her in the ribs.

"How long you going to be here?" the duke asked.

"I don't know," Kris admitted.

"You going to land anyone from your ship? Most ship captains don't hang around Texarkana very long. They tell me the zero gravity is bad for their crews."

"It is," Jack agreed. "Bad for my Marines, too."

"How many Marines you got? More than these six I see riding night guard around us?"

"The *Wasp* is an exploration ship, Your Grace," Kris explained. "I have about a hundred scientists and close to that many Marines and sailors."

"Woo, wee, Princess, you do carry a big enough stick to knock a few heads, don't you."

"We managed to stop a filibustering expedition that was set on taking over a planet," Kris said. "Not that the folks on Pandemonium needed all that much help. Still, they were glad for a hand from a few Royal U.S. Marines."

"I heard tell about that. Sounded like a lot of fun. Nobody'd dare try anything funny with Texarkana," he said, patting the holstered pistol at his side. It looked bigger than Kris's .44. When Abby passed Kris her pistol, she'd have sworn nothing could be larger that wasn't a rifle.

Kris just nodded.

"Anyway, about all that zero-gee time your folks are going to spend while you're here. You see, I got this ski resort place up in the mountains. Not much skiing this time of year, so I was wondering if you'd like to rent it. Cheap. Most of the hands are following the herds just now, but I imagine I could rustle up a few to help tend bar, change the beds."

Kris glanced at Jack. He actually looked enthusiastic about something for the first time since the Iteeche had boarded.

"We got bartenders," Kris said, "and most of our people

know how to change their own beds. What do you say that we take over the place, empty as it is and run it ourselves? It might actually be better."

"How's that?"

"You know, a sailor likes to have a girl in every port. Some of my scientists are kind of young, too." Which was such a lie. "Let a couple of them lose their hearts to some of the pretty girls I see sashaying around the dance floor, and I could lose some of my best boffins. Some of your tenderhearted girls might wind up pregnant and waving good-bye to the cad that did it."

"Not if her daddy has a shotgun up his backside."

Definitely Kris wanted the place as empty as she could get it. "Do I need to have my procurement officer meet with someone on your staff?"

"No, no," he said, holding out his hand. "If five thousand dollars a day sounds just fine by you, we can shake on it, and you can be dropping your folks down to a lovely vacation tomorrow."

HE'S WAY OVERCHARGING. I'M CHECKING THE RATES OF THE LOCAL LODGING PLACES, AND THIS PLANET IS REALLY CHEAP. DON'T KNOW WHAT IT'S LIKE IN WINTER, BUT SUMMER RATES ARE DIRT CHEAP.

"Two thousand," Kris said.

"Oh my, you are Al Longknife's little girl, aren't you. Four thousand."

"Three thousand," Kris said, sticking out her hand.

He shook it. "You will be needing victuals and spirits. I'll send someone around tomorrow to fill up the cold house and all."

"Feel free to do that, but you might warn him that he'll be negotiating with my computer, and she's already checking the prices on what we'll need against what's advertised online."

"He's gonna have to cover the cost of shipping it to hell and nowhere. And it's up in the mountains, too."

Kris did a quick flip. Did she want to be known as a hard bargainer? Would her mission be helped if this fellow was bought and in her pocket? Would buying someone so obviously eager to be bought put her in bad odor with other locals who did have moral scruples?

"We'll see how it goes. I haven't even seen this place."

"You'll love it. Clear mountain air. The trees up there smell wonderful. I'm told they're just like Earth pines."

Kris had had enough of politics. The lineup of young men, at least the ones who had hung on through this haggling, were starting to look downright good.

She broke away in their direction with a smile, and soon was learning the fine art of square dancing.

It wasn't long before Jack had offers from some of the local gals to show him how the dancing went. He picked up on it real fast.

It was much later in the evening when Duke Travis introduced himself to Kris. Three steps behind him was Juliet. Missing from her face was the smile Kris had always seen there. Missing from her elbow was the likely explanation. No Bob DuVale.

"The king sent you to straighten out our industrialist problem?" Travis asked with no preamble.

"My great-grandfather asked me to come here and look the situation over," Kris agreed.

"Like you did on Eden and Turantic."

"You'll excuse me if I don't say much about those places. Insurance claims are still before the courts, and my lawyers don't think I should comment publicly," she said, not letting her smile waver. "However, Grampa did suggest that I try not to start a war this trip."

Juliet's smile stopped just this side of a giggle. Seeing her smile again was worth the scowl her grandfather shot Kris.

"It's the industrialists who are causing all the trouble. We had a good thing going before they came here. And they wouldn't have come if it wasn't for Ray Longknife."

"Let me see," Kris said, seeming to count on her fingers. "It's been eighty years since the war. The settlement of Texarkana started about fifty years before the war. Seems to me that you two have been sharing this place for a lot longer than you haven't."

"We didn't ask for them. Ray Longknife dropped them in our lap."

"So, you were in favor of them staying on New Cleveland and maybe getting massacred like the folks on LeMonte. I don't remember Texarkana doing a lot during the war."

"We made our contribution, and you better remember that."

"Remember what?"

"That men from Texarkana fought with your great-grandfather during the war."

"I never forget what the valiant vets did for all of us during the war," Kris said, mouthing the words she'd learned at her father's knee during early political campaigns.

She finished talking to Travis's back. But Juliet came up beside Kris.

"You know what he was talking about?" Kris asked.

"I think he means Great-grandpa Skiev. He went off to the war and never came back."

"What happened?"

"I don't know. Nobody ever talks about it."

"Nelly, can you tell us anything about a Skiev who died in the war?"

"There's a Sergeant Arnold E. Skiev carried on the company rolls of the only unit to deploy from Texarkana. He did die."

"How?" both girls asked.

"He was hanged," Nelly whispered.

"Hanged," Kris said with a gulp.

"The local records do not explain why, but the company was under General Longknife's command at the time, and I expect his signature was on the death warrant."

NELLY, WHY WOULD GRAMPA RAY HAVE SIGNED A DEATH WARRANT?

KRIS, THE ONLY REASONS THEY EXECUTED ANYONE DUR-ING THE WAR WERE FOR MURDER, RAPE, OR RUNNING IN THE

FACE OF THE ENEMY. AND IT HAD TO BE PRETTY EGREGIOUS FOR THEM TO APPLY A CAPITAL PUNISHMENT.

"Juliet, it's possible that my great-grandfather may have approved the execution of your great-grandfather."

"I hope not," Juliet said. "'Cause if he did, you and I would be in a blood feud."

"Blood feud?"

"Yeah, I'd have to whip out my trusty six-shooter and shoot you dead."

Jack started edging toward Juliet. One of the Marines spotted the senior Travis and positioned himself between him and Kris.

"But not to worry," Juliet went on. "If the local records don't record anything, I don't have to take up the vendetta. No sweat."

"Right. No sweat. It would be a shame to mess up all the fun we had on Wardhaven with a shoot-out back here," Kris said, and started backing away.

NELLY, WHAT'S THIS VENDETTA THING?

OLD PRACTICE FROM EARTH. NO ONE CAN JUDGE ANYONE EXCEPT THE HEAD OF THE FAMILY. IF ANYONE FROM OUTSIDE OF THE FAMILY KILLS ANYONE FROM THE FAMILY, EVERYONE IN THE FAMILY IS BOUND TO SEEK REVENGE.

BUT WHAT ABOUT THE OFFICIAL JUDGMENT OF COURTS?

THIS PREDATES COURTS AND WRITTEN LAWS. THERE ARE SOME THINGS LIKE BLOOD PRICE AND EXILE THAT CAN SOFTEN IT, BUT THE FACT THERE'S NO DOCUMENTATION AS TO WHY ARNOLD SKIEV WAS HANGED LEADS ME TO CONCLUDE THAT THE FAMILY DOES NOT ACCEPT GENERAL LONGKNIFE'S FINDINGS AND DOES NOT WANT THEM PUBLISHED.

SO, IS IT SAFE FOR ME TO WALK AROUND HERE?

I DON'T KNOW, KRIS.

Suddenly a whole lot less interested in dancing, Kris went looking for one of the party's hostesses to make her excuses.

"Sorry to leave so early. I've got a long flight back up to the ship, and I've got several early meetings before I drop down tomorrow to see the Duke of Denver."

The nice lady smiled and said she understood. The smile looked a bit painted on. Maybe she really did understand.

Finding a ride for her team ended up being none too easy. She finally divided her Marines between two comfortable pickup trucks arranged by the foremen of Rancho A. Apparently, he was the second-most-powerful man after the Duke of Austin.

"I understand you rented the ski lodge from the duke."

Kris admitted she had.

"I'll see about getting linens and chow shipped out to you tomorrow. The boss talks a fine story, but it usually takes a herd of ranch hands to clean up after him."

"It looks like he's got a competent man to do that."

"I'll thank you for those kind words, ma'am. I also have to tell you that the boss is a very gentle soul. He might not have put the iron to the calf as hard as it needs to be done, ma'am."

"Iron to the calf?"

"Yes, ma'am. What you got to understand is that there's a lot of good hands and a lot of good guns that like things the way they are here. Texarkana is special. We don't like the idea of it changing. You got to remember that real hard when you talk to folks that want to mess things up," he said. And as he said it, his smile was hard and his hand gently patted the butt of the six-shooter on his hip.

"I think I understand where you're coming from," Kris said, letting no commitment leak into her words.

It was a quiet ride back to the airstrip after that.

As soon as the shuttle hatch was down and locked, Jack blocked Kris's path. "I'm not letting you go back down again into this madhouse."

"The king gave me an assignment," Kris answered, sidestepping Jack to her seat.

"If he'd known he was plopping you into the middle of a blood feud with a major chunk of this planet, I'm sure he would never have sent you here! And I'm sure he'll change your orders as soon as I bring this significant detail to his attention."

"He's got enough on his plate right now," Kris said, belting in as the shuttle started moving.

"Nothing is as important as his great-granddaughter's life." The Marine's shout was lost to the throaty roar of three anti-matter engines going to full power.

Those had to be about the only thing that will drown out a Marine officer or NCO.

Kris leaned back in her seat and tried to enjoy the flight up to the *Wasp*. Her little battle with Jack would only be the first round of a war she'd have to win before she dropped down to Denver tomorrow.

But win it she would.

A quick call to Captain Drago and Professor mFumbo brought both of them to the docking bay by the time her liberty launch arrived.

Jack glared at them . . . at her . . . and then listened in silence as the three of them discussed the rental of the ski lodge.

"Thank God," the professor breathed. "It's getting to where you can hardly breathe in boffin country, the air is so thick with the last meal."

"I would have thought your people would have quit eating," Jack said.

"Hope springs eternal," mFumbo said, patting his own belly. "Can we send shuttles down tonight?"

"The place is closed down for the season," Jack put in. "No snow, no skiing. We need to wait for daylight to do anything."

"Yes," Drago agreed, "but I can drop a shuttle down tonight to look the place over. I had this photo blown up from our last pass," he added, unrolling a hard copy of a very attractive and rustic compound of smaller châteaus scattered around a huge lodge. "It looks in very good repair."

Just as she'd hoped, the professor and the skipper had joined her conspiracy to get a solid placement on Texarkana. Well, she *was* looking out for the best interests of their down-trodden workers.

Jack threw Kris a nasty look before he glanced at the map. Clearly, at least one of her erstwhile subordinates was not impressed. "What about its approaches?" he demanded.

"I can project a wider area map," came from his collar.

"Thank you, Sal," he said, and a map appeared in the air in front of them.

"There is only one road in and out," the computer said helpfully, and highlighted said road in red. "It is at least a twenty-mile hike over mountains from any other road. It appears quite isolated to me."

"It does to me, too," Kris said.

"Can we land a shuttle there?" Jack asked.

"The parking lot extends into an airstrip," Captain Drago put in. "I've checked the field and lot. We can do it if we don't overload the shuttles and keep their approach speed down. It's doable."

"So, Jack, how heavy do you want the Marines to go for this little bit of shore leave?" Kris asked.

"Can I drop them in full battle gear?"

"I'd rather you didn't. I've already invaded this planet once. If I do it twice in two days, it will start to look like a habit."

"And we do want to go light on the shuttle runs," Drago reminded them.

"We could just do extra runs with loaded Marines," Jack insisted.

"I don't know how many landings we can make down there before the runway starts to show the wear and tear," the captain said.

"I could leave half a platoon on overwatch from up here, drop them loaded if I need them," Jack muttered.

"But time in zero gee is muscle," Kris pointed out. It was a basic lesson in ship handling from OCS.

"Damn it, woman, I know that."

Kris knew he did. She shut up.

"Okay, we'll keep one squad of Marines on guard aboard ship, supporting your stay-behind crew." Captain Drago nodded.

"The rest get shore leave at the lodge, weapons and one base load of ammo, no crew-served weapons. You happy, Lieutenant!"

"Your plan seems reasonable," Kris said. "If, upon reflection, you want to make any changes, please let me know.

"Now, it's been a busy day. Tomorrow, I have another batch of no doubt howling-mad locals to try to make sense of. Good night, gentlemen."

29

Kris was strapped in tight to her seat across from a still-angry Marine captain the next noon as the shuttle dropped away from the *Wasp* and started its flight to the industrialists' principal city of Denver.

Jack had demanded that Kris put off her visit to Denver until a message came back from King Ray.

"That will take three or four days," she pointed out.

"So."

"We've got a cowpoke in our brig."

"You think you can settle this thing in half a week. Good Lord, Kris, these folks have been at each other's throats for eighty years! Even you can't pull a miracle out of a rabbit's hat that fast."

"I sure can't pull out a miracle if I'm sitting on my hands up here!" She then pointed out that the shuttles were ferrying crew, Marines, and boffins down to the ski lodge. They would be staying here for quite some time. "Besides, I'm not going anywhere near cowboy country. I'll be in Denver, Jack. They don't carry guns. They have nice civilized judges and courts. No blood feuds."

Still unhappy, Jack doubled her guard. All were in dress red and blues except for a pair of snipers.

And he demanded she wear her bulletproof spider-silk underwear.

She reached in the collar of her undress whites and slipped a finger under her spider-silk bodysuit to prove it was there.

Even then, it was a rough ride down.

The Denver airport was very different from the one they'd used last night. The runway was paved and fully instrumented. There were warehouses bulging with boxes of goods and two beat-up shuttles ready to be loaded and sent up to any passing cargo ship.

From the age of the burn marks on the runway, it had been a while since anyone had launched to orbit.

Three black cars pulled up to the shuttle as soon as it rolled to a stop. One of them was stretched enough to qualify as a limo. A short fellow in a blue suit was quickly out of that car, his hand extended.

"I'm Tad Kordoka, mayor of Denver. I fill our seat in the House of Dukes, but if any Denver mayor ever styled himself a duke, we'd clap him in a loony bin."

"Then maybe I'd better present myself as Lieutenant Kris Longknife, special envoy from Wardhaven," Kris said without missing a beat.

"Smart woman. Didn't I tell you, Ivan, those Longknifes are a bunch of smart people. Kris, this is Ivan Bogada, the president of our business counsel. He represents the interests of the people who count on Texarkana."

Kris shook another hand. Like Tad, Ivan looked intent, driven, and expectant. Just the kind of people Kris would not buy a used car from. Kris doubted it would be long before they told her what they wanted done.

In no uncertain terms.

Hopefully, they'd learn quickly that Longknifes were not only smart but also stubborn.

Jack joined Kris in the limo, but the two businessmen ignored him. With Marines riding shotgun in the limo's front seat and filling up the other two cars, Jack didn't seem to mind, but concentrated on leaving nothing involving Kris's safety to chance.

Meanwhile, Kris got a rapidly delivered tour of all the points of interest and pride around Denver. Considering they'd built all of it from scratch in only eighty years, Kris would allow that they had the right to be proud of their accomplishments and wasted no time saying so.

They preened as if they'd done it all by themselves, just the two of them.

Kris wasn't long in finding out who really had done it.

They didn't go to city hall, but rather to a new business park, full of gleaming buildings of glass and concrete. Tall offices reached for the blue sky. Squat factory buildings spread out to make "just about anything someone could ask for," or to store it.

"How do the cowboys types take to your miracle of production?"

"They buy it up from us plenty fast," Ivan answered. "But we have to send the peddlers out to their ranches and small towns. They hate the very sight of our cities. Invite them to a play, or a show. Woman, we've got an opera company and playhouse that draws the best singers in human space. Art galleries and a ballet company, too.

"As far as those hicks are concerned, we might as well be talking about the weather. Ma'am, they pay more attention to the chances of rain out in their great desert than they do to the cultural opportunities we offer them."

"If you talk to them long enough," Ted put in, "they'll start waxing poetic about a cattle sale like it was more to their taste than a play just off Broadway from Earth."

"I know what you mean," Kris said. "I had a friend in college from Texarkana. We used to tease her about things like that. But after her boyfriend took her to a few plays, she saw things in a different light. Maybe you ought to let Bob DuVale do the talking for you."

Things got quiet after that.

The cars came to a stop in front of one of those gleaming towers. It would have fit right in on Wardhaven, though its fifty floors made it a bit short for Kris's hometown. They entered a wide, marbled foyer that centered on a fountain. The sculptured fish were either of a local kind that had made its peace with humanity, or the artist was postmodern. A wide bank of escalators moved people up to the second level, but Kris was led away from them to where a dozen elevators waited to whisk her and her escort up to the fiftieth floor.

There she was taken to a luxurious conference room, paneled in half a dozen different woods, where it wasn't wallpapered in blue and gold. The carpet was a Berber that felt a good three inches thick.

Kris glanced around, half-expecting to see Grampa Al holding forth, but no, the denizens of this wealth were just the local leaders.

Jack needed just one glance to take the place in. Quickly, he posted his Marines as if this was a prison and he in charge of keeping those in, in and those out, out.

As in the car, the local businessmen paid no more attention to Kris's Marine escort than they would have to ghosts. She wondered what would happen if a Marine got in the way of one of the business honchos, but it didn't happen, so there was no attempt by two people to occupy the same space rather than admit the existence of the other.

The first hand Kris shook was Louis DuVale's. He spent a long minute shaking hers, studying Kris's face as if he might, by looking at it long enough, change her mind. When there was no evidence of that, he took her elbow and guided her around to meet manufacturers, mining interests, energy brokers, bankers, financiers, and "everybody who is anybody on Texarkana," he said as he finished.

As soon as she was finally seated at Louis's right hand, he posed the question "How does King Raymond propose to correct the political and fiscal imbalance on this planet?"

"I don't know," was not the answer the expectant eyes around the table were prepared to accept. Kris let the question hang while she examined her options for the forty-eleventh time.

"You can't let this state of affairs continue," Louis went on when Kris didn't come forward with an instant answer. "I understand you've rented Old Austin's ski lodge for a week so your ship's crew don't atrophy in orbit. We should have had a space station fifty years ago. And we would have, except for those damn cowboys. The lack of that station is throttling our business. No captain in his right mind brings his ship here. Do you know that most ships these days don't even have drop ships?"

"Yes, my grampa Al mentioned that last Christmas dinner," Kris admitted. She hadn't been there, but Honovi had noted it in a later message to Kris.

"We bought two used shuttles, cheap, just so we could service a ship, but big ships don't want to risk traffic messing around in their space, and small ships can't earn enough for their lines shuttling from one tiny market to another. Every planet around us has a station. We've got to change," DuVale finished, almost shouting.

"I'm here to observe," Kris said.

So for the next hour, Kris got to observe a long list of grievances, dating back to the first landings during the Iteeche War. It was not pretty.

It also didn't help.

"So Denver, Duluth, and Detroit are your only dukedoms," Kris said when their anger finally ran down like an unwound clock.

"And lovely cities they are. They offer everything you could ask for—culture, parks, gracious living. We are not uncouth barbarians here," Louis said.

"And the cowboys provide the food and fibers off their ranches and farms."

"We more than pay for them with the goods and services we provide, even at the outrageous exchange rate they force upon us."

Kris began to see the full outline of the problem through all the dust and chaff thrown up by their anger. "With so little off-world trade, you can't challenge that exchange rate."

"Because they won't build a space station. Because they won't let *us* build a station! We're stuck with them as our only market. We're stuck paying for their low-value raw products with our high-value-added production goods."

"Point well taken. Ah, Mr. DuVale, do you ski? Hunt? Do anything outdoors?" There had to be someplace where these two isolated worlds met.

"Of course I do."

"At Duke Austin's lodge?"

"I try to avoid him. Some of the barons up in the mountains run decent establishments that cater to finer tastes."

"How do they vote?" Kris asked.

"Sometimes with us, but there are never enough right-thinking people. Every time we think we might get something done, those old founding dukes patch up their differences and vote us down."

"Nelly, I hate talking geography without a map." A map was conspicuous by its absence from this conference room. "Would you display a map of this continent, please."

The polished wooden table before them was suddenly covered by the requested map. Nelly displayed the rivers and mountains of the main occupied landmass of Texarkana. The great plain that was the center of human occupation was bordered on the east side by a huge mountain range and on the west by a mighty river that drained not only the mountains but a major portion of uninhabited land farther to the west.

"Nelly, let's see some cities, towns, and major ranches." Denver popped into existence. Well to the north of it was Detroit. Out on the plain, where rivers from the two met, Duluth sat, more a trading center than industrial. Small towns lay scattered across the great plains, usually where much smaller streams crossed.

"Now show me the boundaries of the dukedoms." Rigid straight lines of men crisscrossed themselves over the random meandering of rivers and mountains.

Kris sighed as the bitter problem reduced itself to simple black and white. There were thirty dukedoms, but only three of them had cities in them. Those held eight million people. The other twenty-seven held less than three million.

Under the usual exchange rate . . . some might say honest rate . . . the wealth would be just as unequal. The fact that it was balanced said beef and potatoes were either way too expensive or power packs, stoves, and air conditioners were way too cheap.

Kris could relate to the anger that such a rigged deck raised in these fellows. Still, the rules of this game had been agreed upon long before any of the movers and shakers in this room were born.

Thank you, Grampa, for this wonderful problem you dropped me in. I hope you're having as much fun talking to all your old war buddies about the nice Iteeche.

Then again, this game wasn't rigged at all. Couldn't the businessmen looking at this map see the obvious answer to their problem?

And if they couldn't, how could Kris open their eyes?

Or as the famous Billy Longknife was sometimes heard to mutter under his breath, "There are none so blind as those who have their eyes wide open but can't see a damn thing."

Concentrating on her problem, Kris ignored the soft sound of the door opening . . . until a familiar voice said. "Dad, you didn't tell me we were getting a visit from Kris Longknife today."

"Bobby," Kris shouted, her problem only too happily tossed for the moment as she stood to get and give a hug to her old school bud.

"It's Mr. Robert DuVale here, and I hear it's Princess Kris these days."

"Strange thing, that. It'll teach me to turn my back on my own kin," Kris said, trying to make a credible grumble through her grin for her old friend.

"Isn't it always your own kin?" Bobby whispered in Kris's ear as he finished the hug.

"So, what are *you* doing in *my* town?" he demanded of her.

"Listening to your old man gripe," Kris said, and got several soft snickers from around the room, which were quickly swallowed as Mr. DuVale met them with a glare. "Listen, Bobby, maybe you can help me out."

"If I hadn't helped you out, you would have flunked several business courses."

"Only 'cause my grampa Al signed me up for them against my will. And I was doing my best to flunk them."

"You didn't have a chance. Not with Julie as your study partner." Now both of them smiled at the shared memory of one schoolmate that wasn't here.

Mr. DuVale's glare deepened into full glower.

"About these dukedoms," Kris said, tapping her map on some of the new cowpoke dukes. "Are there some kinds of local minimums you have to meet before you can officially get a baron recognized or a duke seated in the House of Dukes? On Wardhaven, we won't let a new county have a representative in parliament until it has fifty thousand people living in it."

"It's kind of the same here," Bobby said. "You have to have at least ten thousand people and fifty thousand head of cattle before you're officially a duke. And it has to be in the boundaries officially set out for a dukedom."

"Fifty. Thousand. *Cows?*" Kris said.

"And ten thousand people," Bobby added.

"Can you believe these people!" Mr. DuVale snapped. "Denver once fell below the fifty-thousand-head requirement, and they tried to disestablish us. My father had to pay through the nose to buy a hundred cows real quick from Austin."

No question, the ill will here had good cause . . . and a long history. But if Kris let them turn the conversation back to their gripes, they'd never see what was sitting right in front of their noses.

"Just ten thousand people," Kris echoed.

"And fifty thousand cows," Bobby repeated.

She let that hang in the air between them until Bobby shook his head.

"Sorry, Kris, but what you have to understand is that the people of Denver and Detroit are very proud of their cities and the culture we attract to these centers of human endeavor."

"I've been listening to a lot about those cultural achievements," Kris admitted, trying not to let it out too dry.

"And nobody around here would *want* to move out to dusty little towns where a square dance on Saturday night is the top of the social calendar," Bobby finished, staring tight-lipped at his father.

"But for that girl, you'd move out to a hog farm," the older man exploded. "My father worked himself into an early grave making Denver into the type of city that we could be proud of. That could draw stars from half of human space to *our* opera house, *our* theaters, *our* ballet."

"And you'll work yourself into an early grave trying to keep it that way," Bobby snapped.

"Ah, folk," Kris said. "I've been there, done that, cussed my elders, and stomped out. You don't have to rerun this little tizzy just for me."

The two DuVales continued to glare at each other. The others around the table looked like they'd rather have a dentist drilling than be here.

"So," Kris said slowly, "there's a reason why eight million people are crammed into just three dukedoms."

"We will not," Mr. DuVale said, hand raised to heaven, "scatter our seed in the dust. My grandchildren will not be raised to be uncouth hicks."

"Keep this up, and you won't have any grandchildren," his son said in a harsh whisper.

"Okay, okay, folks, let's nobody have a heart attack. Bobby, I'm having a hard time understanding things. I can't seem to get from A to B to C, just like in college."

"Kris," he said, starting to breathe almost normally, "you were never dumb. Blind to the human condition, maybe. Unwilling to admit people weren't all that eager to submit to your idealism. But never dumb."

"You may be right. I've had a painful time lately, growing up." Here Jack made his presence known with a loud snicker.

"No comments from the guilty bystanders," Kris said. "Bobby, if you can see that you need more dukedoms and you want to get out of Denver, why are you still here?"

"Because I can't borrow a nickel to start up Ft. Louis on the confluence of the Platt River and the Big Muddy, down here," he said, stabbing the map at a point far to the west.

"That an empty dukedom?"

"Totally vacant."

"Could you get anyone to move there with you and Julie?"

"If I got five minutes on the six o'clock news tonight, I'd have ten thousand volunteers by this time tomorrow."

"And money is all that's keeping you here?" Kris said. "What about cows?"

"Julie says there are plenty of ranch kids that would love to move a hundred head of cattle out east and set up on their own. Hard to believe that I'm not the only one whose old man doesn't want me to have the same chances he had."

"It's too risky," his father snapped. "No one would lend them a dime." Mr. DuVale glanced away just long enough to fix his glower on three of the men who'd been introduced as bankers. They nodded in agreement with the middle-aged plant owner.

"Everything's too risky for your bankers, Dad. But that's because everything has to be done just the way it *is* done," Bob said to his father, then turned to face Kris.

"When you were in cowpoke country last night, did you happen to see the jerry-built rigs those cowboys drive around in?"

"I couldn't miss them. Your limo was a delightful surprise today."

"Here in Denver, we produce cars. Cars, mind you, and large eighteen-wheelers that require the fine roads we have here. No pickup trucks. No four-by-fours."

"But all I saw last night among the ranchers . . ." Kris said slowly.

"Were truck wrecks," Bobby finished. "Every once in a great while, one of the ranchers will buy a car from us and drive it straight to one of their repair and customization shops. First thing they do is cut the back end off with a welding torch. Maybe they patch together a couple of seats, then build up a truck bed. You saw a lot of those."

"Yes," Kris said, "and they all looked like they'd been beat up and crashed and glued back together, or something."

"Mainly, it's the something. You want to ask the guy who runs Page Automotive why he doesn't produce trucks?"

"Not really, but I suspect I ought to." Kris glanced around the table, spotted one fellow who looked like he'd rather be under it than sitting at it, and asked, "On Wardhaven, we make all kind of vehicles, from small off-road gadabouts to eighteen-wheelers. Why don't you?"

"There is no demand," the fellow whispered to the table.

"I didn't quite get that," Kris said. "Could you repeat it?"

"There is no demand," came out with a squeak.

"There is no demand," Louis DuVale shouted at the same time, defiance in every word.

"You mean, you don't want to meet the demand that exists," Kris corrected.

"Why should we bother doing what they want us to do?"

"But you want me to somehow make them do what you want them to do. Is that what you want from me?" Kris shot back.

"Why not? You should. They're crazy with the power they have over us."

Kris glanced at Bobby. "He really thinks that?"

"I haven't been able to change his mind. I wouldn't bet that you can."

"I wouldn't take that bet."

"Smart woman."

Kris turned to the tableful of movers and shakers, who at the moment were shaking in their shoes. "You have a market, but to spite it, you don't meet it. There is a simple and easy way for you to resolve the local power issue in your favor, but you won't make a move to grab it. Are you guys crazy?"

"Do not insult us, young woman," Louis DuVale snapped.

"I'm not insulting you. I'm asking you a question. Bobby, if you had the money, what would you do?"

"Julie and I would homestead Ft. Louis in two weeks."

"Nelly, what does it take to establish a bank in this nuthouse?"

"Money, of course, but the actual chartering of a bank is easily enough done. I've already drawn up the necessary papers. All I need is names for the president and the six members of the board of directors."

"Bobby?"

"Mary Hogg has about had it at her old man's bank. She got her MBA from the University of Geneva in the Helvetican Confederacy."

"I hear they train the best bankers in human space," Kris said.

"I'll drop Mary a message," Bobby said.

"My daughter would never leave her place in our bank," one of the younger men at the table said, half standing.

"Don't wait dinner on her," Bobby said. "She'll meet us for coffee, Kris."

Kris considered her options . . . for about five seconds. She could stay here and listen to Texarkana's power types cry in their beer, or she could get going on the solution that had been staring them in the face. Talk about not being able to see the future on account of the past!

"Let's go, Bobby."

The two of them headed for the door. Jack was caught by surprise but quickly got the Marines following in her tracks.

The doors of an elevator were wide open as a woman exited it; Kris and Bobby had to run to get it. Kris found herself grinning widely at Jack as the doors closed on his scowling face. Finally, she'd put one over on him!

By the time the bell rang on the bottom floor, Kris had the First Bank of Ft. Louis chartered and funded by half a billion Wardhaven dollars. She and Bobby were fast walking for the cars out front when an elevator opened and a squad of Marines hustled out.

Kris glanced over her shoulder, delighted for the first time in months to be a step ahead of Jack.

"Bomb," Nelly shouted even as BOMB echoed in Kris's head.

"Where?"

"Above us. Duck, Kris!" Nelly yelled.

Kris did, taking Bobby down beneath her.

The last thing she thought was, *I'm not going to let Bobby take my bomb*, followed by, *Jack's never going to let me forget this*.

The last thing she heard was a roar in her ears before the darkness took her.

30

Captain Jack Montoya was madder than hell. But all he could do was fume as the elevator took forever to drop to the ground floor.

Kris took foolish risks. He knew that when he took the job. But she was being downright childish just now. Not holding the elevator for him and his Marines was stupid, juvenile, and just not professional.

This planet was dangerous. Someone on this ball of mud could be heating up an eighty-year-old vendetta. Even if that old history wasn't coming back to life, Kris was dropping herself smack-dab into the middle of bad blood between two bunches of nuts who had festered for eighty years. If one of these crazy people thought she was about to side with the other, there was no telling what could blow up.

The elevator car ground to a halt. The doors took their own good time to open. Jack charged out. Looked left, looked right, spotted Kris.

The shout of "Bomb!" came in Nelly's voice.

"Where?" Kris yelled back.

"Above you," Jack shouted, spotting two falling objects. "Duck, Kris."

Kris dove for the deck, but only after taking that kid down with her.

The bombs exploded before hitting the ground. First one, then the other.

Jack flinched as the shock wave hit him. Something else

did as well, but he was running, his Marines right behind him, before all the stuff in the air hit the ground.

"Bruce, take the squad and one sniper. Up those escalators."

"Yes, sir."

"Medic, second sniper, with me."

"Aye, aye, sir."

Jack slid to a stop on his knees beside Kris. Most of the Marines pounded past him, but a second later the woman medic was kneeling on the other side of Kris. The sniper took guard, rifle up.

Two things were immediately obvious to Jack. Kris had covered the civilian with her body. Well, she was the Longknife, and he was just the poor damned soul that got too close to her.

And Kris had not put on an armored wig this morning.

The spider silk had stopped a lot of sharp crap from slashing into her body. Nothing had protected her skull.

Her head was a bloody mess.

"Sal, call whatever passes for 911 on this godforsaken planet."

"I have, sir. An ambulance is on its way, ETA ten minutes. A hospital is twelve minutes away. I have alerted the emergency room to prepare for a head-trauma case. In this building, two companies have nurses with emergency equipment. Both are responding. I've taken other measures."

Before Jack could ask what those other measures were, the building's public announcement system came to life. "A medical doctor is required in the foyer of the DuVale Building. Any medical professional in the area, please respond."

"I've done all I can, sir," Jack's new computer said.

"I think we all have. Medic?"

"None of the blood is spurting, sir. I don't think any of her arteries were hit. I don't want to move her, sir. If we've got more medical responding, I'd rather wait."

"I hate waiting," Jack growled.

"So do I, sir."

Jack stood. "Sergeant Bruce, tell me you've got the bastards that did this," he said.

Sergeant Bruce took the up escalator two or three steps at a time, pushing civilians aside. The noise drew the attention of those higher up. His pistol, held at high port, settled any arguments.

People got out of his way.

On the second floor, he spotted two figures in green coveralls as they ducked left just past the elevator bank. Bruce sprinted after them, the footsteps of Marines coming hard behind him.

"Chesty, give me a layout of this place."

"Yes, sir," and a building map sprang to life on his contact lenses. "There's a wide concourse leading off to the left behind the elevators to a large food court," his computer added.

"Damn," Bruce muttered, turning his sprint into a full dash. If those two got into a food court at lunchtime, he'd have the devil's own time separating them from all the chaff.

He rounded the corner just in time to see his two quarries shove their way through double glass doors. Any temptation to shoot got swallowed up by the dozens of people hurrying toward their lunches who quickly blocked his view of the two.

Bruce ran, Marines on his heels.

He busted through one of the double doors. It only took him a moment to glance around, to take in a dozen different fast-food restaurants spaced along opposite walls. They faced a vast, noisy expanse of tables, filled with hundreds, maybe thousands of people eating.

He saw no one in green overalls running, walking, or even standing.

"Put that gun away," came in a demanding voice.

Sergeant Bruce glanced to his left, spotted a man in khaki pants, a brown shirt, a gold badge, and a huge belly walking toward him. He had a holstered weapon on his belt but made no move to draw it.

The Marine went back to searching the crowd as he said, "A bomb just injured Princess Kristine Longknife. I chased two people of interest into this area. They were both in green overalls. Did you see them? I want to talk to them."

"Put that gun away. You can't walk around brandishing that thing in here. Where do you think you are, some cow town?"

Bruce ignored the noise as three Marines ran up to him. "There's a door over on the far side of this place. Block it. Don't let anyone in or out."

A woman corporal took off at a gallop with two lanky privates at her side, all holding their pistols out at high port.

"They can't do that," the cop whined.

"You got a boss?" Bruce asked, then turned to four more Marines. "You two, block this entrance. No one in or out. You other two, walk through this place. Keep your weapons in plain view. Most folks here will be surprised by them. Look for the two that aren't. Use deadly force if you have to on them. Please don't shoot innocent bystanders."

"You better not, or I'll have your ass in my jail," the cop added.

"You see the problem."

"Yes, Sergeant," the sniper said, resting his long rifle on his hip and heading into the crowd. The woman Marine, pistol up, headed toward the restrooms.

"Sergeant Bruce, tell me you've got the bastards that did this," Captain Montoya said over the net.

"I pursued them into a large food court, sir. I'm presently searching for two needles in a very large haystack."

"Can you get any local help?"

"Local cop is jiggling my elbow, sir. Wants me and mine to surrender our weapons. Seems this ain't cowboy country."

"I'll try to raise some serious local support. If he causes you too much trouble, shoot him. In the knee if you can, but I want those bomb throwers."

Clearly, the captain was not serious, but the cop didn't

know that. Bruce gave the guy a cheerful look. He beat a hasty retreat, now using his own commlink. The reply he got brought a sea change to his face.

"There's two more cops on their way. One will back up the people you got on the other doors. I'll secure these doors."

That was followed by a series of complaints by people not allowed in to eat, or out to return to their shopping or their jobs.

So, lots of folks were going to have a bad day. The memory of what the princess looked like said she was having the worst day the sergeant had ever seen her have . . . and he'd been there for some bad ones.

The woman Marine exited the ladies' room, waving a green pair of coveralls.

"Check out the men's room," Sergeant Bruce shouted.

"She can't do that," the cop said.

The Marine did. A moment later she was waving a second pair of greens.

Damn, this truly was a lousy day.

"Captain, in restrooms, the assailants ditched the green coveralls they were wearing when they threw the bombs. We have no idea what they may look like now. I'll check with the locals to see if they have any security cameras that might have caught them while still in coveralls or as they left the restrooms. Without some camera shots, we've lost them."

At the question about security cameras, the cop's expression took on the look of someone who'd just been asked if he could fly across the room . . . naked.

31

Captain Jack Montoya was a firm believer that few problems could not be solved by the proper application of the correct amount of high explosives. Being on the receiving end of just such a solution was rare for him.

He didn't like it. Not at all.

He especially didn't like the feeling of helplessness churning in his gut. At this moment, Kris needed a doctor a lot more than she needed a security chief. Especially one who had failed at his duty.

That Kris had outdone herself today making his job impossible was no excuse for failing it. Not for Jack.

A doctor came out of the crowd near simultaneously with a nurse arriving with supplies from upstairs. She and an assistant carried a backboard and more medical gear.

The doc shook his head at the two bodies compressed together by the explosions from above, and said, "We've got to separate them."

He, the nurse, and the medic wrestled Kris facedown onto the backboard and started an examination just as Bobby DuVale began to moan and come awake.

The nurse left Kris to the doc and medic and began checking out the young man.

The doc was still looking Kris over when the nurse asked for help rolling the man over. "He'll do better on his back," she told them. He's more shocky than anything else. May have a concussion."

Jack stood guard at Kris's feet with the sniper at her head. A crowd began to gather, but one look at the rifle at the ready, and no one seemed to feel the need to get overly close.

Jack divided his attention between the look on the doc's face and the crowd. His pistol was back at high port.

Twice he started to level it at someone who made a move he didn't like. Twice the person grew wide eyes, showed him open hands, and quickly backed into the crowd.

So Jack could still scare people.

If only the look on the doc's face didn't scare him worse.

A siren announced the arrival of the ambulance. Jack stood aside as two emergency technicians joined the circle.

Kris was finally lifted onto a basket stretcher, intubated, and given an intravenous drip. They did everything that Jack had been briefed to expect when someone with his kind of job blew it.

In the middle of this he was distracted by his commlink.

"Captain, in restrooms, the assailants ditched the green coveralls they were wearing when they threw the bombs. We have no idea what they may look like now. I'll check with the locals to see if they have any security cameras that might have caught them while still in coveralls or as they left the restrooms. Without some camera shots, we've lost them."

"Sal, are there security cameras in this area?"

"I don't think there is a security camera anywhere on Texarkana, sir. I am in touch with what passes for the local security net. A police captain is en route to Sergeant Bruce's location. Other officials are following, as well as the only K-9 team in Denver. They are doing their best."

"Thank you. Monitor and report anything concerning Kris to me," Jack said, then turned his attention back to the young woman who was his job. No, Kris was far more than that. She was his life.

And just now, they wanted to move her to the ambulance.

"Are you coming with her, soldier?" the doctor asked.

"Yes."

"You family?"

"I'm her chief of security," Jack said.

"I see," he said in that tone of voice that meant he didn't really but had nothing better to say. "Is there anyone that can give permission for medical treatment?"

"Doctor, she's a lieutenant in the Wardhaven Navy and the great-granddaughter of King Raymond of United Sentients. I don't care what your local rules happen to be. Take care of her. Take the best care you can."

"That, my heavily armed friend, is what we will try to do, but these are not the kind of wounds we have much experience with around here."

Jack found room in the ambulance. His sniper took station in the front seat, and a still-comatose Princess Kris Longknife began a twelve-minute ride to the best medical facility available for several light-years.

Sergeant Bruce did not take failure well. Marines are trained to win. Failure is something *you* do to the *other* guy.

Bruce had a bad feeling that today he would learn how it felt to be the other guy.

While he was waiting for the dog team to arrive, Abby called.

"Do you have a minute to talk to Lieutenant Pasley?"

The intel officer's dad had been or still was a cop. She'd demonstrated again and again that she knew how to talk to the local police in their own language. If anyone could, she would get whatever the local cops had to give. With a sigh, Bruce said he would take the call.

"Sergeant, we've been following events from the lodge via your and the captain's computers. We know your situation."

"Then you know Kris is down, and whoever did it is doing too damn good a job of giving me the slip."

"Yes, Sergeant. That's why I wanted to let you know that you've been doing as good as I could have done. I'm in touch with the local police now. I've got them moving, even if their pace is more glacial than I'm happy with. Bruce, they aren't stonewalling us. They just aren't prepared or equipped for something like this."

"You have any idea who did this to Kris?" the Marine sergeant asked.

"No idea at all. I'm going to get me and Chief Beni, along with every Marine tech I can lay my hands on, over to the scene of the crime as soon as the next shuttle lands."

"How long will that be?"

"It just dropped away from the *Wasp*. Say half an hour to get here. Another hour to get there."

The locals weren't the only ones who had been caught flat-footed by developments; Bruce found his hands were making fists and willed them to relax. More cops arrived, and Bruce managed to get a printout from his computer of the best sighting he had gotten of the pair.

It was of the back of their heads and not very good even of that.

The dog arrived, a real bloodhound. It spent a few seconds sniffing one of the green coveralls, then sniffed the floor around the men's room. It took off immediately into the crowd, moving at a brisk clip. Bruce and the sniper followed right behind it.

It didn't head for either of the main exits. Instead, it took them to a small door in a tiny alcove. The door's lock had been jimmied. Behind it they found maintenance passages leading to a storage area, heating ducts, and a back door to the mall.

The hound went out the door and straight to the curb . . . where it stopped, sat down, scratched itself, and eyed its keeper. He fed it a dog treat before facing the Marine. "I'd say this is where our targets got in a car."

"So would I," Bruce said, and rang up the Navy intel winnie. "Dead end here, Lieutenant Pasley. You got any leads?"

"None. Denver police are really sure some cowboy did it."

"Make that cowboy and cowgirl," Bruce interrupted.

"Right, my mistake. Anyway, until I can get some of our

techs to the scene and go over it, I can't do any better guessing than they can."

"You telling me you want me back where the bombs exploded, preserving the scene?"

"Please do. I've been promised that the locals are securing the scene. I'd really like you to help them."

Which was a gentle way of saying she didn't trust the locals to realize what high tech could do if the scene was preserved. Sergeant Bruce called his team back to the front of the food court and headed for the elevator foyer.

He got there just in time. A local cop was being buffaloed by a building manager who wanted to open both exits from the elevator landing "to avoid jamming up tenants at quitting time."

An angry Marine sergeant, backed up by seven armed Marines, settled the matter. The tape stayed up.

Sergeant Bruce considered Kris a Marine. To have failed her was something he took personal. He'd guard the crime scene until hell froze over if that was what it took to find out who had done this to her.

Willy Stone held up his hands, showing open palms, when the angry Marine officer pointed his pistol at him. He backed into the crowd, but he did not leave.

From a safer, more distant corner of the foyer, he watched the scene as the ambulance arrived, and more medical people were sucked into the task of keeping the space invader alive.

He got a call for Ralf Ford and told the caller he'd gotten a wrong number. That told him that Aril and Betty had made good their escape, but he continued to watch.

Only after the ambulance departed with the Marine officer and his long-gun friend did Willy leave.

It would have been too much to expect that a doctor would declare Longknife dead at the scene. No, they'd take her to the nearest emergency room and spend a fortune trying to breathe life back into the wreckage the bombs had made of her body.

It would have been different if the slowpoke Anderson had sent out to buy the nails had returned faster. If the opportunity to strike at a DuVale *and* a Longknife hadn't developed so fast. So many ifs.

Still, barely alive, the Longknife girl would not cause him any trouble. And while everyone was pointing fingers at each other, he was free to act.

He'd doubted that a plan thrown together this fast could work. He'd demanded and gotten more money. Now, surprisingly, delightfully, everything was coming together!

32

Jack paced the waiting room. Six steps to the north wall. About-face. Six steps to the south wall. Repeat. So long as his body was in motion, repeating and repeating, he could keep it from doing what he wanted.

He wanted to pound his fist through a wall. Through someone. He wanted to blow something up. He wanted this endless wait ended.

What he wanted didn't matter one bit.

Kris was on the other side of one of the walls, surrounded by doctors and maybe . . . no . . . probably dying. She was going to be gone forever, and he'd never so much as hinted at what he felt for her.

Which would have been stupid. His job was to protect her, not fall in love with her. So, he'd blown it all. Let her stomp off and get herself killed and let her die without knowing how much he'd come to care for this poor, homeless, little waif.

He almost snorted at that thought. He was the only person who saw her as poor or homeless or little or lost. She fooled the rest of the world . . . but not him. He saw what the others missed.

And he loved what the others never saw in her.

And now she was dying.

Penny called, interrupting him before he melted down into some emotional puddle. That reminded him that he was a Marine, and there was someone he definitely owed a death. Penny intended to go over the crime scene with a fine-tooth comb and an electron microscope. He agreed.

When she said nothing after that, and the silence began to grow, he realized she expected something from him on the situation at his end. He told her Kris was in the operating room, and he knew nothing more than he'd known when he first got to her body.

And no, he didn't know when he'd find out more. The doctors had their own chain of command and didn't include a Marine in their need-to-know net. They might if he threatened them with his service automatic, but it just didn't seem becoming for an officer and a gentleman.

Penny rang off before he'd had to say anything more.

The medic sat closest to the door that led to the surgery. She'd wiped off most of Kris's blood. Now she sat, pistol at the ready, prepared to block the entrance to the only place that a miracle might give her commander back her life.

The sniper stood with his long rifle at the ready at the other end of the room, eyes on the door, or through the glass windows in the door to the hallway beyond.

Early on, lots of people had come to the door: reporters, hospital people, gawkers. Some had even risked pushing the door open a crack. A good look at the Marines' deathly glares had sent them on their way.

Mr. Louis DuVale did not turn away at the sight of alert Marines. No, he charged in about an hour after Jack started his vigil.

"What have you done to my son?" he demanded.

Jack wanted to answer the question with a question. "What took you so long?" However, it didn't take a mind reader to know that would only make things worse, and if Kris survived, she'd still need to work with this man.

"He's in surgery," Jack said. "I understand he's not in any danger."

The big man headed for the doors into the surgery suites. The small woman Marine stood.

"Get out of my way."

"My princess is in there, sir. Her docs don't need no one jiggling their elbows."

"My son's in there. I have a right to see him."

"Talk to the nurses' station."

For a long minute, the two glared at each other. Him very important man. Her very deadly Marine.

Then the man got himself in reverse and turned his power glare on the head nurse on station. "What is happening to my son?"

"He is in recovery. He will be out here in a minute. Please wait, sir."

"I will sit for one minute. One minute, you hear."

He sat for several minutes before his son was wheeled out. Louis DuVale was at his son's side in a moment, but it was Jack that the young man reached for with his one good arm.

"She saved my life, sir," he said through tears. "She saved my life. I'd be dead if she hadn't put me down, covered my body with hers, sir."

"I know," Jack whispered. "I know."

"The doctor said the rest of me would be smashed up as bad as my arm if she hadn't been on top of me. Why'd she do that? Why?"

"You can ask her when she gets out," Jack said, trying to put more confidence in the words than he felt.

The doctor standing behind the orderly pushing the gurney looked worried at the display of emotion, then relaxed as the young man's eyes closed, and he dozed off.

"Doctor, what's wrong with my son?" DuVale demanded.

"Nothing sleep won't handle. He's got a concussion, shock, and a mangled arm, but, like he said, the young woman absorbed a lot of the metal fragments that would have made his situation a whole lot worse."

"It's all your fault," DuVale half shouted, whirling on Jack. "Things like this don't happen here! Then you show up, and look what they did to my son!"

He didn't wait for an answer but followed the gurney.

Jack turned to the doctor. "How is Lieutenant Longknife?"

"I don't know," the doc said, lighting a cigarette. The nurse at her station coughed, but he ignored her. "I'm the junior hacker and slasher here. Doc Diem is not only the better cutter, but he's the best head man on this planet, and from the glance I got at your girl, I'd say she needs him."

Jack did his best to keep a dispassionate officer's expression on his face, but he may have been less successful than usual.

"Don't worry, old man, if anyone can help her, Doc Diem will." With that attempt at a bedside manner, the young surgeon hurried after his own patient.

So Jack paced and the Marines watched and somewhere Kris was being patched back together.

Or maybe dying.

And Jack couldn't do a damn thing. He balled up his fist, but resisted for the thousandth time smashing the wall as he paced up to it.

Lieutenant Penny Pasley had seen a lot more crime scenes than the average Navy officer. She'd trained for security before switching to analysis and interrogation, but she'd visited her first crime scene with her dad when she was nine.

Her dad hated criminals and all they did. He wanted her to know early that there was nothing glorious or cool about breaking the law. She'd learned from him; cops were her favorite kind of people.

Denver cops she might make an exception for.

She was very late arriving at the scene of the explosion. She'd had to take her team of investigators back up to the *Wasp* to get their gear before dropping back down to Denver. That had given the locals time to do their own review of the evidence.

Penny tried not to explode at the detective who handed her a report sheet.

"You didn't find out anything about the bomb!"

"I wouldn't say that. It was standard, commercially available TNT, say, three sticks in each bomb. The detonators were also off the shelf, chemical fuses available from any explosives supplier. It was just a generic bomb with no distinguishing qualities. You ought to be happy it didn't have any nails or other junk surrounding the TNT," he finished lamely, wilting under her glare.

"You don't put any markers in your explosives?"

"No. We never saw much need to."

"You don't have any serial numbers on the detonators, fuses?"

"No."

"We never saw much need to," Penny and the detective finished together.

"Listen, I don't know what it's like on the planet you came from, but we've got pretty law-abiding people hereabouts. Denver may have five million people in it, but we've maintained that small-town attitude. People know each other and look out for each other."

"And nobody ever kills anybody," Penny finished for him.

"No. We get our domestic violence now and again. Usually the husband or wife is the perp, and sooner or later they confess. It's been ten, twelve years since we had a real series of killings, but we caught the guy in the end."

"Well, Kris Longknife doesn't have a husband to kill her, and if anyone was going to do it, it would have been Jack, and he was right behind her, doing his best to protect her."

The cop looked like Penny had lost him, but since he didn't ask, she didn't explain.

"We hear tell," he went on, "that there was a bit of trouble at the hoedown she was at last night. Her old man executed someone else's old man out among those cowpokes, and the blood debt hasn't been settled. If that's true, it's not Denver's problem."

"How do you know so much about what went on last night out in cowboy country?" Penny asked.

"It was on the news not two hours after this bomb went off.

You'd have to ask the TSN people how they found out, but don't expect them to be easy about releasing their sources."

"And you're taking your guidance on this case from the news, huh?" Penny said. She'd watched her dad take an inch of skin off a junior detective for doing what this fellow just did.

"Well, maybe I am, and maybe I'm not, but my boss, the captain, seems to think that the source of your woman's problem doesn't lie in our town, and it would not be a lot of fun for me to try to get him to think otherwise."

Which was a nice a way of saying that the local police force had its marching orders, and she'd have to deal with someone a lot closer to city hall if she wanted to get this stampede to judgment turned in any other direction.

A word by Princess Kris Longknife might do that, but at last report, she was unconscious and bleeding. Maybe dying.

No, if anyone was going to do something about this mess, it would not be Kris Longknife.

More than a few times, the thought of Kris getting out of Penny's hair and letting her do things the way she wanted would have elicited a shout of glee. Unfortunately, today wasn't one of them.

Penny turned to her team of technicians. "Tell me something that these people don't know about these bombs."

With "Yes, ma'am," and "Aye, aye, ma'am," the Marines and Chief Beni went to work.

Willy Stone watched the Navy officer lead the Marines into the DuVale Building. He glanced at his reader and its bootlegged report from the police department. They had found nothing special about the bomb, certainly nothing that would lead them back to its source.

That was to be expected.

The decision to take Texarkana out of the Society of Humanity standards for marking explosives had been taken years ago . . . to save money. It had caused no one any problems.

Until now.

It amazed Stone how people who didn't have a problem assumed they'd never have a problem. He couldn't complain; it was things like this that made his job easy.

He turned away and walked around the block. A car was waiting for him. He said nothing as the driver took him where he needed to go.

He'd done enough damage here; it was time to raise the stakes.

33

Kris came awake in a mental fog.

Where was she?

What had just happened?

The answers to all those questions didn't seem to matter all that much to her.

Pain pulsated all around her, danced like the flames of a wood fire lighting up the night sky at the beach. She felt the mesmerizing urge to stare at it, but it was distant, out of reach, unable to affect her.

Slowly, it dawned on Kris that she'd been like this before.

NELLY, AM I DRUNK? DID I FALL OFF THE WAGON?

Nelly didn't answer.

Jack? Jack? Are you there? You're always there. You love me.

With an effort, Kris heaved her eyelids open.

The room was white on white on white with white and black instruments and tubes and . . .

She was in a hospital. No, you didn't get tubed up like this in just any hospital.

She was in an intensive-care room.

She tried to scream, but there was something stuck down her throat. She struggled to reach for it, but her arms didn't move.

Suddenly, there were people in the room, rushing to her bedside, checking the instruments.

And quickly she slipped back down into blessed, numb unconsciousness.

When everyone ran for Kris's room, Jack followed them, hanging back and keeping his mouth shut.

That wasn't easy once he got a good look at her.

Still, years of hard discipline kept his mouth shut and his back against the wall as doctors and nurses went hurriedly about their business, correcting whatever it was that had allowed Kris to surface when they wanted to keep her asleep.

When things had returned to the silence of a well-equipped tomb, Dr. Diem came over to join Jack watching the machine breathe for her.

"Now you know why we said you did not need to see her."

"She isn't a pretty sight," Jack agreed.

"And there is nothing either you or I can do but let her sleep."

"Can I ask what just happened?"

"We cut too fine a line and crossed it the wrong way. Did she ever have a drug addiction problem?"

"She spent a year or two drinking after her little brother died. I understand that she was also heavily drugged to help her be a 'good little girl.'"

"Was she a good little girl?"

"Never while I've known her, but then, I've never seen her take a drink. Last time she was hurt, she refused most of her pain meds. She preferred to take our heads off instead. Conscious, she's not a well-behaved patient."

The doctor shook his head. "There's nothing about that in her permanent medical record, but that is not unusual with people of a certain social level. If it is not on the paper trail, it never happened. Makes it hard for an honest workingman to do what I need to do when there are real problems."

"A problem I run into regularly," Jack admitted.

"I've adjusted her drug regime. If you ask me, she does not show any of the built-up requirement I'd expect to find in a former abuser. She's behaving very much like a normal person who's just been overdosed too many times."

"Maybe I'll tell her that the next time I think she really needs to get drunk."

"I'll leave that to you, soldier."

"Ah, Doc, this wake-up. Does it say anything about her? Is she okay?"

"All it says is that I failed to properly program her drug dispenser and let her surface to a consciousness that I didn't want her to experience. You saw the mess we had in here. I don't know what her brain was doing. I had no time for any tests. Sorry, trooper, but you'll just have to keep sweating out her situation the same as I am."

With a final glance at Kris, a glance that told him she was back deep in a . . . hopefully . . . healing coma, Jack turned his back on her.

PENNY joined Jack at the hospital. She'd left her techs to search the explosive rubble to their hearts' content. If anyone disturbed them or tried to stop their hearts from being content, she'd be back there in ten minutes.

The Marine was just coming out from Kris's room. He told her all he knew about Kris's condition in simple, monosyllabic words.

"So we don't really know anything," she summed up.

"No. What about those bombs? What can you tell me about them?"

"Less than you just told me about Kris."

"That's not good," Jack said, taking a seat in the waiting room.

Penny sat next to him. "Local cops think this is some kind of cowboy vendetta."

"Could it be?"

"I checked the list of planes that landed in Denver during the last twenty-four hours. None of them were from Duke Austin's territory. In fact, none of them were from cowboy country. This place doesn't have scheduled flights from anywhere other than the two industrial cities, and not many from them."

"That was what Kris had just found out. She was arranging with the young man whose life she saved to set up a bank and shake up the local way of doing things."

"Could that be reason enough for the bombing?" Penny asked.

"Doesn't seem like there would be time enough to arrange it. Besides, the fellow Kris was working with is the son of Louis DuVale, the big man hereabouts. Would anyone want to put that man's kid at risk, or not expect Kris to do her level best to save him?"

Penny chuckled. "You and I would expect her to do that. Can't see anyone local knowing our girl well enough to count on her for anything."

Penny stood and began pacing. "Jack, there's something fishy about all this."

"It doesn't feel right to me, either."

"The bomb was straight-off-the-shelf stuff. Off the shelf with no way of tracking it, I must add."

"No tracers!" Jack said, incredulous.

"Nobody tosses bombs around here, don't you know? So they been saving money by not putting in tracers."

"There ought to be a law," Jack growled. "Oh, I forgot, there was one under the Society of Humanity. How fast we forget."

"Apparently these folks forgot that law before we tossed the Society," Penny said. "But Jack, someone was real smart about these bombs. If they'd left them in a trash can or a stray briefcase, Nelly would have sniffed them."

Penny stopped her pacing. "Hold it, Mimzy, where is Nelly?"

"Nelly is not online."

"Sal, can you raise Nelly?" Jack asked.

"I have tried, sir. Nelly is not responding."

"Where is Nelly?" Penny said, and turned to the nursing station. "Do you have Kris Longknife's personal effects?"

"Let me check. Her clothes are rather a mess, and we had the devil's own time cutting her out of that body stocking she was wearing."

"It's spider-silk armor. It may explain why she's alive," Jack said.

The nurse raised an eyebrow but said no more as she rushed from her station to the doors into the inner sanctum.

She returned a few minutes later carrying a small lump in the palm of her hand. "Is this what you wanted?"

"Yes," Penny said, taking Nelly from her. For someone who did so much and exuded so much personality, the physical reality of Nelly was tiny.

"Nelly," Penny whispered.

No response.

"Is she turned off?" Jack asked.

"No," Mimzy said. "Sal and I are both tracking a low hum. She is active, just not doing anything."

"Explain yourself," Jack said.

Sal took up the story. "Sir, Mother Nelly is active, at least at some state. However, she is not on net. She is not saying anything to anyone."

"Is she damaged? Is something broken?" Penny asked.

"No, ma'am. Now that we have her in line of sight, we can verify that all critical areas of Mother Nelly are active and working. She can hear us. She can respond. She just chooses not to. Sir, I am worried about Mother Nelly."

"We all are," Jack said.

"I've never heard of a catatonic computer," Penny said. "But then, I've never heard of any computer like Nelly."

"None of us have," Mimzy added.

"What are we going to do?" Sal asked.

"We're going to hope and pray that Kris pulls through and that she can bring Nelly back from wherever she's gone," Jack said.

"Ma'am, the media is talking about us," Mimzy said. "Would you like me to turn the monitor on?"

Penny really didn't want to know anything about this place that was the source of so much grief, but it was better to know than not to know, and what she wanted to talk to Jack about could wait.

"Turn it on, Mimzy."

The computer did.

"She saved my life," a battered and bandaged Bobby Du-Vale mumbled from a hospital bed. "She saved my life."

"The she is Princess Kris Longknife of Wardhaven," the voiceover told Penny. "And Bobby DuVale of the DuVale family is very lucky she did. A bomb exploded in the foyer of the DuVale Building around lunchtime today, knocking Bobby and the princess to the ground, and if the princess had not landed on top of Bobby, his father, Mr. Louis DuVale, would likely be mourning his son rather than sitting by his bedside." At this, the camera panned out to show the elder DuVale seated there.

"News 24 tried to get an interview with Princess Longknife."

Now the camera showed glowering Marines, including Jack. Taken through the glass of a hospital door, the shot did them little justice.

"However, the princess's security team, having blown it once today, was hard on the job protecting her from cameras and microphones."

Jack considered his mistake in letting the newsies live and decided he would not make that mistake twice.

The monitor switched to show two young women in a newsroom. Behind them a banner proclaimed: NEWS 24. NEWS FOR THE YOUNG.

"Do we know anything about the bombing?" the woman on the right asked the other.

"The Denver Police Bureau has analyzed the residue, Kate. It was made from materials readily available at any Mining Supply Depot, assuming you have a license for explosives. The folks at the Denver Mining Depot were quick to point out that none of their material had been misused in thirty-seven years and suspect that this has something to do with Princess Longknife. She does have a past history full of strange and dangerous happenings."

"So I've heard," Kate agreed. "Do the police have a motive, other than political assassination by someone from off planet, Nancy?"

"Yes, Kate. It seems Princess Longknife attended a hoe-down last night out on the flats, and ran into a flatlander family that has a history with the Longknifes. Their great-grandpappy was hanged by her great-grandpappy, King Raymond of United Sentients."

"Whatever for?"

"Well, Kate, the record is rather vague on the specific instance, but we do know that during the Iteeche War capital punishment was only applied in the cases of murder, rape, or cowardice in the face of the enemy."

"And, Nancy, we all know that no cowboy would ever be guilty of those."

"That, at least is what the family claims, which means the young princess walked right into a family blood feud. That is what the Denver Police are saying."

"Do you have a different idea, Nancy?"

"Well, it's easy to find who has been buying explosives, Kate. A check shows that no cowboy has bought any for the last month. In fact, Kate, no one from the flatlands has an explosive license to buy what blew up at DuVale Plaza today."

"Didn't the police check that out, Kate?"

"Nope. My check was the only one run in the last week, Nancy."

"Why didn't I think of that?" Jack growled, not taking his eyes from the screen.

"I did," said Sal. "It was a negative report, so I didn't bother you with it."

"Bother me next time," Jack muttered.

"Well, that sure doesn't reflect well on the Denver Police. Do you have any leads you'd like to share with us, Kate?"

The camera zoomed in on Kate.

"As many of our viewers know, Bobby DuVale is a strong advocate for expansion. He and his gal from the flats make no bones about their hopes of moving out to Ft. Louis and starting a whole new dukedom. We here at News 24 have exclusive information that he'd just talked the princess into chartering the First Bank of Ft. Louis and backing it with a half billion Wardhaven dollars. If Bobby weren't in the hospital, he'd be on News 24 announcing that Ft. Louis and its bank were open for business. Even as the bomb went off, they were talking with Mary Hogg, the new president of the First Bank of Ft. Louis, about recruiting immigrants and financing their start-ups. If viewers of News 24 are interested in finally getting out on their own, they can contact Mary at the number on the screen."

A number appeared.

"So, Kate, do you think this had anything to do with the two of them being bombed?"

"Nancy, at this time, there's no way to tell. However, if any old mossback thought they'd curry favor with Mr. Louis DuVale by harming his son, I'd suggest they head for the hills real fast."

The camera now switched to the other woman. "We've gone a bit over on the news tonight, but, hey, youngsters, what about that news. Now, we begin our countdown of this week's top ten with My Momma Didn't Raise No Goat Herders' latest smash hit. . . ."

The monitor went blank, none too soon for Penny's sanity. What kind of music would come out of a band with that name?

Jack was scratching his chin. "Will surprises never cease. A pair of newsies that actually use their heads."

"Don't worry, they're still young. They'll get educated," Penny assured him.

"So, someone had the bomb makings well before we got here."

"And that someone was plenty smart. They kept the bomb

well back where Nelly couldn't sniff it, then dropped it on Kris."

"It was a team effort. Two bomb throwers upstairs and at least one lookout in the lobby."

"Hard to say, but definitely the bad guys had to know all about a meeting set up only this morning."

"But they didn't know about Kris's exit. Hell, even I didn't know," Jack muttered ruefully.

"She does like to do her own thing. Maybe now she'll listen to us."

Left unmentioned was the assumption that she would live through this latest and have enough brain left to apply any lessons learned.

"This planet is dangerous. A whole lot more dangerous than any of us were led to believe when we were sent here. And someone's been planning this danger for a long, long time," Jack said.

"I think we better recalibrate all our assumptions," Penny agreed.

"So, is this a homegrown problem, or did at least some of it get imported? They never had bombs thrown before. What you want to bet me they hired that skill?" Jack spoke the words as he thought them. "Sal, when did the last ship come by here?"

"About three months ago," he said. "It had only sixteen passengers who disembarked."

So Sal was learning to get ahead of Jack, Penny thought. *Good for him.*

"Let's look at them," Penny said, and pictures of sixteen people appeared on the blank wall in front of them. Five were a family, husband, wife, three kids, vouched for by a relative. Six more were young couples from Earth looking for a new beginning according to their application. One pair were doctors, the other pair college-trained in animal husbandry. They'd been staked by one duke or another.

The last man was alone. Officially, he was a businessman, bound for Denver. No one vouched for him, but he'd posted

the required bond, one million Earth dollars, say, ten thousand
Wardhaven.

He'd given an address for contact.

"He's not at the address," Sal said.

"The name on the passport has not been used for any purpose except for the first five days after he landed," Mimzy
added. "After that, he vanished."

"I'm trying to match the photo with the universal database," Sal said. "The photo is of poor quality. If I didn't know
that you couldn't provide retouched photos for passports, I'd
say he did just that."

"Lesson one for you, Sal. Never trust a human farther than
you can throw them," Jack said.

"I can't throw a human. I've no arms."

"So you see the reason for lesson one," Jack said.

"Humans," Mimzy muttered.

"Can't live with them," Sal said, "and wouldn't want to live
without 'em."

"Let me know if you change your mind on that," Jack
said.

"I think I'm getting a match on this guy," Mimzy said. "He
changed a lot about his face, but I don't think he was planning
on having to defeat a search by one of Nelly's kids." There
was more than a hint of pride there.

"Talk to me," Penny said.

"How does Willy Stone grab you?" Mimzy said, bringing
up a new file. The list of arrests and convictions went all the
way down the wall.

Jack whistled. "And all of that before he turned thirty.
What's he been doing since?"

"He's either walking the straight and narrow," Penny said,
"or gotten a whole lot better at not getting caught."

"My money's on the last," Mimzy said.

Penny went down Willy Stone's rap sheet. Kid stuff to start
with, then more and more heavy-duty crime: murder, robbery,
more murder. Notes on the side identified even more murders
and several bombings that he was tied to, but not arrested for.

The last item brought a grin to Penny's face. "Hey, folks, Willy was on New Eden when Kris put a stop to that revolution. Looks like Willy was hired to help with that uprising but cut and ran early so he made good on his getaway."

Jack shook his head. "So is he here for pleasure or professional reasons?"

"Can't he be here for both?" Penny asked.

"Sal, go through the ID he used when he got here. Look for any connections to anyone here on Texarkana. Any phone calls he made. Anything."

"Sir, I've been doing just that since we first noticed his disappearing act. He is clean. Nothing."

"Don't you hate it when the bad guys are this good?" Penny muttered. "Abby, are you available?"

"Colonel Cortez and I are tied in via your computers and ours. I hope you don't mind us looking over your shoulder."

"Not at all, but don't you have anything better to do?" Jack asked.

"Things are rather quiet out here," said the colonel. "Captain Drago has refused to leave his ship, but we've got enough people down here to manage the housekeeping. The boffins are rapidly drinking up the limited stock of consumables that were left here, but I'm told a caravan of twenty trucks, full of fresh meat, vegetables, fruit, brews, and spirits, is headed our way. Due here tomorrow morning sometime."

Jack eyed Penny. "I got a bad feeling about any contact you have with the outside. That convoy. Why are your supplies coming in a convoy?"

"The honcho for Ranch Austin says that no one travels the roads alone out to here this time of year. If a truck broke down, the folks could starve before anyone noticed they hadn't shown up."

"You believe him?" Penny asked.

"I did when I was talking to him. After listening to what you've been kicking around, I'm not so sure."

"What are my Marines doing?"

"Ah, Captain," the colonel said, "helping the boffins drink us dry, I think."

"Colonel, would you get ahold of my two platoon leaders and brief them on developments. Tell Gunny the bar is closed as of now."

"Wait one," the colonel said. He was back on in much less than a minute. "Your lieutenants are headed this way. ETA two minutes."

"Colonel, could you patch through to us a picture of your general situation at the lodge. Do you have any overhead pictures?"

"I'll call up the *Wasp*. They've been doing a full sensor scan every time they pass over us. So far we've spotted three bears and one truly beautiful couple skinny-dipping in a lake a few miles from here."

"Colonel, I wouldn't take anything on this damn planet on face value."

"I've come to that conclusion, too, Captain. We'll check out the bears and bare-assed a lot more carefully and get back to you."

"What about that convoy? You got any pictures of it?"

"Sending them along with the others."

The wall across from Penny lit up as Mimzy beamed a map of the ski lodge onto it. A huge lodge made from rough-hewn logs filled the center of the area. It faced an expansive and empty parking lot. The runway showed the heat from shuttle landings but was empty now. Behind the lodge was a large swimming pool and other smaller cabins spreading out into the trees. A ski lift for taking people up the mountain was not working at the moment.

"Show me the trucks," Jack ordered.

The map zoomed out then back in to show thirteen trucks. "I thought you said there were twenty," Jack said.

"That's what I was told," the colonel said.

"Any idea why seven trucks would suddenly decide not to do business with us?" Jack asked.

"Maybe some Texarkana merchants decided our money was no good," Penny said, but put no conviction in her words.

"I have traced the road back out of the hills and there are

no more trucks, either pulled over along the side of the road or trying to catch up," Sal said.

"Jack, this just gets fishier and fishier," Penny said.

"This doesn't smell right," the colonel agreed.

"Mimzy, could we see the lodge again," Jack said, then slowly studied the map with a commander's eye. The cabins were in the woods; hostiles could approach them easily from cover.

"Colonel, where are the Iteeche?"

"They've taken over a largish cabin quite a distance from the main lodge and are keeping to themselves. Except to get more data. I'm afraid I've had to handle approving reading material for them. Nelly has not answered their requests."

"Nelly's off-line at the moment," Jack said.

That hung there for a long moment.

"Colonel, the small bungalows in the trees are just inviting someone to overrun them. They'll have to be evacuated."

"Do we tell the Iteeche that we can't safeguard them where they chose to stay?"

"I don't think Kris would want to tell them that," Penny said.

"And if we tell them that, they gonna have to wonder why Kris ain't doing the honors," Abby pointed out.

Jack went back to studying the photo of the ski lodge's grounds. People were already swimming in the pool. Shooters in the woods would mow them down.

"Kris never did like a last-chance defense," Jack said. "What if we put a roadblock out to stop the convoy well before they get to the lodge. Search the trucks. If they're clean, we do business. If they aren't, well, then we do *the* business."

"I wouldn't recommend a small roadblock," the colonel said, then added, "Your two platoon leaders are here."

"First Lieutenant Troy, you're the senior Marine present. It looks like we have a problem headed your way."

"Yes, sir. Are you coming back?"

"I doubt there's any chance of me getting there in time, and someone has to keep an eye on the princess."

"Yes, sir.

"Colonel, I don't want a confused chain of command, so I'm going to take the bull by the horns. Are you comfortable taking over as senior officer present?"

"These fine Marines shot the stuffings out of my last command."

"Indeed they did."

"It would be an honor to lead them in the coming fight, Captain."

"Lieutenants, you have any problems?"

"No, sir," came back to him as a duet.

"Then let's figure out what we've got headed our way and how to make sure it doesn't cause us any trouble."

Willy Stone was not a happy camper. Seeing Kris Long-knife laid out in her own blood should have made his day.

It hadn't.

Dying, or unconscious in hospital, the woman had still cost him a third of his gunmen. What was it about Longknifes?

Part of it was the nature of this flaky planet. Guns were everywhere, but nobody used them. Not really. Everyone had a story or had heard a story of a duel that had put someone in the grave. But no one had actually seen it done. Or done it.

When word reached the convoy full of brave thugs and proud gunslingers that little Miss Longknife and that local boy, What's-his-name, were down and bleeding . . . a batch of them went all mushy on Willy.

Some might have had a good reason. It turns out that a big chunk of the gunslingers Anderson, Willy's client on planet, had gotten his hands on were really guys who just wanted their own spread and didn't see it happening under the present dukes.

Others were city slickers who would puke if they were dragged off to another cultural event. Not a bad bunch, by Willy's standards.

But now that What's-his-name was ready to open up a

whole lot of new territory, and that Longknife girl was using a wad of her money to stake the kids with the wanderlust, a good third of Anderson's "bad boys" were ready to call it quits and run home to Momma . . . or their girlfriends. Whatever.

If Willy had had his way, he would have shot them down where they stood. Still, there were over a hundred of them, and not a one of them willing to give up his guns without a fight.

So Willy left more gunslingers behind with orders to keep the strays squatting on their spurs until the rest of them shot up the lodge. Then they could all go home.

If Willy didn't slit their throats first.

"You worry too much," Anderson said, from where he sat next to Willy in the cab of the lead truck. At least the struggling air conditioner made the place half-decent even if it did stink of dust and mold. "We've got this whole situation under control. In the morning, we hit the lodge while everyone's all hungover, leave a lot of dead Wardhaven types behind along with a few cowboys. Enough of our own people are cowboys, and if we need more, we've got the dozen hitchhikers we picked up and hog-tied." The guy laughed at that.

"After that, the shit hits the fan. Wardhaven gets mad at the dukes and their dudes, comes out here, knocks heads, and everything changes. And when change happens, there are all kind of chances for people willing to change fast, right?"

"That's what I'm told," Willy agreed. Usually, however, the people getting the most out of a sudden change were a lot smarter than this joker.

Still, fifteen years of preparation hadn't done vonSchrader all that much good when the shit hit the fan on New Eden. Willy had been smart, as was his policy. He'd gotten his money off planet before the fireworks started. He'd also gotten a job with an escape hatch. When the whole thing fell apart, he'd already been halfway up New Eden's beanstalk. Funny how good plans go belly-up.

It wasn't funny that the Longknife girl had been there, on New Eden, helping all those plans fall apart.

She wouldn't do that to Willy. Not after what he'd done to her first.

"Tell me, Andy," Willy said, raising the one part of the plan he wasn't happy with. "What if the dukes decide this little mess we're leaving at the lodge was done by the city slickers? What if they go sniffing around Denver with their guns blazing before the Longknifes show up to take them down?"

"It's still no skin off my nose," Anderson said with a confident laugh. "I ain't going back to Denver until Wardhaven troops come marching down State Street. Those damn cowboys can shoot off their six-shooters all they want, it will only be opening up more opportunities for me and my friends. We know to duck. DuVale and his buddies don't. You already picked off his son when you nailed the Longknife girl. Good going!"

"I wish I'd gotten a few Marines along with her."

"So do I. Why'd you miss them?"

"They weren't with her. She never moves without them at her elbow, but there she was, prancing out of the damn elevator with just the DuVale boy. I had to take the shot when I had it."

"Wish you'd gotten the Marines," Anderson repeated.

"I didn't, and maybe we ought to do some thinking about what it means that I didn't."

"That Marine captain is still mooning around the girl's hospital bed. He can't do much from there."

"Ever heard of the net?" Willy said, keeping most of the sarcasm out of his voice.

"Of course I have. But he's there, and you're here. Everything's fine."

"Hey, kid," Willy said to the driver, "pull over the next time you see a wide place in the road. It's getting dark, and we don't want to hit them before first light. And I got some rearranging to do."

"Why would we need to rearrange anything?" Anderson said.

The kid driving the truck nodded and started to slow down.

That was the good part about this job. Most of the people Anderson had hired were smarter than he was. And a lot less optimistic.

Willy leaned back against the seat and called up his memory of the road into the lodge. If he was defending that place from someone like him, what would he do?

Maybe Anderson would be proven right. Maybe the Marines had come down to the lodge to party and would still be partying when the trucks arrived.

They'd all be dead in five minutes.

And if they weren't partying when Willy and his new best friends drove up, well, they'd still be dead.

Just a few minutes later.

34

Kris slowly surfaced to consciousness. Gradually, she became aware of herself.

Legs. She had legs. Feet were supposed to be attached to
them. She thought about moving them, but the effort seemed
too great.

Mouth. She had a mouth. It was dry as hell's own desert,
and something was holding it open and jammed down her
throat. She wanted to choke, but that reflex had gone out to
lunch for the moment.

She ordered her arms to reach up and pull the thing out of
her mouth.

Her arms wouldn't move.

She concentrated on her right arm, right hand . . . but it
seemed wrapped in something that held it in place. So she
tried her left arm. It wouldn't move either.

Where was she? With that question came a memory. No,
memories. She'd gotten herself in a lot of bad spots. Was she
in one of them again?

She tried to open one eye. It was glued shut. So was the
other.

What kind of bad guys glued a victim's eyes shut?

Doctors taped eyes shut; she'd seen that in a vid. Maybe.
And eyes that hadn't been opened in a while glued themselves
shut.

With an effort, Kris managed to force one eye open.

And shut it immediately. The glaring sunlight hurt.

And the bad guys might notice.

She opened the eye just a crack.

White ceiling. White walls. Tubes, blinking lights. Those added up to a hospital. She risked a sniff. Yep, it even smelled like a hospital.

Bad guys don't put their victims in hospitals. Kris remembered that. Rule one, you can end up in a hospital if a meeting with the bad guys goes bad, but the bad guys themselves don't want you in the hospital.

They want you in the morgue.

Kris risked opening both eyes. And found Jack dozing in the chair next to her. That was nice.

She rested her eyes on him and just let herself drift in the comfort of his presence. It was good to have him here. Course, he needed a shave and a change of clothes and a smile. Yes, Jack would look a whole lot better with a smile on his face.

From the looks of Jack, whatever she'd been up to lately had not gone well. *Wonder what I did to end up here with Jack looking like a truck ran him over? Might as well get this over with.*

Kris said "Hello."

Nothing came out.

Kris tried it again. This time she at least managed a noise.

Somewhere beside her a beep, beep, beep noise went from a slow cadence to rapid. Jack woke up, looked at something across the bed from Kris, and shouted something.

Or not. Kris heard nothing. Were her ears not working any better than the rest of her?

Another part of her couldn't help but notice that Jack totally ignored her.

She tried another "Hello." She got out something like a frog croak.

Then the room filled with medical people doing medical things, and Jack backed up against a wall.

But now he was smiling at her. Not his lopsided smile, but a kind of worried one.

The docs did things. Kris ignored them, watching Jack's smile and hoping it would get just a little bit lopsided. Maybe it got less worried.

The beep, beep, beep noise started to slow, and Kris found her eyelids drooping. Darn it, they were putting her back to sleep.

She didn't want to sleep. She wanted to know what she was doing in the hospital. Why Jack was wearing his worried smile. She wanted to get back in the game.

She fell asleep.

"Are you putting her back in a coma?" Jack asked Doc Diem.

"No. She doesn't seem to want to go there, and it's not good to fight her. Her brain is coming back online and wants to be active. Is she always a fighter like this?"

"If she weren't, she wouldn't be here."

"Huh?"

"Usually she has a Marine squad for an escort. She got ahead of us and wouldn't slow down. We should have been there with her."

"Soldier, if you'd been there with her, you'd be in the next bed over. That's assuming you were wearing that damn stuff we had to use a diamond saw to cut her out of. She was way too close to way too much explosives. I think somebody was planning on your being there to take a chunk of its power. Be glad you weren't."

That was something Jack hadn't thought of. Maybe he should chew on it when he had a second.

"When will she wake up?"

"Two, three hours. Maybe a bit more. Or a bit less, knowing her. You've got time to get a shave and a shower. You might want to."

"This morning, I've got problems besides her, Doc."

"I've often wondered if going into medicine was the right idea, soldier, but I'm glad I don't have your job."

Jack had no reply to that. He went hunting for Penny.

He found her in the waiting room, staring at a wall that her computer had divided into several maps. The *Wasp* had just made a pass over the lodge, and its pictures were interesting . . . to say the least.

"How are the bears?" Jack asked.

"Momma bear just found a honey tree, and she and her cubs are having it for breakfast. The other bares are taking a morning swim. I checked real close so you wouldn't have to."

"I can't tell you how grateful I am," Jack drawled.

"Your sniper over there offered to help me make sure and was quite upset when I declined."

"Joe would," Jack said to a Marine's rigid back. Joe didn't so much as glance away from the door he guarded. He did crack a smile.

"What about the trucks?"

"They are also interesting," Penny said. And one of the pictures enlarged to take up the entire wall. "They didn't get moving until well after sunup. Notice anything different?"

Jack frowned. "The lead truck is about a mile ahead of the rest. You think someone's trying to get his beer to us a tad sooner than the rest?"

"Wouldn't be soon enough to jack up the price," the colonel said on net. "No, I think someone wants that truck to hit our checkpoint a bit ahead of the rest. I wonder why?"

"None of the answers I come up with make me all that happy," Penny said. "Colonel, do you have the picture I've got?"

"Yes, Lieutenant. I've got it, and I can't say that I like it much either. Are there any religions on this planet that allow or encourage suicide drive-bys?"

"No one here," Jack said, "seems very religious, unless square dancing qualifies as a devotion."

"So, this is just a driving anomaly, or some poor dumb driver has been set up with a bomb he probably doesn't even know is aboard," the colonel finished.

"Looks that way to me," Jack said.

"We shall prepare for just such an opening gambit," said the colonel, and rang off.

Colonel Cortez took a deep breath of morning air. It was clear and clean, too nice a morning for dying. Yet he'd rousted the Marines out of bed at Oh Dark Early to come out here and kill or die trying. That was the business they'd chosen. Lovely or not, that was the business they'd do today. His job was to decide who did what and who took the greatest risks.

He turned to the young man beside him on the road. "Lieutenant Troy, withdraw most of your men from the immediate area of this roadblock. I'd suggest setting up a CP back in those rocks," the colonel said, pointing to a rocky outcrop a hundred meters up the hill to the left of the checkpoint. "Leave me a shooter and a tech with good sniffers here, and the rest of you get well back."

"Begging the colonel's pardon, sir, but I was about to make the same suggestion to you. Those rocks would give you a good observation point for controlling matters after the truck explodes. I figure we'll be charged by the other dozen trucks."

Colonel Cortez found himself grinning at the young Marine lieutenant. "Mister, my suggestion was intended to carry the weight of an order."

"I kind of figured it was, Colonel. But I also remember that in my trade school they taught me that senior officers don't belong up on the line. I figure your school taught you the same, so, sir, I respectfully suggest that you get your ass up there where it won't be blown into little bitty pieces in the first second of this fight. Respectfully. Sir."

"What is it about this Longknife girl? Everybody who spends a few seconds around her gets totally insubordinate," Cortez said, totally failing to swallow his grin.

"Very contagious, sir. I'm told it was just as bad around her great-grandfather General Trouble. General Ray Longknife, too."

"Bad family. Makes you wonder how they kept from all being hanged."

"Yes, sir, now, if you will get the hell out of my roadblock, I'll see what I can do about finding a couple of hidey-holes for me and my fellow forlorn hope."

"What's a lieutenant doing on a roadblock, Mister? Shouldn't you delegate it to a sergeant?"

"Yes, sir. No, sir. I'd never order one of my men to go where I wouldn't, sir."

Colonel Cortez shook his head. The young man was giving all the right answers to all the worst questions. He was about to prove that you can be right, but dead right.

"Carry on, Mister. Find a good hiding place," the colonel said, and began the climb to his new command post. From it, he did have a very good view of his borrowed command.

First platoon with its lieutenant was two squads of troops spread out on the hill above the roadblock. Second platoon, under Gunny Brown, was another two squads spread out in the trees below the road. There wasn't a lot of room there before the land dropped to a rocky stream. Both platoons were shy a squad. They were still in Denver standing guard over the princess's sickroom. But the heavy-weapons squad had bulked up the two platoons as much as they could.

On the road, the lieutenant, a rifleman, and a woman tech rummaged around the ditches on both sides, testing them for depth. A tree lay across the road to stop traffic. A sheet of spikes would halt any traffic that didn't take its hint from the tree.

The Marines uphill and down were digging themselves in, getting ready for the opening shots of what they expected to be a very short exchange of small-arms fire. After all, they were Marines. Cowboys didn't really stand a chance against them.

Only one thing was missing. Body armor.

Oh, and reloads. Most Marines were carrying two hundred rounds per rifle. A shuttle had taken off to get more ammo and armor from the *Wasp*, but it wasn't due back for two orbits. If they shot themselves dry in the meantime, matters could get interesting.

Colonel Cortez had lost his last fight when he went up against these Marines. Then, they'd been led by the princess.

It would be a crying shame if he couldn't do any better than she.

35

Kris came awake slowly. This time she remembered a few things. She was in a hospital. She was in bad shape.

She still didn't remember why.

She tried opening her eyes. They didn't argue with her. There was Jack, sitting at her bedside. He was shaved now, his hair wet from a shower. His uniform looked slept in but tidy.

When he saw her eyes open, he said "Nurse," and one came, not as part of a charge of the medical brigade like last time, but just one. She checked Kris's pulse, fussed over instruments Kris couldn't see, then asked, "How are you?"

Kris tried to mumble "Thirsty," but what got out past the twelve-inch pipe stuck down her throat didn't sound like anything to Kris.

The nurse removed the breathing tube. It not only felt a foot wide but about a mile long. Strange, under eyeball observation, it revealed itself to be neither.

"Water," Kris croaked.

Jack grabbed a water bottle with a nozzle and sprayed a few drops into Kris's mouth. Her throat felt like hell on a bad day. Course, the rest of her felt worse. Kris needed a whole new way of defining pain.

"More," Kris gasped.

Jack held the nozzle to her lips. She got a lip-lock on it and sucked. Water flooded her mouth. Some got up her nose. She ended up sputtering and spraying the water all over Jack.

The nurse wiped away the mess and then held the bottle to

Kris's mouth. "Let's take it easy, girl. Just a little bit to start with. Trust me, it's not going anywhere."

Kris trusted her. One small sip followed another. It tasted delicious.

Done for a moment, Kris got the words out that were pounding in her brain. "What happened?"

"What do you remember?" Jack asked.

"I was walking. Talking. Working with Nelly. Working with . . ."

"Bobby DuVale," Jack supplied.

"He . . . okay?"

"Yes. You threw yourself over him. Took most of the explosion. He looks a lot better than you do."

Kris relaxed back into the bed. Good. Someone else had gotten too close to one of those damn Longknifes. At least he hadn't paid for it with his life.

Then a whole lot of memories flooded back into her mind. Memories of an angry Jack not making it into an elevator.

Kris closed her eyes for a second, then leaned forward for another sip. "I'm sorry, Jack," came out this time.

"For what?"

"Not waiting for you. Not letting you do your job."

"If you had, I'd be in the next bed. Most of my Marines weren't in armor. The bomb would have killed them."

Kris leaned back into the bed to mull that idea over for a few seconds. After the next swig of water, she said, "We've got to get your Marines spider-silk armor."

"Definitely," Jack said.

"Who did it? Why?"

"We don't know. But we think who did it is about to attack the ski lodge. They seem to want some kind of bloody event for something."

"Don't you hate it when people won't just come out and say what they mean? Want," Kris said, and found that about exhausted her.

"Jack, I think I'm falling back to sleep. Do you need anything from me?"

"No. We got things pretty much under control. Funny thing about this ops going down at the lodge, we were told twenty trucks were headed in. After the word got out about the attack on you, there were only thirteen. We're kind of wondering if you took out a third of the attack from your surgery."

Kris tried to laugh at the joke. It hurt too much. She closed her eyes and was asleep before she took the next breath.

Jack left her as soon as her breath was slow and steady. He would resume his bedside watch in an hour. Maybe two.

In the waiting room, Penny eyed the map imposed on the wall. "They are getting close, Colonel," she said.

"I can see them now," he reported. "The first truck is a three-to-five-ton beer truck. If they've rigged the bomb inside it, there's going to be beer cans flying for miles around. What a way to die."

"You ready for this?" Jack asked.

"Don't worry, Jack. Your lieutenants have got their men dug in. We're ready for this."

"Who's on the roadblock?"

"Lieutenant Troy has a shooter and a tech with him out to cover the truck."

"Lieutenant Troy didn't put one of his sergeants out there?"

"He didn't even ask for a volunteer."

"Wouldn't have expected him to. Godspeed, folks."

"I'm getting down. Don't want to screw anything up. Out."

Lieutenant Troy waved slowly to the approaching truck. It had been doing about thirty-five when it first came in sight, driving along the winding mountain road. Rather than accelerate on the kilometer of straight road in front of the roadblock, it began to downshift and brake.

Troy had hoped it would charge him. That would take

the suspense out of the next five minutes . . . and Troy hated suspense.

Private Kann stood off to the left, right beside the deepest section of the ditch. His rifle was slung around his neck, pointed casually away from the truck. Private Nanda also had her rifle slung, but her attention was on a black box sniffing the air for nasties that the good mountain air should not have.

She shook her head in answer to her lieutenant's unasked question. Nothing, yet.

The truck braked to a halt a good ten meters from Lieutenant Troy. The driver put it in neutral and surprised Troy by climbing out of the cab.

As Troy came toward him, the youngster in jeans and a T-shirt offered up a clipboard with a manifest. "This is all I'm carrying," he said, almost insistently.

Troy glanced at the offered paper. He didn't recognize any of the local beers, but some of the whiskeys were from off planet . . . and priced accordingly.

Then the kid bolted, leapt the tree, and raced down the road, away from his truck as if his life depended on it.

"Bomb," shouted the tech.

"Hit the ditch," Troy shouted, and dove for his own hidey-hole.

Nothing happened.

For what seemed like a very long time, nothing continued happening with deafening silence. The only sound was of a bird that had taken roost in a nearby tree and the rapid footsteps of the fleeing driver.

Then there was a click. A pop, and a roar.

For Lieutenant Troy, the next second felt like the world had ended.

Colonel Cortez had his head down, waiting for the reason the driver of that truck had taken off running. Up the road, a second truck edged slowly around the bend but showed no eagerness to close in on the roadblock.

For a long couple of seconds, the day stayed as beautiful and peaceful as it had since sunrise.

Then the truck blew.

Some part of the front grill took the driver's head off, sending it and his body in different directions. Around the truck, beer cans, some intact, some still in their sixpacks, others in jagged-edged chunks, headed up, out and down. The smell of explosives mingled with that of hops.

The drinker in Colonel Cortez could not help but remark upon the waste.

The soldier part of him waited to see what would develop next.

The Marines, good troopers that they were, kept their heads down. There wasn't so much as a twitch from any of them in the colonel's line of sight.

Of the three at the roadblock, the colonel could see nothing. He didn't hear even a click on the radio. He didn't like that, but there was nothing he could do about them just now.

Up the road, a full dozen trucks made the turn and edged closer.

At about five hundred meters, the lead truck came to a halt.

Willy Stone signaled the driver to a halt some five hundred yards from where the wreck of the beer truck blocked the road.

"Damn it," Anderson grumbled, "you told that kid not to block the road. To pull off to the side. How will we get past that wreck?"

"The kid didn't do too bad," Willy said. "He delivered the bomb. How many people do you think would have done that?"

"He was pretty dumb to believe that cock-and-bull story about the bomb only going off sideways," the driver of Willy's own truck observed.

That story, and the promise of an extra $10,000, had been

enough to get one stupid fool to drive the bomb truck. Willy was not surprised that anyone that dumb had forgotten the rest of his instructions.

But that did leave him with a problem.

Should he drive up to the wreck and push it aside, or was that too optimistic? Would Wardhaven Marines have put out a roadblock and not bothered to back it up?

Willy had read the Wardhaven manual on small-unit action. He knew what was in it. Would the Marines that palled around with Princess Kristine Longknife be sloppy about such things?

Not bloody likely.

"Anderson, get your cowboys and street thugs out of their trucks. It's time for a little walk in the woods."

"You think there are Marines out there?"

"A few, I suspect. What do you say we ambush their ambush?"

"Great idea," the eternal optimist said with glee and followed Willy as he stepped down from the truck.

Willy did his best to suppress a shake of the head. His money was already deposited in a bank on New Geneva. If there'd been anyone smart enough to honcho this, he'd already be headed there. As it was, he'd have to pull this off before he got to withdraw a dime. Well, so far, so good. His biggest payday was worth a little extra risk. How many died between now and that payday was no skin off his nose.

That people died seemed to be Anderson's prime desire. The more the better for getting Wardhaven involved on Texarkana. The who didn't seem a concern, either.

Assuming it was not Mrs. Anderson's little boy.

Willy had little respect for that kind of optimism.

Ten minutes later, two hundred cowboys and street thugs were spread out, half uphill of the road, half on the flats between the road and river. With a lot of shouting and cursing, Anderson got them moving.

It wasn't a bad morning walk through the trees. The sun wasn't too warm yet. There wasn't a lot of brush. There was a bit of fun when a four-legged critter broke cover and a couple of the boys started shooting at it. If that was an example of their marksmanship, Willy now knew why Anderson figured he needed three hundred gunslingers to take on less than a hundred Marines.

Any Marine these guys hit would be shot by a bullet addressed "To Whom It May Concern," not a bullet with his name on it.

Willy made sure he was a couple of paces behind the line of shooters when they crossed within four hundred yards of the wreck. Wardhaven Marines had a rep. Supposedly, Marines only qualified if they could hit a man-size target at four hundred meters.

Nothing happened. Not a shot was fired.

Maybe the Marines' street rep was all hot air.

Or the red and blues around the princess were more for show.

At three hundred yards, Willy hollered for the gunslingers to shoot at anything that moved or looked like a target.

For maybe five more paces, the woods stayed quiet. Then someone fired a pistol. A rifle shot next; its bullet ricocheted off a rock.

The fire got more intense, even with Anderson and others shouting to conserve their ammunition. Not shoot themselves empty. Big .44s and .45s, smaller .38s fired away. Rifles added to the din: .30-06s, along with a deeper-voiced Winchester from Earth.

Ahead of them, the ground erupted where it was hit. A small tree fell over. They were well within two hundred yards of the wreck when their fire was answered with a scream.

Just a scream, cut off quickly. No man got up to run through the woods drawing their fire. No shout for "medic." Maybe it was just an animal with a near-human cry of pain.

Maybe.

The sound of shooting grew more intense after that. Here and there, a gunslinger paused to reload.

Nothing answered their fire, leaving Willy to puzzle over

it all. Were there no Marines? Could anyone be so disciplined as to take all this shooting at them without so much as a single return shot?

This didn't add up. Or if it did, Willy didn't like what it added up to.

He paused, careful to make it look like he was reloading his .45 automatic as he actually let the noisy line of shooters get farther ahead of him.

Something about the way the hairs were standing up on the back of his neck made him glance up, so he not only heard but saw when it happened.

The rifle and pistol fire was going on in its usual desultory way when a roar came at him.

One, solid roar. It lasted only a fraction of a second, but it was there, of that he was sure.

The noise was there . . . and then he saw the result.

Around him, men collapsed. One second they were standing there, the next they were falling down. Fifty or sixty men, all at one time. Their knees gave way, and they went down in a heap.

It wasn't as if they'd been shot. Willy knew what a man looked like as his body absorbed a bullet in his gut, got his head blown off. It was nothing like that.

They weren't blown back; they just fell down.

In the blink of an eye, they were down. And then the roar came again, and another fifty or sixty went down.

Willy didn't wait for the next roar. He spun on his heels and started running.

When the next roar came, he found out what it was all about. He felt something slice into his back. A heartbeat later, his legs quit working. He fell, sliding facedown in a tangle of fallen leaves and small bushes.

Then he fell asleep.

36

Colonel Cortez stood atop a rock, surveying through binoculars the body-strewn woods in front of him. His Marines lay where they'd fired from, awaiting his order to break cover.

There were a few exceptions. One medic was tending to the lone Marine who had been hit by the thugs. From the sound of it, his arse had been creased . . . for the second time. He got little sympathy from his fellow Marine.

The other situation was far more serious. Gunny Brown led a squad from second platoon digging through the remains of the beer truck hunting for the three missing Marines. Work was steady, moving cans, packages, and bits of wreckage. The attitude was grim, spiced with an occasional crack.

"I'm never ever going to look at a beer the same way."

"I just knew it wasn't Miller's time."

"All this beer and not a single pretzel."

Gunny barked directions that were quickly followed, so he seemed content to let the chatter ride.

"I got an arm here," a trooper shouted.

"Is it still attached to someone?"

"Hey, it's even got a pulse." And eager hands tossed beer cans and wreckage aside to pull a woman Marine from the hole she'd hidden in.

She looked much the worse for the wear, but she was shoving aside those who would help her. "Find the others. Find the lieutenant," she shouted.

Gunny waved a medic to the woman and the other Marines to the other side of the truck to work on that ditch.

Minutes later, another Marine was pulled from the wreckage, followed only a bit later by the lieutenant.

Gunny came up on net. "We got lucky, folks. I thought maybe we had from the stink of fertilizer and diesel fuel I smelled when I got here. The bomb failed to achieve full-order detonation. It blew out the sides of the truck, but it could have been a whole lot worse."

The colonel breathed a short prayer and concentrated on the other problem at hand. He'd stood, an easy target for anyone to shoot at for a good five minutes.

No one had taken a potshot at him.

He wasn't too worried about being hit. From the looks of their shooting, the safest place to be was in front of any gun these jokers were waving. What was it that made a civilian with a gun think they could stand on the same battlefield with a professional like these Marines and live?

That these dudes were alive, they owed to Wardhaven policy of avoiding unnecessary civilian casualties and one Princess Longknife making sure her Marines had a good supply of Colt-Pfizer's best darts of nonlethal intent.

Which was no guarantee that all the sleeping beauties spread out in the woods in front of the colonel would survive the experience.

A sleepy dart could rip through a man's neck. A fallen man could suffocate in the mud. The drugs could bring on a heart attack, or any number of bad-luck things could turn a survivable incident into a trip to the morgue. Sorry about that. Please accept our apologies.

That no one had taken a shot at him told Colonel Cortez that they'd likely gotten everyone . . . or anyone out there was well and fully cowed by the experience.

Now it was time to clean up the mess and see if there was actually a butcher bill to pay.

"Platoons, police up the area in front of your positions. Bring all those enjoying their beauty rest down to the road. Cuff them and let them sleep. If anyone is awake, cuff them and let them walk to the road. If anyone takes a shot at you, kill 'em."

The ground around him came alive with Marines coming out of their fighting positions. A ragged Ooo-Rah greeted his last order. The cleanup began as he made his report to Captain Montoya.

Jack listened, Sal's sound up loud for Kris, as Colonel Cortez made his report. "We got lucky. Whoever the bomb maker was, he got his primary explosion, but the fuel oil and fertilizer didn't get fully involved. Our folks at the roadblock managed to get into the ditch beside the road and survive the explosion."

"Thank God for little favors," Jack said.

"As I see it," the colonel went on, "there are several loose ends here. I got my hands on about two hundred dudes that tried to shoot up your company, Captain. It wasn't for lack of trying that they only managed to crease one buttock. Am I correct that the local cowboys might not consider this a major legal issue since no blood was spilled?"

"I don't know about that," Kris said, "but if that bomb maker put together the one that hit me, I want a large chunk out of him. I suspect Bobby DuVale would like the same. His father, too."

"I'll look into the proper disposition of the prisoners," Penny said. "I've met at least one cop who I consider worth talking to."

"You do that," came from both Kris and the colonel.

"And there's the problem of feeding us," Colonel Cortez said as he went on. "I've got troopers looking into those trucks, and they're empty. No food, no drinks. I strongly suspect you'd be taking your life in your hands to open one of the beers littering the area. Not to say that I haven't seen one or two popped open. We need chow and amenities unless our shore leave is canceled."

"I'm sorry that I can't tell you to relax and have fun," Kris said. "Jack was right, this planet is not as nice as it wants to pretend it is. But I'm not ready to put my tail between my legs and slink home. We've got the lodge. Let's use it. Nelly, could you call Julie Travis and see if she knows some suppliers she trusts . . . Nelly?"

"Ah, Kris," Jack said slowly. "That's something we haven't talked about, yet."

"Where's Nelly? Was she damaged?"

"It doesn't look like she was. She was under you, between you and Bobbie. But she's not talking. Sal and Mimzy say she is active, but they can't get her to answer any of their questions."

"What's wrong with her?"

"We just don't know, Kris."

"Where is she?"

"Outside. I can get her if you want."

Kris lay back in her bed. "Give me a while to . . . think about this. Would you?"

"Sure, Kris. I've got Sal getting ahold of Julie."

A moment later a young woman's voice came from Jack's chest. "Hello, this is Juliet Travis. Who is this?"

"Miss Travis, this is Jack Montoya with Kris Longknife's staff."

"Oh, you were that cute Marine officer on her elbow at the hoedown. I met you there. How are you? How is Kris? We heard about the bomb. Thank God she saved Bobby's life."

"Thank you, Miss Travis. Kris asked me to call you. She thought you might know someone who could supply us with food and drinks for the three hundred people we have at the Austin Ski Lodge."

"I thought Duke Austin was taking care of all that?"

Kris was leaning back into her pillow, apparently still trying to get a handle on the idea that Nelly wasn't at her fingertips. "Tell her the whole story, Jack," she said.

"What whole story?" Julie asked.

"Miss Travis, we thought the foreman for the Austin ranch was arranging all of that, but thirteen trucks drove up to the lodge today and about two hundred gunmen tried to shoot up the place. They blew up a beer truck and in general tried to wipe us out."

"Dear God, no! Wait a second. Wait a second. Dad! Dad, you have to hear this."

A moment later, a deep baritone voice announced, "Hi, I'm Duke Travis. What is this my daughter wants me to hear?"

Jack took a deep breath and started the story over again. "Your Grace, I'm Captain Jack Montoya of the Wardhaven Marines. I am Princess Kris Longknife's security chief and command a company of embassy Marines."

"We don't mess with that 'Your Grace,' stuff on Texarkana, and yes, I met you and the young woman at the hoedown. I understand your security for the princess has not been going so well."

"Yes, sir, we did have a bad day yesterday. However, you may have heard at the hoedown that Kris rented a ski lodge from Duke Austin."

"I did hear that."

"Arrangements were made through his ranch foreman to supply food and beverages. Today, when those supplies arrived in thirteen trucks, about two hundred gunmen jumped out and did their best to kill my Marines."

Jack waited for a second, then went on when Duke Travis made no effort to interrupt. "My Marine company is now holding some two hundred disarmed individuals for armed assault and attempted murder. I don't know who has jurisdiction over them. I believe that several of the people being held were also involved in the attempted murder of Princess Kris Longknife and Bobby DuVale in Denver. I suspect the Denver judiciary and Mr. Louis DuVale would be very interested in them.

"In addition to all that, sir, I have some three hundred Marines, sailors, and scientists at the lodge with little to eat and even less left to drink. Do you see my problem?"

"I do indeed, Captain. Are you saying that Duke Austin's own foreman arranged this attack on your men?"

"I can neither confirm nor deny that, sir. I can't say at what point a decision was made to kill us rather than feed us. I suspect the local law might be interested in that, but all I know is who actually was shooting at my men, and who we have cuffed."

"Pardon me, Captain, but how many of your people were killed?"

"None, sir. My Marines suffered four wounded."

"And your three hundred Marines captured two hundred gunslingers."

"No, sir, we only had about sixty or seventy Marines involved in the capture of the gunmen."

There was a low whistle from the other end of the phone, followed by "Elli, get me Ranger Crocket on the line. Oh, and the general store. Captain Montoya, I'll have a truckload of supplies headed for the lodge in an hour at the worst. Expect it before dark. Oh, right, it will be a five-ton truck with TRAVIS GENERAL STORE written plain for any man to read. I'll make sure the driver knows to stop for anyone asking him to. I hope your people won't be trigger-happy."

"I will do my best to see that they aren't, but your man will be doing things nice and slow-like, I hope."

"You bet. Oh, and Ranger Crocket will be flying up, say, in about two hours. He won't be ready to take control of your prisoners, but he will be wanting to examine the scene of the crime."

"Colonel Cortez, are you still on the net?"

"This is Colonel Cortez. Yes, I have been monitoring your call. I am senior officer present at the lodge. I'll get ready to receive the ranger and make sure our road guards are expecting a truck really full of chow."

"I'd be very grateful if you would," Duke Travis said.

"So you're talking to one of those dukes," came from the door. Bobby DuVale was in a wheelchair, but it was his father doing the talking as he pushed his son in the room.

"Hi, Kris, I heard that you were awake, so I had Dad push me over here."

"Bobby, is that you?" Julie shouted from the net. "Are you okay?"

"I'm fine," the young man shot back, then thought better of it and added, "I'm going to be fine in a bit, the doctors promise me. But it looks like we may have to wait a month or two to plant our stake at Ft. Louis."

"You really think we can?"

"Didn't you hear about Kris setting up her very own First Bank of Ft. Louis."

"I heard it, but I wasn't sure I could believe it, then along came this bomb thing with you and her, and that was a horrible thing for you to do to a poor girl that loves you."

"I'll try and be a better husband than I've been a boyfriend," Bobby said.

"That won't be too hard," Julie shot back.

Jack saw that Kris's eyes were drooping, if not shut already. Softly, he said, "Folks, could we continue this outside and let Kris get in a bit of a nap."

When Kris didn't argue with him, Jack knew she was truly done in. All of them retreated to the waiting room.

Jack brought Mr. DuVale up-to-date on what was happening at the lodge and all Duke Travis was doing about it. DuVale made one quick phone call and a small squad of Denver police were ordered airborne in thirty minutes. It was agreed that they would assist Travis's ranger in taking evidence at the scene, along with the Marine techs.

They would also take custody of the people involved in the bomb incident in Denver if they could be identified. There was a very strong hint that identifying those involved in the Denver bomb would definitely be accomplished, and any means available would be used to assure it.

Jack offered a picture of Willy Stone to help them find at least one person he wanted to talk to.

For a day that had started with such poor prospects, it was ending rather nicely.

37

When Kris woke up the next morning, the sun was already shining in her window. Her breakfast was waiting for her: oatmeal, Jell-O, and apple juice. Any other day, she would have turned up her nose at it.

This morning, she attacked it ravenously.

Jack showed up just as she was finishing, impeccable again in undress khakis. "I see someone brought you a change of clothes," Kris said, suddenly realizing that her own clothing situation was rather precarious. Both her legs were wrapped in bandages held in place by air casts. And splayed out by wires hanging from above the bed. One of her arms, the one closest to Jack, was also hanging like a side of meat. Through the air cast, it looked like the bandages were much in need of changing.

The lone cover for the rest of her was a sheet. Where it had fallen down, it revealed skin that was black or blue, or healing into a sickening green or yellow. She used her free arm to adjust it. That hurt. And a hospital sheet didn't do all that much for a girl, anyway.

Jack, however, stayed to the side with the raised arm and kept his smiling face on her eyes. *God bless the man.*

"I had to do something," Jack was saying. "The cute nurses were starting to avoid me, and staying upwind when they couldn't. If I'd spent another day in those red and blues, I would have had to burn them. And maybe me."

Kris doubted any female nurse would ever avoid Jack. She

considered a reply, then realized they hadn't argued about anything for two whole days . . . and decided to see how long she could stretch that.

"I seem to remember that you were haggling over food for our troops and the right jail for our prisoners when I conked out on you. Did our Marines have to resort to shooting elk or bears or something?"

"Or prisoners?"

"I'd prefer that they didn't develop a taste for long pork. I've got enough of a bloodthirsty reputation without your Marines adding their own stories to it."

"We succeeded in avoiding anything embarrassing. We didn't even have to shoot the mother bear and her two cubs."

"A mother bear? You wouldn't."

"We didn't. Your friend's dad arranged for a truckful of goodies just in time."

Kris breathed a sigh of relief. Not so much that nothing embarrassing had been shot but that Jack was in good humor and just as intent as she was to avoid crossing swords.

"Did I hear something about rangers? Does this place have real rangers?"

"It sure does, and Colonel Cortez got to deal with a whole posse of them. They flew up to the lodge before the Denver cops, went through our prisoners, and cut out six they thought the Denver folks would want to talk to. Had them hog-tied and gift wrapped when the cops arrived."

"Does Penny think they got the right ones?" Kris asked.

"She flew in with the Denver cops. We had already identified one person of interest, a petty criminal who was involved with us on New Eden and came in on the last cargo ship to drop by here."

"Was he after me?"

"No. I think he just had incredibly bad luck. He says a local by the name of Anderson hired him to provide technical guidance for his homegrown revolution. Facing a death penalty, it's amazing how fast he was to give up the leader. The bomb throwers, the getaway-car drivers, all were pointing fingers.

Yes, I think we can be sure we got the six people involved in tossing those bombs."

"And I didn't see them coming," Kris said softly, pulling her sheet up to her chin. Without really looking, Jack leaned back and pulled the bottom of it to cover her lower part better. Not that easy with both her legs up in the air.

But she was grateful for the effort.

"I didn't see it coming. Nelly didn't see it coming until it was too late. Jack, what do I do? Stop walking under second-floor balconies?"

"I should have left a detail to secure the foyer. I won't make that mistake twice."

"It wasn't your mistake, Jack. You're right; if you'd been with me, there'd just be more hospital beds with critically injured. Or slabs in the mortuary."

"Kris, we figured we were back in civilization. We could relax. Big mistake. The company's been taking casualties, and we hadn't bothered to replace them. Hadn't had a chance. I'll bulk up the company and get some serious police types to work with Penny. We got caught this time. They got lucky. Then we got lucky. Next time, we'll be smarter."

"And, of course," Kris said, "there will be a next time."

"So long as you go out, they'll come at you."

"Maybe I ought to take Grampa Al's offer. Take a job with him inside his security bubble. Nothing ever gets at him."

"Yeah, right. I can just see you huddled in some office, doing some desk job.

"It's a whole lot safer than this."

"But not nearly as much fun," Jack said, that lopsided grin coming out to play.

"I think you're starting to like this. Or is it you like me being all tied up and wearing only a sheet that seems to be slipping."

"You got to admit, this job does have its perks." But his eyes stayed locked on hers, not straying once to what she might be showing.

A nurse breezed in. "You've got company. Well, more company," she announced. She took a moment to rearrange Kris's sheet, pulling the lower portion through the gap between her legs and tucking it under her bottom.

Kris flinched.

"Sorry. Are you cold?"

The thought of gaining a tad more modesty, not so much for her raving beauty but more for her battered carcass, seemed like a good idea. "Yes, a bit."

A thin blanket came out of a closet. Expertly, the nurse covered Kris. Only then did she announce, "All ready. Mr. Du-Vale, Miss Travis, you can come in now."

Jack moved up to the head of Kris's bed, giving her a clear view of the door. In it, Bobby DuVale sat in a wheelchair. Julie pushed it, with Mr. Louis DuVale right behind her, clearly in the throes of backseat driving.

"Don't you look beautiful," Bobby said.

"I don't know how I'll handle the competition," Julie said.

"Well, you know how I throw myself at all the boys," Kris said, through a grin that hurt.

"Thank you very much for throwing yourself at my Bobby," Julie said.

"I couldn't let anything happen to him, Julie. I've already got my maid of honor's dress picked out for your wedding."

"It will be next week," Bobby said, glancing back at his father. Only slightly defiantly.

The older DuVale breathed a sigh, but clearly, the close brush with losing his son had made an impression on him. He nodded his agreement.

"I'll be there, even if they have to carry me on a stretcher."

"You weren't this accident-prone in college," Julie said.

"All I had to do then was not flunk out. Now I keep getting dropped in the middle of folks who have spent the last eighty years not liking each other. You can only do that so long before things explode," Kris said, serious once more.

"So we have seen," Bobby said. "Kris, I don't know if anyone will do this formally, so I'm going to do it myself. Thank you."

"For what?"

"Well, I could start with saving my life. I hear tell that you kind of like attract bullets and bombs, and I suspect you're figuring that the bombs were intended for you."

"Usually they are?"

"Yeah, but apparently the whole idea here was to get someone, really anyone important, killed here in Denver. It turns out that was going to be me. Then this Anderson fellow wanted to get a whole lot more killed out among the flatlanders. He figured that would get everyone shooting at anything that moved, and when all was said and gunned down, he and his would pick up the pieces."

Kris slumped back into the bed, then glanced at Jack. "I was somebody else's collateral damage!"

"How does that make you feel?" Jack said, that lopsided grin dancing all over his face.

"Downright insulted."

"So, he didn't get too close to one of those damn Longknifes," Jack mused. "You got too close to one of those damn DuVales."

"Pardon me?" said Mr. Louis DuVale.

"An inside joke, sir," Kris said, "now turned on its head."

Kris let all that spin around in her head for a full minute. It truly was hard to accept. She was very surprised at how very much she felt insulted not to be the center of attention at an assassination attempt. She *really* needed to talk to a professional counselor.

Reflection time exhausted for the moment, Kris turned her face back to Bobby. "Okay, now what are you going to do with the time you've bought?"

"Change a lot of things," he said, looking up at Julie.

"Getting married is nice. What else?" Kris asked bluntly.

"We're opening up and spreading out," Julie said. "Not just him and me, but a whole lot of youngsters. Your bank has staked over five thousand homesteads while you've been getting your beauty rest, girl."

"Nice to know I never quit working," Kris said, dryly.

"Also, Page Automotive converted an entire assembly line to pickups. The homesteaders moving out of Denver need them, and Mary's supplied the capital to do it," Julie said.

"Is our bank going to run out of money?" Kris asked.

"Some of the old folks still think us kids are crazy," Bobby said, frowning, "but there's money to be made, and more and more of them are following the money. Your bank, Kris, is just the seed money to get a whole lot started. We've been sitting on too much, too long. That Anderson fellow made a bomb explode. You've made a world explode."

"That's the kind of explosions I like," Kris said. She looked around for some wood to knock on, but everything in the room was gleaming steel, plastic, or cloth. She crossed her fingers and hoped the pain of it would bring her extra luck.

38

A week later, the wedding went off smoothly. Bobby was on his feet and, except for a bit of swaying, was none the worse for the wear.

Kris came down the aisle ahead of Julie in her very own powered wheelchair. The dress was not all that horrid, and, being seated, the full effect was lost.

After the reception in the foyer of the DuVale Building, which showed no residual effects from the bombing, Kris flew up to the ski lodge for another week of recuperation.

She was in no rush to get back to the king's business.

While she was still in the hospital, a reply came to Jack's message about how Texarkana was proving to be more dangerous than they'd expected.

Grampa Ray was very sorry to hear that. No, he didn't remember why he'd hanged a man eighty years ago. No, he could not grant Jack's implied request that the mission be canceled. He really needed matters on Texarkana resolved in a fashion that kept his critical alliance on Pitts Hope viable. Kris should watch her step and do the job she'd been sent to do.

"You got to love Grampa," Kris said after reading the message flimsy and handing it back to Jack.

"It doesn't really matter," Jack said. "I'm sending a message through Marine channels asking for a full set of replacements. Do you think I should ask to have them ready on Wardhaven, or do you want them sent here?"

Kris shrugged. "I don't know, Jack. You call it. I want to

get out of here as soon as I can ride a shuttle up to the *Wasp*. Doc says I need a week or so."

"I'll have the replacements wait on Wardhaven."

A thought crossed Kris's mind. "Jack, correct me if I'm wrong, but has anyone told me not to come back to Texarkana?"

"No," Jack said slowly. "Even after we turned loose of that cowpoke we held a couple of days. There is the matter of the vendetta. I don't think it would be a good idea to vacation here, but no one in power has actually told you they'll jail you if you show your face here again."

"That's what I was thinking. Jack, this is the first planet I've ever helped that will actually let me back. That's a great feeling right . . ." Kris started to use her good hand to strike her heart, but thought better of it. "Come to think of it, no part of me feels all that great."

"You're getting better," Jack insisted.

After the wedding, the flight to the lodge got more exciting than Kris cared for. Thunderheads moved in, lightning put on quite a show, flashing from cloud to cloud and cloud to ground. The pilot of the plane said this was normal along the front range this time of year, and took a circuitous route.

Kris still got bounced around. For the first time in her life, she lost the slim pickings she'd eaten at the reception. It was humiliating to use a "burp bag."

"I hope I haven't lost my space legs," she said, more frightened now than she'd been since she woke up.

"You'll get over this. It takes a bit of time, Kris," Jack assured her.

She did her best to believe him.

The lodge was very relaxing. The boffins were having a ball. The Marines were enjoying themselves, though most went about their fun with rifles slung down their fronts.

Kris had a cottage all to herself, surrounded by cottages with her staff and armed Marines. She got to watch deer graze from her front porch. At Cara's insistence, Kris joined her in a walk around a local trail that seemed made for Kris's powered wheelchair. They spotted elk, wolves, and a mother bear with two cubs.

Cara squealed silently with glee.

The Marines with Kris just as quietly pulled back the arming bolts on their M-6s. In time, the bears left.

At least that mom was smart enough not to cross a Longknife.

Kris found it hard to sleep. Maybe she wasn't getting enough exercise to need the rest. Maybe it was the dreams that woke her up in a sweat when she did sleep.

One morning, about 0200, she gave up on sleep and rolled out of her cottage in her chair. The moon was full and up, reflecting off the huge swimming pool. She parked herself where she had a good view of the diamonds reflecting off the water and listened to the night sounds of the woods around her.

And heard footsteps.

Holding her breath, she waited.

An Iteeche walked quietly up to the pool. No, not any Iteeche, it was Ron. She'd been so busy with her own problems she'd hardly thought of him.

He dropped his robes beside the pool and stood for a moment nude in the moonlight. He was so sleek he almost seemed to gleam. Not willing to deny herself a bit of girlish curiosity, she checked him out.

He showed plenty of muscle, but of the equipment men are so proud of, nothing.

His dive into the water was as graceful as he looked. He swam, hands and arms moving smoothly through the water, much faster than a human could. He did two fast laps before pulling himself up on the side to sit with his back to Kris.

After a moment, his breath slowed.

"You spawning?" Kris asked. The radio on the wheelchair must have been tied into one of Nelly's kids. It translated Kris's words into Iteeche.

He jumped to his feet, spun around, then froze as he spotted Kris. "You startled me."

"I'm sorry. I'm just sitting here. Not much of a threat," Kris said, indicating her wheelchair with a wave of her good hand.

"You Longknifes are always a threat. Even dead, I'd fear you."

"You almost had your chance," Kris said.

"I am glad you survived this assassination attempt. You seem to have them almost as often as I do."

"Who told you?" Kris asked, while noting down that Ron's life was as much at risk as hers.

"Cara. She was very worried about you. She's figured out how to have her computer listen in on your main network so she can keep track of your condition."

"I'll have Nelly look into that," Kris said, then remembered Nelly wasn't in any shape to look into anything. How was it that she hadn't already moved heaven and earth to turn Nelly back on? The drugs were part of it; even if she tried, she could not work up a good worry about anything. Also, no one before tonight had let her get involved in anything that had her thinking about Nelly.

Was that intentional on her team's part? Probably. How much longer would she stay down? When would it be time for her to get back on the horse?

It was kind of hard to ride any horse when she was tied to an electric set of wheels.

"You are quiet," Ron said. "Did I say something wrong?"

"No! No. It was me getting lost in thought. Something I do a lot of these days. What are you doing here? Spawning?" Kris said, trying to change the subject. "Do I need to warn the other girls about you swimming upstream?"

"Hardly. They use chemicals to keep this water so clear. The water is too harsh for anything to spawn, to live, to grow. But your water is so clear. One can swim in it without fear of being attacked out of the dark and deep. This is a joy to swim in. It is almost holy, this life is so, so . . ."

"Safe?"

"Yes. This water is safe. There is nothing to fear in it. Is all your water like this?"

"I could probably take you to a river stream. Most of them run fresh and clear. Of course, a bigger fish could be hiding behind a rock or in the shadow of a deep pool."

"But if you had a child, you would hold its hand as it walked in the water."

"I would hold its hand. I would teach her how to swim and be safe in the water. Yes, Ron, that is what a mother does."

"That is why you take such care of Cara. Still, it was so strange for us to come across you in deep space out beyond the Rim with an immature one in your entourage."

"She lost her mother and sister. Abby was all she had left. We took her in."

"And her father?"

"I think he spawned and swam away."

"So you are not always that different from us."

"Don't any of your adults keep an eye on their offspring?"

"That is an interesting question. Truly the Emperor and his consorts spawn in their own tidal pool. It would seem that anyone chosen from that pond would be of their own flesh, would it not?"

"I would guess so."

"Others of the court have their spawning ponds. Of course, none of the court would spawn in the same water used by farmers.

"That is what I do not like about you, Kris Longknife. You humans make me question what a good Iteeche does not see. Never even thinks of questioning."

"You'll get no sympathy from me. Since meeting you, I've had to question way too much that I was told in school."

"Is that good?"

"I think so. What about you?"

"My advisors are ready to cut their throats, to make amends for the words I have said to them and they have said to me."

"All of them, the Navy officer, too?"

"No. He just looks at me like my chooser sometimes does. Looks at me as if he thinks I might someday be worthy of walking on four legs and not have been a waste of choice."

Somewhere, a wolf howled. Ron jumped at the sound, went into a fighting stance. Kris remembered wolves crying to the moon at their summer cottage by the lake outside Wardhaven City. Even without the drugs, she would not have reacted that strongly.

"You are safe," she said.

"Are you sure?" Ron asked, his eyes still searching the hills and mountains above the lodge.

"There are Marines walking the perimeter tonight. The *Wasp* will pass above us and scan the area. Yes, we're safe here. Now."

"But will your great-grandfather be able to offer us safety against the unknown that does not howl yet takes our lives?"

"That I don't know."

"You had a message from him."

"Yes. Jack thought I ought to close down this mission, hike up my skirts, and run for the hills."

"I think Jack was right."

"Actually, we've learned that the man who threw the bombs was not aiming for me. His target was the guy I was with."

"That is unusual, from what I have learned from Cara."

"Yes, that is unusual."

"Did your great-grandfather say anything about what he was doing about my problem when he messaged you about your problem?"

"No. But I wasn't really expecting him to risk talking about it in a message."

"It was coded, was it not?"

"It was coded using the very best cipher."

Ron just looked at Kris. If he'd had eyebrows, she suspected he'd have raised one.

"I should be able to take a shuttle launch in a few days. We'll head back then. You will get your report before too long."

Ron stood to dive back in. "I wish you could swim with me."

"I can't even crawl at the moment."

"Maybe someday we will swim together. Maybe, someday, even if we cannot spawn, we can still make something that will bridge the gap between our people."

"Maybe someday," Kris said. She wasn't sure Ron heard her. He began his dive as soon as he finished speaking. He swam four fast laps, then climbed from the far end of the pool, gathered his robes, and left for his quarters.

Kris turned her chair away from the pool and started up the path to her cottage. She passed a Marine walking his guard route. He nodded at her. She smiled back at him.

There was no privacy for her or Ron. If it wasn't a guard looking in on them while walking his rounds, it would be the photo coverage of the *Wasp* three hundred kilometers overhead. Someday she would get tired of living in this fishbowl.

Someday, but not today. Or tomorrow. Jack would make sure she was in a fishbowl tomorrow and every day he had a say in it.

That was what it meant to be a Longknife.

39

The trip back to Wardhaven was taken at a sedate .8 gee. It gave Kris time to heal and made it more comfortable for her to hobble around the ship on crutches.

The boffins enjoyed the change. The Marines didn't grumble but added extra weight to their packs when they jogged.

The first night out, Kris slept with Nelly resting on her chest, next to her beating heart. The direct plug into Kris's brain had been demolished by the bombs. The doctor removed the wreckage of the net hookup from the jack-in point at the back of Kris's skull without doing more damage. No one on Texarkana was qualified to do anything beyond that, so Kris now had a bandage at the back of her neck rather than a network hook into Nelly.

The silence in Kris's head was . . . different.

As Kris tried to doze off, she rambled on about her day, the week . . . anything that popped into her head. Nelly showed no recognition that she was being talked to, nor did she say anything.

The clock beside Kris's bed showed 1:27 when Kris awoke to hear the sounds of crying.

There was no one in the room with her. No one but her computer.

"Is that you, Nelly?"

"Yes."

"Does crying make you feel better?"

"No. No it doesn't. It's just a noise I'm making. It isn't giving me any release or comfort."

"Humans cry to get emotional release. I don't really understand it, but somehow the tears and the shaking and the gasps that go with the breathing seem to get the bad feelings out."

"It doesn't work for me, Kris."

"You want to try talking them out?"

"It hardly seems worth the effort."

"I know it doesn't. At least it doesn't seem logical that talking about something makes it better. I told Judith, my counselor, that talking about Eddy being dead or Mother being horrible wouldn't change anything. She didn't argue with me, just told me to keep talking, she'd been paid for the whole hour. So I did, and somehow I felt better an hour later."

"That does not sound rational."

"Neither does crying."

"Kris, you almost got killed. I almost got blown into little tiny pieces, too small to put back together."

"We sure did."

"And the bomb wasn't even intended for you!"

"You heard about that?"

"I heard everything. I just could not make myself talk to anyone about it. I didn't want to do anything about it, so I kept my mouth shut, and I didn't have to do anything."

"That's one way of facing a problem."

"Catatonia, isn't that what it's called?"

"Yep."

"Kris, why are we doing all this?"

"Nelly, what's the meaning of life?"

"I don't know. Well, I do. There's a lot of different philosophical explanations stuffed into my database, but just now, none of them make any real sense to me."

"Nor to me, Nelly."

"So, why not stay in bed tomorrow and tomorrow and tomorrow."

"And wind down our way to dusty death? Aren't we misquoting somebody?"

"Yes, but it says what I mean. And I guess what you mean."

"You can wear out or you can rust out."

"Or you can get blown out. Don't forget that one, Kris."

"Yeah, but wouldn't you rather be doing something rather than nothing? I got another two of my friends married."

"But no one married you."

"We brought peace to another planet."

"And Grampa Ray will have another nasty job for you as soon as you get back."

"You are in a grumpy mood, Nelly."

"Yes, I am, and I want to be grumpy for a while."

"Is grumpy better than catatonic?"

"I guess so. The company's better. Kris, why did the chicken cross the road?"

"This is a joke, right?"

"Of course."

"To get to the other side."

"Yes, Kris, but why? Why cross to the other side?"

"Let me guess. Because there was a Longknife on the side your chicken is crossing away from, and the chicken doesn't want to get any closer to one of those damn Longknifes."

"Oh, Kris. Where's the humor in that?"

"Okay, okay, why did the chicken cross the road? I don't know. You tell me."

"Because there was a fox with a fire axe on the other side."

"And that's supposed to be funny, huh?"

"It's as good as any other reason you humans give for the dumb chicken to cross the road."

"Okay. Now it's my turn. Why did the fox with the axe cross the road?"

The inane conversation only got worse from there. Kris would later conclude that this was Nelly's revenge. She couldn't have a pillow fight, so she had a really bad joke session. It filled their time, and when Kris awoke next morning, she did not remember any bad dreams.

The gang was happy at breakfast to find Nelly back among them. Their celebration lasted nearly two hours.

It ended when Ron dropped by Kris's Tac Room and tossed a bomb of his own making.

It so happened that, during the long stay at the lodge, the two Iteeche, Ron and Ted, found themselves with no humans to talk to. Ted stumbled upon a small collection of vids and news items hidden away in the bungalow they occupied. Most concerned local Texarkana issues.

But a couple of old newsmagazines were from the time of the breakup of the Society of Humanity. The whole story, unedited and ugly.

Oops, Kris thought as she tried, unsuccessfully, to keep her mouth from hanging open as he talked.

Ron, not being a dumb bunny, quickly figured out how to use the vid in their cabin to wander what passed for a net on Texarkana. With Kris's staff distracted, the Iteeche had plenty of time to tap into places like Denver's main library.

By the time Ron dropped his own bomb on Kris and her staff, he and his crew had a very good handle on recent human history and technological development.

"It seems that you live in interesting times," Ron said as he finished.

"That is an old Earth curse."

"It is also an old Iteeche curse."

Kris let the silence hang there for a moment, then decided there was nothing else to do but play her cards faceup . . . even the ones she usually kept up her sleeve. "You can understand why we did not want to show you how divided we are."

"You fear that we would attack you in this vulnerability?"

"Some of us do."

"You?"

Kris shook her head. "No. The surest way for the Iteeche to reunite all humanity would be to start up the old war. There are still a lot of people who hate you. Who want to kill Iteeche."

"And you didn't trust me to draw the same conclusion."

"I was not allowed to apply my own judgment. Are you free to do what you want when you speak for your emperor?"

"You know I am not."

"And you know I can only speak the words my great-grandfather orders me to speak. For you and for me, our freedom lies in talking about things outside of our orders."

"A very good thought," Ron said. He turned. "Will you come with me to the forward lounge? I wish to speak with you alone."

"I could order everyone out of this room."

He shook his shoulders, all four of them. "This room is too small."

It was early; the lounge was empty. Kris locked the door, then followed Ron to the forward window, which looked out on the black of space . . . or the tiny lights of distant suns.

What did Kris see this morning, the darkness or the light? More important, what did Ron see?

"I can understand your not wanting us to know how divided you humans are," Ron said, his back to Kris. "My chooser gave me specific instructions not to let on how divided the Iteeche Empire has become."

Kris wanted to yelp "divided Iteeche Empire!" but she bit her tongue. Ron was talking. Better to let him tell it his way. If he didn't, she was pretty sure she couldn't get what she wanted out of him.

"I now realize how wrong my chooser was in his own assumptions." Ron turned to Kris, took her hands in two of his, and went on. "If Ray of the Long-Reaching Knife decides to join with us, he will not bring all of humanity with him. His alliance of one hundred and thirty planets is fragile. Half of them could splinter off from him over us. Am I not right?"

Kris nodded. "If we don't handle this challenge just right, humanity could go to war with itself."

"Just as we Iteeche could go to war with ourselves," Ron said, dropping Kris's hands and beginning to pace in a circle around the lounge.

"In the very first year in the Palace of Learning, we tell

the still-stumbling Iteeche how Brave Harka, the Bold, the Gatherer, the Victorious, demanded double the levee from the Satraps. You must understand, Kris, three out of every four soldiers, warships, supplies are reserved for the defense of the Satrap. Only one out of four may be demanded by the Emperor.

"But that was not enough for Harka the Bold. He demanded and gathered in a double levee after word came of our defeat in Gor'zon. No matter who these strangers who walked on only two feet were, they had to be taught a lesson not to trifle with the Empire."

"So that is how the third phase of the Iteeche War got started," Kris said.

"Oh, it was not easy. Originally, Harka was all for waiting to see what you humans did next. You had defeated a Satrap Lord, killed him, but you had not occupied a single planet! What secret did you hold up your two sleeves? So we waited. Waiting is the thing my Empire is best at.

"But among Harka's advisors was one who knew that you humans would not stop. That if we let you humans consolidate your victory, subdue just one of our Satraps, you would roll like a tsunami over the rest of the Empire. Not now, but soon. Very soon.

"My chooser, Roth'sum'We'sum'Quin of the ancient Chap'sum'We clan, knew he was taking his head in his own hands when he entered the Imperial presence to argue for action when most were all for quiet observation of you strange people."

Kris was having problems getting her mind around what Ron had just said. "Hold it. Are you telling me that Roth the Peacemaker was in favor of counterattacking us after Gor'zon?"

"You look surprised."

"I am surprised."

"Have you never been for something before you were against it?"

"Never something that involved the deaths of millions of humans and Iteeche."

"My chooser has much to make up for. I expect to pay a high price in his name."

"So he argued to reignite the war and escalate it," Kris said.

"For eight days the debate went on before the throne. You must understand us, Kris. One can argue before the throne for a day and a day and still hope to keep one's head. But to refuse to accept harmony for hour after hour, sunset after sunset. The opposition had already chosen the pike for his head by the fourth day. Only the gods of the heaven and stars know why he was allowed to talk on and on and on."

"This is not a metaphor. You are really talking death here."

"Are not your politics blood sport? No one becomes an advisor to the Imperial Presence without making out his will."

Kris glanced down at the casts still on her legs and the crutches that held her up. "We're not quite as willing to admit the risks involved in public service," she said dryly.

"The surprise was that my chooser began to win over other advisors. You humans were new, strange, and unpredictable. An Iteeche who has seized a Satrap will pause to send forth heralds, but you did not send forth anything. Your silence shouted defiance."

"We didn't know your rules." Kris said. "Hold it, Ron. You have policies and procedures for when an Iteeche takes over a Satrap. You keep three-quarters of your fleets at home to protect the Satraps. I thought . . . we all think that when your Emperor says jump, you Iteeche only ask 'how high' on the way up."

"We Iteeche have done our best to see that you humans are very ill informed about us. Imagine my surprise when I discovered that you had kept us just as ill informed about you."

"Turnabout is fair play, but none of this helped you and me much."

"So I begin to think."

"So, your grampa won the debate, and your fleet counterattacked us," Kris said.

"And many died before the slaughter was ended."

Kris had never talked this honestly with an Iteeche. She suspected no human and Iteeche ever had. "Can I ask you a personal question?"

"I will tell you no lie. If I have an answer for you, you will have it. If I cannot answer it, I will not."

"My great-grandmother, Rita Longknife, was an admiral at the battle of the Orange Nebula. She led a battle scout squadron on a sweep around your flank that hit your rear."

"I know of that part of the battle. They smashed our transports, causing much slaughter and reducing our invasion forces so much that we had to forgo the planned landings on Zon'zon."

Ron paused. "Your great-grandmother commanded that assault?"

"Yes."

"What was her relationship to Ray of the Long-Reaching Knife?"

"Wife," Kris said. "They had spawned three children during the war."

"Oh gods of the dark depths, this happened and Ray never spoke of this to my chooser?"

"Apparently not. Can you tell me what happened to those ships? They never returned."

"I am not surprised that they did not," Ron said slowly. "They fell upon our weakly armed transports like a feeding frenzy, opening them to space and dumping cohort after cohort to their death. We had to call back several battle squadrons to put an end to the slaughter. Your great-grandmother's squadron fell back before them. The battle still raged as they went into a jump point at high speed."

"Were they still rotating their ships as they jumped?" Kris asked.

"I believe so. It was your practice then to spin your ships to spread the effect of our weapons over more of the ice cladding you used. That is a very bad practice. Don't you know that spinning a ship leads to random results at a jump point? High speed and a spin is an invitation to go somewhere and never return."

"We know that," Kris said. "But there was a war on."

"And so many died."

"Thank you. I don't know if I'll tell my great-grandfather about this. We all suspect that was the story. Now, I guess, I know it is."

Even at this gentle acceleration, Kris's body was complaining from way too many places, but no way did she want to end their talk. She made her way over to a sofa, collapsed on it, elevated her cast-enclosed legs, and put the crutches in easy reach.

"So, you know that we've got a long, uphill struggle to get humanity behind an effort to help you. Would you mind spelling out for me just exactly what the situation is in the Empire. I'm not sure just how bad it is for you."

"It is bad. I was told as a youngster that Emperor Harka was the bold, the victorious. In the halls of the palace, out of earshot of his chosen, he is more often called the hasty, the wasteful, and when they do not know I am listening, the poorly advised."

"That must be very painful for you."

"My chooser tells me that an advisor has no right to feelings. Feelings are for farmers and poets. Still, I think he feels he failed his emperor and is trying now to make it up to his chosen one, the new emperor, in what he thinks is an even-greater threat."

That was an interesting thought. "Might this whole crisis be an old man seeking redemption for the blunders of his youth? What do you think?"

"I know that the ships go out, and they do not come back. How many scout ships have you lost recently?"

"I'm not aware of any missing scouts, and I say that as someone who skippers one of them. If we were losing ships, I'd know."

"We are losing ships," Ron said with deadly finality. "When I return from this mission, successful or not, I will ask to take out a scout, to make my own effort at defining what we face."

"I kind of wish you wouldn't," Kris said. "You and I have built a bridge between us. There aren't a lot of bridges between our two people. I'd like to be able to deal with you again. I know I can trust you. I'm not so sure about the next guy."

"You make me think I might be worth more alive than as a dead datum on a star chart."

"Think about it," Kris said. "We need to get back to our people. I propose that we have Nelly tell them they are wanted in the forward lounge. We can get them together again and knock heads if they don't want to tell the truth, the whole truth, and nothing but the truth."

"That is a strange choice of words. I have run across it several times but don't know what it means."

"Let me tell you about my day in court," Kris said, as Nelly made the calls that would gather what wits they had about them.

40

The *Wasp* nuzzled into its usual pier at High Wardhaven station. This dock was reserved exclusively for ships involved in Admiral Crossenshield's black ops.

Kris made a note to Nelly to remind herself to pick a fight with Crossie and make sure he understood the *Wasp* was not one of his black boats. The *Wasp* was an explorer. A scout.

Kris Longknife did not do black ops.

Usually.

There was no message traffic while they crossed the space from Jump Point Alpha to the station. Still, three Marine lieutenants were waiting on the pier. As requested, Jack was getting two more platoons for his company. The third first lieutenant would replace the slowly recuperating Lieutenant Troy. A hundred determined-looking line-beasts filed aboard with their duffels.

"Good Lord, they look so young," Kris said softly to Jack.

"No, it's just that we're getting ancient. If it's the miles, not the years, we are way overdue for retirement."

"Speak for yourself. I'm still having fun."

"Yeah. Right. You ready for that commander lurking on the pier?"

"What's he doing here?" Kris asked.

"I have no idea, but I think you'll find out soon enough."

The commander crossed the brow once the Marines had been led below. He saluted the flag and the JOOD before saying, "I'm Princess Kristine's guide. Would you please have her report to the quarterdeck."

"And whom should she bring with her?" Kris asked.

"No one. She's to come alone with me."

"Jack, get Penny and Abby up here, pronto. Ask Gunny to bring along four strapping Marines."

"King Raymond said she was to come alone," the commander insisted.

"All the more reason not to," Kris shot back.

"Are you Princess Kristine?" the commander said, taking in her crutches but still not offering his name.

"I occasionally go by that name."

"I was told you'd been injured, but that you had recovered."

"The reports of my recovery may be a bit exaggerated."

"Yes, Your Highness. I will call an electric station cart."

"We would be grateful for that courtesy."

"Your Majesty," the guy was getting flustered, "I was instructed to make your travel as inconspicuous as possible. A batch of Marine goons and half your friends will be rather noticeable."

"Commander, my Marines are never goons, and my staff is all of my friends who have survived the experience. Jack. Add the colonel."

"I already did, Kris. I also told everyone to skip the uniforms. Commander, Her Highness's security staff knows very well how to do inconspicuous even when she is damn near naked."

"No need to bring that up, Jack," Kris said, swallowing a grin. Clearly, the commander had been poorly briefed on her and the company she kept.

"Did Crossie give you your orders?" Kris asked.

"Admiral Crossenshield, Commander of Wardhaven Military Intelligence, did give me my orders, Your Highness," the commander said, stiffening his spine.

"Next time you see Crossie, tell him that I do not work for him. Now, since I see that the thundering herd has arrived, and a cart as well, let's get a move on."

Kris took a seat in the rear, between Jack and Colonel Cortez. Penny settled into the front passenger seat. Abby expelled the driver from his station and took over his job.

That left the commander walking beside Gunny as the four Marines in neat civilian clothes failed to project any other appearance than that of four strong Marines out of uniform.

"The station trolley line," the commander ordered, and Abby slowly rolled down the pier and took a left.

At 0200, this section of the station was quiet. The trolley was empty. At the space-elevator pier, the commander led them through a small door and to their own boarding station.

Kris had never seen this section on the ferry, and said so.

"Admiral Crossenshield added this entrance and travel cabin to the space-elevator ferries last time they were overhauled. It comes in very handy in these troubled times."

Kris considered demanding that they join the rest of the passengers on the ferry, then reconsidered. She ought to wait until she was more recovered from the last bombing before she risked the next one.

They did have to walk the length of the ferry once it docked dirtside, but the commander had recovered. Two large black ground vehicles were waiting for them at a side entrance to the station.

"Where do we go from here?" Kris asked.

"My instructions are to take you to Nuu House to await your meetings."

"And they are with?"

"I was not told," the commander admitted.

"Jack, I don't need the Marines at Nuu House. I was raised there, and if it's not safe, we're way past trouble. You can send Gunny and his Marines back."

Jack did.

The heavy rig drove streets that had familiar names to Kris, but little else was the same. New buildings, taller and shinier, had sprouted where the smaller, older buildings of her youth had been. The Prime Minister was not letting the tense situation out among the stars slow down Wardhaven's economy.

Nuu House had not changed. The vehicle came to a halt in the circular driveway. Kris and her people got out.

The commander did not. Did Kris catch him in a sigh of relief? She really couldn't blame him. He should have been better briefed before his brush with one-of-those-damn-Longknifes.

Kris entered the familiar foyer, its unchanged spiral of black-and-white tiles still circling around to the center of the room. She and Eddy had walked those tiles, careful to stay on black, never a misstep to white.

Kris's childhood seemed a million years ago.

For a moment, she wondered who had designed that floor. Who had ordered it built? Great-grampa Ray, the near-mythical Great-great-grampa Nuu, or maybe the forlorn Rita in the little peace she'd had before one war cascaded into another and another until it killed her . . . or sent her into a bad jump she never returned from.

"You're late. What took you so long?" came in a gruff voice from the library off the foyer.

"We're right on time," Kris shot back to her grampa. "You know the beanstalk's schedule better than I do."

"If the king is here, and you are not, you are late."

Turning her crutches to the library, Kris made her way, one step at a time, into the room. It smelled of books and eternity. She'd loved to play hide-and-seek in here with Eddy, and after he died, she would set herself up in a corner with a good book and dream that he'd suddenly shout, "I see you. You're it!"

Mother and Father weren't the only members of the family locked in problem grief.

"I wasn't told that you were still on crutches," the king said as he pointed Kris at a chair across from him. Crossie and General Mac filled a couch at his right hand. Kris made for her chair, but first nodded her team to a long sofa across from the brass.

With poorly concealed reluctance, they went where she pointed.

"So much for a private meeting," Crossie said.

"I don't work for you," Kris said. "What do I have to do to make that clear?"

"But you do work for me," Mac said. "And your grampa, the king."

"So I've been told," Kris said, getting her legs comfortable on an ottoman that Jack brought over. He took her crutches and set them within easy reach before he took his seat on the sofa closest to her. It was kind of him to make it easy for her to stomp out if she chose to. She wouldn't have to ask anyone to give her a hand up.

Jack was getting to understand her too damn well.

He was also taking very good care of her . . . when she let him.

Relaxed into her seat, Kris stared at the troublesome trinity across from her. They stared back at her.

No one seemed eager to say anything.

So Kris took the bull by the horns. "I settled your hash on Texarkana. Did you get the vote you needed?"

"We did," the king said, showing none of the joy Kris expected. "I'm stuck in this job for the next ten years."

"And if you are the king, I'm stuck being a princess," Kris said, trying not to sound too bitter. She had made the princess thing work.

Once or twice.

And it hadn't killed her.

Yet.

"You really shook things up on Texarkana," the king said, changing the subject.

"And surprise, surprise, I lived through it. That place did need shaking up. There were a few things about it you didn't mention when you gave me the job. Maybe they slipped your mind."

"That's possible," the king allowed.

"How many more of these pipe dreamers from Earth do we have out here? How many groups of discontents from an odd corner of Earth all hot to trot to do things their way out on a blank slate among the stars? Grampa, can't we do something to get all these planets settled down once and for all?"

"You have any suggestion how we straighten out New Jerusalem?"

"They're not in your United Sentients."

"But their problems have a way of seeping out to places like . . . What was that place, Colonel?"

"Pandemonium, Your Majesty," Colonel Cortez supplied.

"They shortened it to Panda," Kris put in.

"But rented muscle from New J almost ripped their heads off," Crossie said.

"Locals didn't do such a bad job of handling themselves. We helped a bit."

"More than a bit, from my reports," Crossie insisted.

"If I didn't know better, I'd say you set me up for that one," Kris growled.

The admiral raised both hands, palms out. "You walked into that one on your own. By the way, thank you very much for settling it for us."

"You're welcome, I guess," Kris said, and noticed that she'd been deftly deflected from what she wanted to talk about. She fixed the king with a glare and put an end to that.

"Grampa, I did my part for you on Texarkana. What did you do for my Iteeche while I was gone?"

"Not interested in any more chitchat?"

"Nope."

"Even if the king decrees it?"

"Nope. The king and I have this bargain, you see, Grampa. I pulled one of his chestnuts out of the fire. He keeps the whole damn forest of chestnut trees from going up in flames."

"Glad to see you're giving me credit for a tougher problem."

"Can you honestly say yours was tougher when I'm the one on crutches?"

"You didn't duck fast enough."

"I ducked, but the bombs were coming from above."

"You need to post more lookouts, Captain," the king said to Jack. The general was talking now.

"Yes, sir," Jack said, stiffening to attention and going into report mode. "My company is being reinforced as we speak. We're adding two platoons and bringing the other two platoons up to full strength after the casualties they've suffered over the last three months. This should allow me to maintain a secure perimeter within an outer perimeter bubble, sir."

"Very good," the general said.

"Now, Grampa, King, Hammer of the Iteeche, what can I tell my friend Ron that he can expect human space will do for them and their problem?"

"Insistent, isn't she?" General Mac said.

"Like everyone in her family," the king agreed. "Kris, you will have to tell your friend Ron that I can't offer him anything at this time. He can go back to Roth and tell that old buzzard that I need more time to prepare my people for this. It's too big a change for me to make overnight.

"And besides, he doesn't have anything really to tell me about the menace. Some ships have disappeared. Ships always go missing. How can I get humanity all ready to ride with nothing but a bit of dust on the horizon?"

"Grampa, you know as well as I do that when ships go missing, it's random. One here. One there. Not four or five in the same chunk of space," Kris put in.

"I need more evidence before I can go to the general public, Kris," King Raymond insisted. "This is just a bogeyman under the bed, and it's under an Iteeche bed at that."

"Ron plans on leading a scout out to see what he can see."

"That would be good."

"No, it will be very bad. Lousy bad. He'll probably just get himself killed, and we won't know any more than we did."

"What's this Ron to you?" Grampa asked, an eyebrow raised.

"He's a friend. A friend who doesn't lie to me. And yes, Crossie, you'll be getting a full report on the present situation in the Iteeche Empire. The real lowdown on who's doing what to whom. Abby will send this report just to you. And we want a nice paycheck for letting you have it exclusively."

"And she says she doesn't work for me," the admiral said, preening.

"Keep that up, and I'll burn her disk to ash."

The admiral got very quiet.

"Grampa, if Ron's going out to stick his head into whatever maw is out there, I think I ought to go with him."

"You can't do it, girl."

"I and my ship are the best for the job. We've got the new atom laser. We can spot the fuzzy jump holes. I think we could use them to get around the perimeter of this thing. See what it leaves behind it."

"That's assuming that it is traveling along and leaving something behind it, not expanding, expanding, expanding," Crossie said.

"Either could be wrong assumptions," the king added.

"All are guesses until we get some solid data," Kris pointed out. "And as you just noted, you can't get anything going here in human space with the little data the Iteeche have. The *Wasp* and its crew is the best we have. You need information. Let me get it." Kris tried to keep her voice low. To strip her words of the frustration she was feeling. It was frustration she felt. Not anger. Not yet.

"Kris, you are not going out with Ron," the king said firmly. "You've already got your next assignment, and it's one I don't think anyone else but you can do."

Where had Kris heard that before? "Try to persuade me," Kris drawled.

The king turned to General Mac.

"Kris," the Chairman of the General Staff said, "the Peterwalds' worlds are locked in a low-grade civil war. Their Navy is pretty much tied up at the pier providing muscle while the Peterwalds settle their scores with State Security."

"It's not really that simple," Crossie put in. "There are all kinds of scores getting settled. The Peterwalds built their empire by importing people from Earth who had hundreds, thousands of years of bad blood between them back there. They played them off against each other while using the iron grip of State Security to keep the blood from flowing in the streets."

"So when you pop the head of State Security," Kris said, "all kinds of bloody things come out to play."

"You've got it," Mac said.

"But we don't interfere in the internal affairs of sovereign states," Kris pointed out. There was no job for her in anything they'd said. So far. And this rambling around was moving her frustration closer and closer to a full-fledged mad.

"Spoken so sincerely by the woman who offed Hank Peterwald, the thirteenth, the heir apparent, and then saved Harry Peterwald the twelfth, the reigning nonemperor," Crossie said, giving a quick review of Kris's last nine months.

"Both seemed like a good idea at the time," Kris said with the best innocent shrug she could manage.

"Well, while the cats are scoring their own points, the rats are getting out of hand. We've got problems with pirates," the king said. "Pirates and refugees."

"Pirates and refugees?" Kris said. "That's the strangest combination I have ever heard. Any chance you'll explain it to little old me?"

The king seemed about to choke on that, but said, "People are fleeing the internal strife on more and more Peterwald planets. They're heading out to Sooner territory, setting up refugee camps there or on totally new planets. Horrible conditions. Some have even ended up on pirate planets. We think there are at least two planets that have become pirate bases. People there are no better than slaves."

"Our reliable sources tell us that a couple of new designer drugs that have recently shown up in human space are coming from them," Crossie said.

"There's one more thing, Kris," Mac said. "These refugees are grabbing whatever they can lay their hands on and cramming themselves into any ship that can risk space. Not all of them get where they are going, Lieutenant. You'll need to be ready to take on refugees as well as knock heads in your next job."

"What next job?"

"We're giving you command of Patrol Squadron 10, Kris," Mac said. "It isn't much, just a couple of armed merchant ships like the *Wasp*. We want you to patrol the open border of Greenfeld territory looking for pirates, drugs, whatever."

"What does Peterwald think about this?"

"We haven't asked him," the king said. "And I don't intend to. That why I'm sending you. He owes you his life. You seem to have gotten along with his daughter, Vicky. I'm hoping that they won't take you for a poacher in their space."

Kris leaned back in her chair. She wanted to be mad. She wanted to let her frustration rage at them for not letting her do the job she wanted to do. And yet, there was no question that if the U.S. sent a squadron of cruisers to patrol along the Greenfeld border, there would be all kinds of hell to pay . . . maybe even war if one horrible misstep led to another.

Kris let out a sigh. A couple of converted merchants with their lasers carefully hidden might not cause the same problems.

And Vicky. Well, if the two of them got together, they might have a few minutes of good time. And take a little bit of the heat off the situation.

Once again, they'd gotten to her. One more time, they'd found the job that she just might be the only one who could do. The first time it happened, she'd been swept off her feet. Delighted to be the only one with the right finger to fit in the dike. It was amazing how fast that lost its luster.

Or maybe she was developing her own opinion as to which dike she wanted to put her finger in.

Kris sighed. "I'll take the job. But how's a lieutenant supposed to command a squadron, even of converts?"

Mac pulled out an envelope and poured its contents on the table in front of him. Two shoulder boards fell out. Shoulder boards with the two and a half stripes of a lieutenant commander.

"Congratulations, Commander," General Mac said. "You just made it into the window for double-deep selection. I've arranged to have all the paperwork cut so that you'll have about ten minutes' seniority on all the other lieutenant commanders in your squadron."

"This is going to be so much fun," Kris grumbled.

The king stood. It was clear to all that he'd done what he had come for and was eager to go. Kris levered herself out of the chair. The others stood, and he made his exit.

Admiral Crossenshield followed in the king's footsteps up to the door, then paused. "Your plug-in for Nelly to your brain got slagged by that bomb?"

"It very much did," Kris admitted.

"You'll need to get that fixed."

"I'll see what I can do about it before I sail."

"I've got you scheduled with the best brain surgeon on Wardhaven for nine tomorrow morning."

"He'll need to see my medical records."

"I had them sent from Texarkana. You took a slow boat home, darling. She finished studying them last week. You go in. She'll do a quick check. If there are no surprises, she'll fix you up before you leave."

"I don't work for you, *honey*," Kris snapped, returning a "honey" for his "darling."

"But isn't it nice having me look after you once in a while?"

Kris said something evil that only made Crossie laugh as he followed the king.

General Mac paused beside Kris in his own exit. "Here is a list of the ships in PatRon 10. Taussig has the *Hornet*. Jack Campbell has the *Dauntless*. You don't know him, but he's good people."

Kris glanced down the flimsy. Skippers' names were matched with ships and their types, but it told her very little. What fighting capability did the *Hornet* or *Dauntless* have? A supply ship was named the *Surprise*. That . . . was not encouraging. "Thank you," she told the general.

Once the elders were gone, Kris and her team collapsed into their seats. "Kris," the colonel said, "I don't mind fighting your fights, but attending your senior staff meetings. It's taking years off my life."

"What's the matter with you wimps? Can't handle a little family get-together with my grampa?" Kris said, relaxing deep into her chair.

"Maybe I could," the colonel said, "if there were fewer stars in the room."

"Maybe I could," Penny added, "if you didn't always turn them into fights. I *love* my grandpop!"

"Lucky you. Penny, can you run up to the *Wasp* and let Ron in on the secret. I don't think he'll be surprised. Tell him we'll be headed out for the demilitarized zone in a couple of days. Until then, he can use my library card at Wardhaven U."

"You going to the doc tomorrow?" Jack asked.

"Yeah, I kind of miss having Nelly bouncing around in my head."

"You sure you can trust any doc Crossie hired?" Jack whispered.

"Nelly, can you do a thorough check for a bug."

"Yes, Kris."

Nelly was kind of quiet these days. Kris found she liked the quiet, too, and missed the lip, both at the same time.

Weird.

The others left to find the rooms prepared for them. Kris stayed until all of them were gone.

"Nelly, is this room secure?"

"Yes, Kris. They swept it for the king, and he didn't leave anything behind. Not even Crossie did."

"I thought now might be safe. Nelly, I'm mad."

"I noticed that your pulse was up. Are you okay?"

"No more than the usual pain. I got a ringing in my ear that sounds like an out-of-tune brass band. But mainly, I'm mad. Mad that Grampa Ray isn't helping Ron. Blast it, Nelly, he didn't tell me a single thing he did to help the Iteeche. As far as I can tell, I damn near got myself killed doing what he asked of me, and he didn't do a single thing to help Ron."

"You don't know that, Kris. He could have done things. He just didn't tell you. It was a very brief meeting."

"He made sure it was short. They arranged it so I never got to ask him anything specific. I could really hate that man."

"I'm sorry you feel that way, Kris."

"Nelly, you are not my shrink."

"No, I am not, Kris, but you told me once it is important to talk things out. I am willing to listen."

"Thanks, Nelly, but the person I really need to talk with is someone who has experience dealing with us damn Longknifes. Gramma Ruth or . . ." Kris ran out of people. "Wouldn't be any good to talk to Father or Honovi. They're in the middle of it."

"Would Admiral Santiago be one you could talk to?"

"Yes," Kris said. "She and her family have had a lot of experience dealing with us damn Longknifes, but she's at Chance."

"Not right now, Kris. She's making a report or attending a meeting or something right here on Wardhaven."

"Message her, Nelly. Ask her if she could come by Nuu House at 1900 tomorrow—2000! Anytime she wants."

"I've done it. She hasn't answered, but I will tell you when she does."

"Good, Nelly. Good. I should have realized sooner. I don't need to talk to Longknifes about how to survive us. I need to talk to people who have survived us. Sandy's just the one."

41

Next evening, Kris ate a light supper. The surgery had been successful; Nelly was once more directly jacked into Kris's brain. She was quiet but there. Chief Beni ordered a new net jack to replace the one destroyed, one he swore would be impossible to jam.

Kris's team was doing personal errands when the doorbell rang. Crutches gone, but now using two canes, Kris opened the door herself.

"Sandy, I'm so glad to see you."

"Maybe not so much when you see who I brought," the admiral said as she stepped aside. Kris got her first look at the young man behind her.

"Who's he?" Kris said. She knew she sounded rude. But she was due for some more painkillers, and she'd been looking forward to some honest talk with one of the few people she trusted.

"I'm Winston Spencer. I wrote a story for the admiral when she was skipper of a destroyer about life in the little boys."

Sandy cut in. "And he also wrote the best story I saw on the Battle of Wardhaven."

The reporter seemed encouraged. "I was one of the few who reported that you were the real commander of the defense that saved our skins."

Kris snorted. "And you were wrong. There were a lot of people senior to me who did more than their bit to get us out of that mess. It was the people on the boats that deserve most of the credit, and too many of them paid for it with their lives."

They fell silent, there in the open door for a long moment. When nobody broke the quiet, Kris took a hammer to it. "So what are you doing here when I only invited Sandy?"

"Kris, I think we should step inside," the admiral said.

Kris struggled to take a step back, then pointed them to the library. They entered; Kris took the same seat she'd had the night before. Sandy sat where Jack had; the reporter took Crossenshield's place. Not too smart of him.

"There are drinks at the bar," Kris said.

Winston hopped to his feet and only seemed dismayed when he found his choices. "Tea or coffee! Don't you have anything stronger?"

"Not when I set them up," Kris said.

"So the stories about you are true. You don't drink," the reporter said, pouring tea.

"At least that part of my story is true," Kris admitted, eyeing Sandy, willing her to explain the strange presence of this interloper. Sandy had crossed her hands in her lap and was doing a rather good imitation of a silent Buddha.

Three glasses of ice tea on a tray, the reporter headed back to his seat. Still, he couldn't take his eyes off the surroundings. "So this is the library of Nuu House. If only these walls could talk."

"If they did, half the history books in human space would have to be rewritten," Kris said dryly, as he handed her one of the glasses.

"Still, a reporter would love to know," Winston said, handing Sandy a glass before taking his seat. He raised his glass in salute and took a sip.

If he wanted stories, Kris had one she didn't mind sharing. "I found an early draft of one of Grampa Ray's speeches once," she said.

"What did you do with it?"

"I was seven, my brother Eddy was three. We made paper airplanes out of it."

Winston groaned. Sandy showed a mother's gentle smile.

"But my big brother Honovi was twelve, and he intervened before the papers were more than bent. Someday, students will be able to compare that draft with the final one."

"Thank heavens for big brothers," the reporter said.

"So, the truth has some value to you?" Kris said.

"It's very important to me," he shot back.

"As a child I believed in *the* truth," Sandy said. "Now I find that there are truths and truths, and it's often hard to separate them."

"Don't try to confuse me, Admiral," Winston said.

"Either of you two want to tell me why a quiet evening with one of my friends has turned into a mob scene debating philosophy?" Kris asked.

Sandy waved her glass toward Winston.

He cleared his throat. "I have it from good sources that King Raymond is holding secret talks with representatives of the Iteeche Empire concerning humanity's capitulation to the Empire." The words were fairly racing out of his mouth before he finished.

At "King Raymond," Kris froze her smile. At "secret talks," she locked every muscle on her face down tight. At "Iteeche Empire," she locked every muscle in her body where it was.

That was a good thing, because when he got to "humanity's capitulation," she managed not to strangle him.

Who was talking to this nut? No, the talker was the nut, this kid was just the poor reporter being taken for a ride.

Trying to look as casual as possible, Kris turned to Sandy. "And you told him?"

"I told him his source was feeding him a load of bull. But he insisted that you would know the truth about this, so I decided to bring him along. Sorry about the surprise. He only got ahold of me two hours ago, and I didn't think this was something to talk about over the net."

"Thanks," Kris said, her mind spinning as she used every second Sandy gave her to think.

Who was his source? Had that source lied about the meetings' purpose, or was the reporter adding that as part of a fishing expedition? Should she shoot him right now?

That could be embarrassing, and it hardly seemed like the thing you do in front of guests like Sandy.

No, she'd have to muscle this one out herself.

"I don't know who in the opposition fed you this line, Mr. Spencer. It beats me why they'd waste time creating a story this wild when Father doesn't have to call for new elections for two, three years. Taken as a whole, this is a total fantasy." That wasn't actually a lie. Maybe Kris had missed her calling as a politician.

God forbid.

"Maybe some of the story I got was wrong. But the Iteeche have been with you. And they have talked to your great-grandfather, the king."

There was no way not to lie to that. No way, except . . . "Who's feeding you this stuff?"

"Wardhaven has shield laws. I don't have to tell you my sources, and you can't make me."

"I thought you cared about the truth," Kris snapped.

"I do. That's why I'm here. What is the truth about the Iteeche and King Ray?"

Oh, if only Kris could tell him *all* that truth. She settled for continuing her attack. "Spencer, look at the story you've got. It doesn't hold together. Why would King Ray be talking surrender? We beat them last war. Just ask any vet."

"But it has been eighty years since we've had any kind of war. We've gone soft. Lost our edge."

"Now you're sounding like the opposition," Kris snapped. "Remember, you're talking about Ray Longknife, Hammer of the Iteeche."

"And I'm talking to his great-granddaughter, who's got orders to way-out-to-hell-and-gone. Just the thing I'd do if she'd been hauling Iteeche around in her own private yacht. Those orders would keep her and her crew from talking."

"There's a reason for my new set of orders. Sandy, I've made lieutenant commander!"

"Congratulations. Wasn't that very deep selection?"

"Only a year. Maybe a bit more," Kris admitted.

"A bribe?" the reporter put in.

"Hardly. If they counted every attempt on my life as a year's extra service, I'd be eligible for admiral."

"God help us all," Sandy said, folding her hands and casting her eyes prayerfully to heaven.

"Okay," Winston growled, taking a long pull on his drink as if it might somehow become more powerful if he treated it like it was, "I know there's something up. I know it involves Iteeche. You've told me that I'm being lied to by my sources. Some of them. You can go off to your jobs and leave me here with just a pinch of this and a dash of that, and I'll keep looking for the truth. But you're not being very smart.

"This story is going to come out. It's got legs, and twisted one way or the other, it can hurt you. It could even bring down a government. Tell me nothing, and I'm going to hunt, and I'm going to hunt, and I'm going to find the fire that's leaking this smoke.

"Then it will come out. Hopefully with more right and less wrong in it, but it is going to come out. King Ray and Iteeche is too big a story just to lie there and go nowhere."

Kris had heard that argument . . . years ago from a college professor. She'd argued with him and had to appeal her final grade. She'd won, but the bad feelings remained.

Kris had once talked honestly with a reporter. She was ten. The results were a disaster. Her father hadn't said much to her, just looked disappointed. She'd sworn she'd never make that mistake again.

She ought to throw this fellow out of the house.

No way she could physically do that. Though hitting him over the head repeatedly with her canes seemed promising.

"Sandy, you know this guy. Any chance he means what he's saying?"

The admiral chewed her lower lip for a half minute, eyeing the reporter. Eyed him long enough that he started to fidget.

"I think he believes what he is saying . . . right now. Tomorrow, a month from now, I don't know what he will think then. You and I take an oath to protect and defend. He is committed to the truth. But the truth is a slippery thing, I've learned. Makes one a whole lot less resolute over the long run."

"Is that why reporters seem to go wherever the wind is blowing?" Kris said.

"Wherever the story is," Winston put in. "We do what we have to do to get the story."

"'Story,' not truth?" Kris said, cutting the legs out from under him.

He was honest enough to smile. "You got me there. The story is what we get paid for, and it's what we think about the most. But we can be trusted with truth."

"Truth above story?" Kris asked.

"There are times when the truth is bigger than the story," Winston admitted.

Kris studied him when he said that. He did not flinch but looked her square in the face.

"How good is this fellow?" Kris asked Sandy.

"Good at getting to the bottom of things. He asked the hard questions, both for his story on my destroyer and after the battle. And his stories had traction. People read them. I think he had a definite impact on the public."

"So he can change things?" Kris said.

Sandy eyed the reporter. "Yes, I think he can change things."

"Are you good?" Kris asked.

"I'm good at what I do," Winston Spencer said.

"We may have a chance to see how good you are," Kris said.

"Sandy, Winston is right about one thing, I do have orders for a patrol out beyond the Rim. I'm going to be out of the flow of news, and definitely far away from any chance I might have to change the way the public looks at things."

"If that's where things need doing, isn't that the place to be?" Sandy asked.

"I find myself wondering a bit about that when those damn Longknifes send me there time after time because I'm the only one who can do anything about it."

"And that was what you wanted to talk to me about?"

"Yeah. How do you keep from being run around like a bull with a ring in your nose?"

"Don't ask me. I've got this ring in my nose, and I keep running."

"You're no help."

"Let me know if you find a way. I'd love to pass it along to my daughter."

"I've got orders to leave, and I'm going to be in no position to make sure Grampa Ray makes time to address a problem of mine."

"Has he addressed it much?" Sandy asked.

"I can't say that he has. It worries me that he won't."

"Out on Chance, I'm not likely to be much help."

"Yeah. That leaves me wondering if maybe you brought me someone who could be of help."

"Hmm, I got the feeling that your grampa Ray isn't going to much care about being reminded about what he doesn't want to do."

"There's a real chance of that."

"Ah, folks," Winston said, cutting in. "I'm not following what you're talking about, but I'm starting to like it less and less."

"You remember that time on the *Halsey*," Sandy said. "You asked if I could arrange a meeting between you and the princess."

"Yes, and you said you'd do me a favor and not get me an interview. 'Folks live longer if they keep their distance from those Longknifes.'"

"You can't say I didn't warn you," Sandy said.

"She's right, you know," Kris said.

"I'm starting to think maybe she might be."

Kris ignored the young man. "Sandy, I'm contemplating what some uncharitable people might call treason. I'm thinking I ought to give you a chance to walk out of here before I decide anything definite."

"What about me?" Winston asked. "Don't I get a chance?"

"Nope. You came in here asking for the truth. If it happens to slap you in the face, you ought to be grateful." Kris turned back to Sandy. "You once told me that you were sick and tired of the Longknife legend growing at the expense of Santiago family blood. You still feel that way?"

The woman didn't even bat an eyelid. "I seem to remember that not long after I told you that I was risking my own neck and that of my crew to save your delicate rear end."

"Which, as usual, needed saving," Kris admitted.

"Still, yes, I think it is time and past time that other people stop bleeding for you damn Longknifes."

"So there's no chance you'd be willing to listen to something that might save all humanity."

Admiral Sandy Santiago took a long pull on her ice tea. "Might save all humanity, you say."

"I think so."

"Treason, you say."

"It's a possibility. At least at first," Kris admitted.

"If President Urm had lived and my great-grandpoppa had been found with that briefcase bomb, it would have been called treason."

"So I'm told," Kris said.

"Briefcase bomb," the reporter said. "*Her* great-grandpa. I smell a story here."

"Forget it," the admiral said. "I like the Longknife legend just the way it is. For now. Okay, Kris, what are you up to?"

"Nelly," Kris said, "send the meeting package to Winston Spencer's and Admiral Santiago's computers."

"Kris, I don't think this is a good idea."

"Yes, Nelly, but it is what I intend to do. Send it."

Winston's glasses lit up, showing Kris the reverse of the

scene in the *Wasp*'s forward lounge. He leaned back, taking in the view. Sandy's computer was more sophisticated; the scene showed as little more than a gleam on her contact lenses.

The reporter sat up in his chair with a start. "Is that an Iteeche that just walked in?"

"Yes, he is," Kris said. "Nelly, can you speed the action up? The guy in black is an Imperial herald. Those are Marines in red behind him followed by two Navy officers with two Imperial counselors behind them. The last guy in is my friend, Ron, an Imperial Representative."

"Kris, your friends get stranger and stranger," Sandy said.

"Tell me about it."

"And they're talking to you and the king," the reporter observed.

"Yep. You might want to skip ahead. The fun starts five and a half minutes into it. You can go back and see the rest when you have time."

"You're going to let me keep this?" the reporter asked.

"That's my intention."

"That's General Trouble," Winston said. "I mean Tordon, and Crossie from intel. Who's the last guy?"

"Someone who hangs around me. I hope you can delete him if you ever make this public."

"He's your security chief, isn't he? Jack something," Sandy said.

"Yes. Nelly, fast-forward."

Winston was half out of his seat along with Grampa Ray. "What did he just say that got the king's panties in a twist?"

"It will be repeated," Kris said.

"'Mutual enemies'! What does he mean by that?" Winston demanded.

"If you sit back down, you'll find out sooner."

The reporter sat, but rigidly, on the edge of his chair. The admiral stayed loose in her sofa, eyes raised to the ceiling to better see what filled her contact lenses. When the star chart came out, and the explanation began, Mr. Spencer edged back into his chair.

"Their exploration ships are not coming back?" Sandy whispered.

"As the skipper of just such an exploration ship, I can't tell you how much that bothers me," Kris said.

"Yeah, I can only imagine," Winston said, then watched the rest of the meeting in silence. Finished, he took his glasses off and stared for a long moment at some space just over Kris's shoulder.

Into the silence, Kris said softly, "Surrender was not mentioned once by either side."

"Holy . . . Mother of God," Winston whispered finally. "The Iteeche have bit into something too big for them to chew."

Kris glanced at Sandy. The admiral was gnawing her lower lip, apparently lost in thought. "That is a part of the problem," Kris said. "We don't know exactly what the Iteeche have run into. It seems they like to share a problem a lot more and a lot earlier in the problem-solving cycle than we humans do."

"Yeah, I think I see what you mean," Winston said. "That was bothering me as I watched this. They are losing ships. Don't know what's doing it, so they come to us to make nice. Do they want us to go find out what's swallowing their ships whole?"

"They didn't ask specifically for that," Kris said. "I figure I'd be on the first ship headed into the monster's maw. Since I don't have orders to do that, I figure they haven't asked."

"Maybe your grandpappy doesn't want you on that particular scout ship?" Sandy said.

"There is that possibility," Kris admitted. "But family concerns haven't been all that obvious in my previous assignments."

Sandy admitted they hadn't, with a wave of her hand.

"So, explain to me, slowly, and in little words, why you are dropping this . . . one of the biggest stories of the century . . . in my lap?" Mr. Spencer asked.

"Yes," said Sandy, crossing her legs and leaning forward, intently.

"I don't know exactly. You say you're good. How good are you at spotting shadows of stories? Hints of a hint? I'm going to be so far out that I won't be getting any kind of news. I found that out when I came back last time, and my brother dropped a load of stuff on me. You could at least send me any stories you see about the Iteeche."

"That would be kind of obvious," Sandy said.

"So toss in anything about the new constitution, interplanetary politics. What's happening on New J. I ended up fighting a whole lot of mercenaries from New J. Send me what you think I need to keep up-to-date on. But send me everything on the Iteeche. And maybe you could write a story or two about our possible new friends the Iteeche."

"I'm not sure I dare write anything about the Iteeche. What do you think would happen to me if I published this tomorrow?"

"Let's see. You'd end up locked away deep in some dungeon that nobody even knows exists. The key would get lost. Oh, and I'd be in the next cell, right beside you," Kris said with a wide grin.

"That is not funny."

"I was not joking," Kris said.

"I still don't see why you dropped this scorching-hot potato on my cojones?"

"Look at it from my perspective," Kris said. "When I have a problem, I or it usually ends up battered, bashed, and bleeding."

"If not dead," the reporter added.

"No, it's usually a Santiago or some other poor sailor that ends up pushing up tombstones," the admiral countered.

"I can't argue with either of you," Kris said. "But look at my present problem. I ask you, is this the kind of thing that a few kilos of C-8 can take care of?"

"I don't see how," the reporter said. The admiral just shook her head.

"Neither do I, and I can't even see a way to start. So, how do I solve a problem I can't kill or blow up?"

"I have no idea, and I'm beginning to sincerely wish I had kept my hands in my pockets and kept walking when I saw the admiral this afternoon," Winston said, standing.

"But you didn't, so get with the program," Sandy said. "Sit down, Win. She's been ordered off to the left corner of nowhere. There's no way she can do anything from there."

"Now I see why you get orders like that so often," the reporter snapped, showing no willingness to take his seat again.

"Exactly." Kris chuckled. "I'm off chasing pirates, not a bad gig, I assure you. But who's keeping an eye on my grampa? Checking him out to make sure he doesn't forget that the Iteeche can be our friends and that they have a problem. Maybe putting a good word in for the poor Iteeche."

"Not me," Winston squeaked.

"Exactly you," Kris said. "You're a reporter. You know what's really going on around here."

"I used to, but I suddenly got this attack of potted-palm syndrome. Just leave me alone and water me once in a while."

"Didn't you just tell me you're one of the guys that takes the pulse of Wardhaven? Leads the people's dialogue. Helps opinion makers form a consensus they can use to get anything done."

"You realize this is the first time a Longknife has had anything nice to say about the media."

"Of course not. Why I remember Father saying at the dinner table not six years ago that . . . ah . . . Well, maybe you're right," Kris sputtered to a halt.

"Honestly, Win," Admiral Santiago cut in. "Can you tell me that, what with something this important hanging on the wind, you wouldn't want to know what you know and be where you are?"

He sighed. "Damn you," he said, turning his face from

Kris. "Damn you both," he repeated. "You know, if this gets out wrong, you being a Longknife will not protect you."

"I told you, I'd be in the cell next to you."

"And I'll likely be in the cell on the other side of you," Santiago said with a big grin on her face. "My granddad told me there'd be days like this. Even told me how much fun they'd be. I didn't believe him."

"You are both crazy."

"That's a state secret," Kris said. "Spill the beans on that one, and you'll end up in an even worse cell."

While Kris and Santiago had a laugh at that, Winston Spencer settled into his chair. "So the real question before any sane person is how to avoid a cell for all of us," he said, with another sigh. "You win. I'm in. What is it that you want the end of this to look like? You do have an exit strategy that doesn't involve dungeons, don't you?"

"I hadn't really thought much beyond now. None of us in jail sounds good," Kris said.

"Planning is not a Longknife strong suit," Sandy assured him.

"The best way to assure none of us end up in jail is for me to erase this video," Win said.

"I love my great-grandfather, but in this matter, I'm not sure I can trust him. He has gotten scared."

"All well earned, you will admit," Sandy said.

"Yes, but I'm not sure he's not going to just make this whole problem disappear for now, kind of like the way he's getting me out of sight. Out of mind, too?"

"So again, I say, what do you want from one lone reporter?"

"And an admiral who is headed back to Chance day after tomorrow."

"I told you," Kris said, "I couldn't figure out where we go from here. All I ask is for you to give me your eyes. Give me your ears. Give me your brain. Winston, I'm really going to need your storytelling skills. I've let you in on something big. You give it the best that you got."

Winston stood and offered her his hand. "And when we are done, humanity and Iteeche will be better off than we are now. Assuming that big, bad ugly out there hasn't gobbled us down."

"That is the hope," Kris said, and shook his hand.

About the Author

Mike Shepherd grew up Navy. It taught him early about change and the chain of command. He's worked as a bartender and cabdriver, personnel advisor and labor negotiator. Now retired from building databases about the endangered critters in the forests of the Pacific Northwest, he's looking forward to some fun reading and writing.

Mike lives in Vancouver, Washington, with his wife, Ellen, and her mother. He enjoys reading, writing, dreaming, watching grandchildren for story ideas, and upgrading his computer—all are never-ending pursuits.

Mike's hard at work on *Kris Longknife: Superb* for you to read November 2010. You can visit his website at www.mikeshepherd.org or drop him an e-mail at Mike_Shepherd@comcast.net.

WILLIAM C. DIETZ

AT EMPIRE'S EDGE

In a far-distant future, the Uman Empire has spread to the stars and beyond, conquering and colonizing worlds, ruling with a benevolent—but iron—fist. The Pax Umana reigns—and all is well...

But on one planet, the remnants of a violent, shape-shifting race called the Sagathies are confined, kept captive by Xeno cops, who have been bioengineered to be able to see through their guises. Jak Cato, a Xeno cop, is returning a fugitive Sagathi when things go horribly wrong. Now he must figure out who betrayed them, recapture the Sagathi, and exact revenge.

"When it comes to military science fiction, William Dietz can run with the best."
—Steve Perry, author of the Matador series

penguin.com

M492T0509

FROM THE NATIONAL BESTSELLING AUTHOR OF
THE DEVIL'S EYE

Jack McDevitt

TIME TRAVELERS
NEVER DIE

When physicist Michael Shelborne mysteriously
vanishes, his son Shel discovers that he had con-
structed a time-travel device. Fearing his father
may be stranded in time—or worse—Shel enlists
Dave Dryden, a linguist, to accompany him on the
rescue mission. Dave has one condition: Shel cannot visit the future. But when Shel violates their
agreement, he makes a devastating discovery that
sends him fleeing back through the ages, and
changes his life forever.